BLOOD AND GOLD

The Legend of Joaquin Murrieta

Jeffrey J. Mariotte

and

Peter Murrieta

Blood and Gold
Copyright© 2021 Gathering String, LLC
Cover Designer Jorge Gutierrez
Sundown Press
www.sundownpress.com

This one's for Marcy, who puts up with me despite everything, and to Peter with great thanks.

~JJM

To Aliza, who is my best editor in life, as in writing. And Dan, who fights for justice like Joaquin. To Jeff, for riding with me. And to all the Joaquins in every generation.

~PM

"When the legend becomes fact, print the legend."

~John Ford

1

July 1847, Trincheras, Sonora, Mexico

Joaquin was floating.

Trincheras was a small village, nestled in a valley with the towering peaks of the Sierra Madre mountains flanking each side. Most of the men in town were off fighting against the United States intervention, but at fifteen, Joaquin was still too young to take up arms. Besides, his father and his older brother Jesús had joined Santa Anna's army. They'd made Joaquin promise to stay behind and take care of Joaquin's mother and sister.

So far, although the Americans had penetrated deep into Sonora, the fighting had not reached the village. But with the men away, people were anxious just the same. During the day, they went out and tried to live normal lives, but at night they went into their homes and bolted the doors and prayed that they'd make it to morning. Rumors had spread of American soldiers rampaging through small towns in search of women, liquor, or treasure, even if there were no battles to be had or Mexican soldiers to be found. Caution was the watchword of the day, and after more than a decade of skirmishes between Mexico and the United States, it was baked in.

But that caution meant that after dark, a young man could

move about unseen. After his mother and sister went to bed, Joaquin often slipped out of the house and went to the hacienda of Don Ramon Feliz, the village's wealthiest man, who owned a huge rancho at the southern tip of the town. Don Ramon was rich enough that both of his children had their own rooms. Joaquin had only to tap on Rosa's window, and within minutes, she would sneak outside.

Tonight, he and Rosita, as he always called her, had gone to the stables and walked hand-in-hand amidst the finest horses Joaquin had ever seen, making plans for their future together. When the church bells rang for ten o'clock—the hour every night that Rosita insisted she had to be back inside the house, because her father would soon check the bedrooms—she had wrapped her arms around him and pulled him close. He felt that her whole body—her entire being—was embracing him. Then she pressed her lips to his for a kiss that seemed both eternal and far too brief. Finally, she had squirmed from his grasp, flashed him a smile full of love and promise, and rushed back inside.

That kiss! He could still feel it on his lips, taste her on his tongue.

She was a year younger than him, too young to marry, but he would have married her in an instant had Don Ramon allowed it. Even without marriage, he knew she was the one he would be with for the rest of his life. They'd been friends since childhood, and he had always thought she was the loveliest creature he'd ever seen. As she grew older, as her body matured, she only became more stunning. And it wasn't only her beauty that attracted him, it was her spirit, her wit, her gaiety, her fierce intelligence. He wanted to breathe in every aspect of Rosita, inhale her and never exhale again.

That kiss.

He headed home, sticking to the shadows, avoiding the moonlit sections of road. Floating.

Nobody was out. A few stray dogs roamed the night. A couple of pigs. A chicken that looked lost, head bobbing up and down as if searching for a clue in the dirt or in the stars.

He was halfway home when he heard hoofbeats, approaching fast from the east. This time of night, who could it be? Was the war finally coming to Trincheras? It didn't sound like a lot of horses, but definitely more than one. As they drew nearer, the riders started whooping.

Joaquin stood in the shadow of a building, but anybody riding down the street would see him there. He eyed the surrounding buildings and spotted three barrels standing in front of a shop. Racing across the road—out in the bright moonlight for only an instant, but too long for comfort—he ducked behind the barrels just as the riders swung into view. There were only two, but they made enough noise for a dozen.

A nudge from behind startled Joaquin, and he barely kept himself from crying out. He turned to see a scrawny street dog sniffing him. "Go away!" Joaquin whispered.

The dog looked at him. Joaquin shoved it, but the dog only shook its head and stood its ground.

"Have it your way." Joaquin grabbed the mutt and wrapped a hand around its snout, wrestling it into his lap. The beast squirmed and whimpered, then settled.

Now the riders were close, actually between the buildings lining both sides of the village's main road. They slowed, walking their horses down the street. Both men wore absurd three-cornered hats and boots that reached to their hips. They were indeed Americans, or so Joaquin assumed, with skin even lighter than his own. He was learning English, so understood some of what they were saying.

"Don't this town got any ladies? Wake up, people! Come on out and let's see what y'all got!"

No one answered. Joaquin risked a peek out between the barrels. One of the men was tall and lean, with a full, red beard drooping down to his chest. The other was shorter, heavier, with a sparse, dark beard. He wore an expression that reminded Joaquin of a little boy whose favorite toy had just been snatched away as punishment for some transgression. He said something Joaquin didn't understand, but from the tone, he guessed it was a string of curse words.

Then the man dropped his hand to his hip and drew a pistol from its holster. The tall one chuckled, nodded, and grabbed for his own gun. "Can't wake 'em up one way, we'll do it another," that one said.

Just then, the dog slipped from Joaquin's grasp and started out into the street. Joaquin grabbed for it but missed. He nearly called it, but at the last moment, caught himself and kept quiet.

"What's that?" the heavy man asked.

"Just a old dog," the other replied.

"You gon' shoot it?"

"Naw. Shootin' ain't a bad idea, though."

Joaquin tried to pull his body inside itself, to become as small as possible so that no part of him would extend past the barrel he crouched behind. He didn't know what was in it, but desperately hoped it was something that would stop a bullet, because the wood itself certainly wouldn't.

He plugged his ears so he wouldn't cry out and had just barely done so when the shooting began.

When he took another look around the barrel, he saw that the men were riding slowly down the road, shooting into the adobe walls of the homes and shops, reloading, and shooting again. The pockmarks their balls left wouldn't do much damage, but the noise was horrific, and that was probably the point.

Finally, a door opened in one of the long adobe buildings, and Abuela Espinosa emerged. She wasn't Joaquin's grandmother, but one of the oldest women in the village, and she treated everyone as if they were her grandchildren. He didn't even know her real name; like everyone else, he just called her grandmother. She had straw-like gray hair down to the middle of her back, a hunched back, and a face as wrinkled as dried fruit. She used a stick taller than she was to help her walk, and Joaquin saw that she held it now in one bony fist.

"What are you doing?" she screamed at the men. "There are no soldiers here for you to fight! Go away!"

The men glanced at each other. It seemed obvious that they didn't understand a word she was saying. Joaquin could have translated, but if he stepped out of hiding now, he'd probably earn a bullet for his trouble.

"You got any daughters?" one of the men asked. "Or granddaughters?" They both broke into riotous laughter at that. The other one replied with something Joaquin didn't understand.

"You leave now!" Abuela cried. She shook her stick at them, then lunged and jabbed the tall man's horse in the snout. The horse reared back, startled, nearly throwing its rider. The tall man shouted something back, and when she looked as if she might lunge again, he fired his pistol. Joaquin wanted to close his eyes, to look away, but he couldn't.

The first shot caught her in the forehead. She dropped to her knees and the stick fell from her hand. Blood spattered the stick as she swayed from side to side, struggling to maintain her balance.

From behind her, someone else stepped out the door. It was Pepé, her grandson, a boy of nine years. "Grandmother!" he shouted. "Come back inside! Those are bad men!"

She swiveled toward him, and the moment her ruined head came into view, Joaquin saw the boy's mouth drop open and tears spring from his eyes. Then there were two more shots, one from each man. Abuela and Pepé both dropped to the blood-soaked earth and were still. As one, the men swung their horses around and rode out the way they had come at a gallop.

When they were gone, Joaquin came out from behind the barrels. All up and down the street, other doors opened and people—mostly women and children, all that was left in the town—came out, and within minutes, the wails and cries echoed throughout the night. Nobody paid any attention to the fact that young Joaquin Murrieta, who, at the west end of the village, was in the midst of it all.

2

Abuela had lied.

In point of fact, some soldiers *were* billeted at Trincheras, just not many. They were assigned to guard the mission there, and particularly to watch over the handful of American prisoners held in one of the mission's well-fortified storerooms. By the time they heard the commotion, the Americans were long gone. But the next day, it was the talk of the village, and especially so among the soldiers, who felt that some response was called for. An attack on Abuela and Pepé—on any of the villagers—was an attack on them all.

One of the prisoners was a man named William Wallace Byrnes, or as he had said the first time he'd met Joaquin, "Bill, to my friends." Bill Byrnes had been captured during the Battle of Buena Vista, along with a few companions, and imprisoned at the mission. Before the war, he had worked for the Mexican government, hunting renegade Indians, and he'd learned Spanish while practicing that trade. Only twenty-three years old, he had studied for the priesthood in his youth. Upon learning that, the priests allowed him to attend services and to study at the mission school, to practice his Spanish and to help teach English to the local children. He and Joaquin had quickly become fast friends, and Byrnes often entertained the younger boy with colorful tales of the United States. He liked Joaquin's boundless energy and enthusiasm, his quick wit, and his simple decency, which Byrnes tried not to taint with his usual profanity. It was hard for him to keep it in check, after his years as a manhunter and soldier, but around the priests and Joaquin he made the effort.

On the day after the killings, Joaquin had sought him out. "Why would Americans do such a thing, Bill?" he asked. "An old woman and a child. It was horrible."

Byrnes sat on a wooden bench in the mission's courtyard and gestured for Joaquin to do the same. "I'm sorry you saw that," he said. "You're right, it is horrible. Were the men regular Army?"

Joaquin didn't understand the question, so Byrnes tried again. "What did they look like? Were they in uniform?"

Joaquin described the strange hats, the boots, the full beards, and Byrnes began shaking his head before the boy was even finished. "Regular Army troopers wear light blue uniforms, like mine," he said, touching his own ragged sleeve. "These men sound like Kentucky volunteers. Those Kaintuck bastards have a reputation for stirring up trouble. General Taylor's already threatened to send the whole lot of them home. I guess some of 'em don't learn."

"But if they're not with the army . . ." Joaquin began.

"Many states have sent their own volunteer units to help in the war effort," Byrnes explained. "Some are more professional than others. Better behaved, too. Obviously."

"Your general should send them all home. This war shouldn't even be fought."

"Can't argue with that. Like most wars, I reckon, it's over land and wealth. Those as have the most land have the most wealth, and those as don't get the short end of the stick. They do the fighting and dying for the benefit of the others, who usually stay far from the battlefield themselves."

Not all wars, Byrnes knew. His namesake in thirteenth-century Scotland had fought for freedom from British tyranny, as had his great-grandfather Willie, who'd emigrated to America a hundred years ago and fought at Lexington, Concord, and Chelsea Creek, before being crippled at Bunker Hill. It was hard to make the same claim for this war, though.

"But . . ." Joaquin paused, obviously searching for the right words. His eyes brimmed with moisture, and he swallowed hard, fighting back tears. He had been looking straight at Byrnes, but now he broke away his gaze. ". . . to slaughter Abuela and Pepé, like they were dogs with the . . ."

"Rabies," Byrnes offered. "Rabid dogs. You're right, it's a vicious act. Most men wouldn't do such a thing, but some . . . some men look for any chance to hurt folks. The thing is, if they did it so easily here, shot down innocents and then just turned and rode away, they're not likely to stop. They'll do it again. Maybe already have done."

Joaquin started to say something else, but the mission bell rang, signaling the start of classes for him. After he hurried away, Byrnes went in search of Corporal Alejandro de Santis, one of the few soldiers who spoke English well. Thanks to the priests' intercession, Byrnes had the run of the place during the day—as long as he stayed within the mission walls. Like the other prisoners, he was sometimes taken beyond the mission property on work details, accompanied at all times by soldiers. And like the others, he spent his nights behind locked doors.

He found de Santis just finishing breakfast in the kitchen area and sat down across from him at the long, heavy wooden table. The aromas of fried eggs, beans, and rice hung in the air, and de Santis had a steaming mug of bitter hot chocolate in front of him. He was clearly a man who enjoyed his breakfasts, and probably his lunches and dinners and everything in be-tween. His woolen jacket was folded on the table beside his plate, and his linen shirt was stretched to its limit. The coat displayed a half-inch wide strip of red from cuff to elbow, in-dicating his rank, and its brass buttons shone like new. His barracks cap sat beside the jacket.

"You eat well?" Byrnes asked.

"Very well," de Santis replied with a grin. "It's what I do best."

"I've been thinking about those murders. Last night."

"So have we all. We soldiers are precious few, but we want to form a party to go after the killers."

"Good," Byrnes said. "That's what I wanted to suggest. Also . . ."

The corporal paused his cup before his lips and raised an eyebrow.

"Also, I want to go with the party. I can help."

De Santis set the cup back down hard, sloshing some of the thick, brown liquid over the side. "You are a prisoner. You cannot leave the mission."

"I'd be under guard, accompanying soldiers."

"You would run away at the first opportunity."

"I won't," Byrnes said. "I swear it."

"Why would you do this?"

"Those men are Americans. They're Kentucky Volunteers. I know men like that. I know how they think, how they act. And I'm a good tracker, which is why your government used to pay me to do exactly that. Those sons of bitches brought shame to my country, and they need to pay for their crime."

"But the victims were Mexican. We are at war."

"Damn it, I know that, Ale. I got no hatred for the Mexican people. I joined Taylor's army because I was called to—likely the same reason you wear your uniform. I don't think you hate Americans, either."

"I do not."

"What those bastards did wasn't part of this war. It was murder, pure and simple. They need to hang for it. I'm your best bet to be able to find them before they rejoin their unit, because if they do, you'll never get them. Time's wasting while we sit here jawing about it. Every minute they get farther away."

He watched de Santis take another sip. The corporal's furrowed forehead and unfocused eyes made Byrnes think the man was considering the proposition. Probably trying to figure out if it sounded insane.

Maybe it did. But it was also the only way justice was likely to be done.

"I will ask Lieutenant Ramos, on one condition."

"What is it?"

"You will be unarmed. If you try to escape at any time, you will be killed."

"That's fine."

"I am not finished. Then, when the soldiers return to the mission, all the soldiers captured with you at Buena Vista will also be killed."

Byrnes considered. Six men had been captured together, and all brought to the mission because it was a sturdy building, well away from the battlefield, and had space available. Two other prisoners were currently held on the premises, but those two would, it seemed, be spared. Did five other men deserve to die for his impulse?

No, that wasn't the right question. He had no intention of trying to escape. He only had to make sure that nothing he did gave the impression that he meant to. Going unarmed in a war zone, on the hunt for murderers, was the only thing that gave him pause.

But if that was the condition, he could accept it. "Deal," he said. "Talk to Ramos. But remember, the sooner we get going, the better our chances are."

De Santis drained his cup and put it down, then heaved to his feet and picked up his jacket and cap. "I will ask."

"Thanks, Ale. I'll wait here until you get an answer. That breakfast smells pretty damn good."

● ● ●

Ramos agreed to the terms de Santis had spelled out, and the team was getting ready to leave. Byrnes rushed to the stables to pick a horse, and ran into Joaquin, who tended to the animals when not in class. While they saddled a horse for the hunt, Byrnes told Joaquin about the agreement.

"Why would you do that?" Joaquin asked. "For Mexicans?"

"There are lines that shouldn't be crossed by anybody, Joaquin."

"Lines?"

"Boundaries. Like here at the mission. I can move around inside pretty much anywhere, but if I were to step outside the gates, I'd be shot. That's a limitation, a boundary. A line. Same thing with murder. An old woman has lived her life, and she should be allowed to die when it's her time, not before. And a child still has his whole life to live. Another person can't take that away. Not without paying the price. I aim to make sure these men pay the price."

"For Mexicans," Joaquin repeated. Why would an American do such a thing for the people with whom he was at war? People who kept him locked in a little room much of the day and all night? He couldn't fathom it.

"For human beings. Look, I'll be back in a day or two. It takes any longer than that, we'll have failed. I just wanted you to know so you didn't wonder where I was."

"Thank you, Bill," Joaquin said. "Be safe."

"Do my best," Byrnes said. "All I can do."

Lieutenant Ramos strode toward them, decked out in a dark blue uniform with red lapels and cuffs and a sky-blue collar, a fringed epaulette on his right shoulder, and white crossbelts holding his brass-hilted sabre. A tall shako crowned the whole look. He was a handsome man, dark-skinned, with a thin mustache riding his upper lip and eyes that seemed to take in the whole world. He was, Joaquin thought, the very image of what an army officer should be. "Are you ready, Mr. Byrnes?"

Byrnes checked the cinch on the saddle, the fit of the bridle and halter. He had already packed what little gear he was allowed into a saddlebag. "Ready."

"It's time."

Byrnes mounted the big animal and looked down at Joaquin. From here, the American seemed almost gigantic, his head scraping the clouds. "See you soon," Byrnes said.

"Go with God," Joaquin replied.

"Same to you, pal. Go with God."

3

When Joaquin tapped on Rosita's window that night, he had to restrain himself from pounding so hard he would break the glass. She appeared at the window almost instantly—black-haired, dark eyes flashing, a vision of pure light and loveliness—and shushed him.

He backed away, sat on a rock, and waited. A few minutes later, having donned a simple shift and boots, she came out of the house. He watched her in the moonlight, her dress swishing as she walked, her hair catching the faint breeze, her smile eclipsing the moon itself. He rose from his perch, held out his arms, and she came into them. He closed them around her and kissed her cheeks, her hair, her nose, her lips, tasting her, inhaling her.

Finally, she spoke. "Shall we ride?"

Riding came as naturally to her as breathing. She had been raised in the saddle and had taught Joaquin most of what he knew about horses. He would never be the skilled equestrian that she was, but he was good with the animals. "Let's walk, instead. There's so much I want to talk to you about."

She took his hand and they set off. They could walk for hours and never leave her father's lands. The bright moon illuminated the talk stalks of the yuccas and the rounded shapes of creosote bush and mesquite. "Joaquin, I heard about Abuela and Pepé. You were there?"

"I was on my way home from seeing you. I heard men riding in, and I hid behind some barrels. I saw the whole thing."

"That must have been dreadful! Are you all right?"

"They never saw me. I'm fine."

"I'm terrified. What if they come back?"

"They won't. The soldiers rode out after them today. And you'll never believe it—Bill Byrnes went with them."

"The American prisoner? The one you're so taken with?"

"He's my friend."

"I'm almost jealous of him. You spend more time with him than you do with me."

"Not by choice. You know I'd be with you every minute if I could."

Their hips bumped as they strolled, hand-in-hand. She leaned in once and kissed him on the cheek, then, laughing, dodged when he tried to kiss her back.

"Anyway," he went on, "Bill volunteered to go after those men. The killers. As soon as I described them, he knew who they were—not their names, but what army they're with. He says he knows how they think, and where they'll go from here."

"But the soldiers are letting an American prisoner go hunt Americans?"

"He convinced them."

"He'll escape!"

"He promised he wouldn't."

"And they believed him?"

"It looks like it. They took him. He doesn't have any weapons, though."

"I would be very surprised if they gave him a weapon. A prisoner. An American soldier. How do they know he didn't plan this whole thing? Maybe the killers were just here to draw the soldiers away for an attack."

"They didn't all go. Just four soldiers, and Bill."

"Four less to defend the village."

"Nothing ever happens here."

Rosita dropped his hand and spun to face him. "You *saw* two people *murdered* here!"

"Sure, yes. That. But the war hasn't come here."

"Yet. Why would Bill want to go, if not to escape? Those were American soldiers, weren't they?"

"He says they weren't part of General Taylor's army. They were . . . something else, I forget the word."

"But Americans."

"Yes, they were Americans. Bill says they were bad men, and they need to be stopped."

"Well, I hope he can stop them. And . . ." She reached out her hands again, took Joaquin's, and drew him close. In the nearby brush, a night creature skittered away. ". . . why aren't you kissing me?"

• • •

Two days later, Joaquin had just finished classes when he heard a commotion outside the mission grounds. He hurried to the gate and saw seven horses coming up the road. Five carried people he knew—soldiers from the mission, and Byrnes. The other two horses he'd seen once before, but the men who'd ridden them then were now draped over their backs, arms hanging down on one side and legs on the other.

All the horses looked worn out, their hooves and legs caked with mud. The riders were equally bedraggled: unshaven, unwashed, and weary. Joaquin stood by the mission gate and watched them approach. When Byrnes saw him, he called out and motioned him over. "You're the only one who saw the killings, Joaquin," he said, bringing his horse to a halt and dismounting. He raised a hand to stop the rest of the party. "Can you identify these men as the murderers?"

He led Joaquin to the bodies. They were both clad in uniforms similar to the ones Joaquin had seen that night—he remembered especially the thigh-high boots, which he now saw were lined in red—and those ridiculous hats. The hats were gone now, no doubt lost in the chase or the fight. Byrnes grabbed one man's hair and raised him enough for Joaquin to see his face. It was the heavy-set man with the short, dark beard, easily recognized despite the gruesome hole that had caved in his left eye.

Seeing them brought back some of the terror he'd experienced that night. He had hunted with his father and brothers since he'd been a small boy. He and Jesús had mined for silver. He'd seen animals killed, and people badly injured, but he had never before seen people shot down in cold blood. The memory haunted his dreams, and he found the image of Abuela and Pepé lying in the road, blood pooling around them, penetrating his daytime thoughts as well. He didn't think he would ever be able to shake them.

"Yes," Joaquin finally said, "that's one of them."

Byrnes moved to the other. Joaquin knew even before he lifted the man up who it was—the red hair was a giveaway. But when Byrnes raised him, the long, red beard confirmed it. His head hung at a weird angle. Joaquin couldn't stop looking at the injuries, but he pointed to the red-bearded one. "This is the man who shot Abuela," he said. "I think that other one shot Pepé, but they both fired at once, so I'm not certain."

"You're sure?" Byrnes asked.

"That's them."

"Well, boys," Byrnes said, "looks like we done good. These are the murderers."

"There could have been no doubt," a soldier named Gustavo Parra said. He was stout, with puffy cheeks, tiny eyes, and a perpetual smile. "We tracked them the entire distance."

Alejandro de Santis turned to Joaquin. "Your friend Bill is quite the tracker," he said. "There were times we'd have lost them, but he always picked up the trail. When we finally found them, we surrounded them, but the big one broke away. Bill stopped him—unarmed—and broke the bastard's neck with his bare hands."

Joaquin glanced at Byrnes, who simply shrugged. "He was gonna get away. I had to do what I had to do."

"He plays it down," de Santis said. "But it's true. If not for him, the killer might have escaped. It was very rugged country, and he could have lost us in the hills."

Byrnes shrugged again, and allowed himself a slight grin.

"Thank you for identifying these men, Joaquin," de Santis said. "Now we need to bury them. They're beginning to stink."

"They stank when we found them," another soldier said.

"Stink more, then," de Santis replied.

"Are you going to bury them in the cemetery?" Joaquin asked.

"Murderous scum like them?" de Santis shot back. "No. Unmarked graves in the desert for these two. You're welcome to join us."

Joaquin had seen plenty of burials in the Catholic cemetery, but he'd never watched killers deposited into quickly dug graves. He was a little hesitant, but curiosity won out, and he accompanied the small party out of town and into the rolling hills stretching out toward the Sierra Madre.

The soldiers and Byrnes dismounted, stripped off their heavy shirts, and took turns digging. To the south, clouds piled up one atop the other, puffy white at first but quickly turning a sinister gray. When the men had excavated two trenches a little longer than a man and about hip-deep, Bill and de Santis dragged the killers off their mounts and unceremoniously dumped them into the holes. The men stood around the holes, crossed themselves—Joaquin, too—then took up shovels to start covering the corpses. If any prayers were spoken, they were done silently.

By the time the holes were filled, the rain had started. The first drops were as big as pebbles. In the distance, lightning split the dark skies. "We need to hurry back," Parra said. "We're about to be drenched. Joaquin, take one of those other horses."

Joaquin did as he was told, slipping easily into the saddle. Thanks to Rosita's tutelage, he'd worked with horses at the mission for years, and sometimes helped out at Don Ramon's rancho, so he was comfortable on strange animals, saddled or bareback. The other men mounted up and they rode through the beginnings of the downpour. Despite their speed, by the time they reached the mission, they were soaked. Inside the walls, the soldiers turned the horses over to Joaquin to groom and put away. Byrnes came over to thank him, and Joaquin asked what would become of him, now.

"Back to lockup," Byrnes said.

"Even though you caught the killers of Abuela and Pepé?"

Byrnes shrugged. "That was the deal. As a prisoner of war, it's my duty to try to escape if I can. But as a human, I couldn't let those killings go unavenged. I set the terms of the bargain, and I'm bound to keep them."

"You're an honorable man, Bill," Joaquin said.

"I'm a man, same as any other, I guess."

"I don't think so."

"Well, I hope you don't lose your respect for honor, Joaquin. Seems to fade away in a lot of folks as they get older. Hang onto that, and you'll do fine in life." Byrnes snickered. "Listen to me, babbling like an old lady. I gotta go. I'll see you tomorrow, most like."

Joaquin watched him walk away, into the rain and across a courtyard toward the locked storeroom where the prisoners were kept. Byrnes kept his head up and his shoulders square. Even though he was a prisoner, he looked every bit the free man.

• • •

"It's just so unfair!" Rosita said.

Because the storm had left the earth sodden, Rosita and Joaquin took refuge in one of her father's barns instead of walking or riding on the grounds. She had brought her rosewood guitar out, and sat up against a wall, strumming it and singing Mexican love songs, while Joaquin lay with his head on her outstretched legs and stewed. The distinctive scent of rainfall in the desert mingled with those of mud and damp hay, creating a kind of aromatic cocoon that embraced them and isolated them from the world outside the barn walls. Joaquin would stay right here forever, if he could.

"Unfair how?"

"From what you've told me, Bill is a good man. A decent man. He could've been a priest. I mean, that's not the same as *being* a priest. You *could* be a priest."

"I'll always be a sinner," Joaquin said. "I'm sure of that."

"Even priests sin. They're just forgiven. The point is, he went to school for it."

"Yes, but then he left it," Joaquin noted. "He's killed many people since then."

"You said he killed Indians. Rogue ones, on the warpath,

killing Mexicans."

"Then he killed Mexicans in the war."

"You don't know that."

"Well, he was in battles, right? So, either he did, or he tried to. And then he killed that American."

"Who was a murderer. The village needed justice for the murders of Pepé and Abuela. Without Bill, that might not have happened. He helped us all, and in return, he's locked up, just like before."

Arguing with Rosita was pointless. He'd never known anyone with such a quick mind, even among his teachers at the mission. She was well-read, she studied hard, and she had an innate curiosity that led her to always want to know the *why* behind things. She could argue circles around him and leave him feeling like she'd been right all along. "I give up," he said at last. "It is unfair to keep him locked up. But rules are rules. What's to be done about it?"

"Well," Rosa said, locking his gaze with hers, "if you think it's unfair, help him escape. Men aren't meant to live in captivity, anyway."

The idea struck him like one of the thunderbolts he'd seen that afternoon. "Help him?"

"That's what I said." Rosita picked out a simple tune on the guitar, smiling down at him. "You believe he shouldn't be a prisoner anymore. Well, *you're* not a prisoner. Do something about it."

"But—the soldiers. They'll . . ."

"They'll what?"

"They'll be furious."

"Of course," she said. "But they'll only be angry at *you* if they catch you. It's obvious that you don't want to be caught helping a war prisoner escape, right?"

Joaquin pondered that question, but only briefly. "No, I'd rather not. But how can I help him get away without being seen?"

"How many guards are there at night?"

"There's always one, at least," Joaquin said. "But sometimes two."

"When are there two?"

"When they change shifts. I've been there at night and seen the new one coming on duty sit and chat with the one who's been on duty."

"And you know at what hour that change comes?"

"I do. Always around two o'clock."

She bumped his head with her guitar, laughing. "What are you doing out so late?"

He rubbed his skull where she'd knocked it. "Going home from seeing you, usually."

"You leave here at ten!"

"I don't always go straight home. Usually, I'm too excited to sleep."

"And you stop at the mission?"

"I have."

"Don't you ever spend time at home?"

"As little as possible." His house was small, with only two rooms, and he shared one of those with Jesús and their younger sister, Esmerelda. His parents and his mother's father shared the other. Privacy was nonexistent, and a teenage boy needed privacy.

Besides, Rosita wasn't there, she was here. And anyplace Rosita wasn't was a place he didn't want to stay.

"Anyway," she said, "if you want to help Bill escape, you need to do something about the guards, right?"

"Yes, but what?"

Rosita set the guitar aside and shifted her legs. Understanding her intention, Joaquin sat up, allowing her to rise. Then she crossed the barn and stopped at a cabinet containing medical supplies for the livestock.

"I might have just the thing," she said.

4

Three nights later, the scant light of a new moon barely broke through the cloud cover. Joaquin had enlisted the help of Manuel Duarte, his cousin. Manuel was a few years older than Jesús, almost a decade older than Joaquin. He had been working as a vaquero when a roped cow made a sudden lurch, and Manuel's rope crushed his finger against his saddle horn. What was left of the finger had been hurriedly amputated. Ever since, the men he worked with had called him Tres Dedos, and the nickname stuck. Even Joaquin called him that, unless they were in the presence of other family members. He was a bear of a man with long, unkempt black hair framing a pitted, scarred face on which every feature was oversized. His brow jutted out over his eyes like a shelf. His nose was broad, his lips thick, more accustomed to sneers than smiles. He had a neck like a bull, and was physically stronger than anyone Joaquin had ever known.

Because he was also related to Abuela and Pepé, the army had relieved him from duty so he could attend the funerals and spend some time with his remaining family.

When Joaquin had told him about Byrnes's role in catching the killers, Tres Dedos hadn't been moved. He was glad the killers had been caught, but to him, Byrnes was just another enemy soldier. But Joaquin had pressed, and when he described his plan—well, Rosita's plan, really— Tres Dedos had become interested, if only for the daring involved.

They slipped through the darkness onto the mission grounds, as Joaquin had done many times before, and into the kitchen. Tres Dedos stood watch outside the door while Joaquin lit some candles and by their light, brewed a pot of strong hot chocolate.

When it was done, the rich aroma filled the space. Joaquin filled two mugs, then added a few drops from a bota strung around his neck, being careful not to inhale the stuff. Rosita had said that it was what her father's vaqueros used to put the horses and cattle to sleep when they needed surgery or some other complex medical care. Too much, she'd warned, would doubtless kill a person, but a little bit would only knock him out.

Joaquin stirred the thick chocolate, then risked a quick sniff. The scent of the chocolate overpowered everything else. Good. He went outside and touched his cousin's arm. They left the kitchen door open and the candles burning inside, then hurried across the courtyard to a shadowed niche on the far side, from which they could watch the kitchen door.

It didn't take long for Gustavo Parra, having just arrived to relieve the other guard, to notice the glow from the open door. He went in to investigate, and a couple of minutes later, reappeared carrying both mugs. "Ale!" he said in a loud whisper. "Ale, there's chocolate!"

Alejandro de Santis emerged from the corridor containing the locked storerooms. "What do you mean?" he asked.

"I don't know who made it. There's nobody around, and there are two mugs. One for each of us."

"Well, somebody made it."

"Then they can make more. Do you want some, or not?"

De Santis reached for one of the mugs. "Why not?" He took

a big sniff, smiled, then downed what must have been half of it in a single gulp. Watching, Joaquin's gut clenched. What if the soldier doubled over with pain, or fell to the ground writhing in agony?

Neither of those things happened. De Santis simply thanked Parra, and the two of them headed back toward the storerooms, chatting quietly. Now there were two guards in the way, instead of none, and Joaquin's fears turned from the soldiers' wellbeing to the failure of his plan.

"I don't know about this," he whispered.

"Give it some time to take effect," Tres Dedos said. "I've seen this stuff work on horses. It won't happen right away. It has to spread from their stomach throughout their bodies."

"Yes, I'm sure you're right. It's just hard to be patient."

Tres Dedos blew out an angry breath. "Believe me, I know. I meant to thank you, Joaquin."

"For what?"

"For your help finding the men who killed my aunt and my nephew. If you hadn't seen it happen, they never would've been caught."

"I just happened to be there. I wish I could have done more. If I'd been able to stop it, somehow . . . "

"You couldn't have. You'd just have gotten yourself killed, as well, and then they would have gotten away with it."

"I suppose you're right. Still, I felt so . . . so helpless."

"You were unarmed. There were two of them, soldiers. You're smart and strong, but you're still a boy. And you weren't helpless, you reported it and justice was done. And now you're helping your friend, who actually delivered that justice. I wish I had been here, so I could have caught those bastards myself. I'd have ripped their hearts out while they watched. But I wasn't. You've done all anybody could, and more. I'm grateful."

Manuel's words warmed Joaquin's heart. Ever since that night, he'd been wrestling with guilt over his passive role—hiding behind barrels while two neighbors were slaughtered. He had thought he'd never forgive himself, and he had never dreamed that he'd earn the forgiveness of the cousin he admired so.

He wanted to find something appropriate to say in return, but for once, words failed him. As he struggled with it, a loud thump sounded from the area near the storerooms. Joaquin and Tres Dedos were instantly alert, listening for more.

"Gustavo!" That was de Santis's voice. "What are you doing? Get up, fool!" Joaquin heard a rustling that was probably de Santis shaking Parra, trying to rouse him. Then hurried footfalls that must have been de Santis going for help. A moment later, the soldier came into view, stumbling drunkenly, waving his arms for balance.

"He—Gustavo—he's . . ." de Santis managed. Then he stopped, his eyes rolled back in his head, and he collapsed to the ground.

Joaquin started to rise, to rush over and get the storeroom keys. Tres Dedos gripped his arm. "Wait! Make sure no one else has heard the commotion. When we're sure, then we go set them free."

The first part of the night's activity had been liberating eight horses from the stables and tethering them outside the mission grounds. It'd been an easy task. Joaquin worked there and knew every horse, and his cousin was an experienced vaquero. The effort had a dual purpose—it would provide mounts for the escaped prisoners, and it would deprive the soldiers of animals on which to give chase.

Joaquin really just wanted to release Byrnes, but he and

Rosita hadn't been able to come up with a way to do that. Finally, they'd decided that rather than make Byrnes languish in undeserved captivity, they'd just have to let all the Americans go. Byrnes would make sure the men didn't return to the village to seek revenge on their captors.

Waiting was excruciating. What if one of the priests came out to investigate the noise? Nobody did, though. The night was almost silent; de Santis's soft breathing, the trilling of insects, the rush of some night bird's wings were the only sounds that broke the stillness. Finally, Tres Dedos gave him a nod. "Let's go."

Cautiously, keeping to the shadows, they crossed the courtyard. De Santis slumbered away. They stepped around him and into the corridor, where lantern light showed Parra slumped against a wall, mouth hanging open and a thin line of spittle descending from it. Joaquin went to the barred window of the storeroom door. "Bill," he said in a loud whisper.

He'd expected to have to awaken the prisoners, but he was mistaken. "Joaquin," Bill replied at once. "What's going on out there?"

"We're getting you out, Bill. Where is the key to this door?"

"Parra should have it—Ale's shift hasn't started yet, and the guards always pass it over when they change shifts."

Tres Dedos had heard and was already searching the sleeping soldier.

"Get ready to go, Bill," Joaquin said. "Your friends, too. There are eight horses waiting for you, and everybody's asleep here."

"I don't . . . what do you mean? You did this?"

"Yes. You don't deserve to stay locked up in here. Not after catching those killers. You should be free. Go back to America. Just please, make sure your friends don't come back to the village. You have no enemies here."

"Joaquin, this is crazy. What if you're caught?"

"If you hurry, we won't be."

"I have them!" Tres Dedos announced. He came toward the door carrying a brass ring with three keys on it. "It must be one of these."

Joaquin stepped aside to give his cousin space. The first key didn't fit the lock, and the second went in but wouldn't turn. Finally, the third one turned, and the door swung open.

"Grab anything you want to keep, boys," Byrnes said. "Appears we're going home."

The other men in the storeroom rustled around, collecting belongings, tugging on boots. "Hurry," Joaquin urged. "I don't know how long they'll sleep."

"If you'd given us some warning . . ." Byrnes began.

"I *couldn't*. I didn't know it would work, until I saw it."

"All right, it's no problem. Let's go, boys. Hurry."

The prisoners filed out one by one, following Tres Dedos down the shadowed corridor. Byrnes came out last, and grasped Joaquin's hand in a firm grip. "I don't know how you did this, Joaquin, but I appreciate it. Say, why don't you come with us?"

The suggestion took Joaquin by surprise, but he only had to consider it for an instant. "I can't leave Rosita. She's my world."

Byrnes laughed. "You're what we'd call a hopeless romantic, Joaquin. That's not a bad thing to be."

"I'm a Mexican. Romance is in our blood."

"Well, I know you and Rosita will have a happy future together. I have a feeling we'll see each other again, somewhere down the trail."

"I hope so." Joaquin wanted to say something more, but

Parra moaned and shifted position. Had Manuel's jostling wakened him? As Joaquin watched, the soldier's eyes fluttered open, though awareness hadn't seemed to sink in yet.

"Go!" Joaquin said. "Follow Tres Dedos! I'll take care of him."

The men moved quickly out of the corridor, and out of sight. Joaquin stood there, watching Parra, not sure how to fulfill his promise. He couldn't kill the man. Not only would it be wrong, but it would raise a bigger stink, and ensure that the escaped prisoners had to be tracked down and punished. But Parra was moving around. He raised a hand to his chin and wiped it, blinked a few times. Joaquin made a sudden decision and rushed down the corridor, in the opposite direction from the prisoners. At the first corner, he slapped the wall hard with both hands and stopped, peeking back toward the soldier.

At the sound, Parra lurched to his feet, unsteady as a man on a three-day drunk. He spun awkwardly toward the corner, then noticed the open door. "What?" he said, his voice thick. "Hey, who's that?"

Joaquin slapped the wall once more, then raced toward an open doorway, hitting the walls as he went to try to sound like several people. Parra stumbled after him, calling, "Come back! Stop!"

After that, it was almost too easy. Joaquin had been born in Trincheras. He had been visiting the mission his whole life and taking classes and working there for years. He knew every part of it. None of the soldiers were natives to the town; they'd been here for months, a year at the most. They were stationed at the mission because there was space for them and for the prisoners, but few of them spent their free time exploring the grounds.

Joaquin passed through a doorway that led into a secluded prayer yard. From there, he scrambled up a low adobe wall, then pulled himself up onto the roof of the chapel. Each time, he slowed to let Parra almost catch up, and made enough noise so that Parra might still think he was chasing all the prisoners.

The wall around the prayer yard stopped Parra short. He tried to climb it, but either the drugged chocolate or his own lack of strength held him to the earth. After a little while, he gave up and retraced his steps.

Joaquin dropped down from the roof on the far side of the chapel. He went in through another door, then passed from there into the kitchen. After a minute, he came out the main door, and saw Parra trying to rouse de Santis. Joaquin yawned and rubbed his eyes.

"What's going on?" he asked.

Parra glanced up, confused. When he spoke, his voice was thick, as if he had sand in his throat. "You're the Murrieta boy, aren't you? What are you doing here so late?"

"I couldn't sleep. Neither could Padre Escalante. We were talking, and he wanted some hot chocolate, so I made us some. I left it to cool for a few minutes, and when I came back, it was gone. Now I see you two, and you look like you've both been sleeping on the job."

"That was *your* chocolate?" Parra asked.

"And Padre Escalante's. He's gone back to bed now, though."

"It was . . . I didn't like it. Ale drank his own and most of mine, and now I can't wake him."

"What are you saying? Someone drugged it?"

"And—and the prisoners are gone!" Parra cried, as if he'd just remembered. "They've escaped! I need to sound the alarm. Joaquin, can you ready the men's horses? I don't think the prisoners could have gone very far, so we can still catch them."

"Of course," Joaquin said. "I'll have them ready by the time you rouse the troops."

He went to the stable, which presently contained only three old mares—one of them lame, the other two in their dotage—and a burro. He didn't bother saddling them. Instead, he took a seat on a hay bale and waited for the soldiers, gleefully anticipating the looks on their faces when they arrived.

He wasn't disappointed.

5

February 1850, Trincheras, Sonora, Mexico

Jesús unfolded the letter from his friend Chuy Rivera and read it again. Joaquin had heard it twice now, and read it once himself, but he didn't mind listening again. His brother's excitement was palpable. And contagious.

My dearest comrade, it began. *I pray that you received my last letter, of one month ago, describing my journey to the gold fields. I have not received one from you, but letters are only occasionally brought up from San Francisco.*

Jesús, Joaquin, and Tres Dedos had sat around the table and composed a letter, after receiving his first one. They had sent it within a few days, so even if it hadn't reached him by the time he'd sent this, it might have by now. Joaquin hoped so. Chuy had wanted to go to California when the first reports started coming in of the gold there, just lying on the ground or lining the creek beds, but it had taken him months to prepare for the journey, to persuade some friends to travel with him, and to raise the necessary funds.

Since I last wrote, I have been fortunate enough to have hit a rich claim. Every day, Pablo and I take in at least one hundred dollars in gold. Prices of everything are measured in dollars here, or else in ounces of gold. Last week I turned over a log with my foot and found a nugget half the size of my fist. Would that beloved Mexico had never given away these rich lands.

Jesús went on reading Chuy's tales of his good luck, to which Joaquin could give only scant credence. Finally, he reached the point of the letter.

Jesús, my friend, you must join me in California. My efforts have had excellent results, but Pablo and I are only two men. With your help, working together, we would soon amass enough treasure to allow our families to stop working and enjoy the rest of their lives in luxurious comfort. Our sisters would wear the finest gowns and attract only the wealthiest suitors.

There it was. Chuy had found enough success to urge Jesús to join him in California, and Jesús wanted Joaquin and their cousin Manuel to come with him.

Joaquin been fascinated by America ever since hearing Bill Byrnes's stories of that amazing place, and this could be his one opportunity to see it for himself. The journey would be an adventure never to be forgotten, and at the end of it he would be a rich man.

The Murrieta family had never been rich. Joaquin and Jesús had made some money at silver mining, and Jesús was convinced that experience would serve them well in California's gold fields. Lately, Joaquin had been working full-time with the horses at Don Ramon's ranch—the only profession he'd ever evinced any skill for—but Rosita's father would never allow her to marry an impoverished vaquero, much less one he employed. If he became wealthy, though, Don Ramon would never turn him down.

But the gold fields were so far away, and Rosita was here. How long would he have to be gone, and would she wait for him? Would she be allowed to? What if he came back in two or three years to find her married and with small children at her knees?

No, he couldn't risk it. He would have to tell Jesús that he was on his own. Or perhaps Tres Dedos would go with him. His brother and cousin would have to ensure the family fortunes by themselves, while Joaquin stayed here, working for his beloved's father.

Loving her, wanting her, but never being allowed to marry her.

The letter wrapped up quickly after that. Jesús folded it and tucked it into his shirt. "We have to go," he said. "Think of all that gold, just waiting for us."

"No," Tres Dedos said. "I hate Americans. Always have, always will."

He had been wounded in the war, though not grievously. But he'd often told Joaquin about the friends he had made in the army, friends who had been killed in one bloody battle or another. He had found the body of one of them, mutilated, after the Americans had won the day but then withdrawn from the field. Before the war, he'd been occasionally ill-tempered, and he had always liked to fight. But after the war, the anger he felt toward the nation to the north seemed to have been seared into his soul, like a brand on a calf's haunch. He was given to dark moods, which sometimes passed as quickly as a summer thunderstorm, and sometimes lingered for days.

Jesús, too, had known friends who'd died in the war, but since receiving the letter, he'd been pressing Joaquin. He had enjoyed their mining stint. Joaquin would have enjoyed it more if they'd found a rich vein of silver and been allowed to keep it. But the Sonoran silver rush at Planchas de Plata had played out long before either of them were born, and more recent, local finds had been considerably smaller in scale. Jesús's dreams of becoming a wealthy grandee from mining had eventually faded, but now Chuy's letter, and other news from California's gold fields, seemed to have revived them.

"I need you, Manuel," Jesús said. "Both of you. It's a long trip there, and I don't want to do it alone. We don't have to stay long—a year, at most. Maybe less, from what Chuy says."

Tres Dedos lit one of the thin cigars he had grown to love during the war—to Joaquin, they smelled like horse droppings wrapped in a tobacco leaf—and sat back in his chair, sucking on it until the tip glowed bright. They were on the patio of a cantina at the edge of Trincheras, where Jesús had let Joaquin take a few sips from his mescal. "A year among the Americans is a year too long." Then his craggy face lit up with a grin. "Unless I'm killing them, of course."

"You can't do that," Jesús scolded. "They'd catch you and hang you."

"They'd never catch me," Tres Dedos said, sounding utterly confident. "I'm smarter than all of them put together. Remember that time I crept into the Americans' camp and lit their captain's tent on fire?"

Jesús laughed. Joaquin had heard the story a dozen times, at least, and never failed to be impressed by his cousin's daring.

Then Jesús's handsome face turned serious. He was slender, with light-brown hair and a narrow nose. His eyes were quick and alert, missing nothing. He leaned forward, elbows on the table. "There, we'd be surrounded by Americans, though. It won't be one camp of them, deep inside Mexico, it'll be the other way around. We'll be strangers. Likely under suspicion from the moment we arrive. This letter is all about the riches Chuy has found, but I've heard stories from others about Mexicans being bothered, driven away from rich claims, and worse. That's why I want—no, I need—you two with me. We can watch out for each other, make sure we're all safe."

He put his elbows on the table, spread his hands. "Safe, and rich."

"I do like the idea of being rich," Tres Dedos said. He blew out a stream of smoke. "Maybe I could just kill one or two Americans. Not every day."

"When you're raking gold into your pockets, you won't care about the Americans," Jesús said. "Me, I don't like them either, but I had enough of killing in the war."

"That's where we're different, you and I," Tres Dedos said. "I never tired of it. The more of them I killed, the more I wanted to kill."

"Me, I'm going for the gold," Jesús said. "If you come with me, I suppose I can't control you every moment of the day. I would only ask that you not do anything to endanger our mining efforts. In the long run, which is more important to you, being rich or killing Americans?"

Tres Dedos set the cigar on the edge of the table and drained his glass. "I suppose getting rich. Once we've made enough, then I can kill to my heart's content."

"So, you'll come?"

"I couldn't let you make that journey without me, cousin," Tres Dedos said. "You need someone to look after you."

"What about you, Joaquin?" Jesús asked. "You'll come, won't you?"

The idea of going to California excited Joaquin almost more than he could bear. But the idea of leaving Rosita behind *was* unbearable. Anyway, if Jesús had Tres Dedos, that was all the protection he'd need. Joaquin was a good shot with a rifle, and working with horses had made him strong. But outside of a few fights, he had no experience with combat, like the other two did. What good would he do? He'd probably just be in the way.

He felt pulled in every direction. He wanted to go. But he wanted to be with Rosita, and she would never be allowed to go to California.

He got up from his chair, scooped a rock from the dirt and hurled it as far as he could, toward the north. Toward the United States.

But when it fell, it was still in Mexico.

And so was he.

• • •

That night they borrowed two mares from her father's stables and rode to the foot of the mountains, then climbed to a favorite spot. They sat on a rocky bench with their feet dangling over a swiftly flowing stream. Sometimes during the summer, monsoon storms would swell it into a narrow river, and they'd peel off their clothes and leap in from the bench, riding the current to a pool where they could swim, before returning to the bench and stretching out until the night air dried them. Now, the water was ice-cold, and they had little interest in stripping naked. Rosita had been quiet, pensive, since she had come outside at his summons, and she held his hand as if afraid he would disappear if he let go.

Finally, he asked her. "What is it, Rosita? Something's wrong."

She looked at him and he saw tears glistening in her eyes. "What?" he asked. "Have I done something—"

"Never!" she said. "It's my father."

"What about him?"

"He . . . he's made an arrangement. With Félix Castillo. Do you know who he is?"

"From Hermosillo? The grandee?"

"Yes, him."

"What kind of arrangement. What does it have to do with

you?"

"Castillo's son Enrique is nineteen. Castillo is afraid he'll never have any grandchildren."

"I'm almost nineteen, and I'm not married yet," Joaquin said. His fingers touched his slender mustache, still new to him. "There's no shame in that."

"There is to Félix Castillo. And I'm seventeen now. It's time, my father says, for me to become a wife."

Joaquin felt a flash of hope shoot through him. Was the old man ready to acknowledge his long courtship? But a glance at Rosita, biting her upper lip, tears now streaking down her face, brought understanding. "You mean, he wants you to . . . to . . ." He couldn't finish the sentence. A fist had clenched in his gut, and he felt like vomiting.

Rosita finished it for him. "He wants me to marry Enrique. It's all arranged. There will be a substantial dowry. My father's wealth will be increased, and he'll be able to buy more land, to raise more livestock and get it to market more easily. It's everything he's ever wanted, all at once."

"But what about what you want?"

"Does that matter? How can a girl deny her father's wishes?"

"How can a father wish for his daughter to be unhappy?" he countered.

"It's worse than you think. I once saw Enrique beat a servant because she spilled a little water on the table, while filling his cup. But he moved the cup as she poured, so it was his fault in the first place. I haven't spent much time with his family, but that's not the only time I've noticed his cruelty. Because his father's rich, he thinks he can get away with anything. And the worst part is, he's right."

"You can't marry him, then."

"I don't want to. He's ugly, as well. His skin is pocked, his nose is huge, and his eyes are tiny and mean."

"No wonder he hasn't found a woman of his own."

"Oh, Joaquin, what can I do? You know it's you I love."

The answer struck him all at once—how to solve both their problems. "Jesús and Manuel are going to California, to mine for gold. They want me to join them. He has a friend who's getting wealthy there, but he needs help, and Jesús and I worked the silver mines here."

He felt her whole body tighten up, saw in the moonlight that more tears sprang forth. "You're leaving?"

"No!" he said abruptly. "You don't understand. I wouldn't go without you. Come with us! You don't have to marry that fool. We can leave right away. We can marry, and your father won't be able to do anything about it."

"To California?"

"That's right. We'll go to where Chuy has found gold. We won't need your father's wealth, or Gonzales's. We won't come back until we're richer than both of them."

"Do you mean it, Joaquin? Could that really work?"

"Of course! Why not?"

"Don't we need money to travel?"

"I have a little saved up from working for your father. You could bring whatever you can, and we can earn the rest as we go."

"I . . . I want to. It sounds foolish. Crazy. Like a beautiful dream that can't possibly come true."

"But it can! What's to stop us?"

"If my father finds out . . ."

"Don't let him. We'll just borrow some good horses and go."

"Isn't it dangerous?"

"We'll be with Jesús and Tres Dedos, so we'll be safe. Anyway, there are so many people going to California now, there will always be someone close by."

"When would we marry?"

"Along the way. First church we come to."

"Without permission from my parents? You could be arrested."

He had considered that possibility, though only briefly. "That's a chance I'll take. Once we're in America we'll be out of the reach of Mexican law."

"Should I tell Reyes?"

"I like your brother, but he might tell your parents, out of concern for you. You can write to him after we're settled in California."

She leaned into him, clutching his hands, and he breathed in her fragrance. "Can this be real, Joaquin? Can we really do this?"

"The real question is, why aren't we already gone?"

She laughed, and a dagger of joy pierced his heart. "When?"

"Tomorrow night. We'll take a day to get ready, and then we ride."

• • •

Joaquin didn't report for work at the Feliz ranch the next day. Instead, he gathered the things he thought he would need on the trail: food and water, a change of clothing, a musket and lead balls, a knife, matches and utensils, and a tent— Rosita couldn't be expected to sleep under the open sky, even though he could. He scraped together every peso he could, from his own earnings and from money owed to him by a handful of friends. Jesús was doing the same, and so, he supposed, was Tres Dedos. None of them had ever made such a long journey, so to some extent, they were only guessing at what the conditions would be.

Eating dinner with his family, he and Jesús were both so anxious, so fidgety that their mother asked twice what was wrong with them. They put her off; they'd decided not to tell their parents and Esmerelda that they were leaving for California, but instead to write them from the road.

Until he was twenty-five, a young man was required by law and custom to obey his father's wishes. Joaquin's father might have granted them permission to leave—but he might also have declined it, preferring to have his sons at home. And if Esmerelda happened to tell a friend, word would race through the village like wildfire, and when he went to collect Rosita, instead of a sleepy ranch, he would instead encounter an armed camp.

Finally, darkness fell. Still, he had to wait. When he heard soft snores from his parents' room and he was certain that Esmerelda slumbered, he and Jesús gathered up the items they'd collected and carried them outside as quietly as they could. They placed them close to the wall of the house. The plan was for Jesús to stay with them for safekeeping, while Joaquin fetched Rosita. Joaquin made sure nobody was looking, then raced through the village, following his usual nighttime path to the Feliz ranch.

When he approached Rosita's window, she was there before he even tapped, her smile as bright as the morning sun. She came outside immediately, embraced him, and offered a kiss that took his breath away. Still reeling, he followed her to the stables, where she had placed her necessaries. They'd already chosen three horses—not her father's best, because he couldn't abide that—but not the worst, either. Blanco was a strong white stallion that he would ride. Rosita would take Oso, a sturdy, shaggy brown stallion. For Jesús, they'd chosen Poco, a spirited gelding. Tres Dedos had a powerful mule he rode everywhere, and he would ride that beast, he said, to the ends of the Earth.

"I left a note where Reyes will find it in the morning," she told him. "Asking him to tell Mother not to worry about me, and to let your mother know the same."

"You're sure he won't find it too early?"

"He sleeps like the dead, and it's not where he'll see it when he first wakes. Anyway, at some point, my mother will check my room and see that I'm not there. She'll tear the house apart looking for me if there's no note."

"Well, we'll be long gone by then."

"Only if we hurry up," she reminded him.

He got the message. They readied the horses and lashed her belongings onto hers—including her beloved guitar. She hated riding side-saddle, which was traditional among Mexican women but which she considered too easy, and which didn't give her enough control of her mount. Lithe and athletic, she sprang into her favorite elaborately tooled charro saddle. Raised with horses, she was perfectly comfortable straddling the animal, even with skirts on, and she usually wore boots under her skirts. When he was certain she was ready, he opened the stable doors and led his own outside, with hers following. The night was cloudy, the moon hidden, no stars to be seen. He hoped it didn't rain.

As he climbed into his own saddle, Joaquin reviewed the plan in his head. Across the village to his house, where they'd pick up Jesús and their things. Tres Dedos would be there waiting when they arrived. The Murrietas lived almost at the edge of town, so from there, they were almost at the road that would lead them west across the valley, then angle north.

North, to America.

He couldn't wait to see it.

6

The nighttime ride was long and bitterly cold, but the horses were fresh and a full moon offered plenty of light. By the time the sun broke over the jagged peaks of the Sierra Madre, they could see Caborca lying in a valley, its rooftops just catching the first of the morning light. The Rio Concepción flowed past the southwest corner, its muddy waters stretching like an uncoiled rope, casually discarded, toward the Sea of Cortés. The city was much larger than Trincheras, and a momentary hesitation gripped Joaquin. What if Don Ramon had already raised an alarm? Caborca was a parish seat. Surely if Don Ramon had informed the authorities that his daughter had vanished, this would be among the first places he'd alert.

Well, there was nothing for it now. They were here, and it was the southern end of El Camino del Diablo, the road that snaked from Sonora into California. If they encountered resistance, they would just have to push through it.

The city was still sleepy, but waking up, when they entered it. Joaquin smelled coffee and chocolate and corn tortillas and roasting peppers. Men traveled this way and that, and women stepped outside the doors of their long adobe houses to sweep the sidewalk, or opened windows to air out from the fires of the night before, and to invite the sunshine in. A few people glanced at the foursome, and some bade them good morning.

Soon, Joaquin spotted, looming above the other buildings, a pair of white towers more or less at the edge of town nearest the river. He pointed it out to Rosita and the others, and they made for it, passing the city's central plaza and continuing on for a couple of blocks. When they were near enough to see the whole structure—the two towers and a dome behind it, all gleaming in the morning sun like mushrooms that had sprouted overnight—he knew for sure what it was.

"That's La Purísima Concepción de Nuestra Señora," he said, unable to hide the excitement in his voice. "My father's been to mass there."

"It's lovely," Rosita said, taking it in. The ornate towers faced onto a plaza, and the dome behind them must have covered the nave. "But I don't think we have time for sightseeing, do we?"

"She's right, Joaquin," Jesús called. "Why are you leading us out of our way?"

"It's a church," Joaquin pointed out. "And we need to be married."

"There?"

"As good as anywhere else."

"We don't have time for this!" Tres Dedos grumped. "We need to stay on the road."

"Perhaps in a smaller town somewhere?" Rosita's brow furrowed, and her lips parted slightly. She was worried.

"No, here," Joaquin insisted. "Fray Kino built this town and established the mission. This is a place of history, and our love is historic as well. When our story is written, it'll be the tale of two bold souls who let nothing get in their way, who met life head on and embraced it together."

Rosita smiled, shaking her head. "Nobody's going to be

writing our story, silly. We're just two young fools in love."

He drew his mount to a stop in front of the church. "Wait and see," he said. "You just wait and see."

"Joaquin . . ." Jesús began.

"Trust me, brother. This won't take long, but it's important."

"You can marry in America." Tres Dedos suggested.

"I can't wait that long. It'll be quick, I promise."

He tied Blanco to a rail, then tied off Oso and helped Rosita down. Hand-in-hand, they approached the double doors. Joaquin pulled open the right one and ushered her inside. The interior was cool, the chancel opulent but simple at the same time, with a niche for the Holy Mother and a seemingly life-sized crucifix above. Not full of gold like some churches.

The place was empty, though. "Let's find a priest," Joaquin said. They went back out, and around to the back. There was a door there, but it was locked. They kept going, Joaquin acutely aware that he was sorely testing the patience of their companions—and aware, too, that if he'd told them earlier of his plans, they'd have refused to stop. Finally, they found a small, plain chapel. The inside was scented with flowers and candles, but at first, it also appeared empty. Then Rosita spotted a priest, kneeling and praying. They waited.

When he'd finished his offices, the priest rose. He was young, probably not yet thirty, Joaquin guessed, with a tonsure cut, the top of his head shaved and dark hair ringing his scalp. His eyes were blue and large, in contrast to his narrow beak and pursed lips. He wore light blue robes with a white belt.

"Oh," he said, when he noticed them. "I wasn't aware we had visitors. Good morning."

"Good morning, Padre," Joaquin said.

"You're standing where he did, you know."

"Who did?" Joaquin looked at his feet and saw a tile with words carved into it.

"Fray Eusebio Kino," the priest said. "Most people who come to the chapel are looking for that spot."

A thrill traveled through Joaquin at the proximity to someone so famous, and whose efforts so shaped the very California they were headed for.

"If you haven't come for him, is there something I can help you with?"

"There is, in fact, Padre. We need to be married."

The priest smiled. "Of course, in due time."

"No, I mean this morning. Now."

The smile vanished, replaced by a look of grave concern. "How old are you?"

"I'm seventeen," Rosita answered.

"And I'm nineteen," Joaquin lied. He would be, in a few months. Close enough, he decided.

"You can't marry at those ages unless you have parental permission," the priest said. "Where are your parents?"

"They're home, in . . . in another town. Far from here."

"Does that town have a name?"

"It does, but it's not important."

"Well, I'm afraid I cannot marry you. Not without permission. Come back with your parents, or when you're older."

Rosita fixed the priest with her big, dark eyes. Joaquin knew how hard it was to resist her entreaties when she did that. "Please, Padre, it's very important to us. Isn't it better to be wed in the eyes of the Lord than to live in sin?"

"Of . . . of course it is," the priest said. "But the church has laws, as does Mexico herself. If you can't produce your families or permission, written and witnessed, you should go. And sin no more," he added. "I can hear your confessions now if you want."

An idea started to form in Joaquin's head. He turned suddenly and said, "I'll be right back. Rosa, stay here with the padre."

He walked back outside, to the horses. His initial thought had been to have Jesús pose as his father, but reaching the animals and glancing at their possessions, he had another idea. He drew the flintlock musket from its scabbard, loaded and rammed it, placed some powder in the pan, and carried it back inside at a half-cock.

"What are you up to, Joaquin?" Jesús asked. "You could hurt somebody with that."

That had already occurred to him. "With luck, I won't need to."

"I have to see this," Tres Dedos said with a grin. He tossed his reins to Jesús and climbed down from the mule.

When they passed through the door, Rosita gasped audibly.

"Now, son, we don't allow firearms inside this sanctuary," the priest said. Joaquin heard the slight tremor in his voice, and found it encouraging.

"I've done plenty of things that aren't allowed," Joaquin said. "This is just one more."

"What do you hope to accomplish with that?"

Joaquin thumbed it to a full cock and pointed it at the priest as he drew nearer, resting his finger lightly on the trigger. "I hope to encourage you to ignore your silly rules and marry two people who are in love."

"This is not the way to do it, young man. Put the weapon down."

"I'm sorry, but I can't do that. Step aside, Rosita."

She watched the whole thing with eyes wide and mouth open, an expression somewhere between wonder and glee. Joaquin stopped a few feet from the priest—close enough that he wouldn't miss, but far enough back that if the priest lunged for the gun, Joaquin could avoid his grasp.

"I understand what you think you're doing, son," the priest said. "But it won't work."

"Padre," Rosita said. "My beloved is . . . impetuous. I did not expect him to fetch a gun, but he did. So I cannot tell you for certain that he won't use it, even if I beg him not to. Would you rather be shot dead than to marry two people who ask for it?"

"Would I rather be a martyr than to break my vows? The answer is yes. To marry you against the laws of church and state would be a grievous sin, and I can't do it. He can shoot me if he must."

Joaquin hesitated. Shooting a priest was a serious crime, not to be undertaken lightly. And what would it accomplish? Alive, the man *wouldn't* marry them, but dead, he *couldn't*. He felt foolish, standing here inside the chapel with a cocked musket in his hands.

Then the door opened, and an old woman stepped inside, ensconced in a bubble of light until she swung the door closed again. Her hair was pure white, her back stooped, her face lined with the years she'd seen.

"Señora Alvarez," the priest said. "Perhaps you should come back in a little while."

"No, Señora," Rosita countered. "If you don't want the

padre to be shot, please come forward."

"You wouldn't hurt—" the priest began.

Rosita cut him off. "You don't know what he might do. He's a desperate man, Padre."

Joaquin understood what she was doing. She had always been the cleverer of them. If he was a hammer, she was the sharpest of razors. He backed away from the priest, putting distance between them so the man couldn't try anything. The old woman stood frozen in place. When he was far enough from the priest for comfort, Joaquin spun around and aimed the rifle at her.

The old woman started to turn back toward the door, but Tres Dedos had moved in front of it. She eyed his bulk, then turned around again. "Come, Señora Alvarez. You're just in time to witness our marriage."

She glared at him. Her lips moved, but no sound emerged.

"Señora Alvarez is mute," the priest said. "She comes this time every day, to light a candle and pray."

"It's easy enough to see in her eyes what she'd say if she could," Rosita said. "Now tell me, Padre. Would you be so willing to see *her* be a martyr, in your place?"

"I don't believe you'd shoot a harmless old woman, son."

"Don't talk to him," Rosita said. "Talk to me, if you want to save lives. I don't believe you want to test him. So which will it be, Padre? Her life, or our marriage?"

The priest was silent, perhaps mulling over the possibilities.

"Hurry up, Padre," Joaquin said. "My finger's getting tired, and I wouldn't want to pull the trigger by accident."

"Very well," the priest said finally. "But you'll have to put the gun down for the ceremony."

"That's not going to happen. If it's the first wedding you've officiated with a musket in the mix, then so be it."

"Well, you have to come back up here."

"Come, señora," Rosita said. "Despite appearances, this is a joyous occasion. Two young people in love are sealing their bond before the Lord."

He could read the fury in the woman's ancient eyes, but she did as she was told. Soon they were all standing before the simple altar; Joaquin facing Rosita but with the gun trained on Señora Alvarez, the priest between them and the altar, facing the empty kneelers. Tres Dedos stood in the doorway, watching the scene unfold.

"My dear friends," the priest began. "You have come together in this church so that the Lord may seal—"

"Make it fast," Joaquin interrupted. "Skip the boring parts."

The priest let out a heavy sigh. "Very well. What are your names?

"I'm Joaquin, and she's Rosa."

"Joaquin and Rosa, have you come here freely and without reservation to give yourselves to each other in marriage?"

"Yes," Joaquin said.

"We have," Rosita added.

"Will you love and honor each other as man and wife for the rest of your lives?"

"Obviously," Joaquin said.

"We will," Rosita said.

"Will you accept children lovingly from God, and bring them up according to the law of Christ and the Church?"

"We will," Rosita said again.

"Of course," Joaquin said. "Get to it, Padre."

Another sigh. "Since it is your intention to enter into marriage, join your right hands, and declare your consent before God and his Church."

"Left hand," Joaquin said. He shifted the musket and held it only with his right, still keeping the muzzle pointed toward the old woman. His finger was alongside the trigger now, close enough that he could shoot if he needed to, but reducing the risk of doing so accidentally. He took Rosa's left hand in his.

"I take you, Rosa, to be my wife. I promise to be true to you, to love and honor you, and all that."

Rosita grinned, but he could see the glimmer of tears in her eyes. "And I, Rosa, take you, Joaquin, to be my husband. I promise to be true to you in good times and bad, in sickness and in health. I will love and honor you all the days of my life."

"You should've gone first," Joaquin said. "You know all the right words." To the priest, he asked, "Are we done?"

"Almost," the priest replied. "You have declared your consent before the Church. May the Lord in his goodness strengthen your consent and fill you both with his blessings. What God has joined, men must not divide. Amen."

"That's it?" Joaquin asked.

"Have you rings?"

Rosita took a red silk scarf from her neck, which she'd put on against the chill of the nighttime ride, and wrapped it around Joaquin's wrist. "This will do, for now," she said. Joaquin touched the scarf and grinned.

"You have to take communion," the priest added.

"I think we'll pass on that, Padre. We'll do it later, when we have a little more time."

"There's much more to the ceremony, Joaquin. Readings, blessings, prayers . . ."

"And someone else could walk in at any time. Wrap it up."

"Very well," the priest said. He rushed through the next part. "May the Lord Jesus, who was a guest at the wedding in Cana, bless you and your families and friends. Amen. May He grant that, as you believe in His resurrection, so you may wait for Him in joy and hope. Amen. May the almighty God bless you, in the name of the Father, and of the Son, and of the Holy Spirit. Amen."

"Amen," Joaquin said.

"Amen," Rosita echoed.

"That's it?" Joaquin asked again. He knew there was a lot more to it—weddings he'd attended had seemed to drag on for hours. But he didn't want to stay a moment longer than necessary.

"You're married in the eyes of God," the priest answered. "If not the eyes of Mexico."

"That's all we ask." They weren't planning to be in Mexico much longer, anyway. In California, they knew no one except Chuy, and he would accept their word on it. All he wanted was for Rosita and himself to know that they'd been married in a church.

At last, Rosita pressed the musket's barrel down toward the floor. Joaquin eased the cock forward. "Thank you for witnessing our blessed moment, Señora Alvarez," Rosita said. "And you, Manuel."

The old woman looked at her with a gaze that could burn through walls.

Rosita ignored the woman's glare. "We'll be going now, Padre. We appreciate your assistance."

"Go with God."

Joaquin kissed Rosita, then took her hand and led her toward the door. Before she followed Tres Dedos through, she stopped just inside and turned to the priest. "Tell the truth, Padre—of all the weddings you've performed, which is the one you'll remember for all the rest of your days?"

Unexpectedly, the priest barked out a laugh. "Hah! This one, to be sure."

"That's what I thought. Good day to you!"

Then she stepped outside. Joaquin followed, closed the door, and drew Rosita into his arms for one more kiss.

It lasted a long while.

But not long enough.

7

Riding through the city streets, Joaquin thought of what Bill Byrnes had told him, about men crossing lines. He guessed he'd crossed a few already. He had betrayed his own people when he'd helped the American prisoners escape, though he still felt justified in that. He had stolen Rosita away from her home and abandoned his own. Now, he'd married— illegally, and only by holding a loaded gun on two innocent people. Even now, his stomach was unsettled, his hands trembling. He was not a violent person, but the willingness he'd felt to kill at that moment scared him a little. He was relieved it hadn't come to that.

Line after line after line, and he had crossed them all. Now, he and his new bride, along with his brother and his cousin, were headed toward the biggest line yet—the borderline, dividing what had once been Mexico from what still was. He'd never even been in a city as large as Caborca before, and now he was on his way to another country altogether.

Rosita interrupted his thoughts with her laugh, which always made him think of an angel ringing a bell. "Would you really have done it, Joaquin?"

"Done what?"

"Shot the priest? Or the old woman?"

"They're both happy I didn't have to, I'm sure."

"So am I."

"Did I scare you?"

"A little," she said. "But I'm glad you did it."

"So am I."

The city was fully awake now, its streets buzzing with activity. Joaquin half expected to be accosted. It was almost unimaginable that the priest, or Señora Alvarez, wouldn't have reported the incident in the chapel. But although some people noted their passing, nobody made any effort to stop them, and soon Caborca was at their backs, and the rest of their lives were in front.

The first indication of why the road to the north was called El Camino del Diablo came the next morning. They'd ridden for an hour after leaving Caborca, just to ensure that they weren't followed, then—exhausted by the previous night's long ride and the excitement of the morning—had stopped and put up their tent. Jesús and Tres Dedos had, as he'd expected, slept on the ground, wrapped only in a blanket. After consummating their marriage, Joaquin and Rosita slept until early afternoon, when Jesús finally roused them. They broke camp and rode on until sunset. Determined to travel by daylight for the rest of their journey, they again made camp. Jesús built a raging fire to ward off the night's chill, and after a meal and a few drinks, Joaquin and Rosita slept wrapped in one another's arms.

In the morning, they shared a quick breakfast of beans and rice and camp coffee, then took to the road. Coming out of a mountain pass on a steep, gravelly pitch, Rosita spotted the wreckage of a wagon off to the side. "Joaquin, look!" she said. "Do you think there's anyone inside?"

He studied it. The thing had likely fallen off the road and

rolled down the slope. One intact wheel stuck up into the air, but the other was destroyed. The boards of the side that he could see were caved in, and a brown stain on one of them might have been blood. Looking at it gave him a chill. "It's been there awhile," he said. "No horses around. I think if there was anybody in there, they're long gone."

They traveled on, but he couldn't shake the image in his mind. He wondered what had happened. Maybe a wheel on the right side broke, and the wagon dropped on that side, startling the horse or horses drawing it. Their anxious motions might have nudged it over the edge, and once it left the narrow roadway, it just tumbled down until it caught on the vegetation and stopped. Had it belonged to someone heading toward the gold? And had that person, or that party, continued on without the wagon and whatever it had carried? Or turned back, dreams shattered?

Less than an hour later, they came upon an ox, bloated, its skin taut, four legs pointing skyward. Tres Dedos gave an abrupt shout and jumped down from the mule, running to the ox. "This is how they invented the drum!" he cried. He slapped on the bloat-stretched skin with his open palms, beating out a rhythm, and like a drum, the sound reverberated from inside the beast. After a minute's performance, Tres Dedos threw back his head and roared laughter at the sky. "Ox-drum!" he shouted. Remounting, he sang the rhythm he'd played on the animal's skin, "Dum di di dum dum, dum di di dum," for the next ten minutes or so.

A short time later, they spotted a horse, or the ragged remains of one after carrion-eaters had been at it. A shattered knee bone jutting through leathery skin told the story.

The first human corpse didn't show until the sun was high.

Tres Dedos noticed it first and pointed it out to the others with a nod of his head. Rosita had been looking the other way and missed the signal. Joaquin tried to ride past, hoping she wouldn't see it. But she said, "Oh!" and the tone of that simple utterance revealed both disgust and fear.

Like the horse, it had been visited by animals. What flesh remained, tattered around an up-thrust ribcage, looked like paper. The person's guts had been taken, as had the eyeballs, and the face was so shredded as to be unrecognizable as human.

"He's been dead a long time," Tres Dedos said.

"Not *he*," Rosita corrected. Only then did Joaquin realize that the fabric splayed out beneath the corpse's legs was a skirt.

"Oh," he said, inadvertently echoing her.

Hour after hour they rode, and the farther north they went, the more horror they encountered. Men, women, whole families, slaughtered and left to rot in the sun. Burned-out and looted wagons. Mules and horses and oxen in various stages of decomposition.

Joaquin had seen death before—death and birth and everything in between. He had hunted, and he'd worked on Don Ramon's ranch. But he had never seen it like this. So many bodies, spread like signposts marking the route to California. Jesús and Tres Dedos seemed unshaken by it, and Joaquin knew, from their stories, that they'd seen brutality on an almost unimaginable scale.

They all carried plenty of water—or so he hoped; they'd refilled their empty botas the last time they'd crossed the Rio Concepción, and still had plenty they hadn't touched—but with every league they traveled, the landscape seemed to become harsher, more brutal, laced with empty, rock-strewn stretches.

When he commented on it, Rosita said, "It would be worse in summer, though."

"That's true. But if we run out of water, the season won't matter."

"We won't run out."

"How can you be sure?"

She pointed to the nearest wagon, or what was left of it: a pile of fire-blackened rubble, only the few metal parts still recognizable. "Somebody did that," she said. "Attacked it, looted it, burned it. Whoever did that lives nearby."

"How can you tell?"

"Would they travel far to rob a wagon? Or would they lie in wait until it came their way?"

As usual, she was more perceptive than he. That hadn't occurred to Joaquin, but now that she pointed it out, he couldn't stop thinking about it. He felt they were being watched from every hilltop, and he worried about what was around every blind curve. He stopped, loaded the musket, then remounted and carried it across his lap as he rode, close at hand. Jesús and Tres Dedos had their own weapons at the ready—and both had far more experience in using them on humans than Joaquin, who had never shot anything more dangerous than a rattlesnake.

"Look at all the wagon tracks, Joaquin," Rosita said, her voice light and cheery. "All the hoofprints. Yes, there are dangers out here, but for every dead body we've passed, there must be a thousand people who've traveled this road unharmed. And none of the bodies have appeared very fresh. I haven't even seen many buzzards."

"I suppose you're right."

"Of course I am. That's why you married me, isn't it? For my astute powers of observation?"

"That, and the beautiful smile that lights the darkest of nights. But why did you marry me?"

She laughed, and the sound of it snatched away his fears. "I'm still trying to figure that out," she said. "I guess it's because I love you and I trust you. Yes, this will be a long, hard journey, but we'll be fine. Because we're together, whatever happens."

His concerns didn't vanish, but they lessened. Still, he kept the musket close.

When he heard the clomp of hooves and the creaking of saddle leather from around a bend, he raised it and brought his horse to a halt. "Get behind us, Rosita," he said.

She obeyed. A shadow seemed to have drifted over her normally sunny disposition.

Tres Dedos took the front position, Jesús and Joaquin flanking him, each with a musket across his lap. After a few moments, a man came into view, riding an aged mule. The man was Mexican, older even than Tres Dedos, but not much more than thirty. His hat was gone, and his eyes stared into the distance from a face caked with blood. He didn't even seem to see them at first.

"Sir," Jesús called. "Are you hurt?"

The man didn't answer.

"Sir? Can we help?"

Finally, he noticed them, blinked.

"Turn back," he said.

"What?"

"Go back to wherever you came from. You don't want to

be here."

"Why not?"

"Sand Papagos. Raiders. Bandits. Whatever danger you can imagine lurks on this road."

"Sand what?" Rosita asked.

"Sand Papagos. Natives. They live up there." He indicated a vaguely northern direction with a slight cock of his head. "They see this road as their own treasure trove, and attack those heading north on it to steal their food and trade goods. There were eight of us, all armed. Only I survived, and that only because I had fallen behind."

"Are you hurt?" Joaquin asked.

"They never saw me."

"But the blood . . ."

The man touched his face, as if he'd forgotten about the blood painting it. He looked at his fingers. "After the Indians left, I went to my friends. What was left of them. I must have gotten blood on my hands."

"How far away are they?" Jesús asked him.

The man shrugged. "Half a day's ride, more or less. But they were heading the other way, last I saw them. Farther north."

"Did you see any water up there?" Rosita asked.

"Not as far as I went."

"What will you do now?" Joaquin asked.

The man shrugged again. "Back to Hermosillo, I guess. Somebody else can have my gold. I'd rather have my life."

"Well, I hope you have a safe journey home."

"I hope you turn around. It's not worth it."

"My brother's best friend is waiting in California. Our futures are there."

"God help you, then." The man gave the mule his heels, and the beast carried him toward the south.

When he was gone, Joaquin rode close to Rosita. "Are you sure about this, Rosita? We could go home, too."

"We can't. We've broken the laws. My father would have you arrested, or worse. Anyway, you're right—your future— *our* future—is in the north. In America."

He reached into his pocket, felt the smooth, soft silk of her scarf. He hadn't given it back, and he didn't plan to. Anyway, she seemed to have an endless supply of scarves. "My future is wherever you are."

"Then you'd better head for California," she said with a grin. "Because I am."

• • •

The tracks of those who'd gone before made the road easy to follow. Now and again, they met fellow travelers headed the same way, and the occasional one who'd turned back or was returning to Mexico with his gold. They found water in occasional small rivers and creeks, running down from the ever-present hills and mountains. After a while, there were more than twenty of them, all bound for California, with three wagons between them. Every night's camp turned into a fan-dango, with music and dancing, and people shared the deer or rabbits they'd managed to kill during the day, so no one went hungry.

People shared stories of California, telling what they'd heard from friends or relatives who'd been there. Joaquin heard about a place called Los Angeles, where some wealthy Californios had vast ranches. He had spent most of his savings on supplies before the trip, and more along the way, so he and Rosita agreed to detour to Los Angeles instead of heading straight to the gold fields with the others.

Jesús argued when Joaquin brought up the idea. "We said we'd travel together!" he shouted. Joaquin had led him away from the others, who were singing songs from home and loudly swapping tales of what they would do with the riches they amassed in California, precisely because he feared such a reaction. "A family!"

"It's just for a few weeks," Joaquin said. "You and Manuel have been working longer than I have, and you've saved more. I don't want us to be a burden on you."

"Family is never a burden," Jesús snapped.

Joaquin understood the spirit behind the remark, but he also knew that family could indeed be a tremendous burden. One tried to overlook it, to tell oneself that one did everything for family, without complaint. But these days on the road, free of his father's judging gaze and his mother's fussing and Esmerelda's chatter, he had felt a sense of freedom he'd never known. He loved his family, but their presence could also be a weight that became exhausting to carry.

Anyway, he had a hole card, and he hurried to play it, to end the argument before it worsened. "Besides," he said, "newlyweds need some time to themselves. We don't want to have to hush ourselves every time we make love, for fear of embarrassing everyone else."

Jesús laughed at that, and Joaquin knew the battle was won. "You two are incredibly annoying. Smooching all the time, making eyes at each other, slipping away for your private chats."

"I know. A few weeks, that's all we need. We'll earn some money so we can help with expenses. You and Tres Dedos go ahead and find us a good spot, and soon we'll have enough gold to build a castle out of."

Jesús nodded his acceptance. "One month. No longer. And you'll write to me, at Chuy's address, every week to keep me apprised."

"I promise."

"And you tell Tres Dedos. I don't want him to hear it from me."

"I will," Joaquin said, glad to be done with the conversation. His cousin wouldn't object, once he learned that Jesús had agreed. He rushed back to Rosita to tell her the news.

• • •

Before they split off from the group, the entire party came to a halt. The landscape looked no different here than it had before—open desert, hilly, with lots of low scrub and occasional yuccas piercing the sky—but something was different, just the same. Joaquin walked to the front of the pack, where some of the group's members had gathered.

"What's going on?"

"Just saying goodbye," one of them said.

"To who?"

"To Mexico."

"You're standing in California," another man said. "In America."

"Really? Now?"

"Right now. You're no longer on Mexican soil."

Joaquin crouched, dug his fingers into the earth, pulled up some dirt and rubbed it. "Feels the same."

"It was Mexican not so long ago."

"We should've kept it," Joaquin said.

"Your lips to God's ears. You're a little late, though."

"Seems like I always am. I was too young to fight in the war as Jesús and our father did. I had to stay behind and take care of the family."

"We all play our part."

Joaquin hurried back to Rosita, waiting with the horses. "We're there," he said. He scooped up another handful of earth. "We're in California now."

Rosita's sudden smile was glorious. "We are?"

"That's what they say."

She slid from the saddle, wrapped her arms around Joaquin and held him tight. Even after days on the road, she smelled like heaven. "We made it! We did it, Joaquin!"

"Well, we made it this far. We're not to the gold yet."

"We've done the hardest part, though."

"Yes. Yes, we've done that." Another line crossed, this one the invisible line marking the international border. And marking much more—a new life, together. New adventures, new challenges.

And all of it with the woman he loved.

Truly, his life had just begun, and he couldn't wait to see what it would bring.

8

The attack came less than two hours after they'd split off from the rest of the group, headed for Los Angeles.

They had crossed the Colorado River on a ferry, at the price of one dollar for each of them and another dollar for each horse. Joaquin and Rosita had no dollars, but the ferryman was willing to take pesos. Joaquin didn't know how many pesos would equal a dollar, and the number the ferryman quoted seemed like a lot. But the man said that although the river was deceptively calm, its placid surface hid man-swallowing whirlpools and venomous snakes, so they paid the fee.

Some rough-looking customers had gathered on the far side of the river, playing cards outside of a large tent. At the ferry's approach, one of them hurried to his horse, jumped on, and raced off to the west. Joaquin noticed his brown hat and canvas pants, but mostly his attention was on the animal, a strong, sturdy mare.

He didn't think much about it after that. The trail canted slightly to the northwest, skirting tall sand dunes and leading into a stretch of increasingly steep, rugged hills sliced by narrow valleys. They had just entered the deepest valley yet, when a man stepped out from behind a big rock. Two others rose up on the hillside, having hidden behind creosote bushes. All three held muskets.

The first one—on the canyon floor—wore a brown hat and canvas pants. Joaquin assumed the big mare was close by. "Let's have the rest of that poke," the man said.

"Excuse me?" Joaquin said. He thought he understood the words, but not their meaning when put together in that way. Rosita knew even less English than he did, so she wouldn't be any help.

"Johnny signaled when you was on his ferry," the man said. "You got money left over. We want it, and whatever other valuables you got on you."

Joaquin took in the three men. The three muskets. They were all some distance off. Their primary advantage was that there was little room to maneuver in the canyon.

His advantage was that the slope across from the one the men stood on was steep and thickly vegetated, offering some degree of cover for much of its height. It helped that he'd been riding Blanco for more than a week and had helped to raise the horse from birth. He knew the animal's strengths and his capabilities. He knew Oso, as well, and he had no doubts about Rosita's skill in the saddle. He only hoped he could keep up with her.

"We have little money," Joaquin countered. "Let us pass, or you'll regret it."

"Ooh, tough talk from the greaser," the man said. "Fork over, or we'll drop you where you stand."

Joaquin wished now that Jesús and Tres Dedos had come with them—these men wouldn't have dared such a thing with those two around.

His mind whirled with possibilities. Hand over the money that was supposed to last them until they reached Los Angeles? Or risk their lives with the guns? In his experience, most men weren't very good shots. But how skilled were these particular men?

On the other hand, moving targets were harder to hit.

"Rosita," he said, in low tones, hoping the men didn't understand Spanish. "Follow me, no matter what."

"Of course," she replied.

Without warning, he wheeled his horse around and gave it his spurs, urging it up the steep slope to his right. The animal obeyed without hesitation. Behind him, he heard the hooves of Rosita's mount scrabbling over the rock-strewn surface, following suit.

Shots rang out. Musket balls thunked into the dirt or spanged off of rocks. Joaquin slid to Blanco's right side, offering as small a target as he could—though if the horse was hit, he would still be in danger. Glancing back, he saw that Rosita had done the same. Of course she had—he'd learned the trick from her. Their mounts charged up the slope, at a slight angle from the gunmen. The two men on the hillside ran down to the canyon floor, costing themselves precious seconds, but probably hoping that a more level surface would allow them more accuracy.

The top of the hill had looked impossibly distant, but in fact Joaquin was already approaching it. Another shot came closer than any of the previous ones, kicking up dirt just ahead of Blanco's hooves. The animal shifted course slightly, almost bucking Joaquin from the saddle, but he gripped tighter with his legs and managed to hang on.

Then he was up and over the peak. Rosita had already passed him and gone over it. Below, he could hear the men shouting and scrambling for their own mounts. Wherever they'd been hidden—to make the ambush a surprise—made it inconvenient to get to them at a moment's notice.

The far side of the hill was almost as steep as the one they'd just climbed, and from here, the trail they'd been told would lead them to Los Angeles was out of sight. He still saw the high dunes to the south, and nothing in any other direction besides more hills and canyons. Presumably, once they lost their pursuers—if indeed the men were going to give chase— they could double back to the south and cut across the trail again. But if not, it wouldn't be hard to get lost out here.

"Do you think they're coming?" Rosita asked. She was breathing heavily, her mouth open and her eyes bright, and he was struck with a sudden, almost irresistible urge to kiss her. That would have to wait, though.

"I don't think we should sit around here waiting to find out." Joaquin pointed down the slope. "Let's follow this canyon as far as we can, then see if they're behind us."

"Lead the way," she said.

They started down the slope, more slowly than they'd gone up the other side, leaning back in the saddle. Blanco was as sure-footed as a mountain goat.

After they wound through the canyons for a couple of hours without seeing or hearing any signs of pursuit, Joaquin reasoned that the men had decided they were too much trouble to bother with. They worked their way back to the main trail, but the sun had almost set when they got there. Just in case, they backed away from it and made camp on the far side of a nearby hill, from the top of which they'd have a good view of anyone coming or going.

"So far, California's not very welcoming," Joaquin said, scraping beans off a metal plate with an old fork. "I'm pretty sure that ferryman robbed us, and then his friends tried to finish the job. Are you sure you don't want to go home? It's going to be much harder to do, after this."

Rosita set her plate carefully down on the dirt. "Joaquin, my love, I don't know if you know this, but women tell girls things about marriage that nobody ever tells boys. Older girls tell us even more. Some of it's lies, but most of it's true, I think.

"But what nobody ever told me—and I don't know if it's true for everybody, but it certainly is for me—is how *exciting* marriage is. At least, being married to you is. It's been one thing after another from the time you tapped on my window and we went into the stables."

"One horrible event after another, you mean." Joaquin was certain she was working her way toward telling him that it was over.

"Horrible? *No!* I mean, some of it was scary. But every minute of it's been fun. I never imagined a girl could have such adventures. And watching you take charge of things, make sudden, life-or-death decisions—it's thrilling. I wouldn't want to have missed a moment of it."

Joaquin studied her. These days on the trail seemed to have matured her a little, shaved off some of the childhood roundness that had still marked her features. Now he saw more planes and angles, and they only made her lovelier. He worried, though, hoping she had enough to eat and could bear more nights in a tent, sleeping on the ground. She'd been brought up in comfortable surroundings, with the best of everything at her fingertips. A tent was as good as a house to him, offering just as much comfort and more privacy. She hadn't said anything outright, but every now and then she made a comment suggesting that she was expecting far more luxurious accommodations, once the gold started rolling in.

"So you want to keep going? To Los Angeles, then north to the gold fields?"

"Of course, silly." She laughed. "That's why we're here, isn't it?"

"Yes. That's why we're here."

The urge to kiss her had become unbearable. He set his plate aside and leaned into her, and one kiss led to more. By the time they returned to their dinners, the plates were covered with insects.

Somehow, Joaquin didn't mind.

9

Los Angeles proved to be friendlier. Most of the population was still Mexican, so Joaquin and Rosita felt at home there. Although they knew nobody, it wasn't long before Joaquin found work busting broncos at the rancho of Don Miguel Esparza. Joaquin's skill with horses won him acclaim, and before the month had passed, he'd earned enough money to finance the rest of their trip north. While he tamed and trained animals, Rosita worked with the landlady who'd rented them a room, helping her tidy up, making beds, and cooking. At the same time, she was learning English and studying the American culture, which she found fascinating.

Having been warned by several people about absurdly high prices for mining gear in the gold towns, they decided to buy what they would need in Los Angeles and carry it with them. On Main Street, near the Lafayette Hotel in which they'd spent their first couple of nights in town, they found a store that seemed to have everything they could want. The shopkeeper was grizzled and gray-bearded, an American who claimed that his discoveries in the gold region had paid to set him up in business here, and now he wanted to help out future miners.

"You'll need some pans, for sure," he said. "On account of most of the time you'll be pannin' in the rivers. Say two, for starters. They'd run you eight dollars each up there, but I can let you have 'em for two bucks each."

Joaquin was about to agree, but Rosita cut him off. "Let's say three dollars for both."

"You want me to lose money on the deal, little missy?" the man asked.

"You're a long way from the gold," she pointed out. "My husband was smart enough to want to equip himself here, but I doubt that very many people headed that way do. Probably most wait until they're much closer, and don't have to haul their supplies so far. So you're better off selling us two pans for three dollars—I see that you have plenty of them—than letting them sit here with the rest of your merchandise, hundreds of miles from the gold fields."

Joaquin watched her, frankly stunned. He remembered how she had negotiated with the priest in Caborca. She'd also convinced their landlady here in Los Angeles to cut the price of their room, then made nearly enough working for the woman to pay the difference. Most of what he'd earned at the rancho, they were able to keep.

"All right, three dollars," the man said, a pained expression on his face.

"That sounds fine," Joaquin agreed. "What else?"

"You need good boots, and plenty of 'em. The rivers destroy 'em faster'n you can say 'Bob's your uncle.' Up north they're runnin' forty bucks a pair. From me, fifteen a pair. How many you want?"

"Two?"

The man cocked an eyebrow at him, and Joaquin amended his order. "Three?"

"Five," Rosita said. "At ten a pair." She glanced at Joaquin.

"You'll be standing in the water a lot, you need to protect your feet."

"The lady knows how to pinch pennies," the man said. "That's a good quality in a wife. Not so much in a customer, but good in a wife. Five'll last you a few months. Now, you'll also need a shovel or two, and mebbe a pickaxe. Assumin' you'll want to do some diggin'. Never know if where you land up, the gold might all be in the river, or in the ground."

"How about one shovel and one pickaxe, then?"

"They're ten each up north. Let's do three bucks each. But when that shovel breaks . . ."

"All right, two shovels."

"How you set for clothes? Canvas trousers is better'n wool for standing in a river, but you'll want some of each."

"I already have some of each," Joaquin assured him.

"You got blankets? A good tent?"

"We do."

"Could be after a week or two in the diggin's, you won't mind payin' exorbitant prices for goods. Twelve bucks for a blanket, eight for a coffee pot, six for a fryin' pan, and so on. But anything you can get your hands on here will save you some up there."

"Save me money, yes. But my horse wouldn't appreciate the extra weight."

"Well, that's true, sonny. And a horse up there would set you back three or four hundred, easy. So you don't want to kill the one you got. I'd say, assumin' you already got the basics for livin', that you're set for now. Let's call it an even seventy-five and I'll help you haul everything outside."

"Sixty-five," Rosita said. "And you'll supply some rope to tie these things onto our horses."

He eyed her like she was an annoying insect, a mosquito he might swat before it bit again. But then he blew out a breath and nodded. "Sixty-five."

At the last minute, Joaquin saw a Bowie knife he coveted. Its heavy blade was half-again as long as his hand, flat on its edge until at the last moment it curved up. The upper surface was only straight about halfway, then had a wicked downward curve. It had a silver cross-guard and its handle was made of deer antler. It was heavy, solid, and would serve to skin and cut game, or men if it came to that. It added an extra ten dollars to the price, but Joaquin felt it a good investment.

The shopkeeper was as good as his word, helping to carry their new possessions out to the street and setting them down in the dirt. Once his hands were free, he leaned close to Joaquin and said, in a low voice, "You got yourself a reg'lar spitfire there, son. Best hold tight to her."

"I intend to," Joaquin replied. The man clapped him on the shoulder and went back inside his shop.

Joaquin and Rosita set to work arranging everything on their two horses and tying it into place for the ride north. They were almost finished when a tall, barrel-chested man, with legs like tree trunks and arms to match, strode up to them. He had short-cropped blond hair and a strangely flat face, as if at birth his parents had taken one look and walloped him with the back side of a shovel. A star-shaped silver badge gleamed on his chest, with the words "L.A. County Deputy Sheriff" engraved on it.

"Morning, folks." His voice had a gravelly, growling quality. His eyes were pale blue and coolly appraising. He had the air of a man who got things done, which was a trait that Joaquin admired.

"Good morning," Rosita said. Her English had come a long way in a few short weeks; she still had a strong accent, but she could understand most conversations, and be understood in turn. It had taken Joaquin months working with Bill Byrnes to reach that point.

"I don't believe I've met you all. Name's Schmitt. *Deputy Sheriff* Jakob Schmitt,"

Joaquin extended a hand, which Schmitt took in a crushing grip. "I'm Joaquin. This is my wife, Rosa."

"It's a pleasure. Looks like you're packin' for a trip."

"That's right."

"You a miner?"

An unexpected wave of pride washed over Joaquin, leaving his face flushed. No one had ever called him a miner. But he was no longer a horse trainer. He'd given up his past profession, and his former country, and his old life. He was a new man—and yes, a miner. Even if he hadn't actually started mining yet. "Yes," he said. "I am a miner."

"Is that right?" Schmitt asked.

"Yes."

"Hmm. You pay the tax inside the store?"

"Tax? What tax?"

"The Foreign Miners' Tax? The governor—I disremember his name, starts with a B. Burnett, that's it. Something like that. Anyhow, he just signed it into law, not too long ago. Twenty dollars, every month, from every foreign miner."

Joaquin had heard some discussion of that, but he hadn't paid much attention. California politics were confusing and seemed far removed from his life.

"But I'm not mining yet. I'm standing here in Los Angeles. The gold fields are far away."

"You just told me you was a miner."

"I meant, I will be."

"Look, you can't be a miner one second and not a miner the next. It don't work that way."

Joaquin was tall and muscular, but next to this man, he felt like a dwarf. He went up on his toes, looking past the big man for someone who might be able to help him explain himself. He was having a hard time following Schmitt's reasoning, and a harder time figuring out how to make himself clear in English. "But, you see—"

"All I see's a Mexican who says he's a miner, but he ain't paid the tax. Look, I'm the law in this county. You don't want to see the inside of our hoosegow, you got to shell out."

He and Rosita had already paid the landlady and packed their things. For all he knew, she'd already rented their room to somebody else. Where would Rosita go if he was jailed?

He had just handed over seventy-five dollars to the shopkeeper. On the advice of some men he'd met at Don Miguel's, he'd divided his money into three stacks and put some in a pocket, some in his boot, and some in his saddlebags. He reached into his pocket and pulled out some coins. Schmitt plucked two from his open palm, then two more.

"That's not twenty!" Joaquin said.

Schmitt nodded toward Rosita. "Twenty for you, twenty for her."

"She's not a miner!"

"You ridin' both these horses north, or is one for her?"

"I'm not leaving my wife behind."

"Sure looks like minin' gear on her horse, there."

"Well, yes, of course, but—"

"Then she's a miner."

Arguing with the man wasn't going to help. Joaquin closed his fist before Schmitt took the rest of his money and dropped it back into his pocket. "Are we finished, then?"

"We're done. You leaving town?"

"Leaving the town—and the county—just as fast as we can."

Schmitt grinned like he'd just heard good news. "Sounds like a good idea. You folks have a safe trip, you hear? And thank you for visitin'."

He turned then and strolled off down Main, no doubt looking for other Mexicans to harass.

But at least, Joaquin thought, he did it with a smile on his face.

10

May 1850, Sawmill Flat, California

Joaquin stood in frigid water almost up to his knees. He plucked a few stones and pebbles from his pan and tossed them back into the creek, then bent over and submerged the pan in the running water. The sun was hot on his back, contrasting with the almost painful cold of his feet. Tilting the pan into the current, he swirled it gently, letting the flow wash away the lighter sand and mineral flakes. After a couple of minutes of this, he raised it out of the creek and shook it to level what remained. This action, Jesús had explained, would settle the gold in the bottom of the pan. This was different from the silver mining they'd done back home, but Jesús had learned the technique quickly and taught it to Joaquin when he and Rosita had arrived from Los Angeles.

Then he had to bend again, dip the pan, swirl off more sediment. He'd seen old men doing this, white-haired, grizzled. His back already hurt; he couldn't imagine how they must have felt. The lure of gold, he guessed, outweighed a multitude of discomforts.

He repeated the process a couple more times. Each one made the pan a little lighter. Finally, there was nothing left in the pan but a little water, some black sand, some shiny flecks, and a nugget.

Joaquin sat on the bank, doffed his sombrero, and wiped the sweat from his eyes, the better to examine his prize. A nugget! His first. At its widest point, about as far across as his little fingernail. He'd heard stories of fist-sized nuggets, but those always sounded improbable—happening to someone nobody seemed to know personally, and even then, from the earliest days of the gold discoveries. This was small, a tiny pebble. But its importance couldn't be calculated by size, or even value. It was proof.

• • •

He'd sent Jesús a letter from Los Angeles informing him of their imminent departure from Los Angeles. Jesús had already told him how to find them when they arrived in the Sawmill Flat area, but he'd been reticent about describing the claim. When Joaquin and Rosita arrived late one afternoon, dusty from the road and bleary-eyed from travel, they were welcomed with hugs and laughter and tequila. Although Chuy and Pablo had moved on to what they claimed was a richer digging, Jesús and Tres Dedos had already made friends among the local Mexican community, and everyone was there for the arrival party. Joaquin was so exhausted that within minutes, he wished everyone would go home, and he fell asleep in a corner his brother had prepared for the newlyweds while the partyers roared outside.

In the morning, Jesús took him for a walk, showing him the stretch of the creek that was their claim. Back home in Sonora any water this wide and deep would have been called a river; it was only by contrast to the many large rivers flowing through this part of California that it was relegated to the title of "creek." Cottonwoods lined the far side, shading the water in the afternoons, and through the trees he could see a hillside covered with poppies, an orange blanket so bright in the sunshine that it almost hurt to look at. On the side where Jesús and Tres Dedos had erected a large tent, a grassy slope led down to an earthen bank with a cutaway to make access to the water easier. The air was cool and aromatic, and Joaquin could hear birdsong, blending with the sounds of men at work on claims up and down the creek.

"This is beautiful, Jesús," he said. "I couldn't even imagine this. It's like heaven."

"It's a good spot," Jesús agreed. "We've already found some color and started a little stash in the cabin. I know the place is small—you and Rosita will probably want to find a place of your own, once we're making real money, but you're welcome to stay with us as long as you like."

Sometimes Joaquin wondered if the changes in his life were real. They seemed too good, too perfect, to be happening to someone like him. To have won Rosita's love, and married her, then come to a place like this where his brother and their cousin had already started amassing gold. A few months ago, he had figured he'd grow old in the employ of Don Ramon, pining after Rosita while she married some wealthy land-owner and raised a brood of her own.

Now, though, anything seemed possible. Everything.

"Thank you for finding this place. And for insisting that we come."

"Of course," Jesús said. "I wouldn't want to be here without you."

"It's amazing that you found such a great spot to claim. Was it difficult?"

"That's what I wanted to talk to you about, Joaquin. It's . . . it's complicated, here. For Mexicans, especially. Any foreigners, really."

"I know that. Some of it, anyway." He told Jesús about the

encounter with Jakob Schmitt, and paying the Foreign Miner's Tax. "I suppose you've had to pay that, too."

"We haven't," Jesús said. "You see, officially, we're employees, not miners."

"Employees? Of who?"

"It's a little complicated, but it turns out there's a way that Mexicans can work claims that would otherwise be forbidden to them."

"How does that work?"

"We met a man—he was actually in the American army, during the war, but he seems to have put aside any grudges. As I have. Tres Dedos, not so much, but I convinced him to go along with the plan. Officially, Harry owns the claim, and we're just working it on his behalf."

"Harry? Who is that?"

"The soldier. Harry Love. He made a go of panning for gold, but he turns out to be terrible at it. Standing in the cold water aggravates his war wounds. So the deal is, he can't pan for gold, but he can own a claim. We can't own a claim, but we can work one. We give him a little of everything we find, and he gives us the legal right to work here."

It was a lot to take in. The idea that Tres Dedos sat down to have a business discussion with a former American soldier was itself amazing. The war had been over for years, but not as far as Tres Dedos was concerned.

"Does the American take a lot?" Joaquin asked. "Half?"

"Oh, no," Jesús said quickly. "One quarter. We told him you'd be joining us, so his riches would build faster once that happened. And so will ours. Even at three quarters, we'll still be wealthy in no time."

"I'm not sure if I like working for the benefit of an American," Joaquin admitted.

"If Manuel can do it, so can you. Mostly, we're still working for ourselves. Joaquin, the prejudice against foreigners here is real. They hate us. The way the gringos look at us is chilling, sometimes, like we're not even human. Manuel was on edge all the time, at first. Now he's getting used to it, but I had to convince him not to turn around and go back home when we first got here. It's almost like . . ." he hesitated, grasping for words. "Almost as if they fought to take back land that was rightfully *theirs*, instead of to steal it from us. But it was always ours. And now that they've taken it, they can't stop throwing it in our faces."

Always Spain's, Joaquin thought, after Father Kino came north from Mexico, establishing a chain of missions as he went; missions that subjugated the Indians who had lived here before along the way. Then ours, after we broke from Spain. Each one a conquest of one sort or another. But he didn't say that to Jesús, didn't want to get into a philosophical debate.

His head was swimming. This was all so complicated, so different than what he had expected. He'd thought he would be working side by side with his brother and his cousin, and the three of them would share whatever they made. Now there was a fourth person in the mix—not counting Rosita, of course, who would live on Joaquin's share—and an American soldier, to boot. He tried to look at the positive side of things. "So by working with Love, you don't have to pay the tax?"

"And we're able to work a promising claim. If we didn't have him, we couldn't get near the creek. We'd be out in the hills somewhere, digging for color. But it's far easier to take it out of the water. And if anyone comes around to collect taxes, we just tell them to talk to Harry. Trust me, Harry's not the kind of man people want to tangle with."

"What is he like?"

"He reminds me of Tres Dedos, in a way. He's a big guy. Tough. After the war, he was a sheriff's deputy in Santa Barbara for a while. Then the gold strikes happened, and he came north to get his share. Like I said, he didn't turn out to be very good at it. Lucky for him, we came along."

"Lucky for us, too, I guess." Joaquin had a hard time imagining a white man who was anything like Tres Dedos. But then, he couldn't imagine Tres Dedos willingly entering into a business arrangement with one, either. That was why Jesús had taken him aside to tell him about the deal, he was sure—because Tres Dedos wouldn't have been able to resist giving his own opinion. Joaquin and Manuel both looked up to Jesús; if he was in favor of the deal, they would go along. But Joaquin didn't expect that their cousin was very happy with it.

"Lucky for us, for sure. Harry comes around every few days to check on us and to pick up his take. I'm sure you'll meet him soon."

"I can't wait." That was a lie, though he hoped a harmless one. He had reservations about this deal—suspicions about the motives of any white man who would set up such an arrangement with a couple of Mexicans. He had to be taking advantage of them in some way that Jesús hadn't yet realized. Joaquin resolved to keep a close eye on things, to see if he could spot what was really going on.

• • •

Days had passed, during which Jesús and Tres Dedos had taught Joaquin how to pan for gold. Harry Love had not shown up. Jesus had shown him where the stash was kept, and how they divided it with Love when he came around. It was safe in the cabin, they said, even when nobody was around—finding gold was so easy that nobody stole from anybody else. And, Tres Dedos pointed out, adding in some pantomime to make his point—the few who had tried stealing from other miners quickly found themselves dangling from one of the many stout branches around.

And it was already paying off. Joaquin dug from his pocket the small bottle Jesús had given him, pulled the cork, and dropped the nugget in. It just fit through the opening. Then he carefully separated the gold flakes in the pan from the black sand, pinched the gold in his fingers, and fed it into the bottle. He held it up to the light, eyeing its gleam. Jesús and Tres Dedos had gone into town for supplies, and he wished they were here to see it.

"You got some!"

That was Horace Beeman, one of the five Americans who'd joined forces to work the neighboring stretch of the creek, just down from theirs. He was lean, gangly, with red hair and a freckled face that made him look younger than his thirty-some years. He always wore red suspenders, even when he worked without a shirt. He and his comrades were building a large rocker they called a long tom, to more efficiently separate gold from the other materials found in the creek.

"I did!" Joaquin called back.

"You're a gold miner now!"

That flush of pride Joaquin had felt when the lawman in Los Angeles had called him a miner returned, its impact tripled now that he had actual gold in his hands. He was a gold miner. He'd crossed another line, become a new person.

"Howdy, Miz Rosita," Beeman called. "Your feller done found some color!"

Joaquin rose suddenly, turning to see Rosita walking toward the creek from their tent, her black hair shining in the warm sun, her white dress swaying with each step. Her beauty made him forget, momentarily, about the bottle in his hand.

"Is it true, Joaquin?"

He showed her the bottle. "It is! Not a lot, but it's a start!"

She quickened her pace, her mouth dropping open. "That's actually gold?"

"Nothing else looks like this." When she neared him, he rose and held out the bottle to her. Instead of taking it, she stepped into his arms, wrapped hers around him, and pressed her lips to his. "My miner!"

"My love."

He heard a whoop from downstream. Glancing over, he saw Beeman and one of his companions, Sam Mackintosh, watching. Mackintosh, heavy-set, bearded, and strong as a plow-horse, was the one who'd cried out. Beeman was an anxious type, and when he worked up a good sweat, he cast off an odor that put Joaquin in mind of a decomposing horse carcass they had passed on their way to California. He'd smelled it on the breeze before they could even see it, and the scent had lingered long after they'd passed. He had hoped to forget about it, but Beeman's stench brought the memory back on a regular basis.

"We don't see a lot of kissin' 'round here," Mackintosh said. "You two want to keep at it, be our guests."

That was true, Joaquin supposed. Men outnumbered women by at least a hundred to one, and maybe more. In the short time they'd been here, he had seen male miners dancing with one another, for want of female companionship.

Sawmill Flat was growing fast—the sawmills for which it was named had recently been completed, and operated around the clock, employing dozens of men to produce lumber for all the booming towns around the diggings. Most of those employees were Mexicans, who'd come looking for gold but instead found only tapped-out fields, and happily settled for jobs that paid regular wages, building and then operating the mills. Others were white Americans, working side by side with the Mexicans. And California was a free state, so a few black Americans had joined the labor force as well. Joaquin had even heard about Chileans, Peruvians, Frenchmen, Germans, and others, but still, almost all men.

With the growth of Sawmill Flat had come businesses catering to the miners and millworkers. So far, those businesses were mostly saloons and gambling halls, and two churches, including the Catholic one Joaquin and Rosita attended. A couple of brothels had recently joined the mix, which meant women were no longer completely unavailable—but for most of the men, they came at a price.

And even at that, none compared to Rosita, at least in Joaquin's eyes. He understood why Beeman and the others would admire her. He didn't like the way they looked, sometimes—like hungry dogs eyeing an unattended butcher's counter—but he couldn't blame them.

Rosita flashed the men a smile that they'd still be thinking about in their bunks that night. Then she turned back to Joaquin. "I made you some lunch," she said. "If you're ready for a break."

"My back aches and I smell like fish," he replied. "I feel like I've become at least half-fish."

"So that means yes?"

"I found some actual gold. I don't want to stop—but yes. I could use a break."

"Come to the cabin, then. You can have some lunch, and after I'll rub your back. At least."

"We need a place of our own," Joaquin said. "With walls."

As they walked up the slope, he noticed that Beeman and Mackintosh were still chatting together, pretending they weren't eyeballing Rosita. "I don't want those guys hearing everything we do and say."

"They need some excitement in their lives. Anyway, when both mills are going at once, nobody can even hear themselves."

That was true. Neither was very close by, but the racket carried, muffled only slightly by the trees flanking the creek. As if mentioning it had made it come true, one of the mills started up, and the infernal buzz set Joaquin's teeth on edge. Rosita took his hand and led him into the tent, where the aroma of tortillas and beans greeted him. Once inside, he closed the flap and set down the bottle of gold.

For the moment, this was home, and it was everything he needed.

11

Clouds piled up during the afternoon, and that night Joaquin was awakened by rain pounding on the tent's roof and wind beating ferociously against the northern wall. Beside him, Rosita stirred. "Shh," he whispered. "It's only a storm."

"I don't like it. Hold me, Joaquin," she said. He was glad to do that, and as she moved against his chest, he wrapped powerful arms around her and drifted off again. But water rose outside the tent, then leaked in under the walls. Everybody had to shift toward the center of the tent, and Tres Dedos's snoring—almost tolerable at a distance—turned out to be almost indistinguishable from the thunder outside and the rain hammering overhead.

Rain continued the next day, hard enough to make panning impossible. As Jesús pointed out, "The point of panning is to pour enough water from the pan to be able to see the gold inside. If the pan fills up faster than you can empty it, it won't work."

In the middle of the afternoon, fed up with being inside, he and Tres Dedos put on slickers and rode into Sawmill Flat for a drink. Joaquin and Rosita took advantage of the unexpected privacy and made love.

Something woke him after a while, but he couldn't figure out what. Silence? The rain had stopped, the wind had died down, and all seemed still outside. But no, there was something else, a kind of shambling sound. Bear?

He rolled away from Rosita, catching a glimpse of her lovely, lithe form and a whiff of her scent, as sweet as honey. Still naked, he snatched up a musket, checked to ensure that it was loaded. Whatever was outside, it came closer. Joaquin threw back the tent flap and stepped out, gun-first.

A burly, brown-bearded man stood outside, eyes wide, staring at the apparition before him. He wore a gray shirt, gray pants with black stripes tucked into brown boots, and he'd tried to pull a brown hat down over his mass of hair, but it mostly floated on top of it.

"Where the hell's Jesús and Manuel?" he demanded. "Every hour this claim ain't bein' worked, somebody else is gonna get the gold should be ours." His voice had a gravelly, growling quality. His eyes were light blue, nearly hidden by bushy eyebrows and his bearded cheeks, but lively. "Reckon you're the brother."

Joaquin lowered the gun, suddenly embarrassed by his nudity. Then he felt motion at his shoulder, and Rosita stood there, only a thin shawl draped over herself. The man's eyes widened even more, and a smile formed on his lips. "And you're the wife?"

"Get inside," Joaquin said. She slipped away, and he turned back to the stranger. "Yes, I am Joaquin. Who are you?"

"Name's Harry Love, and this here's my claim. Why ain't it bein' worked?"

"The rain—" Joaquin began.

"Rain's over."

Joaquin glanced at the creek, running fast and high, throwing daggers of light at his eyes. Love was right; the clouds were gone, and the sun was shining.

"It was raining when I . . . went to sleep."

Love chuckled. "Sleep, is it? All right. You're awake now, son. Best get to it."

"I will," Joaquin said.

"Where's your brother and Manuel?"

"They went into town, a while back."

"Our deal says they work ever' day but Sunday."

"That's your deal with them. I'm not part of that."

"If you're workin' my claim, you're part of it," Love said.

"Stop asking me questions, then, and let me put on some pants."

"Please do, son. Ain't nobody wants to look at that."

Joaquin gave up expecting the man to stop talking. He stepped back into the tent and let the flap fall closed. Rosita had dropped the shawl and was sitting up, cross-legged, finger-combing her long, shining hair. "Do you have to go?" she asked.

"It looks like I do," Joaquin said. "And you should get dressed before the others come back."

She showed him a pout that she knew he adored, but he tried to ignore it, and tugged on some clothes. He could hear Love's breathing, knew the American was still out there, waiting.

• • •

Harry Love waited around until Joaquin Murrieta dressed and went down to the creek with a pan. The water was high and probably cold, but Mexicans didn't mind such things. They weren't much different than burros in that regard, or in most others, for that matter. Ill-spirited, disagreeable, and lazy, but if pushed, they'd work hard under just about any conditions.

He was pleased to see that Jesús's brother had finally

showed up. Jesús and Manuel had said that he would, of course, but they'd been saying it for weeks. The presence of a third worker didn't change Love's cut, of course, but the addition should increase the claim's overall output, which meant Love would keep putting away more and more gold. In a way, he was glad he'd been a flop in his own prospecting efforts—it was so much easier to sit back and let others gather up the color, then split the take. He had three claims going at once, that way, and all it cost him was a little supervision once or twice a week, to make sure work proceeded apace.

He had never expected to be in business with Mexicans, of course. That was the most surprising aspect of the whole arrangement. He'd enlisted early, as soon as it became apparent that war with Mexico was inevitable. His experience in the Seminole and Blackhawk Wars, and then fighting with the Texans in their War of Independence, had taught him much about battling savages and Mexicans—and as far as he was concerned, they were pretty much the same thing—and he'd risen rapidly through the ranks. He'd fought at Resaca de la Palma, Monterrey, Buena Vista, and was one of the first soldiers into Mexico City when the American forces had taken Mexico's capital. Shooting Mexicans had become habit, and at war's end, he'd traveled to California to see the brand-new state. Using his reputation and connections from the war, he'd wrangled a job as a deputy in Santa Barbara County, and had stayed there until the lure of gold drew him away.

So, to find himself now dependent on Mexicans—and the team of Nisenan Indians who worked one of his several claims—was quite the turnabout. But one that had a certain poetic justice to it, considering that fighting Mexicans had almost cost him his life at Resaca de la Palma. The wounds suffered there still pained him today, so letting them brave the chill waters and break their backs extracting gold for his benefit suited him just fine.

He watched Joaquin work for a little while, shifting his gaze to the tent now and again, in case that little Mexican beauty showed herself again, then got back onto his horse and rode for home. The sky was clouding over again, and if another storm broke, he didn't want to be caught in it.

Leave that for the Mexicans.

• • •

As the weeks turned into months and summer slipped toward autumn, Joaquin and the others pulled more and more gold from the creek. They filled bottles of it, cut Harry Love in on his share, and still had enough for their needs and to send some home to Trincheras. Joaquin hoarded most of his in the tent until he was able to buy a small adobe house he'd had his eye on, in the shade of an ancient oak. It was almost a mile down a thickly wooded trail from the claim, so he rode Blanco to the creek every morning. Around lunchtime, Rosita would usually ride over to join him for a meal, then head home or do some shopping in Sawmill Flat. Sometimes she made tortillas and sold them, or took in laundry. The rest of the time she spent turning their little house into a real home, someplace he hated to leave once he'd passed through the door. She had decorated it with scarves and blankets, turning it into a wonderland of color in otherwise drab surroundings.

Jesús and Tres Dedos built a small cabin where the tent had stood. The claim didn't look like it would play out anytime soon, so they all expected to stay put indefinitely. Might as well be comfortable. He and Rosita enjoyed their newfound privacy, and he was sure his brother and cousin were glad to get the lovers out from under their noses.

The downstream neighbors had built a long tom to replace

pans and manual labor, but even with that, they weren't as successful. Joaquin heard angry mutterings that he was snatching all the gold from the river before it could reach them, and a few times he saw them shoveling sediment from his side of the line dividing their claims. In the interests of good relations, he didn't say anything, but the more he noticed it, the more resentful he became. Just like they became more resentful every time they saw him, Jesús, and Tres Dedos carry more gold into the cabin.

As Jesús had said, theft was rarely a problem in the diggings. But there were different kinds of theft. If those men were, indeed, scooping up the creek bottom from the claim he worked—Harry Love's claim, legally, but Joaquin had come to think of himself and his brother and cousin as its rightful owners—under some delusion that more gold lay on one side of an imaginary line than on the other, then they were literally stealing his gold before he could get to it. He didn't believe he simply had more gold there. More likely, his slow, labor-intensive method of extracting it revealed more than their back-saving long tom. Had they been willing to pan each day like he and the others did, the five of them could've turned up several times the gold. But they wanted to get it the easy way. And the easy way didn't always pay off.

One late summer morning, when a cool bite to the air and the sun, low in the sky, slanting through tree limbs and casting long shadows hinted at approaching autumn, he rode through the woods to the creek's edge and saw the big Irishman, Jack Bohannon, hauling a shovelful of sediment from the middle of his claim toward the rocker. Jesús and Tres Dedos were nowhere to be seen. Wading through the creek, humming to himself, Bohannon hadn't heard Joaquin's approach.

"Ho, there, Jack!" Joaquin called.

Bohannon spun toward him. The head of his shovel drooped, and the wet muck began to slide off. "Hey, Murrieta," he said.

"You're a little off your own claim there, aren't you?"

Bohannon looked toward the claim marker on the bank. "Oh!" he said. "I guess so, sorry."

His surprise was feigned. Joaquin knew it, and Bohannon didn't take pains to make it convincing. Ferd Wetzl, youngest of the bunch and rail thin, with one blue eye that wandered seemingly of its own accord, stood outside their tent and watched the scene. He didn't appear to have just come out, so presumably he'd also been aware of Bohannon's transgression.

"You weren't here," Wetzl said.

"It's early yet. And whether I'm here or not, that claim is ours. And Harry's," he added quickly, knowing these white men respected Harry Love more than they did him and his relatives. "Do you want me to tell Harry about this?"

"No harm meant," Bohannon said, turning the blade of his shovel over and emptying it. "Nor done."

"Well," Joaquin said, trying to keep a light tone in his voice, "see you don't do it again. Please."

Bohannon gave him a nod and waded back to his side of the line. Wetzl just stayed where he was, eyeballing Joaquin with an angry expression, as if Joaquin were the trespasser here.

In a way, he supposed he was.

12

Two nights later, a fandango was held in an empty space on the edge of Sawmill Flat. A wooden platform had been quickly constructed for people to dance on, using cast-off lumber from the mills. Lanterns were hung from tree limbs. Some of the town's large Mexican population brought their instruments, and in their heads and hearts carried the songs passed down to them through the generations.

Joaquin wore all white, except for a red sash around his waist and Rosita's silk scarf at his neck. Rosita's dress was red, with black lace. He knew, walking into the illuminated space, that they were a striking couple—especially his bride, who drew every eye in the place. Soon guitars were strumming, tambourines shaking, and the rhythmic beat of the dancers' feet on the tarima added percussion, almost drowning out the powerful voice of the singer.

After dancing, whirling, and stomping themselves into near-exhaustion, Joaquin and Rosita abandoned the tarima and took to the sidelines. On the tarima, a single musician plucked a doleful tune on a jarana while a man stood, clenching his sombrero in both fists and reciting a long poem about a love he'd left behind in Mexico. The poet was the almost skeletally lean Luis Tibran, who worked at a mill. He had an acne-ravaged face, and he was normally so shy and quiet that Joaquin was surprised he'd managed to force himself into the spotlight. But his poem was vivid and moving.

Rosita drifted away with some female friends, and Joaquin spotted a group of Mexicans confronting a single man at the edge of the crowd. Joaquin was behind them and couldn't see their faces, or that of the other man, but the way they stood was tense, fists clenched, a couple of them clutching bottles or knives. He didn't want a fight to disrupt the fandango, but he didn't dare take on that many men.

Then one of them shifted and Joaquin saw the man facing them down. Harry Love. He and Joaquin spoke regularly, and met in town for a drink once a week or so. Love was arguing, red-faced in the lantern light. Joaquin still didn't know the nature of the conflict, but he didn't want Harry to be hurt—or for him to use his size to tear through the men confronting him, which was just as likely. He moved up behind the men.

"What's going on here?" he asked.

A couple of the Mexicans spun around. Joaquin recognized one of them, a man named Juan who worked at a sawmill. "This gringo wants to come in," he said. "He wants to drink our tequila and dance with our women. But I've heard about his work in Santa Barbara—he hates Mexicans. I don't trust him."

"I know him," Joaquin said, trying to sound reassuring. "He's my friend. Do you hate Mexicans, Harry?"

"Most of 'em," Love said. "On account of behavior like this."

"It's our party," Joaquin said. "That doesn't mean you can't join us, but you should understand why these men might object."

"I understand, Joaquin. I'm not one of you. That said, I employ a bunch of you, sponsor your work on my claims. There are probably ten or fifteen fellers here work for me. That gives me an interest in making sure they don't get too drunk to work, or hurt in a fight or anything."

"What we do during working hours is your business, but what we do when we're away from the claims is ours."

"I'm not putting anybody on the spot, Joaquin. I'm just looking after my investments."

Joaquin glanced at the other men. The knives were still out, the bottles grasped by the necks as if to use as clubs, or to break and slash with. The tension was like a living thing, as sharp as a rattlesnake's fangs. He had to calm things down or someone was going to be hurt. "Easy, compadres," he said. "Harry doesn't mean any harm. Like he said, several of us only have claims to work because of him. A fandango is supposed to be about fun and brotherhood, not fighting. Let's put down the weapons and all have a drink, what do you say?"

"I say he doesn't belong here," Juan said, lifting the bottle he carried. Liquid sloshed in the bottom, capturing lantern light and throwing it about. The sense of menace in the air ratcheted up. These men hungered for a fight, and the wrong word now would start it.

"If it wasn't for the gold, there would be no need for a sawmill, Juan," Joaquin pointed out. "The only reason you have a job is the gold people like Harry and I take from the earth. Finish what's in your bottle and find yourself a girl. Same goes for the rest of you. Dancing's more fun than fighting, and it can lead to even better things."

Juan chuckled, a lecherous grin working its way across his face. "I think I'll do that," he said. "Come on, guys." Juan turned and walked away, and the others went with him. As Joaquin's muscles relaxed, he realized how tense he'd been; keyed up and ready for anything.

"Thanks, Joaquin," Harry said. "I would've just left if

they'd been friendly about it. But their attitudes made me want to argue with 'em."

"Drink affects people in different ways," Joaquin pointed out. "I guess it makes those men want to fight."

"Truth be told, I am a little drunk. If they'd come at me, I don't know as I would've been able to take 'em on. You just might have saved my life tonight."

Joaquin hadn't thought the situation was that serious, at first. But now he knew that Love was right—he was as ready to brawl as those other men were, and it wouldn't have taken much to set them off.

He tried to lighten the moment. "I might've let them go at you, but I know a couple of them, and I didn't want to see them hurt. I think you could have handled all of them. Maybe even if they weren't half drunk."

Love laughed at that. Joaquin led him to a table, away from the dancers, and fetched them each a bottle of mescal. He put Harry's on the table and sat down across from him.

"I am a little surprised to see you here," Joaquin said.

"Like I said, some of my crews are here," Love replied. "I have to make sure they don't drink too much to work."

"Tomorrow's Sunday. Our day off."

"If men try hard enough, they can drink right through until Monday, then be too sick to show up."

"I suppose." Joaquin took a sip of his mescal. He had never been that drunk. Close, a couple of times, back home. But here in the United States, he wasn't comfortable enough to risk losing control of himself. The potential for violence lingered everywhere, plucking at his nerves like they were guitar strings. He never wanted to let down his guard.

"I'm pleasantly drunk myself, to tell you the truth," Love went on. "Takes a lot to knock me down, and I don't think I'll get there tonight. But things are looking a little blurry, just the same. How about you?"

Joaquin tipped his bottle toward the American. "Just a little bit."

"Good boy," Love said. "I like you, Joaquin." He stopped, put his hands flat on the table as if to brace himself. He looked like he'd taken himself by surprise. "I mean, you work hard. Production has gone up by half since you got here. And your wife's tortillas are delicious."

"Jesús works hard, too," Joaquin protested.

"He does, at that. But that Manuel—he's too much like me. If you're a big man, like us, it's hard to bend over and dip down into the creek. And he always seems to be on the look-out for trouble."

"He had some hard times," Joaquin began. He was going to say, "in the war," but he knew Love had fought on the other side and might still harbor ill will, so he checked himself. "In the past. It makes it hard for him to relax when things are too easy."

"I know that feeling. We're two sides of a coin, him and me. I guess that's why I like you. You're cut from different cloth."

"I appreciate that, Harry," he said with a grin. "You're not so bad yourself, for a gringo."

"Anyhow, I just figured I should tell you that," Love said. "You keep working hard, we'll all get rich, and we'll get along just fine."

"That's my plan," Joaquin said.

"Good. That's good. You're one of the good ones, Joaquin. One of the good ones."

Joaquin didn't have to ask what he meant by that. One of the good Mexicans. The implication, of course, being that most Mexicans weren't good. And along with that, that being one of the "good ones" meant one who didn't make trouble for whites, one who knew his place and stayed there.

He didn't see himself that way, and he was disappointed that Harry did. Still, he couldn't help liking the man who'd made it possible for him and his family to earn more than they'd ever dreamed of having, in such a short time.

After that, he wandered away and found Faustino Carrasco, a white-haired gentleman who'd made his fortune in the early days of the gold fever, then decided to stay in California and sent for his wife, Margarita. Carrasco wore a heavily embroidered red waistcoat, a white shirt, a red vest, and black trousers and boots, and would have looked more at home in Veracruz or Mexico City than in a rugged American boomtown. Drinks in hand, they returned to where Margarita and Rosita sat in a circle of other women. Rosita was talking, and when Joaquin started to interrupt, Carrasco hushed him with a single raised eyebrow.

". . . a new constitution," Rosita was saying. "There'll have to be. The Church still has too much power over our daily lives—"

"The church and the wealthy," Margarita put in. "The landowners won't give up their position of dominance without a fight."

"Of course, there'll be a fight, but it's necessary," Rosita countered. Joaquin wondered what her father, who owned as much land as the rest of the village put together—a man who traced his lineage back to the Spanish conquistadors—would think to hear his daughter so casually arguing against his financial interests. "Rousseau said that men who claim to own land are the worst of us, the beginning of the downfall of decency and a natural life. In so many words, I mean. The highborn treat the campesinos as if they're subhuman, and that can't go on. Slavery must be outlawed. Education must be mandatory, and directed by the state, not by the Church."

One of the other women came back with an argument, but Carrasco inclined his head and drew Joaquin away from the conversation. "I'm so glad you brought Rosa here. We both are." He chuckled. "I mean, we're glad that you came, too, and Jesús and Manuel. But Rosa has become the center of our social circle. She's young, obviously, and not as well-educated as she'd like to be, but her intellect is as keen as any I've known, here or in Spain, and it's matched only by the sharpness of her wit. Margarita loves talking with her. And I confess, I always learn something from her as well."

"If she hadn't come, I wouldn't have, either. I couldn't leave her, like Luis left his woman behind."

"I can see why. The time I spent here without Margarita was miserable."

They sipped their mescal, Joaquin alternating between watching Luis on the tarima and Rosita holding forth with her friends. He'd known Rosita was widely read—Don Ramon had the best library in the district—but he'd never seen her engaged in such a lively political discussion, and certainly never engaged in one with her. One more facet to the woman he loved. Over time, he figured, he would learn them all. And in the meantime, the learning process was itself fascinating.

Later still, the fandango was winding down and people were beginning to stray back to their homes. From the darkness at the edge of the field, he saw Ferd Wetzl, who he hadn't even known had attended, approach Rosita. He took her arm in a firm grip and said a few words. She yanked her arm free, responded with what looked like some stern words of her own, then spun on her heel and stalked away. Wetzl slipped back into the shadows and Joaquin lost sight of him as he moved to intercept Rosita.

"What did Wetzl want?" he asked.

"Oh, he was just being stupid. He's a stupid man."

"Stupid how? What did he say?"

"Nothing of any importance. Don't worry about it, Joaquin."

"When a man like that speaks to my wife, I worry about it."

"Really, my love, it was nothing."

Joaquin scanned the darkness, but he couldn't see Wetzl anywhere. "He has no business talking to you."

"He's a human being, if just barely. I'm a human, too. Any human has a right to speak to another."

"I'm not your philosophy study group, Rosita. I'm your husband. You need to tell me."

In the glow of the remaining lanterns, he saw anger flash in her dark eyes. Then they softened, and she said, "He told me that if I ever need a real man, I should let him know."

Now the anger was Joaquin's. His thoughts went to the flintlock musket with which he'd threatened the priest who'd married him, and which he still used sometimes for hunting small game. His fists clenched of their own accord, and his jaw went tight. "That bastard! I'll kill him!"

She laid a hand on his arm. "No, Joaquin, you won't. I saw him and his friends getting into the mescal earlier. By morning, I doubt he'll even remember having said it, and his headache will be punishment enough."

"But you're—"

"I know. Your wife, who you love and who loves you like nothing else on Earth. Nothing that pig says can change that. But you have to work near them every day, so you should just forget about this. Like I said, I'm sure he will."

"Forget it? Never."

"Joaquin, promise me. There are five of them, and they're Americans. They'd have the law on their side if you started anything."

"I wouldn't be the one who started it, just the one who finished it."

"Please, my love. Let this go. He was drunk, and drunk people say stupid things. He didn't mean anything by it. I've seen him in town coming out of the brothel. He meets his needs there."

"That doesn't make it any better. Worse, really, if he thinks you're that kind—"

Rosita wrapped her arms around him, pulling him close. "Joaquin, there's no way to make it better, and no need to. We only need to forget about it. I was shocked, in the moment, but then I realized he was so drunk he might not even have known who I was. He meant nothing by it."

"I'll try to forget, because you asked. But I make no promises about what might happen the next time I see his ugly face. If Tres Dedos found out, he'd kill him on the spot."

"Just, please, don't tell him or Jesús, and try to stay out of trouble," she pleaded, burying her face against his chest. "If something happened to you, I'd be lost. Destroyed. I couldn't go on."

"Then you know just how I feel, my heart. Promise me this—if he ever speaks to you again, outside my presence, you'll tell me?"

"I swear it, Joaquin."

"All right, then. Let's go home."

"Yes," she said, releasing him but taking his hand. "Let's."

• • •

But he couldn't forget. It gnawed at him, and every time he saw Wetzl at the creek, he had to restrain himself from attacking the man. His enraged glares did nothing to make him feel better. After a few days, he had an idea, and went into town to speak with Harry Love.

He found the man in a saloon, having lunch by himself, and sat down across from him. Love had steak and beans on his plate, and beans and gravy in the dark tangles of his beard. "That looks good," Joaquin said.

"It'll do." He arched an eyebrow at Joaquin. "You ain't workin' today?"

"I was. I found a few decent-sized nuggets."

A grin spread across Love's face, then he jabbed a chunk of steak into it and started chewing. He chewed for a long while. "It ain't boot leather," he said after a minute. "But it's close."

"I need to talk to you about something," Joaquin said, lowering his voice. The saloon was crowded and noisy, and he didn't want to be overheard.

"Seems like you are."

"It's personal. It's about Ferd Wetzl, one of the men working the claim next to ours."

"I seen him. Face like a rat, only more homely."

"That's him."

"What about him?"

"The other night, at the fandango? He approached Rosita and made some crude comments to her."

"I expect that's the only kind he ever makes," Love said. "Especially to women."

"He knows she's my wife. He told her that if she ever wanted a real man, she should let him know."

Love barked a laugh, and a bit of unchewed steak flew from his mouth onto the table. He eyed it, picked it up with two fingers, and stuck it back in. "Appears his idea of a real man ain't the same as mine. What'd you do about it?"

Do? There was nothing he could do. Joaquin was surprised Love hadn't understood yet why he'd come. He spread his hands and caught the other man's gaze. "I'm a Mexican. If I'd laid a hand on him, I might've been arrested, even hanged. If I went to the law, they'd laugh in my face."

Love nodded. "Prob'ly so."

"That's why I've come to you. You used to be a lawman. I thought maybe you could do something, even though I can't."

Love looked like he was considering it. He forked some beans into his mouth, dribbling some of the juice into his beard. He might have been saving it for later.

"Well, you're right about the used-to-be part," he said around the mouthful of beans. "But tryin' to get cozy with another man's filly ain't against the law. It's downright rude, but not illegal. I guess I could make your displeasure known with my fists and maybe a club, but that actually is illegal."

"He wouldn't have to know who did it," Joaquin suggested.

Love laughed. "Take a look at me, Joaquin. I'm kinda hard to mistake for anybody else. Only way he wouldn't be able to identify me to the local law would be if I killed him. That what you want?"

"I want to kill him myself, Harry. Rosita made me promise not to touch him."

Love studied him for a few moments. "You don't look like a killer to me. Your brother, maybe. That Manuel, he's a killer for certain. I'd've hated to have come up against him during the war, because only one of us would've walked away. And it most probably would've been him. You ask him?"

"I couldn't," Joaquin replied. "Rosita made me promise. Anyway, he's Mexican, too. You know what would happen if any of us harmed a white man."

"Can't say I disagree with the policy," Love said. At least he was honest about his bigotry; Joaquin found it a little refreshing. "But I also don't approve of a man like that makin' eyes at a married lady, even if she is a Mex. And I plain don't like Wetzl on general principle. I'll have me a little talk with him, okay? Might bloody him up a bit. But no killin'."

"That's fine. Thank you, Harry."

"I ain't done it yet. Thank me later."

"Oh, I will. Just, please, don't tell Rosita about this. She can't know I put you up to it."

"She's quite the lady, Joaquin. You just keep takin' good care of her, hear?"

"I plan to," Joaquin told him. "For as long as I live."

Love turned his attention back to what remained of his lunch. After watching him eat for a couple of minutes, Joaquin decided that he'd been dismissed. That was all right with him. Watching the man eat, bean juice glistening in his beard, was making Joaquin lose his appetite, and he hadn't had any lunch of his own yet. Satisfied that at least something would happen to Ferd Wetzl, he headed back toward the claim. There were still enough hours of sunlight left to get some more panning done.

13

Harry Love knew where to find Ferd Wetzl come Saturday night. The little rat-faced guy had a hankering for the ladies at Madame Sofia's, a high-toned name for a low-toned brothel in town that was none too picky about its clientele so long as they paid in gold. The only real question was whether he'd pay Wetzl a visit before or after.

After thinking it over for a few minutes, he decided on before. Wetzl would likely be cleaner then; Love didn't think he would want to touch the man after, at least not without some scalding hot water handy to bathe in. He knew the path Wetzl would take and about what time he would leave, so he positioned himself behind a thick-trunked oak tree along the trail, his horse picketed nearby but out of sight.

Wetzl would know who he was; as he'd remarked to Joaquin, he was easily recognized, and if he attacked Wetzl in the dark of night, the man might never know the reason behind it. Joaquin needed a message to be sent, and it happened to be one that Love agreed with.

He liked Joaquin, though. The young man was a hard worker, and polite, and sharp as a well-honed knife. He didn't much like greasers on the whole, and he'd been happy to kill as many as he could during the war, and more than a few since, but Joaquin was an exception. During the time the man had worked for him, they'd had many conversations—

tentative at first, but Harry had started dropping by the claim more often, and they'd become more frequent and more personal. It surprised him to think of a Mexican as a friend, but he enjoyed Joaquin's company more than he did many of the white men he'd met. Fellows like Wetzl lowered his admiration for the whole of the white race, while those like Joaquin raised his appreciation for Mexicans. Rosita even more so—that woman was beautiful and brilliant, and the fact that she loved Joaquin raised his estimation of the young man even more.

Besides, he was in business with Joaquin, which made it personal. Add to that his disdain for Wetzl, and he was glad to do Joaquin this little favor.

He didn't have to wait long. Dusk was falling, filling the space between the trees with gloom that had almost the same effect on visibility as fog, when he heard footsteps coming toward him at a steady clip, accompanied by tuneless humming. Love peered out from his position and saw Wetzl, hair wetted down, an anticipatory grin on his face. He stepped out onto the path.

"Mister Love," Wetzl said. "I didn't see you there."

"I'm here," Love said. "And so are you."

"Well, there's no arguin' with that, is there?"

"No, I don't reckon there is."

Wetzl eyed him with open curiosity. "You out here collectin' acorns?"

"What would I want with acorns?"

"The local Indians seem to like 'em. Thought maybe you had yourself a squaw or something, could make soup or some kinda ointment with 'em."

"No squaw," Love said. "But that does put me in mind of somethin'."

"What's that?"

"Just a little thing that bothers me. Men who try to get with women that belong to another man."

"That is rude, no doubt about it," Wetzl agreed. He smelled like he'd bathed in Bay Rum, but another odor was starting to sneak through—the sour stench of fear. Wetzl was sweating through his shirt, dark circles ringing his underarms and stretching down his sides.

"I hear you've got a history of not respectin' such boundaries," Love said, edging closer.

"Me?" Wetzl gave a nervous chuckle. "You got the wrong man, Mr. Love. I mean, I like the ladies, same as the next. But I'm always willin' to pay the goin' rate, if you know what I mean."

"On your way to Madame Sofia's, are you?"

"That's right. Got the price right here in my pocket, too."

"Well, then, I don't understand. If you're headin' to a whorehouse, why do you make advances to married women?"

Wetzl's face paled, and the vinegary stink came off him in waves. "You must have misunderstood somethin' you heard, Mr. Love. "I don't—"

Love didn't let him get out another word. He took a step toward the smaller man and lashed out with his right hand, putting his shoulder behind it. His fist smashed into the upper part of Wetzl's chest, just below his neck. It would leave a bruise, but if the man wore a shirt, it wouldn't show.

Wetzl dropped back a few steps, staggered, but not knocked off his feet. His face had turned red and he was having a hard time catching his breath. Love moved in closer and pummeled him with body blows, avoiding his face and head, but punishing the man just the same.

After a couple of minutes, Wetzl went down, writhing in the dirt. Love dropped to his haunches beside the other man and spoke in a low, steady tone, not even winded by the effort.

"You might miss your appointment at Sofia's," he said. "But I didn't break anything. Keep your shirt on and nobody'll know what happened to you, except you and me. I'd appreciate it if you'd keep it that way. You understand what I'm sayin'? Long as nobody hears about this, we won't have any more problems. But if I find out you told somebody, why then, this will feel like the best day you've ever had."

Wetzl squirmed. Road dust caked his nose and cheeks where it mixed with tears and snot.

"If you understand, nod your head," Love went on. "If you don't understand, I might just have to try harder."

Wetzl managed a nod of his head. Love pushed his face into the dirt, then rose and threaded his way to the trees to where his horse waited.

The whole way, he could hear Wetzl sobbing.

• • •

The next day was Sunday, but on a hunch, Joaquin rode to the claim and tied Blanco well back from the creek, next to the small cabin. On foot, he approached cautiously, moving through the trees instead of down his usual path. Nearing the creek, he heard the splashing and rattle of the long tom. Edging nearer, he saw Sam Mackintosh and Ben Chambers, both of them shoveling the creek bottom in the claim he shared with Jesús and Tres Dedos. He stuck his head into the cabin. Jesús was sitting up at a table, stitching up a torn pair of pants. Tres Dedos lay on his palette, snoring away. Jesús glanced up, and Joaquin indicated with a nod of his head that his brother should join him outside.

He put a hand on the hilt of the Bowie knife he'd tucked

into his sash, and he and Jesús strode onto the bank. "We've already talked about this once," he announced.

"Haven't talked about it to me," Chambers said.

"Bohannon and Wetzl didn't tell you?"

"Tell us what?"

"That we don't appreciate you men digging up the creek bed inside our claim. You've got your own to worry about."

"Sorry," Mackintosh said. "We was just doin' y'all a favor."

"What favor?" Jesús asked.

"Churnin' up the sediment. So's the gold comes closer to the top."

"Gold's heavier than most," Joaquin reminded him. The lie was so far-fetched it was almost comical. "You churn it up, it's likely to just wind up underneath the rest anyway."

"Well, we'll stop, then," Chambers offered. "Didn't mean to rile you."

"Just stick to your own claim, and there'll be no riling done," Jesús said.

Joaquin turned to his brother but spoke loud enough for the Americans to hear. "Do you think we should tell Harry about this? If it's going to keep happening, he should know."

Jesús shrugged. "Probably. He'll want to know why, if our take is down."

"Look, we're sorry," Mackintosh said again. He had a tremble in his voice, probably because of the mention of Harry Love. Joaquin didn't know any of them well, but he had the feeling that Mackintosh was a man who apologized a lot, for anything or for nothing at all. He was definitely the least aggressive of the five Americans, and according to the rumors, the one who'd put the largest financial stake into the partnership.

From what Joaquin had seen, Chambers was smart,

educated, the natural leader of the outfit. Bohannon was easily the biggest and strongest. Beeman was easygoing and laughed a lot, and of them all, he was the only one who Joaquin almost considered a friend. And Wetzl struck him as a cruel man. He wasn't big or physically strong, like Bohannon, but he was mean and probably clever enough to know how to play the others, to get done what he wanted, maybe even outthinking Chambers at times.

Mackintosh and Chambers sloshed through the water, back onto their own claim. Mackintosh didn't apologize again, at least not out loud, but he caught Joaquin's eye and gave a solemn nod that conveyed the same message. Joaquin waited a few more minutes, then stepped back into the trees and away. He'd wanted to impress upon them that he might happen along at any moment, and if they were working his claim they'd be caught. He believed he had accomplished that. It didn't mean they wouldn't try it again, but they might be less likely to.

Next time, he'd bring the flintlock, to really drive home the point.

14

On Monday, Joaquin returned to the backbreaking labor of shoveling and panning by hand. The Americans were busy on their claim, feeding wet sediment into the long tom and rocking it to separate lighter materials from heavier. Every now and then he heard a whoop, indicating that they'd found some color. He was finding some, too—flakes and dust, no nuggets, but it spent the same.

When Rosita didn't show up for lunch, as they'd planned, he rode to their adobe. As always, the sight of it, sitting within the welcome shade of the oak's spreading limbs, warmed his heart. Knowing Rosita was inside warmed it even more. But today, the house was empty. He stepped outside again, called her name once.

The sound of a horse approaching surprised him. The worse surprise was Rosita, riding Oso. She was crying, though he couldn't read her well enough at a distance to know whether it was from sorrow or rage. As she neared, he saw her clothing was soiled. Then she got close enough to smell, and he knew something was terribly wrong.

"Rosita!" he cried, dropping his gear on the bank and racing toward her. "What happened?"

"I . . . I . . ." she attempted. "I can't even say it."

He caught the reins of her mount. "Come down from there," he said. "Tell me what's wrong. How did you . . .?" He wasn't even sure how to ask the question.

"It's too awful," she said. "Don't touch me."

"Rosita, my heart. Nothing in the world could keep me from touching you. Just tell me."

Finally, she swallowed, blinked, and climbed down from the horse, landing heavily enough to shake some filth from her skirt. "I'm so ashamed," she said. Her voice quavered, and he was afraid she'd start to cry again, but she fought for control. "I was in town, running some errands."

"And what happened?"

"I passed by that brothel, the Silver Lily. Some girls were on the upstairs balcony, calling to the men in the street. When they saw me, they called me some nasty names."

"What names?" Joaquin asked.

"Never mind that," Rosita replied. "Bad ones. Then one of them went back inside. When she returned, a moment later, she had a bedpan in her hands. I wanted to run, but my feet wouldn't move. She dumped it off the balcony, and some of it . . . some of it got on me. They all laughed like it was just the . . . the funniest thing they'd ever seen."

Now the tears came again—great, hitching sobs. He choked back his own pride and disgust and threw his arms around her, pulling her close. She tried to wriggle from his grasp, but he held her tight. The overwhelming stench made his eyes water. "Those whores," he said. "They're worthless trash. Which one was it?"

"It was that big blonde, with shoulders like a man's," Rosita managed. "Her laugh is like the bray of a mule. I've seen her on the street, talking to Ferd."

"Wetzl?"

"Yes, Ferd Wetzl."

Rage bubbled out of him like boiling water from an

overfilled pot. "When I'm done with her, even a blind man would want nothing to do with her. Then I'll thrash those others, the ones who laughed."

"No, Joaquin, you can't."

"Watch me."

She drew back from him then, took his face in both hands, and met his gaze directly. "I know you're angry. I'm furious, too. Furious and ashamed and humiliated. But you can't do a thing to her. If a Mexican man struck a white woman—even a prostitute—he'd be hanged before another day passed. I can't lose you, Joaquin."

"Wetzl, then."

"He wasn't even there."

"He's behind it. He told her stories about you."

"Possibly. Or possibly she's just cruel, brimming with hatred for anyone who isn't like her. They laugh and joke, but that's a hard life. I couldn't do what she does."

"I wouldn't want you to."

"I know. I wouldn't, either. But if you hang, what'll become of me? That might be my only option."

In that moment, Joaquin wanted nothing more than to bloody his fists on the flesh of a white American. Any one of them would do. They wouldn't have done to one of their own kind what they'd done to Rosita.

As much as he hated to admit it, though, she was right. She'd always been smarter than him, and he couldn't risk ignoring her advice now. They could do anything to Mexicans and the law would do nothing. But for a Mexican to raise a hand against them would be suicide. He had seen hangings since coming to the gold fields, seen the way the Americans gathered to watch. When he looked at their faces, all he saw was raw lust. And if he was hanged, who would watch over

Rosita?

Jesús had gone to Sacramento City to send some letters and buy supplies that were too dear in Sawmill Flat, so he couldn't turn to his brother for help. He could tell Tres Dedos, who had, during the war, developed a taste for killing Americans. But the result would be the same as if he took action himself, and he couldn't bear to see his cousin hanged. Could he go to Harry Love again? No. Harry was a friend; the best he had among whites. But Harry had done already what he could. Wetzl had probably figured out that Joaquin had put Harry up to the attack on him, and this was his revenge.

Tears running down Rosita's cheeks tracked through the filth, and he knew what he had to do. Revenge was suddenly unimportant. She was the only thing that mattered. "Come," he said, taking her hand.

"Where . . .?"

"The creek." A foot trail led from the adobe to the creek. This part of it was unclaimed; gold had never been found here, and those who'd tried had quickly moved on.

He led her there, speaking gently, letting love and concern for her tamp down the fury inside, though he still felt it burning in his gut like a hot coal. The creek was wide here, with grassy banks, the current gentle. Without gold to draw them, nobody came here; this was a private spot. He lifted her down from the bank and into the water. "Oh!" she said. "It's cold!"

"You'll get used to it quickly," he assured her. The first step in always felt cold, but the sun warmed the surface water and he'd never had trouble working in it for hours at a time.

Once they were both in the water, he helped her out of her clothing and let it all drift off with the current. He warmed water in his hands and washed her, starting with her hair and working down. He ran his wet hands over every part of her, rubbing where necessary, making sure there wasn't a trace left behind. As he worked, touching and stroking her flesh, he felt arousal taking over from the other emotions that had gripped him. When he met her gaze, saw her parted lips, he knew she felt it, too.

He kissed those lips. When the kiss was over, she said, "Let's go back to the house and warm up, my love."

One problem—he'd abandoned all her clothes to the stream, and it had floated out of sight. She realized what he was thinking. "Don't worry about it," she said. "Just—I don't want to walk barefoot."

He helped her onto the bank, then pulled off his boots, dumped out the water, and gave them to her. She put them on, and like that, naked but booted, Joaquin clothed, soaked, and barefoot, they returned to the adobe. All the way, he watched the muscles working under her smooth flesh, admired the curves and planes and secret nooks that made up her body. When they reached the adobe, they went straight to the bed and he covered her with kisses, letting her know without words that the parts that had been soiled were clean now.

Then she was ready and so was he. She parted her legs and he moved over her, letting her guide him into herself as he kissed her breasts, her neck, her cheeks and eyes and lips. She clung to him, wrapping her strong legs around him and drawing him ever deeper.

When they were finished, they lay where they fell and slept, intertwined and at peace.

• • •

Joaquin ignored the claim and stayed home with her for the next two days. They made love, they bathed in the creek, they walked through the trees and talked and laughed and were silent. In the house, with a fire crackling, he asked her about the philosopher she'd mentioned at the fandango, Rousseau, and she read to him from a couple of the books she'd brought with her from Mexico. Those days and nights together, ignoring the rest of the world, were among the most idyllic he had ever known. If Tres Dedos missed him at the claim, he said nothing.

On the second evening, she played her guitar and sang to him as he reclined on their bed with a bottle of wine. Her eyes were distant, her mouth perfectly formed as she sang the words so softly he had to strain to hear them. She was playing "La Pasadita," a song she'd learned only while they'd been in California, when they heard overlapping voices from outside. Thinking that it was perhaps friends who'd heard the tale and come to look in on Rosita, Joaquin set the bottle down and threw open the door.

The five Americans stood outside. All of them carried guns—long guns for Chambers and Mackintosh, and Beeman, Bohannon, and Wetzl each had pistols. Wetzl took a step forward.

"On account of you abandonin' your claim, we thought you should know that we've taken it over, Murrieta."

Joaquin needed a few seconds to understand what the man had said. Once he did, fury rose in him in a heartbeat. "Abandoning our claim? We did no such thing!"

"You haven't been there in more than sixty hours, Joaquin," Chambers added. "Neither have the others. That's long enough to count as abandonment."

"For fuckin' greasers, anyhow," Wetzl put in.

"The claim is Harry Love's, as you know. We've been working it regularly. I've had to take a few days off, but Manuel—"

"He ain't been around, neither. Word is he's been drunk

the whole time."

"Still, the claim is Harry's."

"Not if it's abandoned. White or Mex, don't make no difference. We can get a sheriff up here, you want us to."

"Fine," Joaquin said, though he knew the chances of an American sheriff taking his side over five of his own were slender. Maybe he could get Harry here before they got back with a sheriff, though. The law would listen to him. "You go fetch one. I'll be here when you get back."

"There'll be no lawmen coming," Chambers said. "There's only you and us. We want you gone, Joaquin. We don't like your kind."

"My kind? You mean, Mexicans?"

"This is America," Wetzl said. "You got no right to our land or our gold. You come here, struttin' that woman of yours around like you're better'n us, like you got somethin' we ain't. I was you, I'd pack up and take off while I still could."

"What does that mean?" Joaquin demanded. His fists were clenched, but he wished he had a weapon of his own in one of them. "You're threatening me?"

"Call it whatever you like," Bohannon said, muscling his way past the others. His Irish accent was still strong; he was every bit the immigrant that Joaquin and Rosita were. The difference, Joaquin supposed, was that he was white, an immigrant from Europe. "But you're leavin'."

Joaquin sensed Rosita moving around behind him, coming closer to the door. He turned his head long enough to say, "Stay back," and that's when Bohannon charged him.

He'd thought there would be more words spoken before an attack came. It caught him by surprise, and he wound up on the floor with Bohannon straddling him, swinging those big fists into his jaw and chin. Rosita screamed, and the other men piled through the doorway.

In the process, one of them bumped Bohannon's shoulder, knocking him slightly off-balance. That was all the edge Joaquin needed. He rammed a fist into Bohannon's throat, and when the Irishman choked, Joaquin bucked him off. He swung at Bohannon's cheek and opened a cut beneath the man's eye.

Before he could take further advantage of the opportunity, someone grabbed his shirt and yanked him backward. Joaquin kicked back with one of his bare feet and heard Wetzl yelp. The little man released his shirt, and Joaquin drove a fist into his stomach. Wetzl folded around it. Joaquin caught the back of Wetzl's head with both hands and slammed it down into his own knee, which rushed up to meet it. Joaquin heard a satisfying crunch, and when he released Wetzl, blood was running from his nose and mouth. He was pretty sure he had broken Wetzl's jaw, which heartened him even in the midst of the brawl.

His Bowie knife was across the room, on a side table near the bed. If he could get to it, he could make short work of the fight. Inside, in close quarters, the other men might be hesitant to fire their guns, lest they hit one of their own. But when he started that way, Mackintosh swung the stock of his rifle against Joaquin's forehead. Bright lights flashed in his eyes, and he felt blood running down his brow. He wiped it with one hand, flinging droplets away, and lunged for Mackintosh's rifle.

Mackintosh evaded the charge, and then Bohannon was back in it. He plowed into Joaquin, his weight knocking the smaller man to the floor again. Mackintosh hit him with the rifle butt as Bohannon held him down, and he felt a boot striking his ribs—Wetzl's, maybe, or Chambers's. Beeman was already past the melee, heading for Rosita.

In a panic, Joaquin struggled against Bohannon's bulk, trying to shake him off or wriggle free, but the man held him tight. The smashing of the wooden rifle stock was taking its toll—blood filled Joaquin's eyes and the room was going dark at the edges. Someone else kicked him, blow after blow from a booted foot landing on his ribs, his hips, and finally his head. Through blurred vision, he saw Chambers behind Beeman, and Rosita beyond them, her back up against a wall. Beeman held her arms and forced her down onto the bed. Joaquin tried to cry out, but his voice wouldn't come. Bohannon's hands closed on his throat, crushing it.

Darkness filled the room, swallowed the world, and then consciousness came flooding back for a moment and he saw Rosita snatch up the Bowie knife and drive it into Beeman's chest. The man howled and yanked it free, backhanding Rosita at the same time. Then Chambers grabbed her arm and twisted it back, breaking her grip on the weapon. It clattered to the floor. Joaquin could see it there, only the length of his own body away from him. Once again, he attempted to break the hold Bohannon had on him, but he couldn't catch his breath, and the darkness returned, consuming everything.

15

The first thing Joaquin heard was a songbird, probably in the oak tree outside. He tried to open his eyes, but the light was too bright, stabbing his senses like a sword. Then he became aware of the pain. Every part of his body hurt, his head most of all. He moved it ever so slightly, and nausea struck; he vomited, unable to avoid getting it on himself. He'd clean up later, after he slept for a few days or until the pain subsided.

Only then did he remember how he'd come to be here.

Rosita!

He forced his eyes open, made himself ignore the agony screaming from every muscle and joint, and drew himself upright.

She was on their marriage bed. Curled into a tight ball, naked, blood everywhere. Moving closer, blinking, rubbing the dried blood from his own eyes, he saw that the bed was in disarray, spotted with the seed of their attackers. A flash of rage passed through him, almost too quickly to feel—there would be a time for that, but this was the time for worry. He rushed to her, sat beside her, scooped her into his arms. Her face was a pulpy mass, eyes swollen shut, jaw dropping open limply, teeth shattered. Bruises, black and purple, discolored her face, her arms, her breasts, even her legs. Not content to have their way with her, the men had brutalized her from top to toe. She still breathed, but shallowly. He held her close, heedless of his own puke on what was left of his clothes.

"Rosita," he said. "My beloved, heart of my heart."

Her eyes fluttered open. "Joaquin," she said. The word was barely intelligible, her voice thick and far away. "Hold me, my love. So . . . very cold."

"I am," he assured her. "I'll never let you go again."

He sat that way for a long time, feeling her breathing slow, then stop altogether. Still, he held her, even after his own arms went numb. She had slipped away, he knew that, but he couldn't bring himself to acknowledge it. An hour passed. More. The sun moved through the sky outside. Birds sang. A curious ringtail peered through the open door, then scurried away. Joaquin wept until he was dry inside, a hollowed-out husk of what he'd once been. Without his Rosita, he was nothing.

Finally, shivering, he lay her down on the bed. She was gone, and unfair as it was, he yet lived. That simple fact created obligations. And the manner of her passing created a separate set of obligations, in conflict with the first. She was a good Catholic, and she deserved a church burial.

But she'd been assaulted and brutally murdered. He knew who'd done it. And they had to pay. The law here would protect them, despite the circumstances, so if justice were to be done, he'd have to do it himself.

He lifted her off the bed and carried her down to the creek, where he bathed her and then himself. At least the cold didn't bother her, this time. As for him? His sunlight was gone from the earth, and he would never be warm again.

When they were both clean, he carried her back to the little adobe. The oak tree that had once offered comfort and welcome now seemed sinister, its limbs like gnarled claws, reaching down toward the house as if to snatch away any happiness contained within. He shuddered, but he passed beneath it and went inside. He snatched a folded blanket from a shelf and, one-handed, spread it on the floor. Rosita would never touch that bed again; it was forever tainted.

He set her down on the blanket, then examined himself for the first time. He didn't think any ribs were broken, but he couldn't be certain; he was tender everywhere, and his trunk was a mass of bruises and cuts. Likewise, his head and neck. The most serious seemed to be the gash in his forehead, caused by Mackintosh's rifle butt. He had lost a couple of teeth, in the back right; he explored the empty space with his tongue. Every muscle in his body hurt, and when he tried to move around, he felt weak, as if every drop of strength had been drained out of him. He had thought that working his claim had inured him to pain, but he was learning that he'd never known real pain before.

After a thorough investigation of his wounds, he dressed and gathered the few possessions he couldn't spare. The silk scarf Rosita had given him on their wedding day. Some of her books, some food and water, all the gold he had. His Bowie knife and musket. A few changes of clothes. A pickaxe and shovel. He looked for Rosita's rosewood guitar, but found it in a corner, smashed into kindling. At the sight of it, he almost wept again, but tears wouldn't come. Sorrow still consumed him, but alongside it in his breast, anger grew. He couldn't bring her back, but he could avenge her death. As he worked, a plan developed, almost without conscious thought.

When he'd loaded everything he was keeping onto Blanco, he rolled Rosita up in the blanket and lashed her across Oso's back. The sun was low in the west now, and he hadn't seen a human being other than Rosita all day. That was ideal, and he hoped to keep it that way. His last act at the adobe was to use the remains of her guitar, and some firewood, lamp oil, and the soiled bedding, to start a fire inside. He hauled their wooden dining table over it, so when the flames leapt high enough, they'd ignite the table. When it was burning briskly, he stepped out of the house, closed the door, and climbed into the saddle. In the half-light of dusk, he rode away from the adobe and toward the cabin Jesús and Tres Dedos shared.

The old Joaquin Murrieta had died in that adobe, along with his beloved bride. A new one had been born in the pain of her loss. That Joaquin forswore the virtues practiced by the old: hard work, honesty, peace. The new one's heart had been hardened, the blood within it frozen to ice.

He saw light through the cabin's one window as he approached. Tying the horses outside, he went in to find Tres Dedos sitting at the table, head buried in his hands. He looked up briefly, his eyes red and bleary, and groaned.

"Oh, Joaquin, I got so drunk. What day is it? Is Jesús back?"

Joaquin couldn't bring words to his mouth. If he spoke, he would break down.

Through the haze of his misery, Tres Dedos seemed to recognize his pain. "What's wrong, Joaquin?" he asked. "What is it?" His brows lifted as he realized Joaquin's physical condition. "What happened?"

Tears began to leak from Joaquin's eyes. The truth was too painful to speak aloud, but he knew he had to tell somebody. "They killed her," he managed.

"Who?" Tres Dedos asked. He scooted his chair back from the table as understanding struck. "Rosa?"

"Y-yes," Joaquin said. He tried to swallow the first sob, but it burst from his throat, as if violently torn from it. "They . . . ravished her and . . . and murdered her."

"Who did?"

Words would no longer come. Joaquin turned his head toward the cabin the Americans shared, and that was enough. Tres Dedos lurched from the chair, unsteady on his feet. "Them? I'll tear their hearts from their breasts and—"

"No!" Joaquin got out. "No, Manuel. They're mine."

"You're no killer," Tres Dedos said. "I am. I can make them suffer."

Joaquin shook his head, wiped his nose. Swallowed again. It hurt, like swallowing fire. He was glad for the hurt, glad for the bruises and cuts and the aches all over his body. He wanted to hold onto that pain, let it fuel his rage. He had thought this over, made his decision, though he knew it would cost him everything he'd earned, and everything he'd become. "They will suffer, believe me. But I want to do it. I need to."

"You're hurt. You're in no shape—"

"Not now. I'm leaving, Manuel. I need to bury her, and I need someplace to hide, to make my plans."

"I'll come with you. You shouldn't do this alone."

"You need to stay here. When Jesús returns—"

"Jesús can take care of himself."

"He's your best friend."

"That's how I know he'll be fine. You can help me leave him a note that he'll find when he gets back. I'll go with you and teach you what you need to know. If you went up against those Americans, well . . . you look like you've already learned what can happen. I'll help you get better, and show you how to deal with them."

"But, Jesús—"

"He can take care of himself," Tres Dodos repeated. "I don't know anyone more capable than your brother."

"You're saying I can't?" Joaquin snapped. Rage welled up

in him, though he knew it was misplaced, directed at Tres Dedos. If his cousin had been at his house when the Americans came, the two of them could have fought them off. There had been no reason for Tres Dedos to be there, of course. He lived here. He and Jesús visited from time to time, just as Joaquin and Rosita visited them, but to wish he'd been there tonight was foolish.

"Not right now, you can't. You will be able to. Soon. I promise."

As suddenly as the anger had come, it vanished, leaving Joaquin exhausted. Spent. He could have curled up and slept for years. "All right," he said at last. "You can come. But we have to hurry. I set our house on fire. I want to get away before anyone sees us. I don't want anyone to tell me I need to go to the sheriff."

"No sheriff," Tres Dedos agreed. "You and me. That's all we need."

He packed a few things onto his mule, and dictated a note that Joaquin wrote down for him. That done, they closed up the cabin.

Through the night, they rode, heading north, avoiding towns, seeking out the empty spaces. At sunrise, Joaquin buried Rosita near the foot of Bear Mountain, north of the gold country, while Tres Dedos watched, his expression solemn. Joaquin shoveled the dirt he'd removed from the hole over her still, blanket-wrapped form, then gathered large stones and built a cairn. Finally, he lashed together a cross of sticks and placed it at her head. Only then did the tears come again, and he knelt by the grave, weeping, until the sun had climbed high into the heavens.

16

Bear Mountain had earned its name due to the abundance of grizzlies stalking its slopes. Trappers had taken many—butcher shops from Sacramento City to San Francisco sold bear meat alongside beef, horseflesh, and pork—and others were captured for the popular bull-and-bear fights that entertained miners on many a Sunday afternoon, but the supply seemed limitless. When gold was found near Sutter's Mill, most men turned away from hunting and trapping for their livelihoods, and the grizzly population had, by all reports, rebounded. Which made it perfect for Joaquin, who had no interest in or need for human company. He both appreciated Tres Dedos's concern and resented it, because he wanted to be alone in his grief. But at the same time, he knew in that state, he was vulnerable. With Tres Dedos along, nothing would happen to him.

Where there were bears, Joaquin reasoned, there were caves. Not trusting the horses' possible responses to bear attacks, he and Tres Dedos left their mounts tied at the mountain's base and went up on foot. The first dozen or so caves they found were occupied—growls or huffs all that were needed to steer them away—but after spending the entire morning searching, they found one that had been abandoned. It was high on a south-facing slope, not far below the peak. Joaquin and Tres Dedos entered cautiously, not trusting that there weren't bears inside, lying in quiet wariness for any edible interlopers.

The opening was high enough for Joaquin, the taller of the two, to pass through, high enough even for a horse to enter, but narrow, and shrubbery growing nearby almost camouflaged it unless a person stopped right in front of it. But inside, the cavern grew wider and the ceiling soared. The open space within was far larger than the little adobe's single room. Along one side a rock bench, about waist-high on Joaquin, ran for most of the length of the chamber. At the rear, a tunnel led off into darkness. There was plenty of room in here for the two men and all three animals, and more, should it come to that.

Anyway, it would do for now. Joaquin had work ahead of him, and he had planning to do.

• • •

From the mouth of the cavern, Joaquin could see the little valley in which he'd buried Rosita, even if he couldn't make out the cairn and cross. It served as a constant reminder of his failure. Working with horses had made him strong, but his months of finding and amassing gold had made his muscles harder than ever, slimmed his waist and swelled his arms, chest, and thighs.

But he hadn't been in a real fight since boyhood, and then his opponents had also been boys, weak and untrained. He'd had no chance against five armed men, and he supposed they must have believed him dead or they wouldn't have left him behind. He should've gone outside to meet them, tried to draw them away from the house and Rosita, maybe led them on a chase and lost them in the woods. But he'd been unprepared for the attack, and unable to defend against it. Rosita had paid the price for his foolishness.

He relived it in his mind, over and over and over. He woke

in the night, writhing and kicking. Would he ever get over it?

No, he told himself. This wasn't something you forgot, something that went away. It was as much a part of him as his hands or his head. In the most important moment of his life, he had failed.

Never again. There would be violence in his future—he was counting on it, and he'd make sure it happened.

Next time, he would be ready.

• • •

They spent the next several weeks on the mountain. Tres Dedos barked orders at Joaquin. He ran down the mountain, following game trails, and back up again. Up, down, up, down. Over and over. Once running down and up again became too easy, Tres Dedos made him do it carrying big stones, then bigger ones.

A river cut through the valley, and every day he swam against the current, a little farther each time. His hair grew long and wild, and his beard took over most of his face. Manuel's face could barely be seen through his wild beard. They laughed loud and hard, ate when they wanted, slept when they were tired, and pissed where they pleased.

Once, Joaquin rode to a town where nobody knew him and bought a new Colt Model 1848 Dragoon, a six-shot, single-action pistol that put every other weapon he'd handled to shame, and a few dozen boxes of ammunition. He practiced with that and his musket until he was a dead shot with either gun.

All the while, Tres Dedos tried to teach him.

"If you're going to kill human beings—" he began.

"I *am* going to kill humans."

"—then you have to treat them like wild animals. Sure, some of them just weep and wet themselves, and tremble while you're doing it. But others fight back with everything they've got. They bite, tear, flail about, and if there's anything that can be used as a weapon, they'll use it. The thing is, you never know which man will submit and which will become an animal, desperate to survive, so you have to be ready for anything."

"I want to see those bastards beg for their lives. I want them to feel like Rosita did, knowing she was going to die. I want them to hurt."

"Then you have to do it up close, not from a distance. It's harder, up close. Looking in their eyes."

"That's what I want. I don't care how hard it is."

"Where's that knife of yours?"

Joaquin fetched the Bowie knife he and Rosita had bought in Los Angeles. Tres Dedos took it from him, felt its heft, balanced it across three fingers. "Very nice weapon," he said. "Do you know how to use it?"

"I've been using it ever since we got here. I've used knives since I was a boy."

"I don't mean to cut ropes or castrate sheep. I mean, on a person. Show me."

Joaquin took the knife back, faced Tres Dedos. He held the weapon in his right hand, his back hunched a little, legs spread wide.

"Stab me," Tres Dedos said.

Joaquin took a step to the side, lifted his left hand for balance and to draw the other man's attention, then stepped closer and drove the blade toward his midsection. Tres Dedos's right hand whipped out, faster than Joaquin's eye could follow, and caught his wrist. Then he wrenched it and brought it down against his upraised knee. Joaquin's wrist spasmed, and the next thing he knew, his knife was in Tres

Dedos's hand, the edge pressed up against his throat.

"First thing to know—if you fight with knives, you're going to get cut. It's going to hurt. If the other man also has a knife, it's almost impossible to kill him without him getting you as well."

"I wasn't really trying to kill you."

"Obviously. Second thing to know—never go at somebody with a knife unless you intend to kill him." He drew the blade away from Joaquin's neck, reversed it, and handed it back.

"You didn't intend to kill *me*," Joaquin countered.

"I did. But I stopped myself in time. You can't do that until you know yourself, know your capabilities. If I'd pressed a little harder, you'd be on the ground with your life ebbing away. But I know when to stop.

"Third thing—you lunged at me with the blade held vertically. Up and down. That would have hurt, if you'd hit me, but my ribs would've stopped it from penetrating too deeply. If you're going at a man's ribs, turn the blade sideways, so it can slip between them."

"Like this?" Joaquin turned the knife in his hand and jabbed toward Tres Dedos.

"No." Tres Dedos demonstrated with his own hand as he talked. "Hold it like you were, then turn your hand, not the knife. Then, after you've stabbed, twist your hand back, so as you withdraw the knife, you tear at your man's insides all the more."

"It's a bloody business, isn't it?" Joaquin said.

"The bloodiest. But if you want to see the terror in a man's eyes, feel his tears against your skin as he weeps, it's the best way to kill him."

"You've done that?"

Tres Dedos looked out toward the horizon. "I've killed men

in just about every way I can think of, Joaquin. I'm not proud of that, but I'm not ashamed, either. I did what I had to do."

"In the war?"

"In the war. Before the war. After, too."

Tres Dedos had never talked to him about this before. If Jesús knew, he'd never said anything, either. Tres Dedos's sense of humor veered toward the macabre, Joaquin knew. But he'd never imagined his cousin as a murderer.

"You must have had good reasons," he said.

"Sometimes. Other times, not so much."

"Jesús told me you fought like a panther in the war. He was so proud of you."

"I'm proud of him, too. He's as brave a man as I've ever known." He turned, eyed Joaquin. "You're stronger, now, than he ever was."

"Do you think I'm ready for them? The Americans?"

"Not yet. Strength isn't everything. It's only part of what you need. Let's keep working."

• • •

Tres Dedos forced Joaquin to practice with a lariat he'd made; his years working with horses had made him skilled with it, but since then he'd had no reason to use one. His experience showed, and soon he could hurl a loop around almost anything.

One day, he sprinted past a young bear, and the bear gave chase. Joaquin had seen how fast they could run, and how handily they could race up trees, so when it started gaining on him, he stopped, turned, and hurled the twenty-five-pound stone he carried. It hit the surprised beast on the snout. The bear stopped cold, blood gushing, and gave up the effort. After that, most of the grizzlies on the mountain seemed to view him as an object of curiosity and perhaps ridicule, but they left him alone and he did them the same favor.

As his body strengthened, it also healed. Working the creek had left his hands stiff and bruised and his back aching. Those conditions were gone. He slept on a bench of stone with only a single blanket beneath him and one on top, and he awoke refreshed and pain-free.

Evenings, he or Tres Dedos built a small fire within the large main chamber of the cave, away from the opening but close enough to allow smoke to escape. They knew it was risky—it could probably be seen like a beacon, from far off in the valley. But they used dry wood, which reduced the amount of smoke. Anyway, there weren't many people out there to see it, and nobody hunting them, as far as they knew. They cooked simple meals over the fire, then by its light they chatted or played cards. Joaquin handled Rosita's red scarf until it started to fray, then stuffed it into a pocket until he remembered it was there and took it out again. He read the books and monographs Rosita had taken from her father's library—not only the philosophies of Rousseau, but also those he came to understand as the Salamanca school, especially the works of Alonso de la Vera Cruz and Francisco de Vitoria. They all argued for the freedom of man from overbearing authority—Rousseau mainly concerned with the power of the state and the wealthy, the others with the rights of aboriginals to their own lands and tribal associations.

In America, as in Mexico, European conquerors had subjugated the natives or were trying to slaughter them outright. Even in the gold region, most of the Indians had either been driven off or put to work for pauper's wages, doing the hard labor that enabled white men to grow wealthy.

The blood of both conqueror and conquered flowed through Joaquin's veins, and although the Church had taught him to value the Spanish blood more than the Mexican, Rosita's books made him rethink that position. Here he was, living like a barbarian or a beast, and—although he missed his beloved with a fierce and endless passion—he was utterly free.

But he didn't know who he was.

He'd been a son and a brother his whole life. When he'd left home, though, it had been under cover of darkness, without a word to anyone there. He and Rosita had written letters to their families from Los Angeles, assuring them that they were safe and happy, but no return mail had reached him, so he had no way of knowing whether those letters had been received, or in what spirit. He still had a brother, Jesús, who had loved him—but did he still? After all, Joaquin and Tres Dedos had slipped away with only a note left behind, one that explained little. What would he think would he when he found out what had happened?

He had been a vaquero, but he was no longer. He had been a miner, briefly, but that was done. He had been a married man, but no more.

Everything that made him who he was had been taken from him or abandoned voluntarily. What was left was an empty shell, with nothing to fill it except the words in books, and the strength of his body. And the friendship of Tres Dedos, who was teaching him to kill.

Joaquin knew his period of mourning in the mountains had to end. The weather was growing cooler by the day. Soon the rainy season would start, the rivers would swell, and mining would come to a halt for several months. If he was going to fulfill the promise he had made to himself, it had to be now, before the Americans who'd murdered Rosita scattered to the four winds.

"It's time," he said to Tres Dedos.

"You're sure?"

"Do you think I'm not ready?"

"You've been ready. One can always be more ready, but I think you'll do fine. They're cowards, anyway—five of them attacking one man, then a defenseless woman. They deserve whatever you do to them, and more. Anyway, I'm ready for a meal in a restaurant, and a drink at a bar. Let's get off this damned mountain!"

• • •

Joaquin left his hair and beard long, to serve as a disguise in case he encountered anyone he knew in the camps. Tres Dedos did the same, although his hand might be a giveaway if anyone noticed it. Joaquin figured that if he wanted to reveal his identity, he still could—his voice hadn't changed, after all, or his eyes. But he wouldn't be recognized unless it was by his choice. He hung his musket and lariat from his saddle, stuck the pistol and Bowie knife in his sash, then he and his cousin rode down from the mountain and back to Sawmill Flat.

The first stop was the claim that had been theirs. The cottonwoods on the far side of the creek were bare-limbed, the hills behind them looking like molten gold in the crisp autumn air. Men were working the claim, and the neighboring one, but none of them were Jesús, or the men he'd known first as neighbors, then as rapists and murderers. One of them stopped, knee-deep in the creek, and turned to them. "Somethin'?"

"Where's the man who used to work this claim?" Joaquin asked.

"Mexican feller?"

"That's right. Jesús Murrieta."

"Last I heard, he headed up to Moke Hill. Some rich diggings up there, folks are sayin'."

"What about the white man, Harry Love?"

The man shrugged. "Took his poke and headed south for the winter. Santa Barbara, I think."

"South for the winter?" Tres Dedos echoed. "What is he, a sparrow?"

"He used to be a deputy there." Joaquin reminded him.

"That's right," the white man said. "He sold me the claim. Not sure I got the best of the bargain; seems pretty played out to me. Still findin' color now and again, though."

"What about the men who worked the next one over?" Joaquin asked. "Chambers and the others?"

"Never seen 'em," the man said. He called to his companions, working farther up the creek and on the long tom the Americans had built. "Hey, any of you fellers seen them as was here before?"

He was greeted with a chorus of negative responses. Looking back at Joaquin, he shrugged. "Sorry. Reckon they either cashed in and moved on, or they gave up and did the same."

"How long have you been here?"

The man smiled. "Kinda lost track of the days. About a month, I reckon. Give or take."

Joaquin nodded his thanks and he and Tres Dedos rode off.

A month. That was about how long they'd been camped out on Bear Mountain, though like that man, he hadn't exactly been counting off the days. Chances were the Americans had abandoned their claim as soon as they'd killed Rosita, or as soon as they'd discovered that Joaquin hadn't died in the attack. And Jesús must have moved on almost as soon as he saw the note. Would he have told Harry? Or was Harry's departure just coincidence? It was true that winter was coming, and Harry didn't seem to like the cold. Maybe he'd made enough from his various claims, and whatever he got from selling them, to give up the mining country forever.

He missed Harry more than he'd expected to, but it was the other Americans he was most interested in. For the last month, he had thought about little but killing them, and now they were gone. They could be anywhere by now. Back east, maybe. Wherever they had come from.

But their gold-seeking efforts hadn't been very successful, or they wouldn't have had to raid Joaquin's claim. Most men who came west to California expended their available resources to get here. Once here, they either struck it rich and went home, or struck out and stayed close. San Francisco and Sacramento City were full of men looking for work. And the growing towns of the gold region were packed with people trying to profit from the gold in other ways, many of them unsavory. Brothels, saloons, and gambling halls had sprouted everywhere, like mushrooms after a rain, as those who hadn't found gold sought to mine it straight from the pockets of those who had.

Considering the relative lack of success Chambers and the others had found, Joaquin guessed they were still in the area. Either working a different claim or trying their luck at some other trade. They might not still be together, but that didn't mean they couldn't be found.

17

During their time on Bear Mountain, Joaquin and Tres Dedos had spent precious little of their gold. They had plenty left, and nothing but time on their hands. They pitched a tent for Tres Dedos among more than a hundred other tents in Georgetown, a place neither of them had ever been before, because Joaquin argued that once people saw Manuel, they wouldn't readily forget. Joaquin could blend in better without him. He was tall, with broad shoulders and a deep chest, but he wasn't the size of a grizzly bear.

On his own, he rode from town to town and spent some time in each, eyeing the locals, stopping in saloons and gambling dens. Miners busily, happily parted with their money, and Joaquin did the same, although with moderation. He was trying to fit in, not to escape the rigors of the mining life. When he won at the tables, which he did with some regularity, he made sure to lose most of his winnings so as not to be remembered.

He also made the rounds of the diggings and the rivers, in case the men had gone to work on other claims. He stopped at the Bear, American, Feather, and Humboldt Rivers, and visited Auburn, Volcano, Pilot Hill, Folsom, Angel's Camp, Railroad Flat, Sheep Ranch, and more. The first of the late-autumn rains hit, soaking him, but he kept at his quest. Every now and then he returned to Georgetown to visit with Tres Dedos, describe his progress, and trade horses.

Finally, at Fiddletown, he spotted a familiar figure. The town wasn't much more than a collection of weather-worn tents spread out around Dry Creek, which indeed ran dry during the summer months but was flowing now. Jack Bohannon was coming out of a saloon tent as Joaquin rode down the muddy track that passed for its main street. Half-stumbling, Bohannon made his way from that tent to another, which he went into and didn't come out of again. Joaquin dismounted and hitched his mount to a rail down the road, then walked back past the tent. From inside, he heard snoring, and not just from Bohannon, but from at least three men that he could determine. Day-sleeping, he figured them for either drunks or night-workers, or perhaps both. Without knowing how many were inside, or whether some might be awake, though, he didn't want to confront Bohannon in there. He had some questions for the man, and needed time with him, undisturbed by company.

At least he knew where one of the men was, and that was a start. He rode Blanco to another town, acquired a tent of his own, and returned to pitch it not far from the one Bohannon shared. He spent four days and nights there, making his way into town from time to time, spending a little of his dwindling gold supply in the saloons and gambling tents, and keeping his eye on Bohannon.

After those few days, he watched Bohannon and three of his companions go into the woods with axes and big, two-man saws. They were timber workers, then, at least until payday, at which time they became drunks. Now the money had run out, so they had to fell some more trees.

The Irishman wouldn't be alone in the woods, though, which meant that quiet was called for. Joaquin left his guns at his tent and the horse tethered beside it, then set off into the trees with just his knife and lariat. The other men had a head start, but once they started working, the noise made them easy enough to locate. Joaquin had been watching his steps, trying to avoid piles of fallen leaves, but the sounds of sawing and men's shouts made that caution unnecessary.

Once he'd spied them, Joaquin settled a safe distance away and waited for an opportunity. It came after about three hours, when the men called a break. They drank from canteens, and a couple of them—Bohannon included—went into the trees to relieve themselves. Most men Joaquin had worked with would have done so side by side with the others, but perhaps when a man slept in a small tent with his work crew, he might value some privacy when he could get it.

Bohannon struck out in the opposite direction from Joaquin's location, so Joaquin had to hurry through the forest, circling around the work site. By the time he closed in on Bohannon, the man was finished and heading back to join the others. Here in the woods, there was little space to use his lariat, but Bohannon was approaching a space where several big trees had already been felled, leaving only stumps and creating a short gap in the forest. Joaquin raced to the gap's edge, getting there moments before Bohannon reached it.

As Bohannon walked past the stumps, Joaquin got the lariat spinning. He was shivering despite the warmth of the day, his hands trembled, and his stomach threatened to explode. He wished Tres Dedos were there to urge him on, or to step in if he failed. But he was alone, and he couldn't risk failure.

As he worked the rope, experience and years of practice took over. Its loop widened with each revolution. Just before his quarry reached the far edge of the clearing, he let fly. The rope soared across the space and dropped down. Joaquin yanked it taut as it fell, and the loop closed around Bohannon's throat, cutting off his startled cry.

Joaquin looped his end around a stout, nearby tree, and gave a brisk tug. He pulled Bohannon, struggling against the rope, backward until he was up against the trunk. Bohannon's face was turning purple, and the hands clutching at the rope around his neck were already weakening. Joaquin wrapped the rope around him a few times, so his arms were bound tightly against his torso, hands at his sides. Bohannon had a pistol and a knife in his belt. Joaquin yanked those and tossed them behind the tree.

Now, Joaquin showed himself, walking around to face the other man. His anxiety had vanished, buried by the lust for vengeance. He loosened the pressure on Bohannon's neck slightly, enough to enable him to breathe and speak, then showed him the Bowie knife, pressing its sharp point against the big man's cheek. "Do you recognize me?" he asked.

"I never seen you in my life," Bohannon managed.

"Look closer. Look at my eyes."

Bohannon did, then shook his head.

"Imagine me without the beard, and with shorter hair. Imagine me working a claim next to yours."

Bohannon swallowed hard as recognition came. Joaquin could see it in the widening of his eyes and the way his flesh paled. "Murrieta?"

"That's right."

"I thought you was—"

"You didn't think I was dead. Or you might have, once, but you knew almost straightaway that I wasn't."

Bohannon didn't answer, but his eyes showed that Joaquin was right.

"I know why you're here," Bohannon said. "But you got to

know, it weren't my idea."

"Whose was it, then? You're the one who attacked me first. You're the one who held me down while the others went for Rosita."

"It was Sam," Bohannon insisted. "He kept goin' on about you Mexicans takin' white man's treasure, and talkin' about what he wanted to do with your woman. We knew we couldn't stop him, so we decided to go with him, to keep him out of trouble."

"You have a strange idea of keeping someone out of trouble."

"Keeping him safe, I mean. He were alone, you'd have killed him."

"You're right about that."

"Do you mean to kill me now? I could call for my friends."

"Try it and it'll be your last breath," Joaquin assured him. "If you want to live, tell me where to find Sam, and I might let you go."

"Might?"

"I'm after the one whose idea it was to attack and kill my wife," Joaquin said. "If that wasn't you, then . . ." He let the sentence trail off, unfinished.

The Irishman's eyes shifted right and left, as if rescue might come from either direction. Not far away, Joaquin could hear the other workers in conversation, not yet worried about their missing comrade. That wouldn't last, though. He had to finish this quickly.

"Where is he?"

"He's over in Hangtown," Bohannon said. "Working in a saloon there."

"You're sure?"

"Last I heard. You'll let me go now, right? I never meant

you no harm."

Joaquin had never thought of himself as someone who could kill an unarmed man, lashed to a tree and defenseless. But if Bohannon lived, he would call out to his comrades, and then it would be four against one. Joaquin summoned the image of Rosita, curled up, ravaged and bloody on their bed, and that made it easier. He reached forward, loosened the ropes around Bohannon's neck a little more and as the big man swallowed, Joaquin whipped the Bowie knife across his throat. Blood spurted forth, spraying him in the face. He blinked it away and kept at it, making sure the cut went from one ear to the other. More blood, more than he'd imagined, wet the forest floor. No doctor in the world could save Bohannon now.

Then he backed away and unwound the rope from around Bohannon and the tree. The big man pitched forward like a felled pine and hit the ground, still twitching, blood bubbling from his neck and soaking the earth.

Joaquin wiped his face and coiled his rope. Tres Dedos had told him it was bloody work, killing a man with a knife. But he'd also spoken of the look in a man's eyes when he knows death is coming for him, and that's what Joaquin had seen in Bohannon's.

It was as intoxicating as liquor. More.

As he moved through the trees, looking for a stream or creek where he could clean up a little more before returning to his tent, he thought about what he'd just done. Bill Byrnes had warned him about crossing this line. Once a man has killed another, he's a murderer, Bill had said. No matter what else he does with his life, that doesn't change. He'll die a killer of men.

But Tres Dedos was a killer of men, and also a good, trusted friend. He didn't see anything wrong with killing. Especially this kind—killing as revenge for a grievous wrong.

Joaquin had killed, and there was no going back from that, no undoing it. He'd ended Bohannon's life, and although it had been difficult at first, imagining Rosita had made it easier. He would probably pay a price later—in his dreams, perhaps, which now were still full of his beloved.

But in truth, he didn't feel all that different. His nerves were on fire, his muscles sapped of strength, but he had delivered justice. Bohannon had participated in the attack on Joaquin and Rosita. If he hadn't been there, Joaquin might have been able to hold off the others. He, too, was a murderer, and of an innocent woman who hadn't deserved to die. Bohannon was only lucky that Joaquin hadn't had more time, because he might've made sure that Bohannon suffered more before he went.

18

Hangtown, near the south fork of the American River, had eleven saloons. Joaquin hadn't thought to ask Bohannon the name of the one Sam Mackintosh worked at. Of course, the entire story could have been a lie, but he didn't believe Bohannon was clever enough to come up with anything so convincing at such a moment.

The plethora of saloons made hunting Mackintosh a challenge, however, and the size of the town amplified the difficulty. Its main street was nearly a mile long, flanked on both sides by wooden or brick buildings containing stores, six brothels, two churches, two hotels, two barbers, a laundry, a doctor, gambling halls small and palatial, a sheriff's office, an assay office, a bank, and said eleven drinking houses. The street itself was dirt, and torn up in spots because, rumor had it, gold had been found right there in the street, so thereafter folks occasionally dug out patches looking for more. The street was constantly crowded, with people going in and out of the businesses or sitting in chairs out in front of them. Others, less reputable or more intoxicated, simply sat in the dirt.

Joaquin wasted no time, because he didn't want Mackintosh to leave town before he got there, or to hear about Bohannon's death. He desperately wanted to tell Tres Dedos what he'd done, but that would have to wait.

Once he'd arrived, Joaquin stopped into each saloon,

bought a drink, and watched. Once he'd viewed every employee, he moved on to the next one. After the third saloon, he started ordering drinks but not finishing them, fearful that eleven in a short span of time would render him unable to do anything useful, even if he did find his quarry.

But after eleven saloons and at least a portion of eleven drinks, he still hadn't seen the man. He would have to return after dark, when new workers might be on duty. He had been seen all over town, though, and with his long hair and wild black beard, he wasn't someone who could pass unnoticed. If he made the rounds again, people would talk.

The striped pole jutting priapically out from the barbershop wall gave him the answer. Stepping inside, he found two barbers chattering away as they worked on customers sitting in high chairs with footstools, and nine more men waiting their turns. He walked out again just as quickly. Sitting in there would expose him to just as many of the townsfolk as sitting in saloons, and perhaps require him to engage in conversation, as well.

He remembered seeing a second barbershop, so outside, he scanned the street in both directions. The other one was on the far end, and the striped pole there was mounted more modestly, parallel to the façade. Inside, a single barber sat in his own chair, holding a copy of the *El Dorado Republican* newspaper in front of his face. Joaquin cleared his throat. When the man lowered the paper, Joaquin could see that he was Mexican. His black hair was short, parted in the middle and oiled down. He had a thin mustache and two gold teeth in front.

"You need a haircut," the barber said. It wasn't a question.

"And a shave. A bath, if you have one. But why are so many people waiting in line at the other place, when there's no line here?" Joaquin asked.

"Those fellows are good barbers," the man replied.

"And you're not?"

"I'm terrible." With a toothy grin, he added, "and I'm Mexican, so most whites stay away."

"Do you talk while you're working?"

"Not if I can help it."

"A shave and a haircut, then."

"I do have a tub, in back. I'll get my girl to fill it."

"Good," Joaquin said. "I've met horses whose back ends smell better than I do."

The barber got out of the chair, folded his newspaper and dropped it on the counter, and seated Joaquin in front of the mirror. Joaquin studied himself. He hadn't seen himself in a real mirror since Rosita's death, only in streams and still ponds. With his face almost completely hidden under a bushy beard and long hair flying everywhere, he reminded himself of Harry Love. He wondered how the man was doing, back in Santa Barbara.

The barber started by draping a hot, damp towel over Joaquin's face, to soften his beard. While that cooled, he whipped his razor along the strop hanging from the chair, sharpening it. He replaced the towel once with another hot one, then dropped them both back into a pail of hot water sitting on top of a woodstove. He grabbed a ball of soap from a basin of cooler water and roughly lathered Joaquin's face. As promised, he worked silently, sometimes grunting or making another small noise as he scraped Joaquin's cheeks, chin, and neck. Joaquin told him to leave a mustache, and he obliged.

He completed the shave by dabbing the many cuts he'd made with a styptic pencil, then slapped some Bay Rum lotion across both of Joaquin's cheeks. That done, he started in on Joaquin's hair, chopping it away with scissors. Joaquin watched large clumps fall to the dirty floor. He left it long in back, at Joaquin's request, and shorter in front.

Once again, Joaquin looked at his reflection. He seemed to have aged over the last several weeks, his face hardened. He had lost some weight and the flesh was tighter over his cheekbones. He fingered the ragged pink scar on his forehead.

"I didn't do that one," the barber said.

"I know." Being hit with the butt of a rifle seemed like an unglamorous way to gain such a wound. "It was a knife," he lied. Then he added a morsel of truth. "Held by a man who lives here, in Hangtown."

"Is that why you've come? I've never seen you here before."

"What would you say if I told you that he'll be dead before I leave?"

"I'd ask you if he's one of my customers. If he is, I'd ask you to let him live."

"He's a white man. You said you don't have a lot of white customers."

"That's true, I don't see many white heads in here. Mexicans, a few Negroes. I don't know how to braid a pigtail, so the Chinese take care of their own hair."

"Can I trust you not to say anything?"

"About the revenge killing of a man who's never entered my shop? Of course."

"His name's Sam Mackintosh. He works in one of the saloons, I'm told, but I don't know which one."

"I don't know the name."

"He's a fat man. Brown hair and beard, lips as red as if he painted them."

The barber shrugged. "I don't spend a lot of time in their saloons. We have a small Mexican district, off the main street.

I do my drinking in a cantina there."

"But you'd tell me if you knew him?"

"I have no reason not to. Besides, you said you're going to pay handsomely for my services."

"I said no such thing."

"Funny," the barber said. "I could have sworn you did, right before you told me you planned to kill somebody."

Joaquin understood his meaning. He reached in a pocket and handed the barber a small pouch of gold dust. "In this Mexican district, is there perhaps a hotel or boarding house?"

The pouch vanished into one of the barber's pockets. "A room could be arranged, sir."

"I think what's in that pouch will cover it."

"I'm sure it will. While you're bathing, I'll make the arrangements."

He whipped the cape off Joaquin and led him into a back room, where his ten-year-old daughter had been busily pouring water into a copper tub set over hot coals. After laying out a towel, he disappeared. The daughter handed him some soap and a scrub brush, then did the same.

Alone, Joaquin peeled off his clothes and climbed in. The hot bath felt luxurious, but he couldn't entirely relax, knowing he'd revealed his plan to a stranger and was soaking, naked, while his pistol and knife sat on a chair across the room. He climbed out, leaving watery footprints, carried the chair over and placed it next to the tub, then got back in. By the time the water turned cool, the barber was back with directions to his cousin's house, not far away.

Joaquin stepped out of the shop feeling like a new man. He collected the horses and rode to the house he'd been told to, a good-sized adobe in a district where all the shops had Spanish names. Arturo Bojorques met him at the door, shook his hand,

and brought him inside to meet his wife Analisa and three sons, young boys whose names Joaquin forgot almost as soon as he'd heard them. When Arturo showed him the room in which he'd sleep, he lowered his voice and said, "You're going to want to visit the Lucky Strike tonight."

"I am?"

"Most assuredly." He spoke with such confidence that Joaquin didn't question him further.

"Thank you."

"No, thank you, my friend. The gold you shared with my cousin will ensure that we can both feed our families for a few more weeks. It's a hard life here, for our kind."

"Why do you stay, then?" Joaquin asked.

The man spread his hands wide, then clasped them together. "Here, at least, some common people achieve success. We stay and work and pray to be among them."

"An honorable pursuit," Joaquin said. "If ever I can do anything more for you, you have only to ask. I am Joaquin Murrieta."

He wasn't sure what had caused him to share his name, when he was desperately trying to remain unknown while he carried out his mission of vengeance. But he trusted this man.

And spreading a little treasure into the right hands, he was finding, could work wonders.

19

The Lucky Strike was a masterpiece of utility over aesthetics. It looked as if the builder only knew how to make straight lines, and did so in one direction until he tired of it, then turned at a ninety-degree angle and continued that way for a while. All of it—floor-to ceiling and in between, including the tables and chairs—was made from knotty pinewood, making it somewhat difficult to distinguish one object from the next. Only a piano, made elsewhere and shipped here, stood out. The interior was a large square, with a bar that came out from the wall near the right rear corner, and a staircase parallel to the left wall that led to a balcony. From the looks of it, soiled doves had their cribs upstairs, but currently, most of them were either engaged in those cribs or down on the saloon floor, tousling the hair and other parts of drinkers who looked like they might rather be left alone.

Joaquin ordered a whiskey from a surly, bow-tied bartender and carried it to an empty table in a corner of the room, from which he could easily watch the bar and see who went up and down the stairs. He'd enjoyed a couple of hours of sleep in a real bed, for the first time since Rosita's murder, then a wonderful meal in the company of a family, all of whose members loved each other. It brought back what he'd lost by leaving home, but also the potential future he'd lost when Rosita was taken from him. He had been, for a few moments, genuinely happy. Now, that had been replaced by grief and fury.

For more than an hour, he waited and watched. A man pounded the piano keys with all the skill of an enthusiastic beginning student. Men played cards, laughed, joked, threatened one another. A fight broke out but was quickly ended.

Finally, a door at the back opened and a liquor barrel walked in—headless, legs beneath it, arms wrapped around its belly. Then it ducked down beneath the bar, and Sam Mackintosh stood up, red-faced and sweating. He wore a stained white shirt and his bowtie hung loosely around his neck.

Afraid he might go back out the door and be gone for another hour, Joaquin rose and started toward him. He feigned drunkenness, weaving between tables, bumping into people, and keeping his eyes downcast so Mackintosh couldn't see his face. As he'd suspected, Mackintosh was headed for the back door, so Joaquin took a path that would intercept him.

But Mackintosh was closer to the door, and one man snatched at Joaquin's arm when he was bumped, slowing Joaquin just enough. Mackintosh was going to make it outside, then who knew where.

"Good fellow!" Joaquin tried to slur the words, to continue playing drunk. "A moment."

Mackintosh paused, just inside the door. Joaquin closed the distance between them in an instant, his hand going to his sash and whipping out the Bowie knife at the same time. Mackintosh's mouth dropped open. His eyes showed recognition, then apology. He started to speak. "Murrieta, I'm sor—"

Still play-acting in case anyone watched, Joaquin took a drunken stumble, catching himself with his left hand on Mackintosh's right shoulder and shoving the man against the back wall. "This is for Rosita," he whispered, as he slashed the knife across Mackintosh's bearded throat, cutting deeply. He made a graceful half-spin to avoid the first spray of blood, which spurted the length of a man and more, and he was out the back door before blood or body hit the floor. A wagon waited in an otherwise empty alley, drawn by a pair of old horses, five more barrels waiting in the bed.

• • •

Sheriff James Hume barged through the front door like a man on fire. He'd been enjoying the comforts of a lovely lady named Millicent Ann when someone had hammered on the door like an oversized woodpecker, shouting about a killing at the Lucky Strike. As he'd buttoned up his pants, Millicent Rose had reminded him that he had paid for her companionship, which he'd had—the fact that he hadn't yet availed himself fully of that didn't entitle him to a refund, regardless of the circumstances. But he had recently fired one worthless deputy, and he'd given the half-worthless one the night off, so he was on duty and had to respond.

"Has anybody fetched Doc Bright?" he demanded as he entered. "If this feller ain't all the way dead, you're 'bout to have one unhappy lawman on your hands. I ain't wastin' any more time on some feller just got hisself knocked silly in a—"

He let the statement drop when he realized that nobody in the place was sitting down. They were all on their feet, crowded around the back wall of the saloon, where the delivery door was. As he'd entered, they began to part, but the stink hit him before the sight did. Blood, lots of it, and the person who'd bled it had soiled himself something ferocious. Then he saw the blood, a small ocean of it. The stout guy who hauled barrels and trash for the Lucky Strike was the source; he was sitting against the wall, legs splayed out, head drooping at a strange angle, his entire front side painted red.

"Fight," Hume finished, because he hated to let a sentence go undone.

He was in for a long night, and none of the rest of it would involve Millicent Ann.

• • •

"That's ripe."

Hume turned to see Tom Springer standing behind him. Springer—in his thirties but already starting to go gray, skinny and clean-shaven, dressed like an eastern college boy—published the *El Dorado Republican*, wrote most of it, and was an eternal pain in Hume's hindquarters. But he couldn't help liking the guy, just the same. Springer had a pad in one hand and a pencil in the other, ready to start writing down every word Hume spoke. "It'll get worse."

"Worse? Really?"

"Fresh dead smells bad, but old dead, when the rot starts to set in? Puts fresh to shame. Not that either one's any kind of rose garden."

"Who is it?"

"Sam Mackintosh. Works here at the Strike, for the last month or so."

"Who did it?"

Hume had already interviewed most of the witnesses, and their stories aligned fairly closely, with a few exceptions that he put down to having over-imbibed. He'd already be back in his office, if he weren't waiting for Chauncey, the undertaker. Chauncey took his work seriously, but Hume felt the same way about his bedtime.

"Young feller," he said. "Long hair, black or dark brown. Mustache. Fair skin. Nobody's seen him around before today. Mexican, mebbe."

"Maybe?"

"Most say Mex. Amos Fairchild says no, he's Chilean."

"How can he tell the difference?"

"Fairchild says it's the smell. Mexicans smell like bean farts, but Chileans smell like pepper farts." He eyed Springer, dutifully noting what he'd said. "You gonna print that?"

• • •

An hour outside Hangtown, Joaquin slowed Blanco's pace. Racing a horse in the dark was always a bad idea, even on well-traveled roads, but he had wanted to put some distance between himself and the town. He hadn't seen any pursuers, however, and was starting to feel relatively safe.

He was sorry that he couldn't stay and become better acquainted with Arturo and his family, but having completed his business here so quickly, he felt it best not to imperil his would-be host any further.

The thrill of his earlier act still coursed through him; his entire being vibrated like a plucked string of Rosita's guitar. He had killed a man, in full view of a crowded saloon. It had been dangerous, to be sure, but he suspected the danger was what made it so exciting.

People would talk about the bold, cold-blooded killing, and that was for the best. He wanted word to spread quickly that Mackintosh and Bohannon had both been slaughtered like the animals they were. He wanted the remaining three men to spend whatever remained of their lives in terror, wondering when vengeance would come for them.

Because it would.

He would.

He had sworn it, and he meant to follow through.

20

"I've done it!" Joaquin said as soon as he entered Tres Dedos's tent.

The other man had been lying on his back, hands clasped on his expansive gut, but he sat up with a grin. "All of them?"

"Two. So far. The first told me where to find the second. But the second went quickly. I never had a chance to ask him anything. I did it in a saloon, right in front of twenty people or more."

"And nobody stopped you?"

"They were shocked. Frozen in place. I could have done five more men before anybody moved to stop me."

"How do you feel about it, Joaquin?"

Joaquin considered for a moment. "I looked into their eyes. Both of them. Like you said, they knew they were dead men. I saw terror. And something else."

"What?" Tres Dedos asked.

Joaquin hesitated. Finally, he said, "Resignation, I think. They knew what they'd done. They knew what they deserved. They had spent every moment between then and the time I found them wondering when it would happen. When at last it did, I think they were relieved to have it over with."

"Some men go that way," Tres Dedos said, nodding. "With others, you can't even see their eyes for the tears. Or they close them, hoping that if they can't see you, nothing will happen. It's stupid, of course. Once death is ready for them, nothing will change its course." He chuckled. "One man, I spared, because he was so certain it was his time. He closed his eyes and was praying. I just walked away. He didn't even hear me go, because he was screaming out his prayers, as if perhaps God couldn't hear them in heaven unless he shouted. I wished I could have stayed around to see his face when he realized I was gone—except if I had, of course, then I wouldn't have been gone. I'd have had to finish him. I think it's better that I didn't, because he's spent every minute since wondering when I'd come back. I doubt he's had a moment's rest."

"I can't give any of these men that opportunity," Joaquin said. "Death is too good for them, but it's all I can offer."

"Of course. But, how are you? No qualms? Nightmares?"

What a question. Some nights he was afraid to close his eyes, lest he relive that horrible night. He had confessed as much to Tres Dedos, and his friend had helped him through those first weeks, in the cavern on Bear Mountain, when he'd writhed and cried out in his sleep almost every night.

"Nightmares, yes, sometimes. I see their faces, watch them die. But they're not as bad as the ones where Rosita dies, over and over. If they crowd those dreams out, that's all the better. I only want to remember the good times with her, not the end."

"I see the faces of those I've killed, some nights," Tres Dedos said. "And of those I've lost."

"Does it ever get better?"

"Time has a way of dulling things. Like the edge of a blade, it only stays sharp if you work it. With memories, I think if you don't hone them, they eventually lose their power. Some of it, at any rate. You'll never forget, but its bite won't always be so sharp."

"I look forward to that," Joaquin said. "In the meantime, I still have work to do."

"Yes," Tres Dedos agreed. "You don't want to leave this task unfinished. Until you're done, there'll be no peace. This, I can guarantee."

Joaquin glanced out through the tent flaps. The sun had already sunk beyond the western hills. "I'll leave in the morning," he said. "If I cry out in my sleep, just ignore me."

Tres Dedos chuckled. "I've long since learned to do that, cousin, believe me."

• • •

"Hey, brother," Joaquin said. "Can I ask you something?"

For the last several days, most of his conversations had begun that way, and always in Spanish. He approached only Mexicans, and because his skin was fair, he wanted to be recognized for what he was. No white American would come up to a Mexican speaking in Spanish. Usually, given such an opening, the people he asked were happy to talk.

Joaquin followed up with: "I'm looking for a man. A white guy, skinny, with red hair. His jaw was broken about a month ago."

The usual response was along the lines of, "I haven't seen anybody like that."

On this day, however, it was different.

He'd been riding along a forest trail outside Culloma when he saw a pair of Mexican men field-dressing a deer they'd taken. He stopped, engaged in some casual conversation, and asked his question. The men exchanged glances.

"That guy who looks like a drowned rat," one of them said,

chuckling. The other one nodded and rubbed his left cheek, leaving bloody tracks where his fingers had been.

"That's him," Joaquin said. "His name is Wetzl."

"He's in Culloma," the second one said. "He's been gambling a lot and doing pretty well."

"I think he cheats," the other added. "I can't tell how, but I'm almost certain of it."

"That sounds like him, too," Joaquin said. "Where can I find him?"

"Most nights, he's at Meyer's," the blood-streaked one said. "At the faro tables."

"Meyer's is in Culloma?"

"Yes. Meyer's Dance Hall and Saloon. It's a huge stone building, you can't miss it."

"Thank you, my friends." Joaquin eyed the deer. "Nice catch."

"You need some venison?" one offered.

"No, thank you," Joaquin said. He reached into a saddle-bag and withdrew a small pouch of gold. "But here, for your trouble. If anybody asks you, you never told me anything."

He dropped the pouch into the hand of the man with the cleaner hands of the two. That man weighed it in his palm, grinned, and said, "We've never even seen you."

"Nor I you," Joaquin said. With a wave, he rode away, in the direction of Culloma.

A man named James Marshall, who worked for sawmill owner John Sutter, had started the whole rush for gold one morning in January 1848, while inspecting the flow of water at the millrace near Culloma. In the American River's South Fork, he'd seen something glittering. He had reached into the cold water and come up with pea-sized nuggets of gold. After having it checked to ensure that it really was what he thought it was, he returned with others, and they found more gold, in the river and along its banks.

From that happy accident, a worldwide phenomenon had sprung, resulting in people from all over racing to California as fast as they could—including himself, Tres Dedos, Rosita and Jesús. Joaquin hadn't been in touch with his brother since Rosita's death. He should head up to Mokelumne Hill for a visit.

But first, he had Ferd Wetzl to deal with.

• • •

The men had not exaggerated. Meyer's was a cavernous space. The air inside was thick with bitter tobacco smoke and the odors of cheap liquor and cheaper perfume, and music—piano and fiddles and an accordion and other, less recognizable instruments played something that resembled a tune. The thunder of stomping feet and clapping hands and the occasional "Hooraw!" nearly drowned it out, which was something of a mercy.

Joaquin had dressed all in black and pulled a black slouch hat low over his eyes. The corners of the hall were shadowed, and he found a table there. From under the brim, he perused the place. The band held court at one end, on a wooden stage about a hand's length above the plank floor. Most of the dancers were congregated in front of them. Tables hugged the walls, and more drinkers bellied up to a bar long enough to accommodate thirty or more, standing shoulder to shoulder. Gamblers plied their trade at twelve or fifteen of the tables, and plenty of working girls circulated, plying their own.

He had been sitting for almost two hours, nursing a couple of drinks and turning down offers of various sorts from the painted ladies, occasionally rising to stretch his muscles, and trying not to suffocate in the smoky air, when Wetzl finally strolled in. One look at him confirmed the hunters' story—he might not have been much of a prospector, but he was apparently a reasonably good gambler. He wore a red silk vest over a white shirt, with black pants and a low-crowned black hat. His hair and beard had been professionally cut, and the beard was thick enough to almost hide the fact that his jaw had been badly set and was slightly out of alignment with the rest of his face. Nobody would mistake him for handsome—miracles didn't happen for people like Wetzl, and the way his chin pointed a slightly different direction than his nose precluded that—but he wasn't far off.

He walked with a confidence that Joaquin had never seen on the creek. Being frightened away from the gold-seeking trade by his own crime seemed to have improved Wetzl's fortunes considerably.

As reported, the man found a seat at a faro table. A couple of prostitutes flocked to his side, and a Meyer's employee in a white shirt with a starched collar brought him a tray of chips. Joaquin couldn't tell for certain, but he believed Wetzl tipped the fellow handsomely. Wetzl said something to the banker, who laughed as he shuffled a deck of cards and placed it in the shoe. Wetzl studied the board and placed his bet and laid his marker on top of it, as did three players who'd crowded around him. The banker drew the soda card and set it aside, then two more, placing one on either side of the shoe. The coffin driver standing beside the banker slid the counters on the spindle, keeping track of the cards. Play went fast, and before long, Wetzl's chips were piling up. Joaquin hoped he didn't want to play all night, because watching from a distance was as dull an occupation as he could imagine.

Fortunately for Joaquin's sanity, Wetzl gave up after less than an hour. His stacks of chips were towering by that point, and he seemed to delight in handing them out to the working girls, to the barmaids who brought him drinks, to the banker and the coffin driver, and seemingly to anyone else who held out an empty palm in his vicinity. Finally, trailed by one of the girls who had seemed to catch his fancy, he cashed in his chips and let her take his hand. She led him through a door, undoubtedly the passageway to where her crib was.

Joaquin followed. Wending his way through the hall took longer than he wanted, and he had to push a couple of men out of his way, earning him glares. When he reached the doorway, Wetzl and the woman were already out of sight. There were only two ways they could have gone, though: down a hall that seemed to lead toward the rear of the building, or up a narrow flight of wooden stairs. He heard a creaking noise from above, so he picked the stairs.

They took him to a hallway lit only by a couple of lanterns in sconces. Doors lined the corridor, but only one was open. He caught a brief glimpse of a black pants leg and a flash of red vest disappearing through it, and then that door, too, was closed.

He took his time reaching it. From behind other doors, he heard the squeak of bedsprings, muffled grunts and moans, forced feminine laughter. Like the great hall downstairs, the hallway smelled of tobacco and drink, but also of sex and sweat. When he arrived at the door through which his quarry had presumably passed, he put his ear to it. He could make out the rhythms of quiet conversation—or perhaps negotiation—but not the words themselves.

Enough waiting. He had wanted to kill Wetzl from the moment he'd seen him, but the man had been the center of too much attention. Now he would get it done. He drew his knife and tried the door handle. It was unlocked. He slipped inside and eased it shut behind him.

The room was small, containing only a bed, a chair, and a little table with a pitcher of water and Wetzl's loot on it. A window gazed blankly onto the dark night outside. The woman lay on the bed, already naked, holding one arm out to Wetzl as if to summon him. Wetzl's vest and shirt were on the chair. He had one boot and one pants leg off, and was standing on one foot, trying to work off the other boot. At Joaquin's entrance, he tried to turn, clumsy and off-balance, and his mouth dropped open. "You!" he managed, before Joaquin slammed into him, shoulder-first. Wetzl went down in a heap, tangled in his own pants.

Joaquin reached down, grabbed Wetzl's bearded chin, and hauled him to his feet. Tears sprang to Wetzl's eyes as Joaquin wrenched his jaw. "What in the blazes are you—" he got out, before Joaquin jabbed the point of his Bowie knife against his chest.

"Hey, hey now," Wetzl said. "Look, I know why you're mad, Murrieta. I would be, too. But we can settle this like white men."

"I'm not a white man," Joaquin reminded him.

"Don't mean we can't be civilized, here. Look, I got money. Lots of it."

"I'm aware."

"So how much you want? All of it? Just let me go, and it's yours."

"Hey!" the prostitute threw out. She was sitting up in bed

now, eyes wide and glistening, as if this were the most interesting even that had ever happened in her presence. Quite
possibly it was. "You promised some of that to me!"

"Quiet," Joaquin said. Then to Wetzl, he added, "You can't
bargain with that. I can take your money just as easily once
you're dead. And you clearly deserve to die."

"Look, I made a mistake, right? We all did. We got carried
away. I regretted it the moment it happened, and I haven't
stopped since."

"You look like you're wracked with guilt. Dressing sharp,
playing faro, buying whores . . . obviously the behavior of a
man stricken by conscience."

"We all got different ways of showing grief, Murrieta."

Joaquin backhanded him across the face with his left hand,
keeping the knife pressed against him with the other. "Spare
me your phony sorrow."

"What do you want from me, then? You ain't killed me yet,
so you want somethin'."

"Tell me where the others are, and I'll let you go."

"Is that all? I don't know everybody, but Sam's in—"

Jopaquin cut him off. "Mackintosh is dead. Don't you read
the newspapers?"

"Ferd can't read," the prostitute said. "He can barely count
to twenty."

"I can so read!" Wetzl snapped. "I just . . . I don't choose
to."

"Chambers," Joaquin said. "And Beeman. Where are
they?"

"You'll let me go, I tell you?"

"I said I would."

Wetzl licked his lips, tasting blood from Joaquin's slap. "I don't know 'bout Beeman," he said. "But I heard tell Ben was over at Auburn, workin' a claim there."

"You're sure?"

"Last I heard," Wetzl said. "I got no reason to lie."

"How long ago?"

Wetzl shrugged. "A week, mebbe. Little longer, I don't know. Somebody said he seen Ben there."

Joaquin studied him for a moment. He seemed to be telling the truth, or he thought he was. He was looking Joaquin right in the eye, not glancing away. Chambers had been the most ambitious of the lot, and Joaquin had heard there was still gold to be found around Auburn.

"You'll let me go now, right?" Wetzl asked.

"I said I would." Joaquin tucked his knife into his sash, grabbed Wetzl by the jaw and the waist of his half-off pants, and yanked him off his feet. He swung the little man once, twice.

On the third swing, he let go.

With a screech, Wetzl crashed through the window, head-first, and kept going. His cry ended abruptly when he hit the ground below with a loud thump. Joaquin knocked out some of the broken glass and looked down. Wetzl's neck was twisted at an unpleasant angle. Broken, Joaquin was sure. If Wetzl hadn't died immediately, he would soon.

He turned back to the little table and scooped up the money. "That's mine," the woman said.

"You never provided the agreed-upon service," he reminded her. But he threw a fistful of it at her. "Here," he said. "It's more than he'd have given you, and you don't need to deal with the unpleasantness of him rutting you."

He started toward the door, tucking the money into

pockets as he went, but before he reached it, he heard a commotion in the hallway. Instead, he turned back to the window, crawled through, and pulled himself onto the roof. People were rushing toward the body, and pointing up at the broken window, but not looking farther up into the darkness above. From there, he could hear the crowd from the corridor bursting into the crib, and the prostitute telling them that some greaser named "Murri-something" threw Wetzl out the window, then took all the money.

At the term "greaser"—never mind the lie about the money—Joaquin was sorry he'd given her any of it. He'd hoped to buy her silence, at least for a few minutes, but obviously that wasn't to be. He dropped down from the roof at the far end of the building, landing on a grassy slope behind it.

The Mexican end of Culloma was only a few minutes away. Joaquin couldn't get to Blanco, tied up in front of the saloon, so he ran there. The roads were quiet, but light still shone through the windows of some of the small houses. Joaquin picked an adobe that looked like it could use some work and knocked on the door. When a man answered, he explained that he was being sought by a mob because he had taken revenge on the white man who'd raped and murdered his wife. The story was true, and the man seemed to see it in his eyes. When Joaquin offered money, he refused, but Joaquin pressed it into his hands. "For your family," he said. "Take it. The man it belonged to is dead."

The man accepted it and brought Joaquin inside, dropping the money onto the table at which his family took meals. "Carlita!" he called. "Come quickly."

A few moments later, a woman came out from another room, wrapping a shawl around herself. "What is it?"

"This man needs our help. He's being hunted."

"Why?" she asked.

Joaquin explained again, and her face softened. "He did that?"

"He did. He admitted it, before I killed him, but I already knew."

"He deserved to die, if anyone does." She crossed herself and whispered, "Forgive me."

"What do you need?" the man asked him.

"Just—it's not safe for me on the streets. If I could stay here for a few hours, until the fury dies down."

"As long as you need," the man said.

"And my horse is still there, at the saloon. Have you a son who could perhaps fetch him? Nobody knows he's mine, but if he stays there when all the others leave . . ."

"I understand. Of course."

"I don't want to put you in any danger."

The man shrugged. "Every day here, we are in danger. But we stay anyway, because what is there to go back to? At home, we struggled. Here, we also struggle. But here we are, where at least there's hope."

"I stay for the same reasons," Joaquin said. And for vengeance, he thought, but he didn't say that part aloud.

While Paco, the Mendoza family's fourteen-year-old son, went to fetch Blanco, Carlita made coffee. Joaquin sat at the table with her and her husband Juan and got acquainted. Their story was not unlike his own; they had come for the gold, found a little, lost some to taxes and more to theft. Now Carlita sewed and did laundry for the miners and Juan cooked in a restaurant, which he had also done at home in Sinaloa.

After a while, they heard running feet and hooves. Paco put

Blanco into a corral behind the house, where the family kept their own mules, two burros, and a goat, then raced into the house, flushed and sweating. "They're coming!" he said.

"Who?" Juan asked.

"The Americans! They have torches and guns."

"I should go," Joaquin said. "I can't be responsible for—"

"Nonsense!" Carlita said quickly. "Nobody saw you come in here."

"But if they search the house—"

"They'll find nothing."

"They'll find me and punish you."

"They'll find nothing," she said again.

Joaquin went to the window and looked outside. He could already see the light from the torches, bobbing as the Americans stormed toward the Mexican district. He doubted that Ferd Wetzl had been particularly popular in town, despite his gambling success—he hadn't been here very long, and he wasn't especially likable to begin with. But he was white and becoming wealthy, and maybe that was all it took.

"They're almost here," he said.

Carlita grabbed his arm and tugged. "Come with me." Joaquin relented, and she took him to another room. He saw fabrics, sewing supplies, and a huge pile of laundry in one corner, waiting to be cleaned. "On the floor," she said.

He understood her meaning then. He crouched down, and she and Paco heaped laundry over him, completely burying him. He could breathe, but the weight was oppressive. A few minutes later, he heard the muffled voice of Juan, opening the door and inviting people inside. Then he heard Americans speaking English as they stomped through the house, looking under tables and in every room. When one of them threw open the door of the sewing room, he looked around briefly, grunted something dismissive, and left.

Joaquin had come to think of himself as some kind of avenging angel, a hero, if only in his own mind. But would a hero hide in a pile of dirty clothes? No, he was just a man—a man wronged, a man trying to take his revenge on those who had wronged him, but a man just the same. He could be hurt or killed. He could be afraid. And he could hunker down in the corner of a stranger's house and wait for the mob to move on.

Because he wanted to live another day. When his revenge was complete, perhaps he would let the mob take him. At that point, he didn't know what else he would have to live for. Without Rosita, without family or country, why keep fighting?

But for now, he still had things to do. And to do them, he had to live.

21

Joaquin stayed with the Mendozas all that night and the next day. The mob had given up the hunt after a couple of hours, but throughout that night and day, Juan said men on horseback still passed by now and again, looking for something. Or someone. Convinced he was the object of the search, Joaquin stayed inside and away from the windows until night fell again. Then, with profuse thanks to his hosts, accompanied by a small pouch of gold, he took advantage of darkness to mount Blanco and ride away from town.

Auburn wasn't far away, just over some tree-topped hills and across the north fork of the American River. He arrived the next morning, took a room in a hotel, and slept away most of the day. That night, he made the rounds of the taverns and saloons, looking for Chambers. He didn't see him anywhere, so the next day he woke early, mounted his horse, and rode around the area. Wetzl had said Chambers was working a claim, so he was probably staying away from the town proper, living in a tent or a cabin somewhere on the outskirts. It could take a while to find someone in those circumstances, but he had some money and nothing more pressing to do.

That day, he saw plenty of miners, some seemingly coming up with color, but no Chambers. He watched men digging trenches in the earth, backs bent to their labors. He saw them wading knee- or hip-deep in frigid water. He saw them shovel heavy mounds of wet earth into sluices. He rode past some sitting in whatever shade they could find, sweat streaming down their exhausted bodies.

He also saw empty bottles littering the trails, and men passed out or working toward it leaning against trees or flat on their backs. Men had gathered here from every corner of the world, in most cases without wives or families or church or any of the institutions that had kept them on the straight and narrow at home. Some had great success, but most didn't, and now they killed the pain and frustration and sorrow any way they could. Joaquin tried not to judge them. They might be as dismayed by his mission of vengeance as he was by their behavior, or more so.

He thought of the money in his saddlebags, and how easy it had been to come by. Kill a man with money and take it. Even after sharing some with the painted lady and more with the Mendozas, he had plenty left.

He had been one of those hard-working men, not so long ago. He'd thought that was the best life had to offer—you work hard, you take what you can get, and you go home to your wife. If he'd still had a wife, he might still believe that.

But the more he watched those men killing themselves for a handful of gold, if that, the less he thought it was the best way to live. There were other ways, after all, that didn't break a man's spirit as well as his back. If as pathetic a wretch as Ferd Wetzl could succeed, how could Joaquin Murrieta not do ten times better?

Once he had finished with Chambers and Beeman, he would explore other means of making a living. Maybe not through theft and murder, but through gambling or some other occupation. The smart men out here didn't dig for gold, they took advantage of those who did.

He didn't find Chambers that day. He went to dinner at a restaurant near the hotel, and while he waited for his meal, he picked up a copy of the *El Dorado Republican* that someone had left on a nearby table.

A headline on the front page blared, "MEXICAN MURDERER ON THE LOOSE?" in huge, bold letters.

Beneath that, somebody named Thomas Springer had written, "Two citizens have been brutally slaughtered in a week's time, and witness statements suggest that both may have been murdered by the same Mexican killer. I witnessed first-hand the gruesome scene in Hangtown, where Sam Mackintosh's throat was slashed inside the very saloon that employed him, in full view of dozens of patrons. The murderer there was described as a tall Mexican man of powerful build, with long dark hair and a mustache. Some reported a vivid scar on his forehead. Just days later, gambler Ferdinand Wetzl was thrown through a second-story window in Culloma, by a fiend whose description matches the first."

Joaquin's hands started to shake, and he lay the paper flat on the table so as not to alarm the diners around him with the sudden rustling. He scanned the rest of the article quickly and saw no mention of Bohannon. Still, the two most recent murders had already been connected, and his description—right down to the scar—published in the area's most prominent newspaper.

He suddenly felt exposed, as if everyone around him was staring, wondering if he was the killer. He had been seated with his back to the front door, and now he imagined lawmen charging through it, guns in hand. That vulnerability was like icy fingers on the back of his neck. Nobody in Auburn knew him, so he had left his guns with Blanco, and only carried the knife at his waist.

If he stood up and ran from the restaurant, he would only draw yet more attention to himself. And the waiter was coming toward him with a plate. Was it a trap? Distract him with a meal, then take him by surprise?

He couldn't run. As the waiter approached, he folded the newspaper so that story was face-down on the table. He casually glanced around as he ate, and saw that the other diners were ignoring him, each involved with his own meal and companions. He wasn't sure how he felt about that. He—Joaquin Murrieta, the Mexican Murderer—sat in their very midst and yet they paid no attention. In a way, it was flattering to be written about in such vivid terms. He had wanted Chambers and Beeman to fear his coming, and now they surely would. It wasn't *he* who should tremble, but *they*, who knew their own role in making him what he'd become.

He had told Rosita that he would be famous one day. He wished she were here to see his prediction come true.

He sliced into his steak with a smile on his face.

• • •

The next morning, he was having breakfast when a man approached his table. The man wore a brown suit with white stripes, a white, collared shirt, and shiny black shoes. His gray hair was slicked down and his face pale. "May I have a word, sir?" he asked.

Joaquin had just stuffed a forkful of eggs into his mouth, so he stretched out his right leg and pushed the chair opposite his away from the table. With a gesture, he bade the man to sit. The man nodded and did so.

"You look like a right sturdy fellow," the man began, skipping any pleasantries that might have been expected. His voice was soft, and he gestured as he spoke, as if to reinforce every word with a wag of a hand or the pointing of a finger.

"My name is Colonel Hiram Moss, and I've formed a company to profit from the mining of gold."

"You and ten thousand others," Joaquin said.

"Ahh, that's where you're mistaken. We are not an assortment of ragtag miners hoping to strike it rich. We are well capitalized, and, with the benefit of organization and scale, we can make a killing on claims others have abandoned. Operations are already underway, but we find ourselves in need of ever more laborers to meet demand."

"So that's what you're asking? Will I come and work for you?"

"Indeed, sir. As I said, you seem sturdy enough. Broad of shoulder, deep of chest, and you have a working man's hands. If you were a miner, I daresay you'd already be at your claim, but instead you're enjoying a delicious meal, which I've so rudely interrupted. So, I thought you might be in search of gainful labor."

Joaquin took a sip of coffee—not as strong as what he'd been used to in Mexico, but not bad, all things considered. "You asked, and I invited you to sit. Not rude at all."

"Well, I'll try to keep it brief. I have no prejudice against your kind. Some folks believe that Mexicans are lazy, but I've found that your people work hard and expect little in return. Admirable traits, I must say."

Joaquin raised an eyebrow at that. "If I came to work for you, I could expect to earn the same wages as a white American?"

Moss's face took on a pained expression. "Well, of course not. Americans won't labor for less than four dollars a day, most of them. We're paying Mexicans a dollar a day and have employed dozens thus far. They seem more than content with it. For purposes of comparison, we also hire Indians for a quarter a day, and they're ecstatic, if sadly undisciplined."

"You're talking to the wrong Mexican," Joaquin said. "I'm otherwise engaged, currently." He stabbed his fork down onto a bit of sausage with enough force to clatter against the plate. Moss's already-pale face turned a shade lighter.

"I see," he said, scooting his chair back and rising quickly. "I'm sorry to have bothered you, sir."

"No bother at all," Joaquin replied. But it was a bother, and he was glad to see the back of the man, heading out the restaurant's door.

After finishing his meal, he set off again, riding in a different direction than the day before. This time, as it happened, his quest didn't take long at all. He didn't see Chambers, not at first. But as he rode along a trail that paralleled the North Fork, he heard a familiar voice.

"Keep it coming, you lazy bastards!" it shouted. "This bitch don't feed herself!"

Joaquin stopped his horse, dismounted, and climbed a low rise. At the top, he crouched close to the ground, so he wasn't illuminated by the morning sun.

Chambers stood beside a long tom. It hadn't taken him long to put together another team, and the long tom looked much like the one he'd abandoned at his original claim. The men had dug a ditch to divert some of the river's flow into their contraption. They shoveled mud and soil into it, and rushing water pushed the stuff through. Screens kept out bigger rocks, and riffles on the bottom trapped the gold, or that was the general idea. They might have used quicksilver to catch more, because the stuff attracted gold. At the end of the day, miners melted it off, and it left behind the gold it had amassed.

Chambers wasn't knee-deep in the river, but working on

dry ground, picking out larger stones that had collected against the screens, or small ones that had passed through. He tore apart clumps of mud with his bare hands, looking for color. As before, it appeared that he'd gathered men who would take orders from him and let him have the easiest end of the business.

Joaquin considered his options. Men were working all up and down the river, so if he attacked Chambers now, he'd have his hands full getting away. This wasn't like killing someone inside a building, from which he could slip away. He could find himself facing dozens of men armed with knives, guns, picks, and shovels, in broad daylight.

He could try shooting from here. He had high ground, on the far side of the river. Some men were working on this side, but not as many, so he'd have a better shot at escape. He thought he'd be able to hit Chambers from here with a musket.

But that had its own disadvantages. He wanted Chambers to know who had killed him, and why. He wanted to see the terror in his eyes. If he killed from a distance, he would lose that.

Alternatively, he could keep an eye on Chambers, and kill him tonight, after he'd retired to wherever he was staying. That way, he could use the knife, and do it quietly. Chambers would know full well who he was and why he'd come.

Yes, that was the best option. Let Chambers live out his last day, then finish him. He backed down from the hilltop and started hunting for a spot from which he could watch his quarry go about his business for the last time.

He found it on another hill, farther from the river but with a clear view. A live oak on the slope offered shade, and—after checking the trunk for ant activity and seeing little—Joaquin settled in with his back against it, while Blanco munched the golden grass of early autumn. He could see Chambers and his team slogging away, but if Chambers could see him, it would only be as a shadowy figure in the distance. He hoped Chambers did suspect it was Joaquin on that hill, watching. The hunch would plant a seed of fear, which would grow throughout the day.

After an hour or so, Joaquin rose, stretched, picked up a couple of fallen acorns and hurled them in Chambers's general direction, though they fell far short. He got some jerky from his saddlebags and washed it down with water, then relieved himself.

This was boring. He craved action, and once again considered simply riding up to Chambers and dispatching him on the spot, in plain sight of the other miners.

That would bring a certain satisfaction, but it wouldn't get him any closer to finding Beeman. His goal was to bring down all five of the murderers, not just four. He needed Chambers alone for that. Instead, he entertained himself with memories of Rosita as he had known her: vibrant, joyful, with the soul of an angel but enough of the devil in her to keep her endlessly unpredictable. Remembering her brought an ache of its own, but also steeled his resolve to carry out the grisly task he'd set for himself.

Finally, as the sun sank behind the western hills, Chambers and the others quit for the day. As they prepared to leave their claim, Joaquin mounted his horse and rode closer. He risked briefly losing sight of his prey, but he hadn't seen any horses around the men, so he suspected they lived in the small cluster of cabins nearby. From the hilltop, he couldn't see all of those, and he didn't want Chambers to get safely inside one without knowing which it was.

He topped a low rise overlooking a collection of structures

interspersed with tents, too small and disorganized to be called a town. Most of the men who'd been working along the river were quitting at the same time—dusk made the gold almost impossible to spot; they needed sunshine for that—and heading, weary and stoop-shouldered, for whatever primitive abode they called home. It took a few minutes, but Joaquin spotted Chambers following a curving path through the cabins and disappearing into one near the edge of the array, halfway up a little hill. The place was barely more than a shack, but Chambers was a relative newcomer here, and it might have been all that was available when he'd arrived.

Joaquin memorized the spot, then settled in his vantage point and waited some more.

Once the sun dipped behind the hills, dark came on fast. The little congregation of homes livened up then, with men gathering around cookfires, making dinner and drinking. After a while, it appeared that the drinking had become the more commonplace activity, and a breeze carried snatches of rowdy song and cackling laughter his way. He remembered laughter, recalled the pleasant sense of sitting with comrades after a day's work and letting go of the strain with a joke or a song or a drink. Would he ever know that feeling again? He had his doubts.

But although Joaquin watched closely, he never saw Chambers emerge from his cabin. Once the night quieted again, he mounted Blanco and headed into the makeshift village. No streets existed, just pathways still muddy from a recent rain, weaving among the structures. Here and there, men too drunk to make it back inside snored, curled on the ground, but otherwise the place was silent, with the aroma of dying embers tinging the air.

Joaquin tethered his mount out of sight of Chambers's

cabin and went the rest of the way on foot. It was also quiet, and dark, as if any occupants were asleep. Waking Chambers wouldn't bother Joaquin; it wasn't as if the man would be rising early to go work his claim, anyway. His next sleep would last an eternity.

Silently, his Colt Dragoon in his right hand and the ever-present Bowie knife in his sash, Joaquin approached the door. The cabin's floor was built on low pilings, as if to hold it above floodwaters during the rainy season, and three wooden steps led to the entrance. They looked flimsy, and would probably creak under Joaquin's boots. He stepped back and made a quick circuit of the building. On the west side, firewood was stacked in preparation for winter. There were windows on the front and east sides, which Joaquin ducked under as he passed, but the other walls were blank. The door appeared to be the only way in. Returning to it, he raised one booted foot and tested the first stair.

Then he was brought up short by a stink that reminded him of a rotting horse.

Beeman.

Chambers wasn't alone in there.

Joaquin hadn't seen Beeman, though he'd been watching Chambers for most of the day. Chances were, he was not part of Chambers's team at all. Which left only one likely reason for his presence—the two men had heard about the deaths of their three former companions and huddled together for safety.

Which called for a reconsideration of his plan. He'd intended to barge through the door, find Chambers in a state of half-wakefulness at best, and demand Beeman's location before killing him. But if they were both in there, threatening would be meaningless. He'd have to be ready to kill immediately—and he would be facing two men, not one.

If he had been waiting for a killer, he would make sure that one of the men was awake at all times, standing guard. Chambers was smart, so Joaquin had to account for that possibility. Of course, it was also possible that both men would be awake—even that, despite his precautions, Chambers had seen and recognized him during the day, or been told by contacts in Auburn that a man of his description had been there.

Instead of climbing the stairs, Joaquin backed away, once more ducking beneath the front window. If someone were near enough to the window, he could have seen Joaquin, of course. But Joaquin had kept his eyes on those and had seen neither shape nor motion. He went silently to the west side, lifted a good-sized split log and a smaller one from the firewood stack, and returned to the doorway. Tucking the pistol into his sash, he took the smaller log in his left hand and the larger in his right.

Then, as nearly simultaneously as he could manage, he hurled the small log through the front window. The moment it left his hand, he spun around, raised a booted foot, and kicked open the front door, throwing the larger log through as it swung wide. Both logs landed inside with a clatter that was nearly drowned out by the booms of two almost instantaneous shotgun blasts, one aimed toward the door and the other blowing out most of what glass remained in the window.

With those blasts roaring in his ears, Joaquin dove in through the open door, landing low and rolling once before springing to his feet well away from the door. In the moonlight streaming through the shattered window, he saw Chambers sitting at a wooden table, trying to insert a fresh shell from an array lined up before him. Joaquin raised the Colt and fired twice; the first shot struck Chambers in the chest, and the second one pierced his forehead, just above his left eye. The man's chair tilted backward, and he slid off.

While he was doing that, Joaquin heard rustling from behind him. He guessed Beeman had also been trying to reload, but on foot and in the dark, without even the moonlight to help. Instead of continuing, he had gripped the shotgun by the barrel and swung it like a club. Sensing what was coming, Joaquin tried to dodge. The gun's wooden stock caught him on his right upper arm, and the shock of it caused him to drop the Colt.

Certain that Beeman was preparing to swing again, Joaquin lunged for him. He could barely see the man, just a dark shape against a black background, but he felt Beeman fall back beneath his charge and slam into the wall nearest the doorway. Before Beeman could resist, Joaquin caught his throat in his left hand and closed the fingers of his right around the Bowie's grip.

"Rosita stabbed you," he said, his voice a furious rasp. "I hope it hasn't stopped hurting."

Beeman tried to speak, but Joaquin's grip on his throat was too tight to allow him any air. Joaquin didn't much care what he had to say, anyway. With his left forearm, he pressed against Beeman's chest and shoulder until he found the approximate spot where Rosita had buried the knife. The man's whimper when he landed on it told him he'd succeeded.

"There it is," he said. "That spot, right?"

Beeman nodded his head, to the extent he was able.

"That's what I thought," Joaquin said. He shifted his arm, raised the Bowie knife, and drove it into the same spot. He felt the point push through flesh, then muscle, and at one point, glance off a bone. Beeman let out a squeal and writhed under

Joaquin's grip, but Joaquin pressed him harder to the wall and drew out the knife. Blood came with it, spurting from the wound and splashing on the floor. Joaquin considered, briefly, letting Beeman live, as a warning to anyone who dared threaten him or his loved ones.

It took only seconds to shake that notion. The only people he wanted to know that he had killed Chambers and the others were already dead. There was no one left to warn.

Instead, he drew the knife across Beeman's throat, and felt himself baptized in blood.

Reborn.

22

After three straight weeks in which the sun in San Jose had appeared as only a pale, cold wafer behind the clouds, Speaker of the Assembly John Bigler was pleased to be in Los Angeles. The sun was bright, the air warm, with no hint of the rains about to descend in force on northern California. He briefly considered advocating to move the capital to Los Angeles, but two obstacles presented themselves: Los Angeles was too close to Mexico, and too far from the gold.

He'd survived far worse winters, back in Pennsylvania, but life in more temperate climes tended to thin the blood. He wasn't certain that he could make it through an Eastern winter anymore, particularly after contracting cholera in Sacramento City.

No, he was in California to stay. And he was an ambitious man who meant to be governor soon. To that end, he was visiting Los Angeles to see how that municipality dealt with the Mexican issue—and also because an increasing number of voters lived there. It wasn't growing the way San Francisco was, but it was on an upward path just the same.

His escort was the town's youthful mayor, Dr. Alpheus P. Hodges. The man was impressive: slender, still in his twenties, he was already a physician and now mayor, as well as the town coroner. He had light brown hair and an impressive set of whiskers for one so young.

They'd started the tour on Monday morning, at the Los Angeles Plaza, in the shadow of the Plaza Church. The bells were ringing when Bigler arrived, and schoolgirls were lined up outside the picket fence, waiting to go in. Bigler had reached the city early the day before, found lodging in a hotel, and stayed inside most of the day, rarely venturing out because the streets were full of rowdy, drunken Indians and other undesirables. This morning, though, all was peaceful.

Hodges arrived a few minutes later, accompanied by a pair of soldiers for protection. After introductions were made, they started across the plaza, only to be brought up short by a procession of more than twenty Indian men, led by a tall, barrel-chested white fellow with short blond hair. He carried a shotgun and had two pistols tucked into his belt. Another white man bearing a Hall carbine brought up the rear. The Indians raised a cloud of dust as they shuffled past.

"What's wrong with those men?" Bigler asked. "They look half-dead."

"They're hung over," Hodges explained. "They work for local men, ranchers and such. On Friday, they're paid in liquor. They spend the weekend drunk, then on Sunday night Schmitt arrests them and corrals them behind the Downey house. By Monday morning, they're sober but hung over. They're being led to an auction block, where their employers will bid for them by offering to pay their bail. Then they'll have to work for those men until the fine is paid off—perhaps a few weeks, perhaps longer. When the debt is finally discharged, they'll be paid for their labors—in liquor again—and the whole process repeats."

"California's a free state," Bigler reminded him. "That sounds quite like slavery to me."

"Ah, but not in the eyes of the law," Hodges said. "Those

men owe a debt that must be repaid. They can't afford their own bail—"

"Certainly not, if they're only paid in spirits."

"—and they'd rather be free than sitting in jail. The system works for everyone."

Except their families, Bigler thought. It was an outrage. But at the same time, devilishly clever, and he understood the idea behind it. Cheap labor and easily controlled workers meant more profits for the ranch owners and others who employed the men. And those were undoubtedly white men—Americans, to whom California now belonged—so increasing their wealth was good for the fledgling state's future.

But something else Hodges had mentioned stuck in his mind. "You said, 'Schmitt arrests them.' Is that the man's name?"

"Jakob Schmitt, aye. He's the fellow in front with the shot-gun," Hodges said. "He's a deputy sheriff for the county, but we let him have free rein within city limits. In fact, if you want to see how we handle the Mexican issue, you'd do a lot worse than watching Schmitt for a while."

"Could I?"

"I don't see why not. I've never known him to be shy."

• • •

After the auction, Hodges spoke with Schmitt, who agreed to let Bigler follow him on his rounds. Otherwise alone, Schmitt stormed through the Mexican sections of the town, up Olvera Street, back down Bath, then up one side of Main Street and back down the other. As he went, he demanded taxes from merchants, told a few people to be out of town before the following morning, or simply snarled until they turned away or ducked inside buildings. To others, he was courteous, even friendly, complimenting women on their dresses or their babies. Everyone seemed to know him, and many stepped aside to let him pass, seemingly out of fear that he might turn on them. At one point, he overturned the cart of a man selling tamales, spilling his wares all over the dirt road. As the man picked them up and tried in vain to dust them off, he apologized to Schmitt and offered cash, which the deputy pocketed.

When he'd finished his rounds, Schmitt invited Bigler to join him for a drink at a saloon on Main Street, which Bigler gathered the Mexicans still called Calle Principal. The place was quiet; at this time of day, only serious drinkers were already at it. Schmitt was as well-known there as he had been on the streets, as nearly everyone in the place greeted him or else tried to pretend he wasn't there. A barkeep brought Schmitt a whiskey without being asked, then took Bigler's order.

"Everyone knows you," Bigler observed.

"Not by accident," Schmitt said, draining his glass and slamming it down on the table. The barkeep heard the sharp crack and hurried over with another. "Makes things easier if they know what to expect when they see me comin'."

"I suppose that's true."

"The point is to make the Mexicans feel unwelcome here. And your criminal element, as well. I want Los Angeles to be peaceable, prosperous, and white. It's an uphill battle, since it was almost entirely Mexican just a couple years ago. And we're close enough to the border that it's easy for more of 'em to come all the time. I roust a few every day or two, collect taxes and tribute from others. When they raise a fuss, I don't mind bruisin' my knuckles, or worse. Every time one gives up and goes back to Mexico, he tells a dozen others about how he was treated in Los Angeles, and that keeps 'em from swarming over. At least, that's the idea."

"Can you tell how well it's working?"

"Well, the town's whiter'n it was last year, and last year was whiter than the one before. I think we're makin' progress, but we still have a ways to go."

"Not just here, but throughout the entire state," Bigler said. "Since the gold rush began, there are more and more white folks coming, and the population balance is shifting. But they've heard about gold in Mexico, too, and I'm afraid the whole country will empty out with people coming north to seek gold."

"You got your Foreign Miners' Tax. That oughtta help."

"It does, but not enough. And it's unpopular in the legislature. I'm afraid it'll be repealed before I'm governor, and able to prevent it."

"Well, I hope you win, then," Schmitt said.

"I certainly intend to. Of course, Mexicans aren't the only problem. We're getting more and more Chinese, for one thing, coming by sea to San Francisco. They mostly stick to themselves, of course, but will that last? And although we're a free state, so far there haven't been large numbers of Negroes. They'll likely stick close to the loving embrace of their masters, I suppose, but some of the free ones from the northern states have been showing up. I don't think we'll have to go as far as Oregon Country did, banning coloreds altogether, but it's worth keeping an eye on. And of course, Indians are a perpetual concern. What I'm driving at is, we need to keep California as white as we can. I like your approach, and of course, Mexicans will always be our main problem because of proximity."

"Naturally," Schmitt said. He'd emptied half-a-dozen glasses during their conversation, making Bigler wonder why the barman didn't just leave the bottle, rather than pouring a new glass and rushing over every time Schmitt slammed another one down. Maybe the lawman tipped well.

"Should anybody wonder," Bigler added, "it's not hatred of the lesser races driving my concern. It's simply good sense to steer the future of our great state in the proper direction."

"Of course," Schmitt said. He considered for a moment, then added, "You ought to go to Santa Barbara and meet Harry Love. He's a deputy I worked with there, before I came to Los Angeles. He taught me most of what I know about dealin' with greasers. I reckon he could teach it to lawmen in other parts of the state, too."

"I'll try to do that." Bigler rose from his chair and pushed it under the table. Schmitt stayed where he was. "I told you I mean to be the next governor. I've already sewn up the Democratic party nomination and am convinced that I'll win. When I do, I'll be calling upon you, and perhaps this Love fellow as well. You have a larger role to play in this state's future, I believe. A man with your talents can go far."

He extended a hand, and Schmitt gripped it tightly and gave it a hard shake. "I'll be headin' up north for Christmas, see my cousin," he said. "In the meantime, I reckon I'm not goin' anywhere until I get a few more drinks in me."

Bigler left him there, glad to have made the man's acquaintance. He was a heavy drinker, to be sure, and he didn't come across as the smartest of men. But he had a way of getting things done that Bigler admired. A man like that could come in very handy indeed, once he was in a position to put said individual to use.

And very soon, he would be in that position.

23

Winter brought the rain, and lots of it. In the northern part of the state, the miners gave up for the season. They hunkered down in cabins or tents, burning whatever dry wood they could gather, playing cards or drinking, writing letters home and rereading those they'd already received, folded and unfolded so many times they were fragile and prone to tearing. Some took whatever gold they'd managed to collect and went home; others followed suit but with empty pockets. Still others went to San Francisco in search of employment, having given up on the dream of easy riches.

In Sacramento City, the Sacramento and American Rivers overflowed their banks, flooding most of the town and ruining tens of thousands of dollars of merchandise that had piled up in the roads for lack of enclosed storage; the carpenters couldn't work fast enough to keep up with the goods flowing into the city, for sale to the region's blossoming populace.

Rivers in the southern reaches flowed faster than ever, creating boom times for the miners there. Joaquin briefly considered heading there himself, trying his luck again. Jesús was making out all right at Murphys Diggings, and Tres Dedos had joined him there. But Joaquin didn't think he could face that—not just the labor involved, but the ever-present reminder of what he'd once had, with Rosita by his side, would hurt too much.

Instead, he holed up in his Bear Mountain cave. There, the rains had turned to snow, and it formed deep drifts that looked like they'd last until spring. The bears mostly stayed in their caves, but sometimes he went outside and watched wolverines scamper in the snow and chase whatever prey they could find. As weather allowed, he continued the strengthening exercises he had developed, and the target practice. Most of the time, though, he emulated the bears and stayed inside. He read Rosita's books, kept a fire going, sometimes talked to Blanco and Oso as if they might answer back.

He read and reread articles about himself in the *El Dorado Republican* and other newspapers from the area. He had torn out and saved every one he'd been able to find. They described a man he barely knew, one who looked like him but was otherwise his opposite. The man in the newspapers was a murderer and a thief. Crimes he had never imagined had been laid at his feet—robberies, assaults, rapes, and more. Seemingly anything that couldn't be explained was blamed on the "Mexican Murderer" with long dark hair, a mustache, and a scarred forehead. A few papers contained sketches, none of which looked exactly like him, but some of which came close.

Reading those, and his beloved's works of philosophy and poetry, made him wonder about who he really was. Was he that man the newspapers pictured? He had killed, certainly, but did "murderer" define him? He couldn't deny some attraction to the sense of power he felt when taking the life of another. But the men he had killed had brought it upon themselves; he knew of no others who he wanted dead. He had always made an honest living, and he wanted to do so again.

The only question was, at what? And where? Could he even show his face in any nearby town? He had no intention of going back to Mexico.

Once the snow eased up, he visited with Jesús and Tres Dedos and made brief trips into various towns, picking up supplies and assessing his own safety. The newspaper stories had ceased, or at least slowed, and nobody seemed to connect him to the person described therein. Still, before he left his cave, he had to convince himself that it was safe, that he wouldn't be attacked, and that even if he were, he could defend himself. He found himself anxious, almost fearful, around white men. He had never been that way before, but now, he eyed every white American he saw with trepidation, half-expecting an attack. He had to take deep breaths and think calming thoughts before he could approach any white man for the first time, and he always scanned his surroundings for escape routes.

After spending time with Jesús and their cousin, Joaquín did some shopping in Murphys Diggings. As he packed goods into his saddlebags, he heard a familiar voice call out.

"Joaquín! Goddamn it, as I live and breathe, it's you!"

Joaquín's hand dropped to the gun at his waist before he turned. Already, he thought he knew the voice's owner, but it wouldn't do to be caught by surprise if he was wrong.

He wasn't. Bill Byrnes walked toward him, arms out in greeting, a broad smile splitting his craggy face. He looked older than Joaquín remembered, but still, he'd know Byrnes anywhere. He was a little surprised that the man had recognized him, though.

Satisfied that he wasn't being called out or exposed as a killer, Joaquín raised his hands, and met Byrnes with a hearty embrace. The other man threw his arms around Joaquín, nearly lifting him off his feet. When he released Joaquín, he was laughing, and Joaquín joined in, his fear suddenly dissipated.

"Bill, I can't believe you're here! What are you doing here?" he asked.

"I can't believe you are!" Byrnes replied. "As for me, Murphys is one of the richest camps around. Seemed like the right place to be."

"For what? Mining?"

Byrnes shook his head. "Tried that. Didn't agree with me. No, I've better ways to make money, and they don't involve breaking my damn back."

"Like what?"

"Let's you and me get a drink and talk about it, Joaquin. Shit, we got a lot to catch up on, don't we? When did you get to California? How fares Rosa?"

Joaquin tried to maintain his happy demeanor, but at the mention of Rosita, he lost control of his own face. Byrnes saw it. "Oh, no. What happened?"

"I'll tell you about it, Bill," Joaquin said. "But only over those drinks."

• • •

Inside a quiet saloon, Joaquin told Byrnes as much of the story as he dared, leaving out his mission of vengeance against those who'd killed her. He described the night they ran away, the wedding at gunpoint, the early days on the river, and Byrnes nodded along, listening eagerly. When he got to the attack, Byrnes's face clouded over.

"Those men should hang," Byrnes said. "Did you tell the authorities?"

"A Mexican's word, against that of five white men?"

Byrnes shook his head sadly. "You're probably right, goddamn it. Still, there ought to be something done."

"It's been done, Bill." Joaquin said.

"What do you mean? They were arrested? Turned

themselves in?"

"I can't say any more than that."

Byrnes studied Joaquin over his glass. His brow furrowed, his eyes narrowed. "It can't be," he finally said, lowering his voice.

"Can't be what?"

"*You're* the Mexican Murderer?"

"Shh. Bill—"

Byrnes let out a sharp laugh. "You are! Goddamn you, Joaquin, you're him!"

Joaquin laid a finger across his lips. "Bill, don't get carried away. I'm the Joaquin you've always known, that's all. I've known tragedy, but I'm still him."

"You're different, though. I can see it."

"I'm older. So are you."

"Well, thanks for pointing that out. But no, it's more than that. You're harder."

"Listen, Bill—" Joaquin began.

Byrnes cut him off. "Let's go for a ride. I'll show you something you've never seen before, never even imagined. We can talk there, away from anybody who might overhear. Sound good?"

"Sounds fine," Joaquin said. Byrnes had stirred his curiosity. Something he couldn't imagine? He thought he had a fairly vivid imagination, so that promise seemed hard to keep. But knowing Bill Byrnes as he did, he suspected his old friend had something up his sleeve.

They rode for hours, heading north, shouting out to one another now and again, but not really talking. The landscape gave way from the rocky hills around Murphys Diggings to thickly forested heights, with higher mountains almost invisible behind the trees. Despite the remnants of snow on the ground, the forest offered every shade of green Joaquin had ever seen, and then some. From a distance, the trees looked tall, but the closer they got, the more he realized how huge they really were.

Entering the forest, Byrnes slowed his pace. It was quiet there, with little underbrush and wide spaces between the tallest trees, with only smaller pines—still large, but not in comparison to the big trees—and a few bare-limbed maples and others Joaquin couldn't name, interspersed between the giants. A carpet of needles over the soft earth muffled the hooves of their mounts. The air itself was the richest of perfumes. Byrnes rode easy in the saddle, at a walk, eyeing the enormous trees with the manner of a man of faith entering a cathedral. Joaquin was stirred, and a little awed, by the majesty of the place.

After a while, Byrnes stopped. The tree behind him was by far the largest Joaquin had ever seen. Its trunk was wider across than man and horse together, wider even than some houses Joaquin had been in. The first branch didn't even break from the trunk for at least twice as high as the tallest building he had ever seen. Its height could not be measured; though he craned his neck as far as he could, the thing disappeared into the canopies of the trees around it. As far as he could tell, it never stopped, but pierced the heavens and kept on going.

"This is . . . have you ever seen anything so huge?"

"Any living thing?" Byrnes asked. "Never. Far as I can tell, this is the granddaddy of all trees. Maybe of everything that lives, for that matter. Somebody told me that, I wouldn't argue, anyhow."

"How did you find this?"

"I was tracking a deer one day last autumn. I could tell from its hoofprints that it was a big one, but I hadn't caught a glimpse of it. It led me into the trees. When I finally spotted it, I could hardly believe it. Sixteen points, at least. Beautiful coat. A spectacular animal that would've kept me in venison all winter. I nearly caught up to it and had me a good shot at it.

"But then I noticed the tree behind it. Ten of those deer could've stood there, in front of that trunk, and not blocked all of it. Once I saw that, I forgot about the stag. It took off, and I didn't worry about it. I walked all around this old thing, eyeballing it, trying to see its top. Couldn't."

"I know. It's too high. It touches the stars."

"Might could, at that."

"It's unbelievable, Bill. Had you described it to me, I'd have called you a liar."

"Wouldn't have blamed you. That's why I didn't bother telling you where we were going. You would've thought I'd gone loco."

"Probably." He turned his head, trying to take in the massive trees. "Rosita would have loved this place."

"She would've, at that," Byrnes agreed. "What do you say we get off these animals and walk a spell, have a little chitchat?"

Joaquin agreed, and the men dismounted. Byrnes rolled a smoke and lit it, then offered one to Joaquin. He'd never developed a taste for tobacco, and he declined. Here among the trees, the smell of the tobacco burning was quickly dissipated.

"First of all," Byrnes began, "I don't care who you killed. From what you said, it sounds like those men were animals who needed to die. Kinda like those Kaintuck fellas back in Trincheras. Men who'd commit an act like that aren't worth a second thought. So, don't think my opinion of you has changed one bit. Anyway, if our most wicked acts defined us, Heaven would be empty, and Hell would overflow. You were always a friend to me, and that's what you'll stay."

"That's good to hear," Joaquin said. "I was worried you wouldn't want to have anything to do with the 'Mexican Murderer.'"

"Far as I'm concerned, it's not murder, it's justice."

"That's how I looked at it, also. And I'm done with it. I'm looking to find honest employment somewhere." That was the truth. He had crossed that line, not once but five times. He meant never to cross it again. As Bill had said, his killings had been in the name of justice, which would have been denied at the hands of the white authorities. He had found the act easier as he'd done more of it, but each time turned his stomach, made him doubt his own humanity. He hoped to settle down, to be safe in the world, and to never kill again.

"You had enough of mining?"

"I have. Jesús and Manuel are still at it, but it's not the life for me. I need something different to do."

"Trust me, it's hard on a white man, too. I turned up a handful of nice-sized nuggets, some flakes, but never enough to live on for any length of time. I mean to use what I got to set myself up in my own business. But it turns out I'm a few hundred dollars shy. I could use a partner."

The words struck Joaquin with the impact of a slap. Bill Byrnes had been the best American friend he'd ever had. Was he going to ask Joaquin to partner up with him? This could be the opportunity he'd been looking for, and he had just fallen into it by chance, because he and Byrnes happened to be on the same street at the same time. But if that wasn't Byrnes's intention, he didn't want to put his friend in an uncomfortable position.

"A business doing what?" he asked.

"Well, it seems men with some money in their pockets get

awful thirsty," Byrnes said. "And if they don't spend it all on drink, they look around for something else to throw it away on. I was thinking about opening a small drinking establishment in Murphys Diggings—nothing gaudy, just a quiet, friendly place where folks could come and drink with friends, maybe."

"What kind of partner are you looking for?"

"Like I said, I'd want a game of chance to strip away the rest of the gold they're carrying. Maybe monte. It's easy, it doesn't take much space, and if you play it honest, people will keep at it until their purses are empty." He dropped the butt of his cigarette into the dirt. "You think you could run a monte game?"

"I could try," Joaquin said. He didn't know much about the game, but he'd seen it played, and it didn't look hard to learn.

"Like I said, I'm a few hundred shy. Can you make up the difference so I can get the spot I'm looking at, and some supplies and product?"

Joaquin considered his financial situation. He'd gone through all the gold he had amassed, and what little he'd been able to take from the men he'd killed. He'd had to dash from Chambers's cabin so quickly that he hadn't had time to look for valuables. "My pockets are as empty as a man who's spent all night at your establishment," he admitted.

"Could you borrow from your brother? Or you got anything you could sell? There's no one I'd rather go into business with than you, Joaquin. I know you to be a man of admirable character and considerable gumption, and you got a certain charm about you. Together, we could do well."

Joaquin ran through a mental list of his worldly possessions. Rosita's books, a few changes of clothes, some blankets and cooking utensils, a pair of horses. He snapped his fingers.

"I could sell a horse."

"If it's a good horse, it'd bring a couple hundred, maybe more. Still a little shy."

"How long until we started making money?"

"Few weeks, maybe. Could be less, but no more."

"Then if I sold two horses, I could buy one of them back, or a new one, fairly quickly? They're good ones, from Rosita's father's ranch."

"They're Feliz horses? You'd get top dollar for those. That'd be enough to put us over the top, I'm sure."

"Do you have a place in Murphys to live?"

"I do, but it's just a small room with one bed. No room for anyone else."

"I could probably stay with Jesús until I can find a room of my own."

"There you go. If it comes to it you could sleep under my bed, but if your brother's close by, that's all the better."

It was a lot to think over, all at once. Selling Oso and Blanco would strand him in Murphys Diggings. And he had grown to love and appreciate both animals, who'd saved his neck more than once. But if Byrnes was right and they'd soon make enough money to buy new mounts, or perhaps to buy back Blanco, then he would have everything he needed—honest work with a friend in a respectable profession, and a horse to leave town on if it became necessary.

"What if I don't get enough for them?" he asked.

"It'll be close, anyway. We can skimp a little on furnishings or product at first, if need be."

"And you're sure there aren't already too many saloons in Murphys?"

"There are a few places with pianos and whores and card games and such. They're noisy and smelly, and yeah, they have a steady trade. But there's no place like what I'm talking about—someplace smaller, quiet, where the owner is the barman and he knows your name and your drink soon as you walk in the door. It's a different kind of idea, and I know there's folks would be drawn to it. I would be."

Joaquin had been in a lot of saloons recently, while tracking down his victims. It was true that there was a sameness to them, and they held little appeal to him. An establishment like Byrnes described might be the kind of place he would enjoy, as well.

"I guess I'm in, then."

Byrnes extended a hand, and Joaquin shook it. "Partners," Byrnes said.

"Partners. Thank you for asking me."

"I owed you. And like I said, I couldn't think of a better partner. Let's get those horses sold and get busy."

24

Joaquin had received fair prices for both horses and put the entire proceeds into a pot with Byrnes's money. They'd acquired the premises Byrnes had in mind, a space considerably smaller than the other saloons in town, but big enough for a bar and a dozen tables, one of which Joaquin appropriated for his monte games. A scale stood at one corner of the bar, to weigh gold for those who chose to pay for their drinks with that. Log walls packed with mud and a second-hand potbelly woodstove in one corner held at bay the worst of winter's chill. The stove scented the air with aromatic pine that cut the stink from two brass humidors, tobacco, liquor, and sweat.

To his credit, Byrnes had created exactly the kind of establishment he'd described. He welcomed everyone who passed through the door, regardless of race or sex. He learned people's names, listened to their stories, and remembered them when they returned. If he thought people would get along, he introduced them to one another. The quiet drinkers could sit by themselves and not be bothered, but those who wanted to talk were able to. They quickly developed a regular clientele, which grew every week.

The sign painter hadn't inquired about the spelling of Joaquin's name, so the wooden sign hanging over the entrance said BILL AND WAKEENS PLACE DRINKS AND MONTE.

Joaquin was, at first, upset about the slight, but he got over it quickly when Byrnes pointed out that at least the whites who were unfamiliar with Spanish customs would know how to pronounce his name.

Some of those who did pronounce it used it to curse Joaquin as a cheat. He wasn't, but he quickly developed the skill to pick up and drop the cards so swiftly, using both hands to confuse the player, that it was almost impossible to follow the red queen. He learned to flip the queen with the corner of another card, so he couldn't be accused of switching it at the last instant. But some men hated to be wrong, and because Joaquin was Mexican, they often didn't bother with the name, but called him "Pancho," "greaser," or worse. Those men were invited to leave the premises and not return.

Instead of buying another horse right away, Joaquin saved his share of the proceeds until he could afford to rent a room in the town's lone hotel. Jesús's cabin was a thirty-minute walk from Murphys, and on these frigid winter nights, to make that trek was to risk freezing to death. Joaquin slept in the saloon, curled on the floor by the stove, until he was able to acquire lodging of his own.

But Jesús and Tres Dedos came into town whenever they could, and Byrnes remembered Tres Dedos from the night of his escape. When they all got together, Jesús often brought news from home, because he'd been writing letters to their parents and getting them in return ever since they'd left. Joaquin hadn't written once since Rosita's death. Guilt gnawed at him, but he couldn't tell them what he'd been up to.

Six days before Christmas, Jesús and Tres Dedos rode in on their own horses, with a mule Joaquin had never seen trailing behind. From a saddlebag, Jesús retrieved a stack of letters bound with string and carried them inside, placing them on Joaquin's monte table. It was a Wednesday, mid-morning, and the place was otherwise empty. "These are all the letters I've had from the family since I've been in California," he said. "I thought you'd like to read them for yourself. But some of them might be hard reading—you hurt them, when you left without a word. I'm not sure Esmerelda's forgiven you yet."

"I knew at the time how they'd feel," Joaquin countered. "I did write them from Los Angeles, and again from Sawmill Flat. After what happened to Rosita, though—I couldn't."

"I understand, little brother. I told them about that, too, as much as I could, and asked them to inform Don Ramon. If he ever sees you again, he'll probably kill you, then bring you back to life so he can kill you again."

"I wouldn't blame him."

"Nor would I."

"He'd have to get in line," Byrnes called from behind the bar. "Since he's been dealing monte, the number of folks who want to kill him has grown calamitously."

"It's true," Joaquin said. "Add in that I'm Mexican and the number is in the hundreds, at least."

"I could do it," Tres Dedos said. "They'd probably elect me governor of California."

"Mayor of Murphys, maybe," Byrnes said. "He's not well-known enough around the state for that many people to hate him."

"Give him time," Jesús said. "Back home he had a knack for being hated on sight."

Unable to hold it back any longer, all four men broke into laughter at the same moment. Byrnes poured drinks, and the men sat around the table, Joaquin thumbing through the letters while the others traded stories of life in California.

The letters were, as Jesús had suggested, hard to read. The pain his disappearance had caused became real in a way that it hadn't before, like an ice-cold knife to the gut. On one of the first letters since he left, some of the words had been blurred by drops of water, which he assumed had been his mother's tears.

By early afternoon, patrons began to filter in. Joaquin put the letters aside and dealt some monte games, and Byrnes got busy serving drinks. Jesús came to Joaquin's side and bent over. "I'm leaving the mule for you, little brother, because you said you wanted to visit some friends in Culloma."

"Yes, the Mendozas. They helped me out when I—when I was in some trouble. I want to take them a gift for Christmas, for their son, Paco."

"You'll go tomorrow?"

"I will, and I'll return on Christmas Day."

"I'll come back that afternoon to collect the mule, then. I just bought her. She's fine for riding, but I mainly bought her to work at the diggings. She's a good hauler, I'm told."

"Thank you," Joaquin said, rising to give his brother a hug. "You're a good brother. I'm glad we're still near enough to see each other sometimes."

"As am I," Jesús said. "Stay out of trouble, Joaquin. We'll see you soon."

Jesús and Tres Dedos walked out the door, and Joaquin returned to the game, where men stood, waiting to have their gold taken from them. This life—one of peace, friendship, and honest work—was what he wanted now. Rosita was irreplaceable, and he felt her loss every day. But if he could never be that happy again, he thought that perhaps he could, at least, learn to be content.

• • •

Joaquin had spent some of his earnings on a Christmas cracker—a paper tube filled with sweets, that would make a popping or cracking sound when pulled at both ends and the sweets fell out. He had been surprised to see it in a local store, where the shopkeeper said it had been imported from Paris, France. He'd immediately thought of Paco Mendoza, and purchased it on the spot.

The next day, he packed that and some fruits and nuts he'd acquired onto the mule Jesús had loaned him and headed out of town. He had only made it as far as Murphys Old Diggings—slightly off-course, but following the road was easier than trying to cut cross-country through these parts, thick as they were with diggings and blanketed with fresh snow—when a man he vaguely recognized called out to him.

"You, there! Ain't you Joaquin?" the man asked. He was a thin man, wiry, with a bulbous nose as red as a cardinal's wing. The cold wind had chapped his cheeks, and his left eye was stuck in a perpetual squint, as if he were forever appraising tiny objects. Under his slouch hat, he had a scarf wrapped around his head, covering his ears against the biting cold. He wore a scowl like he'd been born with it, and Joaquin knew that whatever the man's reason for hailing him was, it wasn't to extend Christmas wishes.

Joaquin reined the mule in. "I am. I know you . . ."

"You oughtta. You took enough of my money at your monte table."

The name came back to him. "You're Mr. Lang."

"Will Lang, that's correct."

"Something I can do for you, Mr. Lang? I have a long ride ahead of me, and it's mighty cold out here."

"A long ride on my mule," Lang said. "What the hell you doin' with that animal?"

"It's my brother's mule! He bought it!"

"The hell he did. That beast was stole from me, three days back."

"My brother is an honest man. He's a miner; he bought the mule to haul things for him."

"A mule instead of a burro? Hell of a tale. You got any more like it?"

"Sir, I'm telling you, my brother bought this mule—"

Lang crossed the distance from him, his gnarled hands bunched into fists. His breath was sour, as if something had crawled down his gullet and died. "Well, he might have did, but I ain't sold it!" He pointed to the animal's right ear, where Joaquin saw a notch he hadn't noticed before. "See that? She cut that on some barbed wire, reaching under it for better grass. I got a little spread off the old Murphys road, and I can show you the section of fence she cut it on. She got a scar on her muzzle there, too."

"Mr. Lang, there's some misunderstanding," Joaquin said, keeping his voice calm. "I don't know who Jesús bought it from, but he did buy it, and I'm certain he had no idea it had been stolen."

"I could peg you for a horse thief right now," Lang said.

He was right; people had started to come out of homes and businesses, curious about the altercation on the quiet main street of Murphys Old Diggings. They were almost exclusively white people, and a Mexican accused of stealing horses wouldn't stand a chance in their company. How could he get out of this mess?

"You could, but it wouldn't be true. You know who I am,

where I work. I'm partners with Bill Byrnes in that place. I wouldn't risk my livelihood and my neck by stealing a mule."

"You might not, but I wouldn't know your brother from General Santa Anna hisself."

"Look, let's meet in Murphys tomorrow at noon. I'll get Jesús there and we'll get this all straightened out. I'm sure it's some kind of mistake."

"Noon? I'll be there. And I'll bring my mule."

Joaquin no longer carried a gun with him everywhere, but he was never without his knife. He put his hand on the pommel and said flatly, "I'll bring the mule."

Lang read the look on Joaquin's face, and nodded, however reluctantly. "You be there. I know where to find you if you're not."

"That's true," Joaquin said. "I'm not hiding."

"Noon, then."

"Noon."

Lang walked away without looking back, his shoulders hunched. Joaquin had to fight back a sudden impulse to charge after him and bury the knife in his back. To accuse him or Jesús of such a thing infuriated him.

But he couldn't. Not only were there plenty of people around, but he was done with that life. He was an honest man now. Disputes had to be settled reasonably, with words instead of violence.

His trip to Culloma was over. He couldn't get there and back in a day, and he had to fetch Jesús, to let him know what had transpired over the mule. Perhaps he had a bill of sale. Or maybe Tres Dedos had witnessed the transaction. Anything to quiet Lang's complaints.

Joaquin was no innocent. He'd murdered people and

robbed them after.

Stealing livestock, though? That, he had never done.

It was one thing to live with one's crimes. It was another thing entirely to be accused of crimes he'd never even contemplated.

He swallowed his rage and turned the mule around, heading back the way he'd come. The sky was leaden, threatening snow, and he had miles to travel yet.

25

The sun was high and flat through the clouds, its light diffused, casting soft, fuzzy shadows where they landed at all. Joaquin, Tres Dedos, and Jesús stood on the road outside Bill and Wakeen's, with the mule hitched to a post in front of the door. They'd been there for about fifteen minutes when Will Lang stepped out of a saloon down the street, accompanied by half-a-dozen white men.

"I was beginning to think you weren't coming," Joaquin said. His anger at Lang's accusation had only grown overnight, and he wasn't inclined toward patience at the best of times.

"I'd be damned if I wouldn't show up to claim my own property," Lang said.

"The mule's mine, and you know it," Jesús said. "You sold it to me yourself and took my money."

"You got anything on paper to back that up?"

"You didn't give me anything."

"I doubt he can read or write," Joaquin said.

Jesús stifled a laugh, but Lang saw it on his face. "Somethin' funny about all this?" he demanded. "I don't think horse thievin' is a laughin' matter."

"The mule's not stolen," Tres Dedos insisted. "And you know it. I was there!"

"You fellers, take a look," Lang said. "Check that cut on the ear and the scar on her face. Whose mule is that?"

The other men gathered around, inspecting the animal as if it were a fine thoroughbred. "That's your mule, Will," one said. "I'd know it anywhere."

The others offered their agreement.

"I don't know any of you men," Jesús argued. "None of you were there when he sold it to me."

"And where exactly did that take place?" Lang asked.

"Why, on the road between here and Columbia, where I met you. You were on a horse and leading the mule, and I stopped you and said I was looking for one, and would you ever sell it. You asked me to name a price. I did, you raised me, and we settled in the middle."

"Boys, have I ever been to Columbia?"

"Not that I know of, Will." It was the same man who'd identified the mule, seemingly the appointed spokesman for the group. He was a big man, with close-cropped blond hair and a strangely flat face. Joaquin stared at him. He'd seen that man before.

"Well, I haven't," Lang said.

"I didn't say in Columbia," Jesús countered. "I said on the road."

"Well, what in the hell would I be doin' on the road from there, I hadn't been there in the first place?"

"I didn't even say which way you were going," Jesús pointed out. "But now that you mention it, you were coming from that direction, and I was going toward it."

"Liar," Lang said. He spat onto the muddy road. "You're a liar and a horse thief."

"I am not!" Jesús's protestation sounded desperate. Only too late did Joaquin realize that it was.

"Fellers, fetch some rope," Lang said. "This thief's got to

hang."

"Wait!" Joaquin shouted. "Surely this can be settled some other way!"

"I didn't steal the mule," Jesús insisted. "I paid for it."

"Will says you didn't," the big man said.

"I say he did," Tres Dedos shouted. He whipped out a big knife from somewhere. Joaquin felt the mood of the gathered crowd change instantly, as if the air itself had caught fire.

A couple of the men dashed back into the saloon from which they'd emerged. "I won't be treated this way," Jesús said. "I'm taking *my* mule and going home."

Lang stepped between him and the mule, drawing a pistol from behind his back at the same time. The big man came forward and grabbed Jesús by the wrists. Joaquin reached for his knife, but three other men swarmed him, one locking his arms around Joaquin's, another snatching the knife from his sash. The third also had a gun, which he waved in Joaquin's face. "You just settle down, mister. We're awful sick of you fucking greasers coming here and stealing our stock. You try anything, you'll get the same treatment as your friend."

"He's my brother," Joaquin said. "And he's a better man than all of you put together."

At the same time, five men grabbed Tres Dedos, two of them hanging onto his knife arm. He surged toward Lang anyway, dragging the men along. Before he could reach his target, two more men joined the fray. One of them slammed a thick wooden club into the back of Tres Dedos's head several times, blood flying each time it was drawn back. Tres Dedos wrenched his arm free with a roar and lashed out with the knife, slicing into the men holding him.

The club came down again and again. Eyes wild, almost frothing at the mouth, Tres Dedos went to his knees. The men around him kicked and punched, and the club struck again and again and again. Finally, Tres Dedos slumped forward and fell on his face in the dirt, blood pooling around him.

The two men who'd gone into the saloon emerged again with a length of rope already tied into a noose at one end. So this had been the plan from the start. Joaquin struggled against those holding him, but they were strong, and the one with the pistol slashed it across his cheek. Joaquin tasted blood.

Jesús struggled, too, but more white men poured out of nearby buildings. What had moments earlier been a small group was turning into a mob, as word of the imminent hanging of a Mexican horse thief spread. They pinned Jesús in place and looped the noose around his neck, then started dragging him toward a sturdy live oak at the end of the road.

Joaquin screamed at them to stop, but any time he did, someone punched him in the kidneys or kicked at his knees and shins. The man with the gun pistol-whipped him again for good measure.

Then the door to Bill and Wakeen's opened, and Byrnes came out, accompanied by two other men. One of them, a regular customer named Ray McPhee, owned the town's butcher shop and served as a constable on the side. The other, Sam Green, was a rival saloonkeeper, but a longtime friend of Byrnes's. "What's going on, boys?" McPhee wanted to know.

"Never you mind, Ben," Lang said. "We're just fixin' to stretch some hemp. These greasers is horse thieves."

"Joaquin's my partner!" Byrnes protested. "You all know him! He's as honest as the day is long."

"He's in league with these others. They stole my mule and tried to deny it."

"He did nothing of the sort." Byrnes caught Joaquin's eye.

"I thought you were in Colluma."

Joaquin tried to answer, but one of the men had such a tight grip on his throat that he couldn't get a word out. The man's hot breath in his face stank of whisky and chew.

"Turn him loose!" Byrnes demanded.

"Look, I'll lock this pair up in the jail," McPhee offered. "When Sheriff Hannon gets back, he'll straighten this all out. If these men are thieves, they're entitled to a trial."

"They been tried and convicted," Lang said. "By us. They're goddamned lousy Mexicans. Why involve the law? You men will stay out of our way, you value your own hides."

"We'll do nothing of the kind," Byrnes said. He started back toward the bar—where Joaquin knew he kept a shotgun, in case of trouble—but before he'd made it two steps, one of the men from the mob drew a pistol and fired it. The top of Byrnes's head blew off in a pink mist, and he dropped to the road. The man with the gun pointed it at the other two. He was a short fellow, with had a narrow face and a dark mustache that drooped to his chin.

"Either of you feelin' brave?" he asked. "White man takes a greaser's side, he gets what he deserves."

McPhee went to his knees beside Byrnes, but offered no complaint. Sam Green just stood there, arms at his sides, inarticulate fury twisting his face.

Tears sprang to Joaquin's eyes as rage and sorrow flooded through him in roughly equal measures. But as if the scent of blood had driven the mob over the edge, a roar went up, and he and Jesús were dragged down the road. When he was able to glance back, he saw Byrnes in the road, still as death, and men holding guns on McPhee and Green to keep them from interfering. Not far away lay Tres Dedos, also unmoving. Others on the street watched without taking sides, which meant they were complicit in condemning him and his brother to early graves.

Curses popped around him like firecrackers, and the stink of sweat permeated the air. Joaquin was put in mind of a sexual experience, for reasons that he couldn't quite grasp until he saw on the faces of some of the men the same kind of ecstatic abandonment that men often wear at such moments. The realization lent him new strength, and he jerked one arm free, then planted a booted foot and turned on his nearest captor, throwing a fist that split open the flesh below the man's eye. He clawed at another man before two others grabbed the free arm and wrenched it behind his back, shoving his face into the muddy road. They dragged him along then, facedown, kicking him as they went.

At the oak tree, he was hauled to his feet and he caught a glimpse of his brother. The noose had been tightened around his throat, and his hands bound behind his back. His face was bloodied, his eyes wild with terror.

The big man who had been with Lang from the start took the loose end of the rope and hurled it skyward. As he did, Joaquin finally remembered who it was—that deputy from Los Angeles, who had made he and Rosita pay the Foreign Miner's Tax. What was his name? He couldn't bring it up. Later, perhaps, but not in the midst of this.

The rope hit a thick branch, some twenty feet up—roughly parallel to the ground for much of its length; scars on the bark suggested that it had been used for the same purpose before—but fell back down. The man tossed it again, giving it more of an arc this time, and the rope draped over the branch, dropping down on the other side.

An ugly cheer went up from the mob. A dozen of them wrestled for position on the loose end, and the victors set to tugging on it. Jesús gave a choked cry as he was yanked off his feet, and he started kicking every which way. The effort caused his body to sway, but it did nothing to slow his upward progress.

Joaquin tried again to break free of his captors, to rush to his brother's side and try to lower him back to earth. It earned him only more beatings. When they dragged him to his feet again, he could hardly stand on his own, but the grips of the men holding him kept up upright. Then Jesús rose above the crowd, still kicking, one boot having fallen off sometime during the ascent. The men stopped pulling him and tied the rope to the tree's trunk. Jesús dangled there, unable to reach the noose around his neck, unable to do anything but kick and writhe from side to side. His face turned from the color of a ripe tomato to that of an eggplant, his eyes bulged, his mouth worked but nothing came out except guttural sounds. Finally, it stayed open, his tongue lolling out, and the kicking stopped. Jesús swayed gently, then came to rest, only turning slightly when a cold breeze blew out of the east.

"Now this one," Lang said, pointing at Joaquin. But with the death of Jesús, the vigor seemed to have drained from the mob. Sensing that there was no spirit left for another hanging, Lang settled for second best. Some of the men who'd participated in the hanging—and the men and women who'd gathered just for the spectacle—drifted away, but enough remained. While the big shovel-faced man cut off a length of the hanging rope, others stripped off Joaquin's shirt. They pressed him up against the oak's trunk, away from his brother, with his bare chest against the rough bark, and tied his wrists together on the other side. Somebody procured a whip for Lang, who began lashing Joaquin's back.

The first few blows knocked the wind out of him. Just as he

regained it, the next landed, and the next. Lang wasn't a big man, but he had the wiry strength of someone who's spent a lifetime working the land. After the first six or seven, his back on fire, blood rolling down his back and into his trousers, Joaquin hardly noticed the remaining blows. Watching Jesús die had dulled his mind. He knew he should be relieved that he'd avoided his brother's fate, but the only emotions he could identify—hatred and rage—supplanted all else.

• • •

Sometime later, a Mexican man—older, late fifties, Joaquin guessed, with white streaking his beard and crevices marking his face—scooped water from a pail in a dented tin cup and offered it to him. Someone had cut him loose from the tree, though he didn't remember it. He had been lying beside it for what must have been an hour or more. He hadn't lost consciousness, but his mind had left his body and traveled across the state, into Mexico, and finally into the depths of the Sierra Madre, that wild and rugged land of secrets and madness, sinners and saints.

He remembered—*relived* might have been more accurate—a trip into those mountains with his father, years before, when his mother was pregnant with Esmerelda and so desperately ill the man feared losing both wife and unborn child. He took Joaquin and went looking for a bruja he'd heard about. When they found her home, the look of it frightened Joaquin so much he tugged at his father's sleeve, trying to turn him around. But he refused, more afraid of his wife's sickness than of a strange house, where rotting goat heads hung from the vigas and the chickens in the yard made a wide circle around the headless corpses of three large roosters.

Inside, they interrupted the ancient crone in some profane act; she had two rooster heads in an iron pan on a stove, so hot that ribbons of smoke wafted from it, and was in the process of prying out the eye of the third with the point of a small knife. She didn't acknowledge the visitors until she had freed the orb and flicked it into the pan, where it sizzled and emitted a green puff of smoke.

It turned out that the rooster heads were for them, part of the process of concocting a potion to heal Joaquin's mother, because the bruja had somehow known they were coming, and why. And although the idea of seeing his mother drink it so terrified Joaquin that he waited outside the house upon their return, she did so and soon the illness left, and Esmerelda was born healthy three weeks later.

When the man bent over beside him and sloshed the cup in the pail, Joaquin blinked and returned to the present, becoming aware again of the agony that started at his back but swelled to engulf every part of his being. He tried to sit up, couldn't. The man dropped the cup back into the pail and took his arm, helping him sit. Every motion sent another lance of pain through him, but be couldn't lie on his stomach forever. When he was stable, the man dipped the cup once more, and this time Joaquin opened his mouth and let the stranger pour some on his tongue.

"Do I know you?" Joaquin asked. His voice was hoarse, and sounded to him like someone speaking from far away.

"No," the man said. "I have seen you before, in town. My name is Bernardo. I saw what they did to you."

At that, Joaquin looked up. Craning his head stretched a muscle in his back, and he flinched at the motion. Jesús still dangled there, twisting slightly on the rope. He had soiled his pants in death, discoloring them. His fallen boot still lay on the earth beneath the tree.

"And to him," Bernardo added.

"My brother, Jesús," Joaquin said. "Help me get him down."

"My friend, you're in no condition to—"

Joaquin lurched to his feet. Unsteady, he threw out an arm for balance and caught himself on the tree trunk. "Help me, or I'll do it myself!"

"Calm down," Bernardo said. "I will help you. But let me do the hard work. You're hurt badly."

"You're an old man. I can do it!" Joaquin grasped at his sash, looking for his knife, but it was gone. Taken by the mob, no doubt, though he had no specific memory of losing it.

"We can do it together," the man said. He dug a knife from a pocket and handed it to Joaquin. "Cut the rope, and I'll hold it."

Joaquin accepted the knife, much smaller and duller than his lost Bowie. Bernardo took hold of the rope, straining to hold Jesús's weight, while Joaquin sawed at its thick, fibrous length. Finally, it snapped. Bernardo grunted at the sudden increase in weight, and Joaquin spun around, dropping the knife and catching the rope. His back felt like someone had thrown oil on it and set it on fire, but they stopped Jesús's fall. Together, they lowered him to the ground.

"I need to bury him," Joaquin said.

"You need a doctor. You're injured."

"I'll be fine," Joaquin snapped. "Will you help me?"

"Bury him where?" Bernardo asked. "The church here won't take a hanged man."

"Not here, where the white devils can spit on his grave. I'll take him out into the wilderness, find a good spot."

"It's winter," Bernardo reminded him. "The ground is as hard as stone."

"What do you suggest? Leave him until spring? He needs

to be buried."

"I can help," Bernardo said.

"Do you have shovels? And horses?"

"I have little, my friend, but I can get them."

"Do it. I'll reward you."

"With what?" Bernardo asked. "No reward is needed. We are all strangers here, in a place where we're unwelcome. If we don't help each other, who will?"

With what? The question drove home Joaquin's situation. He had a little money, but not much. He had his interest in Bill and Wakeen's, but Byrnes was dead. Tres Dedos too, most likely. He peered down the street but saw no sign of Byrnes's corpse, or his cousin's. By now, Lang and his friends had probably stripped everything of value from the bar and burned it to the ground. He couldn't even risk seeing those men again. He would have to kill anyone he saw who had been part of the mob, but in his weakened state, he would most likely be killed, instead.

No, he had to recover and come back when he was stronger.

Then he would kill them all.

26

Bernardo borrowed two horses and a shovel, and together they rode into the hills. Joaquin found a spot on a south-facing slope—so Jesús could look toward Mexico—and the two men took turns digging into the frozen earth until they had a hole deep enough to accommodate the body. As the sunset washed the sky and the valley below with salmon, rose, and gold, Bernardo said a few words over the grave. Joaquin hadn't spoken for hours. He was an empty vessel, stripped of everything but skin and bones and pain.

"Will you be all right, my friend?"

"Let me have one of the horses."

"I cannot. The horses are borrowed, otherwise I would. But they are not mine to give."

"I'll repay you and the owner tenfold."

Bernardo shook his head. "Forgive me, but you do not look like a man with that kind of wealth."

"I will have it," Joaquin promised. "My name is Joaquin Murrieta. This will not be the last you hear of me. I owe you, and I always repay my debts. The friendly kind as well as the other."

Bernardo considered briefly, and finally agreed. He told Joaquin that his full name was Bernardo Alvarado, and where his small farm was outside Murphys Diggings, then he headed for home with the horse and shovel. The lesser of the two animals, he left with Joaquin.

• • •

Once again, Joaquin retreated to Bear Mountain. The snow was too deep at the highest reaches, so he circled at a lower elevation until he found another vacant cave, smaller but still big enough for him and the borrowed horse. There, he paced and tried to think. He ate when he was hungry, slept when he was tired, and waited for tears that didn't come. He could feel no grief or sorrow; he knew no emotion besides white-hot anger. He thought it would subside with time, but it didn't. He was finished with American society, with trying to fit in. He'd given it his best shot, and he'd failed.

He was, he thought, out of options. He had tried to live an honest life, but even that was denied him. He had put on different personalities like so many changes of clothing, and none of them had fit. His last recourse, he finally decided, was to become an outlaw. The only task at which he'd ever been successful had been murder, and now he had more reason than ever to kill.

The idea no longer shocked him. Before, he'd been driven by the need to avenge Rosita's assault and murder and had not even considered whether it was right or wrong, according to any moral code. Now, he knew the answer to that. Further, he knew that he didn't care. Those were ideals he'd cast aside—or that had moved on without him.

Down in the mining camps and the towns, people were celebrating Christmas. Holidays no longer mattered to Joaquin; the passing of days and weeks bore notice only for the opportunities they offered. He stayed at the cave, hunted to survive, melted snow for drinking water, and healed. He could feel the scars crisscrossing his back and knew they would be lifetime reminders of the day his only remaining brother, his cousin, and his friend were slaughtered before his eyes.

For that, and for so much else, people had to pay.

• • •

He started with Will Lang.

Lang had been the instigator. He'd taken good money for the mule, then had accused Jesús of stealing it. To buttress his argument, he'd brought so-called witnesses who had turned a disagreement into a bloodthirsty mob. If it hadn't been for his lies, Joaquin would still be partners with Bill Byrnes, and he, Tres Dedos, and Jesús would still be alive.

The faces of every man in the mob haunted his dreams and his waking hours. He didn't know all their names, but was convinced he would recognize them on sight. Lang, though, he knew how to find.

He still had the horse he'd taken from Bernardo Alvarado. He rode down from the mountain and bypassed Murphys Diggings, instead going to the Old Diggings. The snow had melted, and signs of spring were everywhere: trees beginning to bud, grass greening up, the first of the year's wildflowers showing their colors. Close to town, small farms and ranches and a few mining claims lined the road, and Joaquin watched out for Lang's "little spread." Men who'd spent the winter inside were out in the fields, preparing them for spring planting, so it was easy enough to rule out different properties.

It took days to spot Lang, but finally he did, on a Sunday morning, riding a buggy home from church dressed in what must have been his finest suit. It was brown, mostly, with yellow stripes and patches of almost-brown in the worn-through spots. His expression was sour, a grimace, as if the sun and the emerging greenery of spring had spoiled what would otherwise have been a perfectly pleasant day of hatred, prejudice, and greed. Joaquin noted that the mule pulling the buggy had a notch in its right ear.

If he'd been nearer, he could've taken Lang on the spot. The road was empty for the moment, and any neighboring land-owners were either still at church or inside their homes. But he saw the buggy from a vantage point on a slope, and if he charged down on horseback, the man would surely see him coming.

Instead, he watched, staying just close enough to see where Lang went. His little spread turned out to be only the former. Little, but not a spread, simply a wooden house with a small yard surrounded by barbed-wire fence. Behind the house, it looked as if Lang had been digging for gold. Maybe he'd even found some, but not enough to afford a larger plot of land. Behind the house were two shaded stalls, open to the ele-ments. A horse stood in one, and Lang put the mule in the other when he unhitched her from the buggy. Then he turned away from the animals, opened his pants, and urinated in the dirt beside their stalls.

Just one more reason to kill him.

Joaquin gave him a few minutes to get inside, get settled.

He had no weapons; he'd left his musket and pistol in the hotel room the day he'd been whipped, and he had never gone back. The knife he had bought in Los Angeles had been stolen. But he wouldn't need weapons for Lang.

When Joaquin kicked in the front door, Lang was sitting at a simple wooden table with a steel flask in front of him, the lid unscrewed and set beside the bottle. The man looked up at him, the lifting of that eyebrow over that eternally squinting eye the only indication of surprise.

"Wondered when you'd show up," he said.

"I hope it's been disturbing your rest."

"Not really," Lang tapped the neck of the flask. "This helps."

"You might as well take another swig, then. It'll be your last."

Lang tilted his head toward a rifle hanging from two pegs hammered into the wall. "I have a gun."

"Why not go for it?" Joaquin asked.

"Figgered there's not much use in it."

"Do you want to die?"

"It ain't a matter of wantin' it or not. It's a matter of practicality. I'm half-drunk, and not particularly spry at the best of times. I done plenty of bad in my time, and not so much good as I might have. I got no people to worry about, and no fortune, neither. You tell me, is livin' so much better than dyin'?"

"You're a sad man," Joaquin noted.

"And you're not?"

Joaquin pressed his lips together until they turned white, but he didn't answer. Instead, he snatched the rifle off the wall. "Ammunition?"

"Box on the little table by the door."

Joaquin turned, saw it in the shadows. "I hope you live a long time," he said. "And I hope every day is more miserable than the one before it." Taking the gun and the bullets, he went out the door, leaving it open behind him. To be Will Lang, alive, was worse punishment than dying. He walked to the back of the house and took the horse and the mule, then climbed back onto his horse and headed for Columbia to sell Lang's animals. His brother had been hanged for a crime that hadn't been committed . . . but it was never too late.

● ● ●

With the proceeds from the sale of Lang's livestock, Joaquin was able to purchase a brand-new Colt Dragoon to replace the one he'd lost, and a new Bowie knife with a nine-inch blade. He also bought some clothes and boots, all in black, including an American hat with a wide brim. He added a leather rig for the gun and ammunition, and a sheath for the knife. He'd been used to Mexican-style clothes, but he was in America now, and he found that American-style clothing was more practical. As a concession to his heritage, he had a seamstress sew ornate silver conchos along the outer seam of each pants leg, and he kept his red sash around his waist, covering some of the gun belt but not hampering quick access to the holster.

He was beginning to look the part, but still more was needed. At the same time, a plan was beginning to form itself in his mind, and he would need help to carry it out. He rode from there to Hangtown, to see the barber he had met before, the cousin of Arturo Bojorques.

The shop was as empty as it had been on his previous visit. The barber was sitting in his own chair again, carving away at a chunk of pine.

He looked up when Joaquin entered. "It's you."

"You remember me?"

"You are hard to forget."

"You did me a favor before. I appreciate it."

"If we don't help our own, who will help us?"

"Words to live by."

"You need another haircut," the barber said. He rose from his chair and put the wood and the knife down on a counter, beside scissors, combs, brushes, and an assortment of glass bottles.

"And a shave," Joaquin said. "It's been a while."

"Your clothes are new, but your head looks like you've been living in a cave."

"You're very observant. The clothes are indeed new, and I have been living in a cave."

"I did not mean that literally."

"I do. And I do need another haircut, but I also need information. You seem to know a lot about our fellow Mexicans in this area."

The barber shrugged and motioned Joaquin into the chair. "I know some." He picked up a comb and ran it through Joaquin's hair, where it caught on tangles and bits of cave debris that had become snarled in it. He didn't let it stop him, but yanked the comb through. Joaquin had endured far worse pain, so he sat and tried not to jerk his head away.

"What kind of information?" the barber asked.

"I need to find some men who aren't afraid of a little danger. Men who can help me make some money."

"Digging?"

Joaquin laughed. "I'm not trying to take gold from the ground anymore. I'll let others do that, then take it from them."

The barber switched to scissors and began cutting big chunks of hair. "I might know somebody like that."

"You might?"

"Have you heard of Salomón Pico?"

"Of course." Everyone had heard of Pico. His cousin, Pio Pico, had been governor of Alta California before the war. After the war, Salomón had started raiding in newly American California, amassing a good-sized gang. His activities had mostly been confined to the southern and central parts of the state, not the gold regions, which Joaquin had thought a short-sighted approach. Presumably he had wanted to stay near enough to Mexico to race across the border if necessary.

"I know a man who knows some men who used to ride with him. They've become . . . let's say, disheartened. What I hear is that they think he takes unnecessary chances, and he's becoming too unpredictable. He will either be arrested or killed soon, or else he'll give up and go back to Mexico, they say."

"So they're looking for another situation?"

"I'm only saying what I have heard."

"Can you put me in touch with them?"

"Perhaps," the barber said. He made a few more cuts, then ran his fingers through Joaquin's hair, inspecting his work. "Are you . . . somebody who has something to offer?"

"I could be."

"Tell me your name again."

"I am Joaquin Murrieta."

"I have never heard of you."

"Have you, perhaps, heard of the Mexican Murderer?"

"Him, I've heard of."

"Do you remember when your cousin Arturo hid me?"

"I do."

"Do you remember why people were looking for me?"

The barber put down his scissors and spun a brush in a cup, working up a lather. "Now that you mention it, yes."

"That man's name was Sam Mackintosh. He had done me a grievous wrong, and he paid a price for it. So did four of his friends. Their names were Chambers, Beeman, Wetzl, and Bohannon."

"I believe I have read those names in the newspaper."

"You probably have."

"That was you?"

"It was. Those were personal, though. From now on, it's not personal."

"What is it, then?"

Joaquin considered his answer for a moment, while the barber scraped a razor over his cheeks. "It's my mission in life," he said at last.

"That is quite an ambitious mission."

"It is indeed."

The barber stopped shaving and walked to the door, looking outside casually, then returned to Joaquin's side. "Here is the man you should see . . ." he began.

27

Joaquin had to ride down to the Sonoranian Camp, southeast of Columbia, to meet with a man he knew only as Garcia. He had been curious about the place ever since he'd heard of it. It had been founded by men from his own state of Sonora, Mexico, skilled miners who had employed their skills instead of following those who'd gone before and relying on dumb luck. They had known how to look for gold and how to take it from the earth, and they'd been so successful, it was said, that their riches had inspired the Foreign Miners' Tax. He wondered if he knew anybody there, or at least their families.

The settlement was nestled in a pleasant valley, surrounded by low hills carpeted with the bright green grass of early spring. Like most other mining camps he had seen—except the richest and most developed—it was comprised primarily of small wood homes, a few of logs and mud, and numerous tents. There were even a few structures of brush on the northern edge, such as might have been made by the native population that had no doubt roamed this land before the coming of the Spanish or Americans.

He wasn't supposed to meet Garcia directly, but to go to a particular house and announce himself. From there, he'd been told, he would be taken to where Garcia was. It seemed like a lot of effort to meet an outlaw, but then, if an outlaw was too easy to find, he likely wouldn't be loose for long.

He found the house easily enough. It was one of the larger ones, and along the front façade six chili ristras dangled from the beams. Joaquin rode up to it, dismounted and tied off his horse. Then he checked the way his Colt hung at his side, and the accessibility of the Bowie knife's grip. Satisfied, he approached the door. It opened before he reached it, and a burly man with a long mustache and a mass of dark curls on his head stood before him. His expression was less welcoming than upset by some imposition.

"I'm supposed to meet Garcia," Joaquin said.

"Your name?" The man's voice was ragged, as if his throat had been slashed at some point and never quite healed. He had a scar through his left eyebrow and another one on his chin, but no visible ones on his neck.

"Murrieta."

"The whole name."

"I don't know Garcia's whole name," Joaquin protested.

The man started to close the door. Joaquin jammed his boot against it. "All right. I know I'm the one who asked for this meeting."

The man didn't say anything, just stood there in the half-open doorway, glaring at him. "Joaquin Murrieta," he said. "From Trincheras."

At that, the man grinned. His angry face was less frightening. "I'm from Caborca," he said.

"I was married there."

"At Nuestra Señora?"

"Yes. Without parental permission or witnesses. The priest didn't want to do it, but my bride persuaded him. With some help from me."

The man's eyes shifted toward the sky, as if he was trying to remember some detail. "Help? With a musket?"

"Yes!" Joaquin said. "That was us!"

"People still talk about that. The padre retired not long after that. He said the priesthood was becoming too dangerous."

"I wouldn't have really killed him," Joaquin said, then reconsidered. "At least, I don't think I would have. I don't really know for sure."

"Well, it's good to meet the man behind the legend," the other man said. "I'm Alfredo Punte." He was still smiling, and now he offered a hand, which Joaquin clasped.

"Good to meet you, too. When can I see Garcia?"

"Sorry, right away," Punte said.

He led Joaquin away from the house and made at least a dozen turns, navigating a veritable maze, before they arrived at a small stone structure that smelled of meat cooked over open flames. "In there," Punte said.

"Are you coming?"

"Me? No, no. My part is done."

"You've been taken care of?"

"Garcia will take care of me later," he said, arching one of his bushy eyebrows. "One way or another. How he does it is up to you."

With that, Punte turned and walked away like a man who had somewhere else to be, and wanted to be there in a hurry.

Joaquin put a hand on the Colt's grip and loosened it in the holster, then walked in. The inside was dark, with the only light coming from an open fireplace at the rear. He blinked a couple of times and saw a shadowy form sitting at the darkest table. "Garcia?" he asked.

"Who asks?" The voice was only a low growl, but hinted at the potential to roar like a lion.

"Joaquin Murrieta."

"Oh? Come. Sit."

Joaquin walked through the place, scanning for anyone else hiding in the shadows, but the man was alone. He released his weapon, pulled out a chair, and took a seat opposite the man he assumed was Garcia.

The man struck a match and lit a thin cigar, sucking on it several times to get the tip glowing, and blew out a long stream of foul-smelling smoke. In the light from the match, Joaquin saw the familiar features of his cousin. On the table in front of him stood a bottle of mescal, half-empty, and a glass.

Tres Dedos appraised him for a few moments, as if making sure he was really who he said he was. Then he threw back his head and laughed, rising from the chair, tipping over the mescal as he did. He rushed around the table and threw his arms around Joaquin, lifting him off the floor. "I thought you were dead!"

"I thought you were!" Joaquin shouted back.

"I'm not!"

"I can see that! Neither am I!"

Tres Dedos put him back on the floor and doubled over, laughing. Joaquin barely managed to get back on the chair without falling over. Finally, with tears in his eyes from laughter, he said, "What's with this 'Garcia' business?"

Tres Dedos wiped his eyes and picked up his cigar from the edge of the table. "I thought I'd try being careful, for a while, keep my real name secret. Americans have started calling me "Three-Fingered Jack."

"But you have four fingers on that hand!"

Tres Dedos wagged his thumb. "This one? Some people say a thumb isn't a finger. I think it's basically the same, but what do I know? Anyway, Three-Fingered Jack sounds more frightening than Manuel Duarte, so I don't argue with it. But I thought there might be some use in disguising my real name, anyway. For one thing, why risk disgracing the family? And for another, why make it any easier to find me?"

"So you really are an outlaw now?"

Tres Dedos shrugged. "Seemed time to give it a try. I've been riding with Salomón Pico for a few weeks, since I recovered."

"Then why are you here? I had the impression you were looking for new partners."

"It didn't take long to learn that Pico has lost his mind," Tres Dedos said. "He thinks he's immortal. He's taking crazy chances. Anyone who rides with him is likely to be killed outright, or captured and hanged."

"So you want to keep making money, but you want to follow someone who has a plan. A strategic genius, who knows the region, knows where the money is, and how to get it."

Tres Dedos chuckled. "If you find such a man, let me know who he is."

"I *am* such a man," Joaquin said.

"You're the smartest man I know, Joaquin. And I know better than to underestimate you—after all, the way you killed those men who assaulted Rosita shows your courage and your willingness to do what must be done. But I never thought of you as the outlaw type."

"Nor I you, cousin. But here we are. I've tried my hand at making money in California the honest way, and it hasn't worked. I've become known as the Mexican Murderer. I've killed every man I've set out to, so far, without getting caught, so I believe that my strategic skills have been tested and have proven themselves. Now, as it happens, there are more men who need killing—those who murdered Jesús and my friend Byrnes. That is your duty, as well, so we have that task in common. Once that's done, I see no reason why we shouldn't try to make a living—as you've already been doing, apparently—with our guns and our brains, instead of our shoulders and backs. The two of us would make a fantastic team."

Tres Dedos studied him. Joaquin knew that appraising eye. He was asking his cousin to view him in a new light—as he was now viewing his cousin. Neither had thought of the other as an outlaw until this encounter, and it was no easy shift to make.

Not easy, but seemingly necessary.

"There's more to it than that, isn't there?" Tres Dedos asked.

"You've always been sharper than people give you credit for. Except me, I mean, and Jesús. Yes, there is more, for me. As I said, I have several more men I need to kill. But first, I need to raise some money. And I want revenge on every white man who has ever turned up his nose at a Mexican."

"Now you sound like Pico."

"I haven't questioned Pico's goals. I share them. But my execution would be different. I would strike like lightning. Without warning, never in the same place twice, and with devastating results."

"Sounds good," Tres Dedos admitted. "But can you lead men? Ones who have already shown themselves resistant to rules and rulers?"

"I believe that I can. If I'm wrong, then I would expect those men to kill me and choose a leader of their own."

"As long as you know what to expect."

"I would lean on you for support, cousin, since you've had a taste of the outlaw life. What do you think, Four-Fingered Manuel? Will you ride with me?"

Tres Dedos chuckled. "Did you think for a moment that I wouldn't? I'm just so glad to see that you're alive. I went looking for you, you know. To Bear Mountain."

"That's where I was!"

"I went to the cave."

"I couldn't reach it when I first arrived, through the snow. I found another one, lower down, but on the far side of the mountain."

"I'm sorry I didn't think to look there."

"As am I," Joaquin said. "But we're together now. And there could be no better partner."

"Do you have a plan?"

"I've been thinking of one, while I stayed in the cave. Those two sawmills at Sawmill Flat? Together they employ well over a hundred men. Their payrolls arrive together, once a month. We know when they arrive, and the route that they take. The route is well-guarded, but a team of able men could take it."

"Rich pickings, eh?"

"Rich indeed."

Tres Dedos smiled and nodded, obviously thinking over the plan and grasping its ramifications immediately. "But the workers are Mexicans, mostly, and Peruvians. Some Americans, too. Won't we just be hurting our own?"

"The companies know they have to pay their employees, so they'll replace the payroll. The workers will still get paid; we'll only be stealing from the American owners."

Tres Dedos opened his mouth in a toothy grin. "I like that."

"It won't be easy," Joaquin warned. "We'll have to kill some people."

Tres Dedos laughed outright, a surprisingly loud, high-pitched sound. "Killing? Count me in."

• • •

The next day, Tres Dedos took Joaquin to meet the men who'd deserted from Salomón Pico with him. When he mounted an enormous black stallion, the horse seemed to groan under his weight. Joaquin climbed onto the horse he'd taken from Bernardo, back in Murphys, and for which he still owed ten times its value. They rode away from the Sonoranian Camp, west toward the towering Sierra Nevada mountains.

After about twenty minutes in the saddle, they left the beaten trail and ventured through a thickly forested area, and eventually toward a meadow abutting a towering cliff face.

Tres Dedos rode up beside Joaquin. "Are you ready to meet the boys? You're in for a surprise."

"Are we there?"

"Very nearly. We've been watched for the last ten minutes."

The statement took Joaquin by surprise. He had thought that the dense foliage would have made observation impossible. But as he scanned their surroundings, he noticed that through the overhead canopy, he could see the upper heights of the cliff. If he could see those, he could be seen from there.

"Do they know it's you?" he asked. He trusted Tres Dedos thoroughly, but his previous experiences in California suggested that the state was a dangerous place indeed.

Tres Dedos laughed. "They do. And if I was bringing you here under duress, they'd know that, too."

"You signaled them?"

He held up a half-smoked cigar. "That last cigar I lit, just before we entered the trees? If I'd been a prisoner, leading you here at gunpoint, I'd have thrown it on the ground immediately after lighting it. Because I kept it going, they know I'm bringing a friend."

That was reassuring. He'd known Tres Dedos his whole life, and trusted him intimately. But he couldn't know how cautious his cousin would be now, as an outlaw. Calling himself Garcia and letting Punte act as an intermediary seemed wise, but this business with the cigar was both careful and clever. If they were going to be outlaws together, it was good to know the man took no unnecessary chances.

And what was the surprise he'd mentioned? Joaquin racked his brain, but he couldn't guess.

As they drew nearer, he saw tents pitched in the meadow, with a cookfire in their midst. Flames licked at the carcass of a wild hog, and four men sat around the fire, drinking, smoking, and tending to the meat. At the approach of Tres Dedos and Joaquin, they rose, greeting the newcomers with friendly smiles.

"My friends," Tres Dedos began, "this is Joaquin Murrieta. You might have heard of him described as the Mexican Murderer, last autumn. He has a proposition for us, and I feel it's worth listening to."

"Come," one of the men said. "Sit, have a drink and something to eat."

Joaquin studied the faces. Most were young, all Mexican. Then he spotted one that looked familiar—almost a mirror image of his beloved Rosita, and nearly fell off his horse. "Reyes! Is that really you?"

"Joaquin?" the young man said. "When Manuel said the name, I thought it a coincidence! But now I can see that you're him!"

Joaquin dropped from the saddle and swept Reyes Feliz up in a warm embrace. This was the surprise, then, and what a surprise it was! "How did you—" he began.

"I heard what happened to Rosa," Reyes said, gripping Joaquin's arms so tightly it hurt. "I came north seeking revenge, but ran into Manuel and Pico, and joined them until I could make my way farther north. Then he told me that you'd already finished what I hoped to do."

"I had to."

"Then justice is done. Thank you, my brother." He released Joaquin finally, and wiped a lock of hair from his forehead. Gesturing toward a man Joaquin didn't know, he added, "Look who else is here! My cousin Claudio!"

A double surprise, then! The man he indicated stepped forward. "We've never met," Joaquin said. "But Rosita told me stories. It's an honor. You look like Reyes and Rosita."

Claudio clasped his hand. "People often mistake Reyes and me for brothers. His mother was my father's sister."

"Then I'll consider you family as well," Joaquin said. "The Feliz family was always good to me."

"Until you ran off with the only daughter. After that, my father would've skinned you alive," Reyes said.

"I had no choice. He was about to marry her off to a man she despised."

"She wrote and told us," Reyes said. "Eventually, he cooled off. Until . . ."

"If there was anything I could have done to protect her from that, I would have. To my eternal shame, I was overpowered. I will never let that happen again."

"You all talk too much," Tres Dedos said. "Like a bunch of old women at the market. Let me introduce you to the rest of the group, and we can continue the family reunion later." He pointed out two others, both seemingly in their twenties, scarred and battle-hardened like the rest. "This is Joaquin Valenzuela, and here's Luis Vulvia. Antonio Valenci is up on the cliff, standing watch, but you'll meet him soon."

"I look forward to it," Joaquin said.

"Now, why don't you sit with us, and explain your plan. Gentlemen, I think you'll like this. It involves killing gringos…"

28

From the outlaws' camp, it was only a half-day's ride to Sawmill Flat, so they stayed at the camp, drinking and talking, sharing stories of Mexico and their escapades in California, for a couple of days, then spent three back in the Sonoranian Camp, rounding up four more helpers and some supplies. Having acquired those, they broke camp, saddled up, and rode to a point about midway between the San Joaquin River and Sawmill Flat.

The payroll traveled by steamer from San Francisco, up the bay and across the San Pablo Bay and Suisun Bay, then to the confluence of the Sacramento and San Joaquin Rivers. The boat turned south down the San Joaquin to the Stockton, and there the payroll was loaded onto a pair of wagons for the overland trip. Some of the dozen guards who had accompanied it upriver rode in the wagons; others took turns riding scout, either up ahead of the wagons, watching for ambush, or dropping behind in case someone with ill intent was following.

The wagons traveled from Stockton to the west side of the San Joaquin River through the great valley, so that rivers intersecting the San Joaquin from the east didn't present obstacles. Near the juncture of the San Joaquin and Mariposa Rivers, they crossed over and headed westward into the foothills.

Where Joaquin and the others waited.

A direct assault was out of the question. The payroll guards were trained, well-equipped, and ready for just such a scenario. The scouts had established a routine; after riding ahead as a pair for thirty minutes, one would return to the wagons to inform the people there that the next stretch was clear. Having made that dispatch, that rider would return to his partner, who was waiting in place, and they'd ride ahead for another thirty minutes, at which time the second scout would return with the news. That way, the wagon guards always knew the situation a short distance ahead, and if ever a guard failed to return on schedule, they would know that trouble lurked. Behind the wagons, the rear scouts only rode out for fifteen minutes, checking the back trail, before one reported back. The route avoided narrow passes whenever possible, and the men in and alongside the wagons kept sharp lookouts to every side. They had made this trip often enough to have identified every possible ambush spot.

But that meant they took the same route every time, which was what Joaquin counted on. He was also pretty sure that none of the guards were scouting underneath the usual route. Further, because the guards weren't local men, but dispatched from the San Francisco bank that supplied the payroll funds, they didn't know that as they entered the foothills, several underground shafts crossed their path.

None of the outlaws had made a success of mining, though all except Reyes Feliz had given it a try. But the experienced miners of the Sonoranian Camp had worked underground mines back in Mexico and in California. They knew how to dig shafts, to extract minerals—and, more to the point, how to bring shafts down.

Vulvia and Valenci were stationed on hilltops about twenty minutes away from the chosen shaft. At the first sign of the scouts, one of them would ride to alert the others of the wagons' approach, while the other would stay put, to watch for any change of direction. That would give the work crew almost an hour to prepare the shaft. Joaquin waited with Tres Dedos and Reyes, hidden among a spray of boulders just north of the trail. Joaquin Valenzuela was on the opposite hillside, and Claudio Feliz was inside the shaft with the miners.

The day was warm, the rocks reflecting bright sun, and Joaquin fanned himself with his hat as they traded stories of home. After what seemed like hours, he heard approaching hoofbeats and rose. Antonio Valenci raced toward them, hunched low over his horse.

"It's Antonio," Joaquin said.

Reyes and Tres Dedos got to their feet, stretched, and the three of them climbed down from their rocky perch. They reached the trail at the same time that Valenci did. He reined his mount—a pretty roan, sweating and foaming a little around the bit—to a halt and jumped down. Valenci was thin, light-skinned, with a pronounced underbite. But as a horseman, his skills compared favorably to Joaquin's. He seemed a nervous sort, often stammering and slow to commit to an action, but Tres Dedos vouched for his fighting skills.

"Th-they're coming," he said. "Two scouts, just as you de-described."

"Their system has worked for them for some time," Joaquin said. "No reason to change it." He chuckled. "I mean, until after today."

Reyes handed Valenci a canteen, and the young man drank deep. After he swallowed, he said, "Should I stay here now, or go b-back?"

"Stay," Joaquin said. "Luis can let us know if there's any

change in the route. Sit in the shade and rest for a while." He turned to Reyes and added, "Go into the shaft and tell Claudio and the others to get ready."

"Yes, Joaquin." Reyes hurried off to the shaft's entrance, which was on the far side of the northern slope.

The men had already started treating Joaquin as their leader, and he liked it. He had expected that it would take longer—that until they had made some money by following him, they would look upon him with suspicion. Instead, almost from the moment he had explained his idea, they had obeyed his orders. Only Tres Dedos viewed him as an equal, not a boss. He suspected they had been accustomed to following Pico's leadership—all but Tres Dedos, again—and were most comfortable as followers.

"Come, Antonio," Tres Dedos said, nodding his head toward where they'd been cached amidst the rocks. "We're sitting up there, out of sight from the road."

Joaquin had just told Valenci to sit in the shade, which was offered here only by a spreading oak near the trail. In the rocks, the only shade was under one's own hat. Rather than saying anything about Tres Dedos contradicting his command, though, Joaquin let it go. His cousin was right; Valenci had just completed a hard ride, and he needed to rest for a spell, to be as agile on the ground as he would soon need to be. Better to have him join them in hiding than wait where a scout might suddenly come around the curve and spot him, or force him to seek shelter without notice.

The three of them went back up the slope, where Valenci took the spot recently vacated by Reyes. Tres Dedos had been telling a story about some soldiers he'd killed, back in the war, and he picked it up where he'd left off. Joaquin wasn't really listening; he was running through the possibilities in his head, trying out alternate solutions if things didn't go as planned. The worst case was that they would all be killed, but if that happened, at least there would be nobody left to complain about any flaws in Joaquin's scheme.

While they sat and talked, the scouts appeared. Joaquin and his companions watched silently from the rocks as they rode by, but neither one spotted them. One scout turned back a little later, presumably to report that the way ahead was clear.

They checked their weapons. Among the boulders on the north slope, they had positioned five rifles and several pistols, along with plenty of ammunition. Reyes returned from the mine shaft with the news that all was in readiness there, then he and Tres Dedos moved to the south slope, which was grassy and spotted with a handful of live oaks, and stretched out just beyond the crest with Valenzuela and another five rifles. When Vulvia rode up with the final report, saying that the scouts had reported no issues, and the wagons continued on their usual path, he joined Joaquin and Valenci on the northern side. For a while, all was silent except for the occasional warble of songbirds, but then Joaquin heard the rumble of hooves and wagon wheels growing nearer.

At the mouth of the shaft, Claudio was supposed to be listening for the same thing. The greatest likelihood of error was now—if the timing wasn't just right, the whole effort would be pointless, or worse. None of the men in a position to see the wagons' approach could signal to those in the shaft, so it would fall to Claudio to correctly interpret what he heard, then to race inside the shaft to tell the miners that it was time. Then the miners themselves would have to complete their work quickly, or it would be the last job they ever did.

And there was nothing Joaquin could do but wait. He had

laid out the instructions as clearly as he could, and he was counting on the miners doing their part.

The scout that had returned to the wagons rode past again, and he was just as oblivious to their presence as he had been the first time. They allowed him to pass, not wanting gunfire to alert the men with the wagons. If he didn't get too far ahead, he might return and create a complication, but that would be dealt with if it happened.

Then the wagons came into view, each drawn by a team of four horses, rounding the curve that led between the two hills. As Joaquin had expected, there were two of them, flanked by riders. In the bed of each wagon, two riflemen accompanied the crates that contained the payrolls for the mills. More riders brought up the rear.

Without warning, anxiety gripped Joaquin. He had found men willing to follow him, including the brother and cousin of his beloved. What would happen if his plan turned into a disaster? If he even survived, he'd be right back where he started, friendless and alone. His hands trembled and sweat dripped down his sides. He took a few deep breaths, wiped his hands on his pants and used the ends of his sash to dry his face. Everything would work out.

It had to.

But the wagons were getting closer every moment. Why was nothing happening?

He could make out details on the guards' faces now. One had a gold tooth that caught the sun and flashed like a beacon. Another was as lean and wedge-shaped as an ax head. A third squinted against the sun, his head constantly moving, eyes studying every surface. Joaquin was surprised he hadn't looked up into the rocks yet, because if anyone was going to see them, it would be him.

Then a massive explosion rocked the earth.

With a jet of flame, rocks and dirt shot into the air and rained down. Some of the boulders on the slope shifted, and one started rolling, creating a small landslide. Valenci lost his footing and caught himself on a boulder, giving a little cry of surprise that would surely have alerted the wagon guards if the explosion hadn't deafened them. A plume of smoke erupted just in front of the first wagon, and the earth caved in.

The horses pulling the first wagon panicked, trying to break away from their traces, but it was too late. The two in front tumbled into the sudden opening. The two animals following tried to rear away from it, but the weight of the first two horses and the momentum of the wagon rolling into them from behind pushed them into the hole as well. The screams of the horses were terrible, nightmare sounds that Joaquin, even with all his ranch experience, couldn't have imagined. The wagon came to an uneasy rest halfway into the hole, but the horses beneath it bucked and writhed, making the wagon resemble a small boat on a stormy sea.

The driver of the rear wagon tried to steer his team around it, but his horses were no longer taking direction. As panicked as the first team, they collided with one another and tried to bolt in different directions. The wagon skidded, then tipped over. The crates and riflemen fell out, and the horses dragged the sideways wagon for another minute before they gave up.

The mounted guards fared little better. One fell into the opening with his horse. Another was bucked off immediately, and his skull smacked against one of the fallen rocks, while more crashed down onto him. The horses of the two men riding between the wagons were both hurt or startled by the blast and the crashing wagons, and their riders went down. Two riders well ahead of the blast pulled up and turned around, trying to fathom what was happening. Two more bringing up the rear were able to stop in time to avoid the worst of it. Their horses pranced nervously, making it almost impossible for them to get off an accurate shot. One dropped his rifle in the act of drawing it from its scabbard. The other yanked his and studied the hills looking for what he rightly assumed was a trap.

"This is it, boys!" Joaquin shouted. "Make it count!"

Joaquin targeted the two in the rear first. He fired a rifle, missed, reloaded and corrected his aim. Fired again. This time he hit one man's horse in the flank. That man was already raising his rifle to return fire, but the horse buckled beneath him, throwing off his shot. Joaquin fired a third time and hit the rider square in the chest.

Then the men around Joaquin were firing, too, each targeting a different guard. Tres Dedos whooped as he pulled his trigger, as if to encourage his bullets toward their goal. Heavy fire from both sides of the canyon cut the remaining guards down, wounded if not dead, and some were still struggling to emerge from the exploded shaft.

Joaquin and the others started down from their hiding places, to finish the guards and claim their prize. They moved cautiously, staying behind cover as much as possible—except for Tres Dedos, who cast aside his rifle and charged down the slope, drawing a huge knife from a sheath on his belt.

He reached the first of the fallen guards before Joaquin had even made it halfway down. He caught a fistful of the man's hair and yanked his head up, then slashed across the man's exposed throat with the blade, using enough force to halfway sever the head.

By that time, Joaquin and Valenci were on the canyon floor joined by Valenzuela, Reyes, and Vulvia. They moved from man to man, finishing off any still living with pistol shots to the head. With every white face he shot at, Joaquin imagined they were men from the mob that had hanged his brother. He knew they weren't—these men were innocent, paid to do a job and trying to do it well—but that didn't bother him. They were white and they worked for a bank or a mill, which meant they took advantage of Mexican laborers at every opportunity.

The last of the guards had been hit only in the arm, and a bullet had grazed his temple, knocking him out of the fight. Joaquin realized that he could live. "Joaquin!" he called. Joaquin Valenzuela looked up from where he was crouching at Tres Dedos's side, watching his grisly work. "You know something of the healing arts, yes?"

"A little," Valenzuela answered.

"See what you can do for this man."

"I can do something for him," Tres Dedos offered. "I can cut out his intestines and feed them to him before he dies."

"I want him to live," Joaquin said. "I want him to be able to tell others about what happened here."

"We could make it look like the Indians did it," Reyes offered. "Pico often did that."

"No," Joaquin snapped. "I mean, I understand the thinking, Reyes. But I want the Americans to fear *us*, not Indians."

"I'll do what I can," Valenzuela said.

While he wrapped a makeshift tourniquet around the wounded man's upper arm, all was quiet except for the cries and whimpers of the wounded horses. "Let's put these poor animals to rest," Joaquin said. He went to the opening and fired down at the injured creatures, their coats matted with blood and earth, bones exposed, eyes rolled back in their heads in pain and terror.

Then even the animals were still. Claudio and the miners ventured into the pass, and Joaquin counted heads to make sure they had all survived. "That was perfect," he said. "You men did exactly what you said you could. Whatever's in these crates, half of it is yours."

Tres Dedos looked up from where he was reloading his weapons. "Half? Have you become rich in the time we've been apart, Joaquin?"

"Me? You know I'm far from rich."

"I thought only the wealthy were so generous with treasure that's not theirs."

Joaquin finally understood his point. "We wouldn't have anything without them," he said. "And they risked their lives just as much as we did. They're honest, hard-working men with families. Besides, they'll have to buy a lot of dynamite to replace what they used here. They can have half. We'll have plenty of opportunity to increase our own wealth."

Tres Dedos looked like he wanted to say something else, but he checked himself and gave a nod. None of the other men raised an objection.

Which answered the question Joaquin had been wondering about. He was the leader of all these men—including Tres Dedos. They would take orders from him, even when they disagreed.

And it was just the beginning. He would add more members to the gang, increase their wealth and power along with his own. He had finally found the place—the person—he was meant to be.

Soon, all California would tremble at the mention of his name.

29

The trouble with being a leader of men, Joaquin was learning, was that he had to have someplace to lead them. He had been proud of himself for coming up with the plan to rob the sawmill payrolls, and prouder still that it had worked. But that had been his only real plan. Now, he had a crew of outlaws looking to him for ideas and ways to increase their wealth, and he didn't have any.

He remembered hearing Rosita talking about politics at the fandango, shortly before her death. She knew so much about such things. Why hadn't she ever spoken with him about them?

But he knew the answer to that. He wouldn't have listened. He had thought that he knew everything; or, at least, everything that mattered. If she'd talked about what she'd learned from books, or from conversations with her father's educated friends, he'd have dismissed her insights out of hand. He had always known she was smarter than him, but he hadn't thought it mattered.

It did, though. These men would disagree sometimes. They were rough, wild, and even if they were used to following orders from Pico, obviously—because they were no longer with Pico—there were times when they rebelled against leadership. Pico had much more experience than he did, too. What would he do when they pushed back against his commands? Rosita's knowledge might have given him some insight.

He would just have to do his best, and hope it was good enough. He wasn't as educated as Rosita, but he was a quick learner.

For now, anyway, he had a goal in mind. He had expected to accomplish it alone, but now he had men ready and willing, for the moment, to do what he said. He might as well see if he could put them to use.

"I have to go back to Murphys Diggings," he said. They had left the scene of the robbery—worried that the plume of smoke would attract unwanted attention—and had escorted the miners back to the Sonoranian Camp with their share of the take. They had repaired one of the wagons and used it to carry the money. That night, they'd started toward the camp where he had met the other men the first time, to stash the treasure somewhere safe, but stopped on a hillside about halfway between when darkness caught up to them.

"What's there?" Valenci asked. Valenzuela was tending a fire, and Vulvia and the Feliz boys had gone out looking for something to cook on it. Joaquin, Tres Dedos, and Valenci were leaning on some fallen trees, drinking.

"About twenty Americans who have to die."

Valenci's face broke into a ragged-toothed grin. "Anyone in particular? Or just the first twenty gringos we see?"

"In particular." He explained about the hanging of Jesús and his own whipping, and how he had decided to let Will Lang live. That still left everyone else who'd been part of the mob. Those men had to learn that such crimes merited special consequences.

Tres Dedos grinned. "When can we leave?"

Joaquin's stomach growled. "A more important question: when can we eat?"

A few minutes later, the Reyes cousins and Vulvia returned to camp bearing a few jackrabbits they'd managed to kill. "I hope you're not too hungry," Valenzuela said. "It looks like we won't fill our bellies tonight. Tomorrow at our camp, though, we have some rations put away. We'll eat well before we leave for your revenge."

"I am hungry," Joaquin said. "For food, and then for blood."

"One thing at a time," Tres Dedos said. "The men we're after probably won't die before we get there."

"Are any of them ri-rich?" Valenci asked.

"I don't think there are many rich men there. But whatever they have, we'll take."

"I look forward to seeing those faces again," Tres Dedos said, rubbing the back of his head. "After all, I owe them, too."

"Some I'll want to kill myself," Joaquin said. "But yes, you can have some. Just as long as I can watch. I want them to know why they're dying."

Tres Dedos laughed again. He laughed easily and enthusiastically, throwing his head back and hurling guffaws and spit toward the heavens. "That," he said once he'd brought his mirth under control, "*that* we can definitely arrange."

• • •

The following day, they stopped in the canyon long enough to bury most of the payroll money, after first parceling out some to each man, and to get some of the provisions Valenzuela had promised were there. It was all food that could be safely stored—jerky and hardtack and salted beef and the like—but washed down with strong coffee, it filled their stomachs. They stayed one day, then started for Murphys Diggings. Along the way, Joaquin filled the others in about his plans, and he and Tres Dedos described the men he was looking for as well as they could. Some, he wouldn't remember until he saw their faces. He was confident, though, that when he spotted a member of that mob, he would know it.

He was shocked when he rode into Murphys. Only a few months had passed, but the town seemed like a different place—gloomy and run-down, not the hopeful, happy place he had left behind. More structures had been built, and the hills outside of town stripped of trees to be used as building materials. The sign at Bill and Wakeen's was gone, replaced by a hand-painted sign offering:

DOCTOR/DRUGGIST
POTIONS FOR ALL AILMENTS

Only a few people were out on the street, and they all looked like they wished they were somewhere else.

The oak still stood, though. Was there a sturdy oak left in California that hadn't seen a Mexican hang? He doubted it.

He had left most of the men outside of town and gone in with just Reyes Feliz, who was still so young—in his late teens—that he wouldn't look threatening. Joaquin wore his hat pulled low, shading most of his face, and packed his red sash in a saddlebag. With his fair skin, he could almost pass for white, but the sash would give away his identity to anyone who remembered him. They rode slowly down the main street, Joaquin studying every man's face he saw.

He spotted one man he recognized, an older fellow with thin hair combed back over a balding scalp and a nose that had been broken at some point and never properly set. "That one," Joaquin said quietly. "When he's looking to the east, his nose is looking north."

"I see him," Reyes said. The young man had always had a sharp mind, like his sister. Joaquin thought if he could point some of his targets out to Reyes, then Reyes could come into town with one or two of the others. Tres Dedos could make trips in with other men and do the same. Little by little, they would all learn to recognize the members of the mob, and together they could determine the best time to go after any one of them.

After riding the length of the street, they dismounted and walked into one of the saloons. Joaquin avoided making eye contact with anyone inside, and let Reyes order them a couple of drinks. They sat at a table in the corner, both with their backs to a wall, so they could see the whole place.

Three of the men were inside, including the little man with the drooping mustache who had shot Byrnes, and two others who had joined the mob late. Should he start shooting? No, causing a scene now might make it harder to locate the other men he was after. He didn't want to begin the killing until he had identified as many as he could. Instead, Joaquin directed Reyes's attention to each in turn, but without pointing or even seeming to look at them. Reyes noted each. They stayed for an hour, but none of the other men Joaquin sought came in, so they left and rode out of town to rejoin the others.

"I've seen four of them," Reyes reported. "Later, another of you can go into town with me and I'll point them out, if they're still around."

"Four out of twenty?" Tres Dedos said. "Not a lot."

"People move around," Joaquin reminded him. "Some have probably moved to other towns or left the region altogether. If we don't get them all, that's all right. We'll get enough that anyone else who hears about it will spend the rest of his life in fear, wondering when we're coming. Four is good to start with."

"When can we kill them?"

"You're always anxious for the kill," Joaquin said with a grin. "Soon, cousin. But not until we've found everyone who's still here for the finding. I don't want them going to ground yet."

Tres Dedos heaved a great sigh. "I grow weary of too much peace, that's all. It's been days since I've killed anyone."

"Trust me," Joaquin said. "With me, you'll get your fill."

His cousin's eyes lit up. "That's what I'm counting on."

• • •

Three more days passed. Joaquin went into town with Valenci, with Claudio, and then with Valenzuela, and spotted seven more of the men. Meanwhile, others rode into town in pairs, until everyone had seen at least a few of the men. Joaquin's theory was that strangers weren't unusual in the area, but if the same men were seen numerous times, they might attract notice. Different pairs of men, though, would not be recognized as the same men. And he and Tres Dedos, most recognizable of all to the locals, had to limit their appearances.

They had located eleven members of the mob. Not enough to satisfy him, but Joaquin had to balance satisfaction with practicality. As he'd pointed out, some might have moved on. Some might have died in the interim. He couldn't wait until he had every single one in his sights, because then he would never get revenge on any of them.

No, it was time to act.

Six men, so far, had been tracked to their homes. The first

three killings were easy: follow a man to his home, go inside, kill him. When they had time, they searched the victims' homes for valuables. So far, they had found a few ounces of gold and other currency, several guns and knives, and random foodstuffs to make their camp outside of town a little more comfortable. But those men had been incidental to the death of his brother, not the prime instigators.

Joaquin wanted the big blond man, and he wanted that murder to send a message.

30

Jakob Schmitt thought he had finally gotten his life on track. After the hanging of the horse thief who'd taken Lang's mule, the town fathers, such as they were, had decided that Constable Ray McPhee was too soft on greasers. They'd taken his badge and instead, given it to Schmitt, as a reward for his active role in the event. He had originally intended to return to Los Angeles after visiting his cousin for Christmas, but decided he would stay here instead, earning a better salary than he had down south. And unlike McPhee, he wouldn't have to be a part-time constable whenever business was slow at the butcher shop.

He was given the keys to the jail and the apartment over the jail that had been McPhee's, though he'd rarely used it. Finally, as the biggest slap in McPhee's face, the title of the position was changed from constable to marshal, so instead of Constable McPhee, the law enforcement activities in Murphys Diggings—except whenever the county sheriff deigned to involve himself—were in the hands of Marshal Schmitt.

And for a while, all had been well. He'd broken up some fights, caught a few thieves, locked the occasional belligerent drunkard in a cell until he sobered up. The town was generally peaceful anyway, except on Friday nights. When he was in a certain mood, he found some excuse to arrest a prostitute, and once she was in the jail, negotiated her release on friendly terms. Saloonkeepers gave him free drinks, on the theory that his presence in their establishments would help keep order. He wasn't getting rich, but he didn't have much to spend his money on anyway.

But then, the murders had begun. Three of them, now, spread over six nights. And these weren't barroom brawls with unintended consequences, but cold-blooded killings, in the victims' own homes, which were then ransacked and stripped of valuables. Bodies torn to bits in some cases, with pieces scattered all around. Suddenly, the town fathers demanded action. To make it even worse, he was sitting across the table from a newspaperman who wanted answers, too.

"Why you think anybody in El Dorado County wants to read about some killin's here, Mr. . . . ?" he asked the man, whose name had already escaped him.

"Springer," the man said, pushing his spectacles back up his pointed beak. He'd given his name when he'd invited himself to sit at Schmitt's table, but it hadn't stuck. "Tom Springer. The answer to your question is that if someone's murdering people here, it stands to reason he might not stick around too long. He might move on to a neighboring county. People have a right to be warned."

A warm sense of hope shot through Schmitt, like a fire on a cold night. "Really? You think he'd do that? Move on?"

"It's possible." Springer leaned over the table, as if to share a secret with Schmitt. The marshal didn't mind; the saloon was noisy, and the newspaperman's voice soft. The only thing hard about him was his steely gaze, and those spectacles magnified his eyes so much that Schmitt was almost afraid the man could look right into his soul. "These other murders took place across different camps and towns. The killer used different methods of murder. But many believe—as I do—that they were all done by the same man. Rumor has it—little more than gossip, really, but convincing to some—that the murderer was seeking revenge for a terrible wrong done to his loved one. All anybody knows for sure is that he was a Mexican man, because he committed one of the killings in the plain view of more than a dozen witnesses. At the *El Dorado Republican*, we started calling him the Mexican Murderer, and other newspapers followed suit."

Schmitt was having a hard time following the newspaperman. The big words he used didn't help; neither did the fact that he hadn't eaten since midday, and had decided not to bother, but instead to get a good drunk going. He'd been halfway there when the man spotted his badge and cornered him. "So you think this is the same Mexican?" Schmitt asked.

"Oh, not necessarily. In fact, probably not, if the gossip is to be believed. And several months have passed in the interim. A significant number of gold seekers move from one camp or one claim to another, do they not? Eternally chasing the next big prize?"

"I reckon."

"Just as they do, I'm saying, so can one man kill people in a place, and move around and kill somewhere else. Thus, my question remains. As my understanding is that you are the sole law enforcement authority for Murphys Diggings, what progress have you made in identifying the killer?"

Schmitt worked through what Springer was asking, and thought he understood. "Well, I've talked to some folks, but nobody's seen nothin'."

"Neighbors of the deceased, I assume?"

"Some."

"Or perhaps people who knew the victims, who might know if someone had a grudge against them?"

"Oh, that's a good idea, too," Schmitt said.

Springer leaned back in his chair and steepled his hands, examining Schmitt over his spectacles. Schmitt felt like a scientific specimen of some kind. "How much experience with the law did you have before you accepted this position, Marshal?"

Schmitt considered a moment, but the answer wasn't hard to calculate. "I was a deputy sheriff, down in Los Angeles. Mostly my job was to ride herd on the greasers. I didn't have to catch a lot of murderers."

"Well, those are certainly valid qualifications. I wonder, though, if you've considered the issue of growth."

Schmitt laughed. "I don't think I'm gonna grow anymore." Then, thinking further, he patted his stomach. "Except mebbe here, I don't watch myself."

"I don't mean your physical growth," Springer said. "I mean progress. Murphys Diggings is in the process of growing from a somewhat tawdry mining camp into something resembling a real town. Like many such towns in the area, it may at some stage become truly civilized. But a necessary precondition for such a state is adequate law enforcement. You'll need deputies—after all, you can't be on duty all day and night, can you? Yet, crimes can be committed at any time. If you had some assistance, a deputy might have been on patrol when one of those murders was committed, and could conceivably have interrupted the crime. Possibly prevented it, or at the very least, apprehended the killer."

Again, Schmitt took a few moments to reason out what the man was saying. "I guess so. I've been a deputy before. I should ask if I can hire somebody."

"Perhaps you should," Springer said. "An excellent idea."

"Thanks."

"I can see that Murphys is in good hands."

A flush went through Schmitt. This conversation had, he thought, suddenly taken a different turn. He'd thought the newspaperman was criticizing him, but suddenly he seemed to be complimenting him on his performance. The man was even harder to figure out than that Bigler fellow who wanted to be governor.

Springer stayed at the table a few minutes longer, making small talk, but it seemed he had gotten what he came for. Or he hadn't. Either way, Schmitt figured, he was only being polite now. His hunch was correct; soon, Springer handed him a copy of the *El Dorado Republican* newspaper, bade him a good night, and headed for the hotel where he had a room for the night. He did ask Schmitt to inform him of any further developments in his search for the killer—or any additional murders—and Schmitt promised that he would. But he didn't think he'd follow through on that promise. The newspaperman bothered him, and if he didn't have to talk to the fellow ever again, he'd be better off.

Alone at his table again, he finished his drink, and one more. Then, a little wobbly in the knees but not incapacitated—it took a lot of liquor to knock Jakob Schmitt on his rump—he rose, still clutching the newspaper, which he could make good use of in the outhouse. He thanked the barkeep for the free drinks and headed for his office. He had no prisoners in the cells so had left the front door unlocked, and a brief glance inside told him that nothing had been disturbed. Satisfied, he went out the back door to the wooden staircase leading to his quarters above the office.

He was a little unsteady on the way up, and the railing had given him splinters before. But if he just used it sparingly as he climbed, touching it for balance now and again, he was fine.

His place upstairs was nothing to brag about, but it came free with the badge. McPhee had his own place, a little ranch just outside town where he raised some of the meat he sold in his butcher shop, so he had never lived here. When Schmitt moved in, a layer of dust covered the scant furnishings, and though he'd wiped off spots from time to time, he had never made an attempt to clean the whole place. It had two rooms, a front one with a fireplace and a little stove, and a bedroom behind that. When nature called, he either had to go downstairs to use the outhouse standing behind his office, or just piss over the railing from his front door.

When he opened the door on this night, something smelled a little funny. That wasn't unusual, though; his clothes often got dirty enough to stand up and walk around on their own before he bothered taking them to the Chinese laundry on the far end of town. Anyway, by the time it fully registered in his somewhat inebriated state, he was inside.

Where a man sat at his rough wooden table with both barrels of a shotgun pointed at him.

"Remember me?" the man asked.

Schmitt stopped just inside the door. He bumped it with his rear and it swung closed, startling him and pitching the room into near darkness, with only one window letting in scant moonlight. "Uhh," he managed, but got no further than that.

"Light," the man at the table said.

Someone else—hitherto unseen—struck a match and touched it to a candle, which he set on the table in front of the man with the gun. The man was a greaser, he knew that much right off. He wore all black, at least as far as Schmitt could see. His hat was pulled low over his brow. He had a lean face with a slender mustache. It looked vaguely familiar, but he couldn't place it. He only got a glimpse of the second man, but he looked like a Mexican, too.

"Think back," the man said. "You hanged my brother."

Schmitt had taken part in three hangings since he'd been in Murphys Diggings, but only one was recent, and he didn't remember Mexicans being involved in the two previous. In the flickering candlelight, he remembered the face. This was the man they had whipped, after his brother had stretched hemp.

"You're him. You stole Lang's mule."

"I did nothing of the sort, as I think you know," the man said. His voice was as calm as if they were having a neighborly chat. His hands were steady, too, as were those barrels pointed his way. "And neither did my brother. I'm sure you know that, too."

"Look, mister, all I know's that was Will's mule, and he got it back. I got no quarrel with you."

"I think you do," the man said. "Or at least, I have a quarrel with you."

"Your fight's with Lang, not me," Schmitt said. The newspaper rattled in his hand, and he threw it down on the table just to be rid of it. He still couldn't see the second man, but he heard a rasp of steel and leather and believed the man had just drawn a gun from its holster. The obvious danger had sobered him up fast. He had a pistol at his hip, but if he reached for it, the man could open up with those barrels and cut him in half. "I don't want any part of it."

"You made yourself part of it," the man at the table said. "You didn't have to get involved. Once you were, you didn't have to stay. You didn't have to chop some rope off the length that hanged my brother to tie my hands with. You did all those things, of your own free will. I saw nobody forcing you."

"So you're here to kill me?"

"That's the general idea. But not so quickly. If not for you, my brother would still be alive. I feel you should suffer first, before you die. Give you some time to dwell on your sins."

As Schmitt saw it, he had only one chance. The man meant to torture him and then kill him. And there was a second man who probably also had a gun pointing his way. His only advantage was that he knew the layout of his quarters better than they did. If he could get past them into the bedroom, he could go through that window, which would let him out on the overhang above the marshal's office. There he had plenty of guns and ammunition, and if a fight started, people up and down the street would hear it and pitch in.

If he stayed here, he would die. If he could get outside, though, he had a chance.

He acted as soon as the thought flitted through his mind, out of fear that his face would give it away. He dropped straight to the floor, landing hard on the rough-hewn planks. The shotgun went off, its roar deafening in the little space, but it was still aimed at where he had been. He heard shot tear into the wall behind him.

At the same time that he touched the ground, he grabbed a leg of the table and shoved it toward the gunman. The candle flew off the table, presumably bounced off the man with the shotgun, and went out before it hit the floor. The second man muttered an oath, but he didn't shoot. Schmitt was already moving, yanking his gun with his right hand and wrapping his left around a chair leg as he pushed to his feet. Without slowing, he hurled the chair toward the man with the shotgun. He heard it crash into someone. He snapped off two quick shots at where he thought the second man was and raced for the bedroom. At least one of his rounds hit flesh.

He had, he thought, a clear shot for the bedroom and the window beyond. On the way, he ran into somebody—one of the first two or a third man, he wasn't sure—but he used his weight to bull past the man and keep going. The window was ahead now, moonlight showing his path.

As he threw the window open, he fired twice more back through the doorway, into the front room, to discourage pursuit. Squeezing his bulk out the window was harder than he expected. The opening was smaller than he'd thought, or he was larger. Stuck here, he'd be an easy target, if either of the men inside still lived.

Then some unexpected force tugged him through the gap, and he fell, sprawling on the pitched roof. Schmitt lost his grip on the pistol, and it slid toward the edge, but a booted foot stopped its descent. An ally, then, but who?

He looked up and saw a third man, limned by moonlight. He looked as big and solid as Schmitt himself; shorter, but probably just as heavy. He had a thick beard and a prominent brow, and he wore a serape and a beat-up hat. In his right hand he held a long knife or a short sword, of a size and shape that put Schmitt in mind of a cutlass that might have been wielded by buccaneers in days of old.

Worst of all, he was grinning.

"Going somewhere, friend?" he asked.

Schmitt jerked a thumb toward the window. "Men in there, trying to kill me."

The stranger stepped nearer, scooting the pistol under his foot and craning his head to look past Schmitt. "You don't say?"

"They are," Schmitt insisted. "My gun."

"Oh, this is yours?" With a quick motion, the man skidded the gun behind him and over the edge. At the same instant, he lunged forward, driving that wide, curved blade into Schmitt's gut. He yanked it free again and blood splashed the roof. Schmitt dropped to his knees, hands across his midsection, trying to hold himself together. At the last moment, though, he realized his mistake, because he had just put his throat within reach of the strange man. Moonlight glinted off the blade as the man drew it back, then slashed toward him. He thought he heard his own head slap the roof before his body did, but that must have been an illusion.

31

"I wanted him alive," Joaquin said. He was at the big man's window, watching Tres Dedos finish the job of sawing off the head. Blood ran in rivulets to the edge of the roof, and spattered on the ground below.

"So you did," Tres Dedos said. "But when I heard the shotgun, I figured you'd changed your mind."

"Well, he didn't cooperate."

"Does that surprise you?"

"Make it fast," Joaquin urged. "People will have heard the shots. They'll be here any moment."

"This is my vengeance, too, Joaquin. Jesús was your brother, but he was my cousin and my best friend. I owe these bastards a debt."

Even as he spoke, Tres Dedos snapped the last bit of gristle and raised the head high. "Done," he said.

"Toss it into the street. Right in the middle, where no one can miss it."

Tres Dedos stepped to the edge and gave a gentle toss. The head arced out and dropped in the center of the road.

"Let's go," Joaquin said. "Quickly, now!"

Tres Dedos took a last, long look at the corpse and the river of blood flowing from it, then hurried to the window. Joaquin and Valenzuela helped him through the opening, and they rushed back toward the door.

On the way out, Joaquin spied the newspaper the man had dropped. Moonlight revealed a bold headline across the top, saying "MILL PAYROLLS ROBBED IN DEADLY AMBUSH." He snatched it up, and together the men raced toward horses waiting at the side of the building. They hadn't gone far before they heard the screams of whoever had first happened upon the big man's head.

• • •

Back at their camp, Joaquin read the newspaper article by the light of the campfire.

> MORE MEXICAN MURDERERS. — On the 3rd (Saturday), a cowardly ambush along the trail to Sawmill Flat left eleven American payroll guards dead and one gravely injured. The sole survivor, one Joseph Farmer, a payroll guard in the employ of the San Francisco Savings Bank, located on Montgomery Street in that fair city, reports that the murderers laid in wait, then caused an explosion that created a hole beneath the first of two wagons carrying payroll funds for the primarily Mexican employees of two sawmills. In the confusion caused by the explosion, the murderers opened fire upon the guards, who fought back bravely, but were outnumbered. All of the killers were Mexican, Farmer describes, and seemed to be led by one called Joaquin, who Farmer says was a short, stout fellow with more gold in his mouth than ivory. Several men called out the name of Joaquin, who provided medical

aid that allowed Farmer to live when all
the others had died. As a further atrocity,
one of the killers beheaded a man. That
murderer had only three fingers on his
right hand and is believed to be the outlaw
known as Three-Fingered Jack.

At that, Joaquin hurled the paper to the ground. "Damn
you to Hell, Valenzuela!" he cried.

Valenzuela looked at him with questioning eyes. "What
did I do?"

"This newspaper thinks you were the leader of the attack
on the payroll wagons!"

"Me? Why?"

"It says everybody was calling for Joaquin, and you helped
bind his wounds. So he thinks *you're* the Joaquin everyone
looked to for orders."

"Well, that's not my fault."

He was right. It wasn't his doing, and the realization
calmed Joaquin's anger somewhat, or at least directed it elsewhere. "I know," he said. Then, raising his voice, he addressed
the entire camp. "From now on, we speak English whenever
we're around Americans."

"Always?" Tres Dedos asked. He was sitting cross-legged
on the other side of the fire, with a jug between his thighs.

"Unless we're addressing someone who doesn't speak
English. Or we're in Mexico. There, we're not bandits. In
America, we are, and American bandits speak English."

Tres Dedos rose and came over to sit beside him. He picked
up the newspaper and appeared to scan it, but he couldn't
read English. He was one of the smartest people Joaquin had
ever known, despite this lack. He seemed to know the entire
history of Mexico, from the days of the Olmec civilization

through to the Aztecs, the Spanish conquest after that, and the more recent struggles that led to Mexican independence from Spain, the years of the Mexican Republic, the revolution, and everything that had happened in his lifetime and Joaquin's. He also knew all about plants and animals, all the stars in the sky and how to navigate by them, and he was constantly surprising Joaquin with some new facet of his knowledge. Joaquin had quickly learned to trust him.

"This troubles you?" Tres Dedos asked quietly.

Joaquin turned toward him and lowered his voice accordingly. This was one of the lessons of leadership, he thought. Don't display weakness—even perfectly human weakness—in front of your men. "It does. Perhaps it shouldn't. Pride is one of the deadly sins, is it not? But, damn it, that wasn't Valenzuela's plan. It was mine, and it worked. It paid off handsomely."

"That it did, Joaquin. And the men know it was yours, even if that newspaper is ignorant. They all look up to you."

"It wasn't the newspaper, it was the man I told you to spare. He misunderstood the situation and described Valenzuela as the leader. Now the whole world thinks it."

"I'm sure the whole world doesn't read this."

"No, you're right, cousin. I'm overreacting. It shouldn't matter to me, but it does."

"You want to be famous?"

"I don't care about fame, but I want to be feared. I don't really care about killing the rest of those men in Murphys. They were carried away, part of an angry mob, but they didn't mean my brother any harm. Or me. Many of them knew me, had played monte at my table. They wouldn't have acted against us if not for the instigation of others. I don't care about revenge against them, but I want other Americans to think twice before laying a hand on an innocent Mexican."

"That's a noble goal." Tres Dedos leaned forward, pulled a stick from the fire, and lit a cigar from it. He sucked in smoke and blew it out in a long plume, then tossed the stick back in. Sparks drifted into the air.

"Nobility has nothing to do with it. At home, I had nothing. A tiny house, with a room I shared with a brother and sister. A job working for Rosita's father, which I took only so I could be near her. If I stayed there, I would still be working for Don Ramon, with nowhere to go and nothing to claim as my own.

"Here, things are different. Here a man can make of himself what he will. Here, we can be rich, you and me. We can own things, run our own affairs. Who knows, perhaps one of us will be governor someday."

He laughed, and Tres Dedos joined him before saying, "You, maybe. Not me, not with this face. My mother used to describe me as heartbreakingly handsome, do you believe it?"

"When was that?"

"She said it right before she beat me with the stick she'd named Xavier, after my late father."

"She named a stick?"

"She said it would have been his job to beat me, had he lived. Because he didn't, she wanted me to know that he would have disapproved of me."

"Did she beat you often?"

"Almost daily, I suppose. I was a mischievous child. No doubt, I deserved it."

"What happened to your father? I always wondered about that."

"I don't know. All I know is that I didn't kill him. I didn't start killing people until later."

"Did your mother do it?"

Tres Dedos grew pensive. "Now that you mention it, it is possible that she did. She always did have a mean streak."

Joaquin shook his head. Something about all this sounded wrong to him. "When did all this happen?"

"When I was around nine or ten, I suppose. I hoped I would grow into my nose. I'm still hoping."

You're good with your knife," Joaquin observed. "What's to keep you from taking someone else's face off and wearing it as your own?"

Tres Dedos's demeanor suddenly turned serious, and he pointed the lit end of his cigar at Joaquin. "You, sir, are possessed by genius!"

"I have come to a realization tonight, cousin. I really *don't* need to kill all of the men from the hanging. I want the man who killed Byrnes, but the others don't matter. Let them live, knowing what they did. As with Lang, who's more miserable now than he was before he had Jesús killed, their sins will mark the rest of their pathetic lives. You and I, my friend, have better things to do. Bigger things, and much more important."

"Like getting rich?" Tres Dedos asked.

"That, and other things. I do have one more task to perform before we leave Murphys, but it will be a pleasant one, for a change."

"Can I help?"

"No, this one I should do alone. It won't take long. I'll leave at first light, and be back before noon."

"Perhaps you should get some sleep, then," Tres Dedos said.

Joaquin pointed across the fire, at the jug Tres Dedos had abandoned. "Perhaps first, we should have another drink."

Tres Dedos threw his head back and roared his laughter at the stars. When he was able to contain himself, he fetched the jug, brought it back, and handed it to Joaquin. "As I said, possessed by genius."

Joaquin took a long swig, felt the burn going down his throat and into his stomach. When he finished, he wiped his mouth on the back of his hand and gave back the jug. "Manuel, my cousin," he said. "I cannot argue with you."

• • •

True to his word, Joaquin left the camp on horseback before the sun broke the horizon. When it finally rose, it washed the hills with golden light and stretched his shadow out before him. An hour later, he was knocking at the door of Bernardo Alvarado, who had told him where his farm was before they rode off to bury Jesús in the wilderness.

Bernardo came to the door. He looked older than Joaquin had remembered, unshaven and haggard. He held a mug of coffee in one hand, and Joaquin could smell it as soon as the door opened.

"It's you!" the man said, his eyes brightening in recognition.

"I told you I would return." Joaquin held out a sack of money, proceeds from the payroll job. It was a mixture of American eagles and double eagles, Mexican pesos, Spanish reals and doubloons, and exchange notes from the San Francisco bank. It could all be spent in the mining towns and camps, along with the commonplace gold nuggets and dust, but the sawmills didn't deal in gold.

"What's this?" Bernardo asked, his face registering surprise.

"I told you I'd repay your friend tenfold for the horse. A good animal she turned out to be, too. I'm still riding her." He gestured over his shoulder, toward where the mare waited at the gate. "This is probably more than tenfold, but your friend deserves it."

"I . . . thank you, sir. He'll be delighted. He never expected payment."

"Tell him that Joaquin Murrieta always pays his debts."

The man took the bag, and Joaquin dipped into his pocket for a smaller pouch. "And this, sir, is for you. For your troubles."

Bernardo shook his head. "Oh, that's not necessary, my friend. I was happy to help out a countryman."

"Not necessary," Joaquin agreed. "Except to me. You did me a good turn. I want to do you one. Please, I insist."

"If you're certain."

"I am. Take it, please."

Bernardo did. He seemed pleasantly surprised by its weight. "This is most generous."

"It's no more than you deserve. As I said, Joaquin Murrieta pays his debts. You can tell anyone that, and I will never make a liar of you." Even as he said it, he realized that he owed other debts, here in town. If his word was to be any good at all, he had to see those tasks through as well.

"I will," Bernardo said.

"That's all I ask."

Bernardo regarded him for a silent stretch, then shook his head. "You are a most unusual man."

"So others have said." Joaquin doffed his hat, bowed, and returned to his horse. As he rode away, he noticed that Bernardo still stood in the doorway, watching him go.

• • •

When Joaquin returned to the campsite, the men had broken camp and waited for him, smoking and playing cards. He reined the newly purchased horse to a sudden halt and jumped down from the saddle to confront Tres Dedos. "What are you doing? Why are the tents down? Are you going somewhere?"

"You said we were done here," Tres Dedos reminded him. "You said it was time to move on from this place."

He was right, of course. Joaquin had said that. He hated to admit to being wrong, but even more, he hated to admit that he'd changed his mind. It seemed a particularly egregious form of weakness. How could men follow someone whose whims vacillated without warning? His anger was directed less at Tres Dedos and the others than at himself.

"I've changed my mind. We aren't finished in Murphys. Not until every man in that mob is dead."

Tres Dedos face lit up with a smile that was, if not handsome, at least less fearsome than his usual scowl. "All of them?"

"Every one," Joaquin said again. More quietly, he added, "Beginning with the man who killed Bill Byrnes. And then Lang. A man can take almost everything from another man. His love, his treasure, even his life. The only thing that can't be taken from a man is his word. I swore to kill the men who hanged Jesús, and I will, by God. I owe them that."

Tres Dedos turned to the others and shouted, "Get the tents back up, men! We're staying put!" Then he stroked the handle of his machete, as if it were a favored pet. "My blades will have plenty to drink. I don't know what brought on this change of heart, but thank you, Joaquin."

Joaquin nodded his acceptance of his friend's gratitude. "Never let me forget, cousin. Joaquin Murrieta always pays his debts."

32

July 1851, Central Valley

High summer. The great inland valley and the deserts in the southeast baked under the incessant sun. Winds from out of the east blew hot, dry air westward, but ocean breezes cooled the narrow strip of land near the water, and with June's cloud cover gone, the beaches and shoreline cliffs offered relief and unmatched beauty. In the north, warm days made working outside easy, and cool nights allowed for relaxation and sound sleep. Most of the snow melted from the high peaks of the Sierra Nevada, sending water cascading down the rivers where the big commercial gold outfits worked before emptying into the Pacific. Mountain valleys were still green and dotted with wildflowers from spring rains, and where the hillsides were dry, golden grass shaded by live oaks reminded people why they'd come to California in the first place.

The state was perfect, and it belonged to Joaquin.

• • •

He had killed eight of the men from the mob that had lynched his brother. Six had left the area for parts unknown, and more than those he couldn't identify with enough certainty. He had shot the narrow-faced man who'd murdered Bill, right between the eyes, as that man had done to Joaquin's friend and partner. He had not had the chance to kill Lang, because Sam Green had beaten him to the punch. Green had run into Lang in a saloon in Columbia and called him a no-account lying coward who'd railroaded an innocent man. The altercation had turned uglier from there and ended with Green drawing down on Lang and putting four bullets into him. Green was still in jail in Columbia, but Joaquin had sent a considerable sum to his family, with a note saying it was "from an appreciative friend."

That task accomplished, he and his friends had turned their attention to greater things. Using the connections each man had in California's Mexican communities, they added to their ranks. Some of the men who joined them were outlaws, others had failed at mining or lost other jobs — or never found them. Most were desperate for one thing or another, and hadn't found what they were looking for. Or, like Joaquin, had found it and seen it taken away. Joaquin, Tres Dedos, and Reyes Feliz spoke with each of them, ensuring that they were free of other obligations and hard enough to fight, to kill, and perhaps to die. Mostly, they wanted to know that the men were hungry for something they hadn't found — treasure, ideally, or vengeance.

Soon, the band was thirty men strong, and all answered to Joaquin.

He set few rules, but foremost among them was that Mexican people were to be treated with respect at all times. Those in need were to be helped, if at all possible. Any time a robbery was profitable, a percentage of the take would be handed out to poor Mexicans or those in debt to the Americans. In this way, they would make sure that they were always welcome in Mexican neighborhoods and homes. Their own people would shield them from American law when necessary, hide them when pursued, and inform them of riches for the taking.

One hot afternoon in the southlands, under a cloudless sky

and a merciless sun, Joaquin and Tres Dedos and a few others were riding around the perimeter of a wealthy ranch. Fences hemmed in the land, but grazing behind those barriers were seventy or eighty of the finest horses Joaquin had ever seen, including those belonging to Don Ramon.

"We could sell those for a fortune," Joaquin said. "Up north, or in Sonora, either one. If we sold them for half their value, we'd still be rich."

Tres Dedos laughed. Joaquin loved the sound he made when he did that, deep and gravelly. It reminded him of the devil clearing his throat. "You're right. And they're right there for the taking. I don't see anyone tending them."

"But we don't have room for that many," Joaquin said. They still used the outlaws' original hideout in the near the Sonoranian Camp. "Where would we hide them until we could sell them?"

"I might have an idea about that," Tres Dedos said. "I was talking to one of the new men, Reis Carrillo, and he told me of a place that might suit us better."

Anger flared in Joaquin's breast. Why hadn't Carrillo told him first? Still, everyone knew Tres Dedos was close to him. What one learned, the other would soon know as well. "Tell me."

"It's near Arroyo de Cantua, he says. A canyon, easily defended, with grassy pastureland inside. There's always water running through the arroyo. The walls are steep, hard to climb, and there's only one way in and out."

Joaquin tried to picture the area. Arroyo de Cantua was in the great central valley that ran most of the length of California. There weren't any tall mountains there, but he supposed if the canyon walls were forbidding enough, they didn't have to be that high. It was well-placed, not too far from either the gold fields or the Mexican border. "That sounds ideal. Too ideal, in fact. Why isn't somebody already living there?"

"Somebody was," Tres Dedos explained. "A farming family. They were slaughtered by Indians a few months ago. Burned most of their house, set fire to their fields. Since then, no whites have dared to take it over. It's just sitting there for the taking."

"What about the Indians?"

"They could return, it's true. But if they did, they wouldn't find a peaceful farming family, would they? I believe we could encourage them to seek easier targets."

"Are you sure about this?"

"None of it," Tres Dedos admitted. "I don't think Carrillo would lie to me. But I haven't seen it for myself, and I don't know how long it's been since he was there. I know he once lived nearby."

"How far from here?" Joaquin asked.

Tres Dedos chewed his lower lip as he considered. "Two days' ride, if we hurry. Three, if we dawdle or find someone to rob on the way."

"Well, we always have to allow time for that." He took a last look at the magnificent beasts on the far side of the barbed wire. "Let's hurry."

• • •

The ride north was rushed, across country hammered by the sun, the men's throats parched and their eyes gritty and dry. But when Carrillo showed them the canyon he'd described, Joaquin thought it all worthwhile. It was even better than he'd said. The entrance to the canyon was barely wider than the span of three horses, standing nose to tail. But the walls rose steep and sheer around it, forming natural barriers to anyone who might want to bypass that narrow opening.

Sitting in a huge, grassy meadow inside the canyon were the remains of the farmhouse, partially burned, but stone walls and a chimney still stood, offering at least some shelter from the elements. Tall cottonwoods shaded the house, adding to its appeal.

Whatever crops they'd been growing had been well and truly torched, which didn't bother Joaquin much, as he had no interest in farming. If some of the men wanted to try cultivating those areas again, they were welcome to it. He was more interested in the thick, healthy grass, which would feed stolen horses until they could be marketed. Water trickled down the cliffs from a hidden spring and ran across the canyon before eventually joining with Cantua Creek itself, beyond the walls.

Riding close to Tres Dedos, he indicated a stretch of land toward the rear of the canyon. "We can plant posts there, and run fence between them," he said. "That'll keep the horses pent up, but nobody passing by would see them. And if they come into the canyon, they'll have other problems to worry about."

"We can station men at these high ends," Tres Dedos said. "From up there, they'd be able to watch anyone approaching well before they got close."

"If they can get up there," Joaquin said.

"We can find some who are good climbers. They can affix knotted ropes to trees or brush at the heights, and then we'll have ladders up and down. But no one approaching from the outside will be able to do the same without being seen."

"Good idea. It's a natural fortress."

"Let's hope we don't need one."

"If we don't," Joaquin corrected, "then we're lacking in ambition."

Tres Dedos snorted a laugh, then said, "Somehow, I don't

think that'll be a problem with you in command."

"No," Joaquin agreed. "I'm quite certain it won't. Come, cousin, let's explore our new home."

• • •

The moon, nearly full and soaring high in a cloudless sky, painted the valley with silver. The buzz, whine, chirrup, and chirp of insects filled the air. Joaquin, Tres Dedos, and four others moved slowly across the grass, because the racket stilled when they approached, and they didn't want to alert the men around a dying fire to their presence.

But they were in no hurry. The night was long, and the later it got, the sleepier the men would be. Already two had left the fire and curled up to sleep, their snores soon adding to the general din. That left two awake, smoking and talking softly. Four horses were tethered nearby, seemingly asleep on their feet.

"I can get them both from here," Gregorio Lopez said after a while. "Two quick shots, easy."

Lopez was the best marksman of the group. Joaquin had never seen him miss a target with a rifle, even if that target was at full gallop. Two men outlined by glowing embers would be child's play for him.

"No," Joaquin said. "I want to avoid any shooting until we're done." They didn't know how many other men might be scattered around, though two days and nights of observation hadn't revealed any significant numbers. The ranch boasted plenty of hands, but few stayed out on the range with the livestock. Still, the sound of gunfire on a quiet, windless night might travel far enough for those in the bunkhouse to hear. Joaquin didn't want to bring them running.

They worked their way closer, until when they were less than twenty feet away, one of the men stepped on something that made a sharp cracking sound. Instantly, the two men at the fire shot to their feet. "Who's there?" one asked. He held a rifle loosely in his hands, but didn't know where to point it.

Joaquin didn't move, didn't breathe. He held out one hand to keep the others still.

"Just one of them horses, mebbe," the second man said.

"I don't like it," said the first. "Speak up, you're out there," he demanded.

Joaquin spread his arms, and his men responded by putting some space between them, moving quietly.

But the two at the fire were on alert. Both had guns out, and they weren't going to relax now. One was already nudging the sleeping men with his foot, waking them. This wasn't going according to plan.

"Go!" Joaquin shouted.

At his command, all six charged toward the fire from different directions. The men on their feet fired blindly. The other two threw back blankets and grabbed for weapons. Too late, though; Joaquin's men closed the gap in moments, knives out.

Joaquin's Bowie knife slashed the man with the rifle across his forearm. He cried out and released the gun, and Joaquin closed on him, driving the knife into his gut again and again. Hot blood splashed his hand and chest, and the man tried to claw Joaquin's face, but weakness overtook him. Beside Joaquin, Tres Dedos had grabbed the other gunman from behind and drawn his machete across the man's throat. The other two hadn't even found their footing before they were swarmed, overwhelmed.

"Spare that one!" Joaquin ordered before the last of them was killed. He was bleeding from wounds on his arms and chest, but he would live, Joaquin judged. "Take his weapons."

His men obeyed, checking the fellow for hidden guns or

knives. Then Lopez and Pancho Dominguez hauled him to his feet. He was afraid, but he tried to put on a brave face. "Who are you?" he asked. "What do you want?"

"Just these fine horses," Joaquin said. "We mean you no harm."

The man eyed his fallen companions. "Don't look that way."

"You would've objected to our taking your livestock," Joaquin pointed out. "We couldn't have that."

"You'll have half the county on your trail before sunrise," the man said. "Those shots were heard for miles."

"Perhaps. That's a chance I'll take."

The man studied Joaquin and his companions in the moonlight. When he recognized Tres Dedos, his mouth dropped open. "You're Three-Fingered Jack!"

Tres Dedos bowed. "So I am."

"You've heard of him?" Joaquin asked.

"Everyone's heard'a him. He's a man-killer."

"You honor me," Tres Dedos said with a grin.

"He won't kill you," Joaquin said. He gestured at the man's chest with his knife. "Strip."

"What?"

"You heard me. Take off your clothes."

"My clothes?"

"You ask a lot of questions for a man whose life I've just spared. Off with them."

The man shrugged and unbuttoned his shirt. He was still bleeding, and the fabric stuck to his wounds. He winced when he pulled it away.

"Keep going," Joaquin said.

"You never seen a naked man before?" the man asked.

"Don't make me change my mind," Joaquin said. "If you

want to live, strip and shut your mouth. And hurry."

The man kicked off his boots, dropped his outer shirt and his cotton undershirt on the ground, then unbuttoned his pants.

"Drop them."

The man obeyed. He was lean, rangy, his arms and legs crisscrossed with scars. "You've had a hard life," Joaquin said.

"Who hasn't?"

"Now the drawers," Joaquin said.

"For real?"

"You're not chasing us. If you want to run for the bunkhouse, you can, but it'll hurt."

The fellow shrugged again and yanked off his drawers, tossing them aside. "You like that?"

"Liking has nothing to do with it. Boys, load his weapons and clothing onto their horses. It's time to go."

Dominguez had gathered their horses. He was a veteran of the American War, a cavalry officer, and knew a lot about horses and other military matters. He and Lopez stashed the weapons of all four men, and the naked man's clothes, and then all six of them mounted up. Joaquin leaned out of his saddle, toward the man. "I am Joaquin Murrieta," he said. "One day, you'll tell your grandchildren about this." He glanced down at the man's exposed groin. "That is, if any woman would be interested in a man with so little to offer."

Laughing, he pulled out a pistol and fired two shots in the air, paused a moment, then added a third.

At that signal, men stationed at the fences knocked down two sections to create an opening. Other men, mounted, rode in and circled around the ranch's horses, whooping and firing guns, herding them toward the opening. Joaquin and the others joined in. Stampeding animals in the dark was always dangerous, but it wouldn't be dark for much longer. Besides, these animals were pure profit—if they lost a few, they were still out nothing but time and effort.

By the time the sun crested the eastern mountains, the band was racing north, hooves thundering across hard-baked earth and raising a dust cloud that could be seen for miles. Others were in pursuit, their own cloud visible in the distance. Joaquin had planned for that, too. Eighteen of his men were with him, herding the horses toward Arroyo de Cantua. Twelve more waited at a place where the pass narrowed and crossed a shallow river. The horses charged through, but when the pursuers reached it and slowed, even if only slightly, crossfire from the heights would cut them down and discourage any survivors.

Keeping thirty men happy and earning enough wealth to ensure their continued loyalty was a challenge, but Joaquin was sure that, even if they wound up with only fifty of these fine horses, the quality of the animals would fetch high prices. Those profits would be shared equally, with some left over to be donated to impoverished Mexicans around the state. This was his biggest victory yet, and it was sure to be talked about for months, if not years.

And that—as much as the treasure itself—was the point.

33

Once their brands were altered and the horses sold, Joaquin took his share of the money and visited a tailor he'd heard about in San José. He liked the city. The weather was seldom too hot or too cold. Although it had until recently been the state capital, the population was still mostly Mexican. He could walk its streets and immerse himself in familiar sights, sounds, and smells that made him think of home. And he had plenty of allies there, from men who could walk freely among the legislators in the capitol building to those who could lie at their feet outside, as invisible as poor people anywhere. This way, he always knew what the state government was up to. He'd been told that there was concern about marauding Mexican gangs, but so far, he didn't seem to have been specifically identified.

He stayed in town for a week, waiting for his new clothes to be ready. He ate well and drank freely, visited with old friends and made new ones. He bought some books and sat in the lobby of the City Hotel, on First Street, reading and watching the world pass by. When the tailoring was done, he put on the first of two sets of identical clothing in the shop, and told the tailor to give his old things to someone poor and deserving.

He left resplendent in the first things he'd ever worn made just for him, and they fit him perfectly. Still favoring black to enable him to disappear into the shadows, his shirt was elaborately embroidered and fitted with silver buttons. Over it, a black vest had plenty of pockets for anything he might need to carry, and he had an embroidered black coat to go over that. His pants were snug, the outer seams lined with silver conchos. He continued his tradition of wrapping a scarlet sash around his waist. He wasn't wearing his gun belt now, but he was accustomed to arranging the sash to ensure easy access to the pistol and knife hanging from it. He still needed new boots and a new hat, but he had determined to wait until the clothes were finished so he could choose the ones that would match the best.

Eating lunch, Joaquin noticed that an earlier diner had abandoned some newspapers on a nearby table. He scanned the first, a recent issue of the *San Jose Weekly Visitor*, but it was focused on the activities of the legislature and white society, and he quickly lost interest. But beneath that one was the *El Dorado Republican*, which had written about his exploits before. He picked it up and saw that it was almost three weeks old. Before setting it aside, though, he spotted a story about the horse theft. He scanned it, looking for anything he didn't already know about the horses or their owner, and halfway down found an almost familiar name. "The leader of the band of brigands told Charyn that his name was Joaquin Murriata. Some reports from Murphys Diggings speculate that this is the same man responsible for more than a dozen vicious murders in the Spring, including the brutal beheading of the town's marshal, just hours after this publisher spoke with the doomed lawman."

Murriata. He scowled at that. Somehow, he had to let people know who he was. He understood that some bandits wanted to remain anonymous, hoping never to be caught. He had thought Pico foolish for becoming well known, but as his own fame grew, he had developed a different philosophy. If people feared him before they ever saw him, then that fear would work in his favor. He wanted Americans to scare their children with tales of his doings. Cutting the head off a law-man was a good start—even though that had been Tres Dedos, not him—but only if people ascribed the act to the right Joaquin.

His gut in an uproar, he left his lunch half-eaten and walked around the Mexican part of town, enjoying the music of the Spanish language being spoken, and the actual music of fiddles and guitars and accordions coming from businesses and courtyards. That calmed him. He briefly considered moving back to Mexico, but as quickly dismissed the notion. He had sworn not to return until he was a rich man, and although he could afford his own needs now, he had not come anywhere close to being truly wealthy.

Anyway, those who had mistreated him were all here, in California. Yes, he had killed the men who had personally done him great wrongs, but the environment that had created those men, given them license to do those things, remained. Too many Mexicans were still in California, and as long as they were, Joaquin would stay and fight. For them as much as for himself.

As he walked back to the hotel, an aroma grabbed his attention and he followed it to a panadería, a Mexican bakery called Molinera's. When he entered, the sights and scents of pan dulce, tres leches cakes, bolillo, empanadas, cookies, tortillas, and more whisked him back to Mexico, back to childhood, when his father might be willing to spare a couple of pesos for a treat. A sweaty man behind the counter, his forehead and arms dusted with flour, was putting something into an oven with a large, wooden paddle. In the front of the shop a shorter woman filled a customer's order with a smile. She raised her head at Joaquin and greeted him.

"This place smells fantastic," he said.

"It is fantastic," the customer ahead of him said. She was a stout lady in skirts and an apron, but she gave him a grin as she tucked her wares into a net bag. "You've never been?"

"I'm not from here. I just smelled it up the block."

"You'll love it." She shouldered past him and out the door.

"What would you like?" the shopkeeper asked.

"One of everything," Joaquin said.

She grinned. "Do you want to eat it all here, or take it with you?"

Before he could answer, another woman stepped into view from around a corner, carrying a basket of breads. She was considerably younger than the first two, and beautiful. Her eyes were light brown, almost the color of cinnamon, and sparkled with intelligence. When her gaze met Joaquin's, she glanced away, then returned his look. Her cheekbones were high, her forehead smooth, with heavy brows. Her jawline was pronounced; that and a firm, slightly squared chin framed lush, pink lips curled into a smile. All of it was enhanced by hair like flowing honey, pulled back into a braid that dropped almost to her waist. From what he could tell through her clothes, she was slender, but not overly so.

"Sir?" the shopkeeper asked.

He'd forgotten where he was for a moment. He hadn't been with a woman since Rosita's death. In the mining camps and the towns of that region, women were rare—a handful of miner's wives and some prostitutes were the only ones around, and he hadn't been interested in either. Most of the people he'd spent time with had been men. No woman had caught his attention like this one.

"Hello," he said. The young woman stopped, obviously aware that he was addressing her.

"Good afternoon," she said. "My mother asked you a question." Her accent had traces of Mexico in it, but that was all. She had lived in California a long time, he guessed.

"Your mother?"

The young woman nodded her head toward the older one, still waiting at the counter for Joaquin's order. He looked her way for an instant, but his gaze returned to the younger almost instantly. "I am Joaquin Murrieta," he said. "And you are . . .?"

She gave a brief curtsy and set down the basket. "Antonia Molinera."

"My daughter," the shopkeeper said.

Joaquin looked at her again, searching for some familial resemblance and not seeing it. The older woman was small, dark, her face creased with deep lines. Strands of gray twined through her thick, black hair. Mostly Indian, he guessed, but the young woman had plenty of Spanish blood. Then he glanced at the man working in the back, tall and muscular. What hair he had was clipped short, but most of his scalp shone with sweat. The Spaniard in her came from him, then.

"It's a pleasure to meet you," Joaquin said. "I was drawn in by the aroma, but I was rendered speechless by your loveliness."

"Obviously not speechless," Antonia said. Her voice was stern, but the smile never left her eyes. She was perhaps a few years older than he, but something in her carriage, the planes of her face, and her sly smile suggested that she was far more worldly. Of course, he was no longer the innocent boy he had been when he'd wed Rosita and run away to America, so perhaps he was her equal in sophistication after all.

"Not entirely speechless, at that," he said.

"Sir, what would you like today?" the shopkeeper broke in. "Antonia is not on the menu."

His stomach was no longer the part of his anatomy on his mind, but he had to buy something, or the woman would throw him out. "Her basket."

"Her basket is not for sale."

"Everything in it," he said.

"Everything?"

"And the basket. But only if she'll bring it to me."

The old woman studied him. He was glad he was wearing new, tailored clothes, and hoped she didn't pay attention to his beat-up boots and hat. For the most part, he looked like a well-to-do gentleman.

"I don't think—" the woman began, but Antonia talked over her.

"Of course," she said. "It'll be the biggest sale of the day. Add it up, Mother."

She picked the basket up off the worktable and carried it toward Joaquin. At the counter she did a half-spin that ended with an aggressive thrust of her hip, and she stopped before Joaquin, holding the basket at her waist. "Here it is, sir."

"Delicious," he said. His gaze left no doubt that he didn't mean the breads.

"I'm sure you'll find them so. My father's the best baker in San José."

"I'm glad I happened into his shop, then. I do have a taste for baked goods."

"Is that all?"

"Oh, no. I have a fondness for many of life's pleasures. Perhaps I could see you sometime and we could discuss them."

"I hardly know you," Antonia said.

"With a chaperone, if you wish."

"Still."

"Sir?" he said, addressing the father. "Might I have the privilege of accompanying the young lady?"

The man looked up from his work, kneading dough on a table, and said, "The girl knows her own mind."

"Then I have your blessing, should she agree?"

The man shrugged. "She's been her own creature for years, now. If she agrees, she agrees."

Joaquin turned back to her. She still wore that smile, but he couldn't tell if it spoke of interest or merely patience. "A walk?"

"When I know you better. Not before."

"But how will you get to know me?"

She ticked her head toward the basket of breads. "When you finish those, you'll need more."

The older woman laughed softly, and added, "And my husband is always baking."

34

Joaquin left San José the next morning, without even bothering to acquire new boots or a hat. The warm glow imparted by his new clothes had faded somewhat after his encounter with Antonia Molinera. She hadn't rejected him, exactly, but neither had she taken him up on his obvious advance. He was left wondering if he'd been overly forward, or not direct enough. He had been with Rosita for so long that he had no experience with other women, and he wasn't sure how to approach them. He was naturally confident, and he thought he was handsome enough—especially with his brand-new outfit on—to be desirable to anyone. But women were strange beasts. Even Rosita, who he'd known for most of his life, had sometimes had moods unfathomable to him.

That, and his misidentification as Murriata, combined to sour his own mood. The bread he'd inadvertently bought from the Molineras was as good as it had smelled, but eating it reminded him of his failure, so he wound up giving it to some Mexicans who worked at the City Hotel. By lunchtime, he was starving and wishing he'd kept some of it, which further angered him.

He stopped for lunch and to wet his throat at a roadside tavern between San José and Ojo del Agua. Before entering, he made sure his sash and his coat covered his gun belt, because he didn't want to be caught in a strange place without protection. He found the whiskey watered down but passable, the beef stringy and tough, but the beans pretty tasty. As he ate, he thought he heard someone calling his name. His right hand dropped to the butt of his pistol and he held it there while he cautiously looked around to see who had done it.

No one paid him any attention. He took another forkful of beans and watched. A couple of minutes later, he heard it again, coming from the lips of an American man who hadn't even glanced his way. Then he realized they were talking about the exploits of Joaquin Murriata, the nonexistent outlaw. He stopped chewing and listened.

"That damn Murriata showed his face around me, it'd be the last thing the bastard ever did," one man said. "I'd fill his greaser gut so full o' lead they wouldn't have to dig his grave, he'd just sink down through the dirt."

The man's companion—the one who he'd first heard mentioning him—guffawed. "I'd like to see that son of a bitch myself," he said. "Those folks he killed must'a been some weak sisters, to let some Mex punk get the drop on 'em like that."

A couple of men at the next table overheard the conversation and chimed in, describing the things they would do to Murriata if he were so foolish as to show his face in the area. There were also various theories as to his parentage, his looks, and his sexual practices, which included sheep, goats, dogs, and eventually snakes. Joaquin found that one particularly odd, and spent some time trying to imagine how that would even work. Unsuccessful at that task, he finished his lunch, paid, and prepared to get back on the road.

Joaquin was on his feet when one more white American started in on how he would handle the outlaw Murriata. It had to do with punching the bandit's face into jelly, then cutting off his head and displaying it on a pike outside the man's home.

Joaquin took two steps toward the door, fully intending to leave, but pride stopped him. He had halted beside an empty monte table, so he stepped up onto a chair, and from there onto the table. By that point, the dozen or so men in the saloon were all staring at him. He threw back his coat and drew his pistol. Meeting the gaze of each man in turn, he shouted, "I am Joaquin Murrieta! If there's any killing to be done here, I'll do it! Now, who wants to be the first?"

Nobody went for a weapon. One man's mouth dropped open and beans spilled out onto a shirt that had obviously soaked up plenty of food before. Another made a show of looking down at his hands, which he'd pressed flat against a table so firmly they were going white. The saloonkeeper slowly lowered himself behind his bar until he had disappeared entirely.

"So it's all talk," Joaquin said. "As I thought. Brave Americans, the lot of you."

He stepped down from the table and went out the door. Outside, a new horse waited—one he'd acquired from the ranch theft, and which he hadn't named yet—and he climbed on. As he rode away from the saloon, he wondered if he had really hoped someone would challenge him, give him a reason to shoot. He thought, in the moment, that he had. His finger had rested on the trigger, twitching as if it wanted to pull. But to shoot a man for no reason? Was that really who he'd become?

He couldn't know for sure.

And that uncertainty was more than a little troubling.

• • •

Some of the men had brought their women to the camp at Arroyo de Cantua. Joaquin hadn't objected—a man needed his pleasures, after all, and he knew that the love of a woman could be the greatest joy of all.

But having failed to make any headway with the only woman who'd interested him since losing Rosita made him resent their presence. Some of those men were homely, unschooled, lacking in even the most basic of social graces. *They* could attract a female, and he couldn't? The idea enraged him. Besides, having a woman elevated one's standing, and although he already led them, he knew some made fun of him— when they thought he wasn't aware—for being without one.

So when he saw Sophia Gordo—Pedro Vergara's woman— storming toward him with her skirts bunched up in her fists, her brows arched and a scowl on her plain face, he knew there was trouble coming. Further, he knew he'd have to try to control his temper or he would explode.

"What is it, Sophia?" he asked. Trying to keep his voice pleasant, but not entirely sure that he succeeded.

"It's that bastard Reis Carrillo," she said. From the tone of her voice and the set of her jaw, Joaquin wouldn't have been surprised to see her start snorting and pawing at the earth. "He's got a woman in his tent."

"Reis? Good for him."

"Not good. She's been bawling like a newborn ever since she came. I tried talking to her, telling her it's not so bad here. I even tried to tell her that Reis is a good man, but lying makes my throat dry and I couldn't get it out."

"What's her problem?"

"She's here against her will. He took her from her home,

right in front of her widowed mother and her own lover. She wants to go back."

"He stole her?"

"At gunpoint, according to Pedro."

"Why didn't Pedro stop him?"

"Have you ever tried to stop Reis from doing something stupid?"

Joaquin had to ponder that. He'd seen Carrillo do some stupid things during the time they'd been together, but nothing so destructive that he'd had to intercede. "I think not."

"Once he gets an idea in that thick head of his, it's hard to shake it loose. Pedro didn't want that gun pointed at him, that's all."

"When did they arrive?"

"Late yesterday," she said. "She's been wailing ever since."

"Do you think he's had his way with her?"

"I told him if he did, I'd yank off his balls and feed them to him before he died."

Joaquin didn't doubt that she had, or that she would follow through on the threat. "I'll talk to him," he said. "Thank you for telling me, Sophia."

"Just do something!" She spun in place, still just as angry as when he'd first seen her. She seemed to live her life in that state. He wondered why Vergara liked her, why he'd brought her to the camp in the first place. Then again, Vergara was no prize—he was one of the stupidest men Joaquin had ever known, a brute who'd kill anyone and not lose an instant's sleep over it. But at least he had a woman. That put him one up on Joaquin.

The camp hadn't been deliberately organized, but in the fashion of most human habitations, it had settled into a reasonably efficient shape. Joaquin slept in the single intact room of the old house, where an iron bedstead still stood, rusty but usable. The room also boasted an oil lamp and a copper tub in which he bathed, in creek water heated outside at the fire. Tres Dedos slept outside the doorway, a human blockade against anyone who might try to challenge Joaquin. Those who had tents pitched them around the house in a disorderly maze of every size, color, and description, each far enough from the others to allow some degree of privacy. Most were worn and patched, but each man knew which was his, or which he shared, and with whom. Some of those without tents had constructed little dwellings of tree branches, mud, and whatever animal skins, canvas, or boards they could scrounge. Others slept under the stars.

The house contained a fireplace, and a few fire pits were scattered here and there, including a pair of large ones where most of the cooking took place. The creek provided water for drinking and bathing, and a latrine area had been established downstream.

Carrillo's tent was devoid of color, so long had it stood in sun and wind and rain. It had been patched at least a dozen times, and some tears remained. So did the bloodstains left by the two men Carrillo had killed when he took it, at least in his telling. As Joaquin neared it, he could hear sobbing from within, and a soft voice seemingly trying to comfort the one crying.

"Reis!" he shouted.

A rustle from inside the tent, and bulges appeared on the wall. Then the flap flew back. Carrillo emerged, straightening up as he did. He was tall, gangly, and had to exit the tent hunched over to half his size.

"Yes, boss?"

"Wait over there." Joaquin pointed to a spot a few meters away from the tent. "I'll deal with you in a minute."

Carrillo eyed him with a mixture of concern and suspicion, his thin face elongated even more than usual by a dropped chin and a raised brow. His mustache drooped below his prominent nose, the ends dangling beneath his chin like tiny appendages. "Yes, boss," he said. Then he added, "Does this have to do with the girl?"

"In a minute," Joaquin repeated.

"Yes, boss." Carrillo went to the spot Joaquin had indicated, crossed his arms over his chest, and studied his feet.

The girl's sobs continued, but when Joaquin pulled back the claps and entered, she let out a shriek. "I'm not going to hurt you," he said. His patience was already at an ebb; if she didn't quit with the tears, he was going to lose it altogether.

She nodded her head and swallowed. She was, he had to admit, simply stunning. Blond, with a fair face that could have been sculpted by the finest artist in Europe, her huge blue eyes were its most pronounced feature. They were perhaps exaggerated by the tears still flowing from them, as if from an eternal fountain. Her physique was likewise stunning, slim in spots and curvaceous in others. Barely out of her teens, if that, she was one of the most beautiful creatures Joaquin had ever laid eyes on. For a moment, he considered leaving the tent and congratulating Carrillo on his excellent taste in companions.

But he had set some rules for his men, and if Sophia's story was true, Carrillo had broken one of them. "Don't worry, nothing will happen to you," he said. "What's your name?"

"Sadie," she said. "Sadie Ann Avery."

"Tell me what Reis did, Sadie."

Between bouts of sniffling and weeping, she told the same tale that Sophia had. Carrillo had, she claimed, seen her on the street and decided then and there to take her. Her fiancé had been walking her to her mother's house, and they were almost there when Carrillo approached them, pistol drawn. He forced them into the house, then made her gather a few things she wouldn't want to be without. When her fiancé objected, Carrillo slashed the man's face with his gun, knocking him down and opening a bloody wound. Once she had the few things she needed, he dragged her outside, put her on his horse, climbed up behind her, and brought her to the camp.

"Has he touched you?" Joaquin asked when she finished.

"Of course. I just told you he did."

"That's not what I mean. Do I have to be specific?"

She shook her head. "No, I know what you mean. The brute has put his hands on me in . . . places. But he has not ravished me."

"Do you want to go home, or stay?"

"Home!" she said quickly. "I want to go home, please."

"You don't like Reis?"

"I despise him. He hurt my Franklin."

"Franklin is your lover?"

"He is my betrothed. And he's a gentleman."

"So he has not 'ravished' you, either?"

"Of course not."

Joaquin couldn't contain a snort of laughter. "What kind of man is he? You might be better off with Reis, or someone like him. Someone who knows how to treat a real woman."

The tears started spilling from those enormous eyes again. "Please," she said. "Take me home."

"I will. Or rather, Reis will. With something for your

troubles."

She wiped her nose with the back of her hand and sniffed. "Do you mean it?"

"I am Joaquin Murrieta," he said. "I keep my promises."

She took a few deep breaths. Her mouth was open, her bosom heaving with every inhalation, and for a few moments he thought she might offer herself to him in gratitude. She would be hard to turn down, but he steeled himself against the possibility. Not only would Carrillo forever seek the moment in which he could drive a knife into his heart, but now that he had met her, he wanted only Antonia Molinera.

Who—like this girl and Carrillo—didn't want him.

But he had rules, and one of them was that women must be respected. Only those who wanted to be with his men would be. He would not countenance forcible arrangements. Some of the men groused about this rule, and a couple had even left the band over it, unwilling to give up rape even for the greater profit that came from riding with successful outlaws. He would not bend, though.

"Wait here, Sadie," he said, tearing his gaze away from her. "I'll talk to him and tell him what to do."

"Will you go with us?" she asked.

"Do you want me to?"

"I don't trust him."

Joaquin rubbed his chin. "Come to think of it, neither do I. I'll go with you."

"Oh, thank you," she said, blinking away tears. "You truly are a savior."

"I wouldn't go that far," he countered. "But I will keep you safe."

35

Carrillo didn't like it, but he also didn't dare go against Joaquin. He might come for him later, Joaquin knew—a knife in the back, a bullet in the heat of battle—but those were the chances one took anytime he commanded a group of fighting men. Rules had to be made and enforced, but the very act of enforcement—which commanded respect and made a man into a leader—also made enemies.

That night, Sadie slept in Joaquin's bed. He slept outside the room, listening to Tres Dedos's snores, which could have shaken the roof down if the room had a roof. In the morning, Joaquin, Tres Dedos, Carrillo, Manuel Sevalio, Gregorio Lopez, and Pancho Dominguez mounted up and rode six hours, to a farming community not far from Monterey. Carrillo tried briefly to claim that he didn't remember where the girl's house was, but she spotted a rock outcropping that was familiar, and knew the way from there.

They arrived at a small, wooden farmhouse surrounded by fields cultivated with vegetables, and one meadow in which some sheep munched tall grass. Sadie's mother was sitting at the table, her eyes and nose red from crying, when Sadie burst in. The older woman lunged toward her, knocking her chair over backward. It clanged against the woodstove before it clattered to the plank floor. "Sadie!" she cried. Despite her silver hair and lined face, it was easy to see where Sadie's beauty had come from.

"Momma! I'm home!"

"Are you—" Sadie's mother looked at the doorway and saw the Mexican men crowding through, Carrillo among them. "Have you come back for me, now?" she demanded. "If my husband were alive, he—"

Sadie broke in and pointed at Joaquin, then Carrillo. "Momma, that one's Joaquin. He protected me from that devil, the one who took me. He made him bring me back."

The woman started toward Carrillo, her hands turning into claws, and she eyed a knife laying on a sideboard. Sadie grabbed her, held her back. "Let them speak," she implored.

"Ma'am, I am sorry," Carrillo said. Joaquin had made him practice the words throughout the ride. "I am sorry I took your daughter. I am sorry I hurt her friend."

"Did he touch you?" her mother asked Sadie.

"Not that way. Not the way you're thinking."

"Are you sure?"

"I'm certain. I would know. I would tell you if that happened."

Carrillo reached into his shirt and withdrew a bag of gold nuggets from a previous robbery. Joaquin had known he'd had it, and told him it was the price he had to pay. It was either that, or he'd let Vergara's woman have her way.

He had agreed immediately.

"This is for you," Carrillo said, handing her the bag. "For your trouble."

"Where's Franklin?" Sadie asked.

"He went to the doctor, in Monterey," the woman said. "He was going to try to raise a posse to go after you."

"He mustn't," Sadie said. "I'm perfectly safe. Joaquin made sure of it."

Sadie's mother studied him, and Joaquin could almost see the puzzle pieces fall into place for her. "You're the bandit Joaquin?" she asked.

He gave a little half-bow. "At your service."

"And you protected my daughter from that beast?"

"We have a rule against such behavior," Joaquin said. "He was so struck by Sadie's beauty that he forgot it, but I reminded him. He understands he did wrong, and he'll never do it again."

"Can you be sure?"

"If he breaks the rule again, his punishment will be swift. And painful."

"I think he deserves it now."

"Another rule," Joaquin said. "Everyone gets a second chance. He has returned her unharmed and paid you for your worry."

"Momma, I'm fine," Sadie said. "Joaquin made sure of it." She pointed out Vergara. "And that one's friend, a woman, took care of me as well. Even Reis wasn't so bad. He just frightened me."

"And was nearly the death of me. And Franklin."

"I am so sorry that happened, Momma," Sadie said. She wrapped her arms around her mother, in what was perhaps as much as a preventive measure as an embrace. "Especially for you."

Her mother took a step back and gave her a stern look. "What does that mean?"

"Franklin didn't protect me. He hardly even tried to fight off Reis."

"The man's a ruffian, and he had a gun! What would you expect Franklin to do against that?"

"We have a Brown Bess. And knives. Cast-iron pots. He could have found some weapon. Instead, he tried to use fisticuffs, and Reis got the better of him in an instant. He didn't even have to shoot. I'm only saying, there are men who would have done more."

"Franklin's a good man. He has a career."

"In a bank. He works with numbers, not with his hands. He's soft."

"Mrs. Avery? Miss Sadie?" Joaquin offered another bow. If he listened to any more of this, he'd be sick. "We'll let you two discuss this in our absence. We're sorry to have troubled you, and we're glad to see Miss Sadie safely back in her own home. Should any further harm come to her at any time, you have only to tell any Mexican that I'm needed, and I'll be here. We won't trouble you any further."

Sadie released her mother and took two steps toward Joaquin, then stopped herself, as if only then remembering proper comportment. She curtsied briefly. "Thank you, sir, for your good manners and gentlemanly ways. You won't be soon forgotten."

Her mother started to say something else, but Sadie silenced her with a glance. Joaquin pushed open the door and gestured the other men outside, and with a final smile for the ladies, he followed.

As they walked to the horses, Carrillo said, "I think she liked me."

Joaquin stepped nearer and grabbed the man's crotch in his hand, squeezed, and said, "If you want to keep these where they are, you'll never think of her again."

Carrillo's face blanched, and he swallowed hard and nodded his understanding.

Joaquin relaxed his grip and went to his own horse. As he mounted the big mare, he added, "Everyone in the camp knows by now. And we're all more afraid of Sophia than we are of you."

"I don't blame you," Carrillo said. "I would be, too."

"But you see what you've done? If she doesn't somehow reach Franklin, he'll raise an army to come after us, or try to."

"Everything we do makes them want to kill us," Carrillo argued. "What's the difference?"

"There's no profit in stealing a woman, fool. What's the point?"

"To have a woman?"

Joaquin had to concede that he made a certain amount of sense. "We're in this together," he said. "We steal something, we all share the loot. You steal a woman, she's just yours. Not only is it against my laws, but you can't share her with everyone. If gringos are going to try to kill us, let's make sure it's for something we all profit from."

Carrillo nodded. He looked glum at the prospect of leaving without Sadie.

But his balls were still where they belonged, so Joaquin figured he should be happy with the outcome.

"I saw a bank in that little town on the way here," he announced to the others. "If we're going to be chased, let's at least try to make it worth our while."

• • •

The men fell asleep to the deafening buzz of crickets that night and woke to the racket of grackles, their cries rasping like rusty gate-hinges. The town that they'd passed through on the way was barely that—just a crossing of dirt roads with a feed store, a dry-goods store, the bank Joaquin had spotted, a saloon, and a few scattered homes. The businesses served the surrounding farms. The buildings were sun-bleached and dusty, and when the outlaws rode into town in the morning, they saw a horse tied to a rail outside the dry-goods store.

"If there's any money in that bank," Tres Dedos said, "it's probably less than the price of a bullet."

"It's early yet. When we came through before, there were more people around."

"Do you have a plan?" Dominguez asked. He was quite fond of plans, Joaquin had noticed.

Joaquin laughed. "A plan? Why do we need a plan?

"We've never robbed a bank, Joaquin. I'd feel better if we had a plan."

Joaquin considered whether to slap the man, shoot him, or humor him. Finally, he said, "Here's our plan. We go in the front door with guns drawn, demand the money, and leave. A bank like this will be simple to rob."

"I haven't been in a lot of banks," Tres Dedos said. "Don't they usually have guards? If I had that much money in one place, I'd keep a close eye on it."

"Do you see any guards? Any people at all? Trust me, cousin, this will be the easiest money we've ever made."

Joaquin didn't see any reason to delay. He dismounted and directed Dominguez to stay outside with the horses. He and the other men drew pistols and went in. The inside was almost as dusty as the outside, giving the impression that nobody had been there in weeks. There were two barred windows on the other side of a blank stretch of tile floor, and behind those a doorway, through which Joaquin saw part of a large safe. At first the building appeared empty, but then a man stepped out of the other room carrying a tray of some kind. "Can I help you gentlemen?" he asked. A quaver in his voice suggested that he already knew what they wanted.

"Is Franklin here?"

At that, the man seemed to take some slight relief. "No, not presently. Can I tell him you asked after him?"

"Never mind. That safe is open, yes?"

"You can see that for yourself." The man was slight, with thinning hair and small spectacles perched on a tiny nub of a nose. He was trying to keep his terror from showing, but his lower lip was trembling, and he could hardly hang onto his tray.

"Then you can help us. Or we can get the money ourselves. That's up to you."

"I'll get it," the man said.

"All of it. Sevalio, go back there and make sure he doesn't miss any."

Sevalio nodded and went around the counter. The man had already disappeared into the other room, so Sevalio hurried to catch up. He always wore Mexican spurs with big silver rowels, and they jingled as his boots clicked on the floor tiles.

By the time Sevalio reached the doorway, the banker was already at the safe. Joaquin saw a sudden flurry of motion. "Sevalio!" he cried.

Too late. The next thing he heard was the boom of a shotgun, and the wet splatter as the load ripped a hole through Sevalio's middle, blowing blood and flesh and innards across the room. The banker swung back into the main room with the double-barreled shotgun in his hands, looking for his next target. The first blast still echoed through the empty space and rang in Joaquin's ears, and smoke hung in the air as what was left of Sevalio dropped to the floor.

Joaquin fired first, but three other guns joined in. Joaquin's shot crashed through the man's right lens and into his eye. As his head snapped back, three more rounds struck him. He dropped the shotgun, but stayed on his feet a few moments longer. Joaquin almost fired again, then saw that the life was ebbing from the man as his blood splashed onto the floor. He sank to his knees and pitched forward, his out-flung left hand lying in a pool of Sevalio's blood.

"Get the money," Joaquin ordered.

Lopez was the first one at the safe, stepping through the gore as if it were just spilled water. Carrillo followed. Tres Dedos crossed to the bank's front door and stood just inside, watching the street. Joaquin stayed where he was, watching the other men empty the safe into some money bags they found inside. The jangle of coins piling up was the sweetest music.

It didn't take Carrillo long to dash his hopes. "There's not much in here, boss," he said. He came back through the door carrying two bags. Lopez held one more.

Not much indeed.

"I didn't expect there would be, in such a small town," Joaquin said. "But we needed something to show for our troubles."

They stepped carefully past the banker, who was still twitching on the floor, blood seeping from his ruined eye. Tres Dedos met Joaquin's gaze. "Looks clear," he said. "But that made more noise than a virgin on her wedding night."

"The town's still asleep," Joaquin said. "There won't be any trouble." He shouldered past Tres Dedos and went outside.

The other men followed. Pancho Dominguez looked anxious, and so did the horses.

"Saddle up," Joaquin said. "We need to get out of here."

"Not so fast," another voice said. Joaquin spun around to see two men coming out of the dry-goods store. One was stout, wearing an apron, and his hands were empty. But the other wore the sky-blue pants of an American soldier and had a pistol in his hands.

Someone behind Joaquin fired first, but his shot flew wide, kicking up dirt in the road a dozen feet away.

The soldier fired back, but his round only knocked adobe from the bank wall.

Joaquin and Tres Dedos both shot at once. Joaquin missed, but his cousin's aim was true. A red blossom spread on the man's shirt. He remained upright, though, and fired again, his aim thrown off only a little by his wound.

Lopez cried out. Joaquin didn't dare see if he'd been hit, but he corrected his aim and shot the man in the upper chest. More guns barked around him, and with three more rounds in him, he finally buckled. He squeezed off one more shot on his way down, but it soared into the air and disappeared.

Now Joaquin turned to Lopez. He was bleeding from a gash at his temple, but it looked like a shallow wound. "Can you ride?"

"Yes, Joaquin," Lopez said. "It's not too bad."

"On your horses!" Joaquin shouted. "Let's go!"

He was helping Lopez into his saddle when he heard a rustling behind him. The shopkeeper had snatched up the other man's pistol and held it in two quaking hands. He didn't even seem to take aim, but simply fired into the group of men before him. His first shot hit Tres Dedos's horse in the muzzle, and his second struck Carrillo in the small of the back.

Carillo stumbled. Joaquin caught him and lowered him to the ground. Tres Dedos and Lopez returned the shopkeeper's fire, both hitting him several times. When he dropped the gun, Tres Dedos stormed over to him, holstering his own gun and drawing one of his knives. The man sank to the earth and sat there, tears rolling down his pudgy cheeks, as Tres Dedos approached.

"You're about to be a dead man," Tres Dedos said. "How does it feel?"

The other man mumbled something in return, but Joaquin couldn't make it out. His arms were full of Carrillo, who was bleeding heavily and whimpering from the pain. The horses were making noise, too, stomping and kicking and braying. "Can you get on a horse?" Joaquin asked.

"No, I don't . . . I can't. I can't feel my legs."

"You'll be fine, we just need to get away from here."

"Am I dying, Joaquin?"

"You'll be fine, I said!"

He heard the sound of Tres Dedos's knife cutting flesh and bone, and the strangled scream the shopkeeper gave out cut suddenly short. He didn't want to think about what Tres Dedos was doing. And his reassurances to Carrillo notwithstanding, he was beginning to doubt his own promise. If he released Carrillo, the man would pitch forward or back; his legs seemed no longer to work on their own. He was holding Carrillo up against one of the horses, to help with the man's weight, but the horses were on the verge of panic, and the one that had been shot was down on its front knees, screaming in pain and trying to shake the fire from its muzzle.

"Somebody kill that horse!" he cried, no longer able to

think through the racket. The animal wouldn't survive, and its pain was unbearable. Lopez put a gun next to the roan's skull and fired twice. Blood and bone matter flew from its head, but it went slack and fell onto its side, quiet at last.

"Pancho, help me get Carrillo onto my horse!"

Dominguez joined him, and together they hefted Carrillo up, draping him over the back of Joaquin's horse. Carrillo cried out in agony. "Get some rope!" Joaquin ordered. "Tie his wrists to his ankles so he doesn't fall off. And hurry!"

He climbed into his own saddle, looking this way and that, expecting more townsfolk to come see what the commotion was. So far, all remained quiet.

Tres Dedos mounted up. Lopez finished tying Carrillo onto Joaquin's horse, then did the same. Pancho was the last, trying his best to keep the others' horses calm until they were all ready. Then he scrambled into his saddle.

"Let's ride!" Joaquin shouted, adding, "This town isn't so quiet after all."

36

Fearing the possibility of being tracked back to Arroyo de Cantua, the men rode east, toward the Sierra Nevada. The wide-open space of the valley here would make it easy to spot pursuit, Joaquin reasoned. And if they had to go to ground, small communities scattered here and there could hide them if need be.

After about an hour, he realized that Carrillo hadn't been moaning or whining for some time. "Hold up!" he called, raising a hand. The others reined to a halt around him. Joaquin pulled off his hat, wiped sweat from his eyes, and turned in the saddle. Carrillo was still. Blood had ceased to drain from the wound in his back. Joaquin reached over and gave him a nudge.

No response.

"Is he dead?" Tres Dedos asked.

"I think so."

Tres Dedos jumped down from his horse—once Carrillo's, but when his own horse had been killed, Tres Dedos had appropriated the one Carrillo didn't need—and lifted Carrillo's head. Joaquin couldn't see the man's sightless eyes, but he didn't need to.

"We should dump him," Tres Dedos said. "He's extra weight for your mount."

"We should bury him," Pancho Dominguez said.

"That takes time."

"It's only right!"

"There might be people after us."

"Look back there!" Dominguez said, waving his hand toward the west. "Do you see any dust cloud other than our own?"

Joaquin shielded his eyes against the sun and scanned the horizon. "I don't."

"Then we should bury him. In the army, we—"

Tres Dedos cut him off. "Should we fetch a priest? Find a churchyard? The man's dead. He doesn't care where his body lies."

"His spirit cares."

"Joaquin, my cousin," Tres Dedos said. "It's sweet that Pancho is a pious man. But does he understand who we are? What we do?"

"Of course I do, Manuel," Dominguez said.

"We steal. We kill. We're not exactly the kind of men that priests look kindly on. I doubt your God does, either."

"The Lord despises our sins, but He loves us. We will be forgiven."

"I think there's a limit to what he'll forgive," Tres Dedos said. "We've reached it and gone beyond. You might not have, yet. Perhaps you'd be better off rid of us."

"I go where Joaquin goes. I'm no general. I take orders; I don't give them."

"We have no shovels," Joaquin said, anxious to put an end to the discussion. "And it's more than Sevalio got. But if you want, we can pile stones over him, and you can say a prayer."

"I'd like that," Dominguez said. "We can keep it short."

"We'd better," Tres Dedos growled. He wasn't happy, but he carried the biggest stones of anyone, and when Dominguez spoke, Joaquin thought he detected a tear in his cousin's eye.

• • •

By nightfall they had reached the foothills of the Sierra Nevada. They made camp there, and in the morning, cut north and skirted the mountains until they reached the Sonoranian Camp. Carrillo had a brother there, and Joaquin wanted to tell him the fate that had befallen his sibling. That took most of the day, so that night they slept at the home of Tres Dedos's friend Alfredo Punte. Much of the next day was spent visiting with friends, drinking and laughing and singing songs from home. Heading south, they got a later start than intended, and by the time they reached the ferry landing to cross the Tuolumne River it was almost midnight, and no ferryman was around. A rare summer downpour had swollen the river, and no one wanted to try swimming their horses across it.

"We'll just take the ferry and leave it on the other side," Joaquin said. "The man can swim over tomorrow to retrieve it."

He dismounted and walked down the well-trodden path to the ferry. It was a simple raft, planks set across logs, with wooden railing all around to keep people and animals in place. Ropes linked it to a similar landing on the far side. But heavy iron chains held the ferry fast to the dock, and two huge padlocks joined the chains. Nothing Joaquin or the others carried would break those chains, and although they could try shooting the locks, even that might not work.

"It's locked up tight," he said, returning to the others. "Big chains and bigger locks. We need the keys."

"We need the ferryman," Lopez said.

"Yes, that's what we need. Good thinking, Gregorio. We'll rouse him." The ferryman lived in a little cabin just over the rise. They'd passed his home to reach this spot.

He walked his horse while the others rode, back to the top

of the low hill and over its crest. The cabin stood beside the road, with a row of pines beside it to block the winds from the east. All the men dismounted, and Joaquin pounded on the door with the grip of his pistol.

A minute passed. Joaquin was about to knock again when he heard a shuffling noise inside, and then a key turning in the lock. The door opened a few inches, and a man holding an oil lamp showed his face. "Who's out there?" he asked.

Joaquin pressed the barrel of his pistol under the man's chin. The man was gaunt, with unkempt brown hair, wearing only a long drawers cinched with a belt. His eyes widened in surprise and he bobbled the lamp, almost dropping it. "Your next passengers," Joaquin told him.

"Ferry's closed until morning."

Joaquin pushed the barrel deeper into the man's tender flesh. "I believe it is morning, or near enough. The ferry's open again."

"All right, all right. Let me put some boots on and get the keys." He backed away from the door and started to close it.

"We'll wait inside," Joaquin said. He caught the door and shoved it open. "And while we're here, we'll borrow whatever money you've collected from your previous passengers."

"Borrow?" the ferryman asked. Joaquin could see that he was afraid but determined not to show it. He respected that. "That means you'll give it back. I'll loan you what I got, but you'll be disappointed."

"Well, not borrow, perhaps. Let's have it."

The man carried the lamp into a small kitchen area, with a stove, a cupboard, a table with two chairs, and some pots hanging from nails on the wall. He reached into the cupboard and took out a coffee can, which he emptied onto the table. An assortment of coins and a few demand notes spilled out.

"That's it?" Tres Dedos asked. "You need to raise your

prices."

"That's all I got."

"There must be more somewhere," Lopez insisted. "Don't try to hide it from us."

"I had it, I'd hand it over," the ferryman said. "I don't want to die. It takes most of what I make with the ferry to pay off the county sheriff, and I send some to my wife and boys in Kansas. I should'a gone back there when my claim was a bust, but I fell into this and stayed put. Anyhow, with outlaws all over the place, folks ain't traveling as much, so most days I don't make but one or two trips across."

"I can search the place," Dominguez offered.

"No, I believe him," Joaquin said. "He doesn't sound like a liar to me. He sounds like a poor but honest man."

"Poor, anyhow," the ferryman agreed. "Still, take what's there, just don't kill me."

Lopez took his hat off and started toward the table, intending to scoop the money into it. "Leave it," Joaquin said. "Keep your money, sir. Take us across the river, and we'll pay for our ride."

Tres Dedos eyed him with a raised eyebrow, but he didn't question Joaquin. The ferryman tugged on a wool shirt and some boots, pulled on an old hat, and took a ring of keys from a nail near the door. Thus outfitted, he led them back down to the river. There, he unlocked the raft, tossed aside the chains, and held it steady while his passengers boarded. The trip across the river took only minutes, with the ferryman heaving mightily at the ropes to keep the craft from being swept downriver by the strong current. At the other landing, he again steadied the raft for the bandits to disembark. All the while, he didn't speak a word.

"What's your usual fare?" Joaquin asked, once he was standing on the far bank.

"Two bits a person, dollar a horse."

"So, we'd owe you four dollars and eighty cents? That's not a bad wage for a few minutes of work."

"It ain't much when it only happens once or twice a day, if that."

"No, I suppose that's true. Gregorio, give me one of those sacks from the bank."

Lopez looked like he wanted to argue, but Joaquin thrust a hand at him. Lopez tugged a sack full of coins from a saddle-bag and handed it to him.

"Here," Joaquin said, placing the bag in the ferryman's hands. "This should cover our passage."

"That's too much," the ferryman said. "You don't need to—"

"I insist," Joaquin said. "Your wife and sons in Kansas—do they want to join you here?"

"They want nothing more than for us to be together again. There or here, either one."

"Perhaps that's enough, then. If not, surely it'll be close."

"But—"

Joaquin pressed a finger to the man's lips. "Say no more. You're a poor man. So are we, or we were. I'm a Mexican and you're white, but poverty binds us more than race divides us. Take the money, sir. And thank you for bringing us across. I'm sorry to have awakened you."

"I don't know what to . . ." the ferryman began. He shook his head. "Thank you, sir. You're a right honorable feller."

Joaquin gave a deep bow. "My name is Joaquin Murrieta. If anyone asks who woke you at gunpoint, tell them that. And if they ask you whether Joaquin has honor, be sure to tell the truth."

37

John Bigler—*Governor* John Bigler now, thanks to the intelligence and insight of California's voting public and the backing of some businessmen with money to spread around—dropped a newspaper onto the desk of Senator Thomas Jefferson Green. "*Daily Alta California.* Read the headline," Bigler said. "Never mind, you're probably seeing double, so I'll read it to you. 'Slaughter Near Monterey.'" He placed another paper on top of it, then added a third. "*Daily Union.* 'Bank Robbed, Men Murdered.' This one's the *Sacramento Transcript.* 'Mexican Murder Spree.'" He tossed one more onto the growing pile. "*El Dorado Republican.* 'Murriata Gang Suspected in Robbery-Murder.'"

Green tried to hide a smile, but he failed. "You're keeping the newspapers in business all by yourself, John?"

"Damn it, Green, this is serious business. These gangs are killing people. Whole towns are in an uproar. Something's got to be done."

"If we could direct them to kill the right people, it would make election day easier, wouldn't it?"

Green had an uncanny ability to find humor in any situation, however grave. It was maddening.

Bigler respected the man almost despite himself. Before coming to California to try his hand at mining—as had seemingly every other able-bodied man in the known world—

Green had served in the legislatures of both Florida and Texas. After giving up on the mining life, he had run and been elected to the legislature here. But trying to talk to him about a serious matter was frequently infuriating.

Green, however, chaired the Finance Committee, without which Bigler could get nothing done. A governor ought, Bigler believed, to have enough power to accomplish things without crawling to the legislature every time he turned around.

"Read those stories," Bigler said. "Mexican bandits are running rampant across our state, and we need to stop them. I propose offering a substantial reward, or alternatively, raising a force of our own to go after them. I met a man in Los Angeles, a fellow named Jakob Schmitt, who's good at putting greasers in their place. He's dead, but he told me about another man, name of Harry Love, from Santa Barbara. He might be someone we could—"

Green stopped him with a wave of his hand. He reached down, opened a desk drawer, and came back up with a jug. Spirits of some kind, without which it didn't seem that Green could get through a day. "There's no money," he said. He brought the jug to his mouth, tipped it, and swallowed. When he took it away, he offered it to Bigler, who shook his head. Green shrugged and said, "There's no money for the state's ongoing expenses, much less for anything like what you're proposing."

"McDougall never should've repealed the Foreign Miners' Tax. That was short-sighted. Foolish."

"It never brought in as much revenue as was promised," Green reminded him. "Too many Mexicans just quit mining and went home."

"Good! That's where they belong."

"I'm not finished. Chinese quit mining, too. But home's a

lot farther away. Instead, they went to San Francisco, or Monterey. Some to Los Angeles. Impoverished, they're a burden on the state. Instead of putting money into our coffers, they're draining it."

"Something's got to be done, Thomas," Bigler said again. "Those men—"

Green interrupted. "Trust me, I understand."

Bigler believed he did. The year before, Green had been tasked with leading the California Militia to quell some Indian activity. He'd fought Mexicans across the border, as well. With his slicked down hair and bushy sideburns, he hardly looked like a rugged fighting man, but Bigler knew better than to underestimate him. Even with his drinking and his constant need to find the amusing side of things, Green was a man to be reckoned with.

"If you could take the militia again—"

"My days in the saddle are over, John. I imagine yours are, too. Sitting at a desk all day does that to a man."

"Then—"

"John, John. Listen. Every town of any size has a marshal or a constable of some kind. Every county has a sheriff. Let those men earn their keep. They're paid to protect the peace and wellbeing of their charges. Let them do it, and let the locals pay for it. We cannot." He tipped the jug again, and drank it dry, then set it down on the desk with a loud thump. "It's gotten so bad, Governor Bigler, that I'm forced to buy my own liquor. And that, sir, is a stinking shame."

• • •

Pancho Dominguez had been born with every advantage. His family was moderately wealthy in a nation where most people were either very rich or very poor. Castilian blood had given him light skin, light hair, and green eyes. He learned to like fine food and fine women almost equally, though if he'd had to choose one to give up it would have been women. He did well enough in school without having to work hard at it, and he became an officer in the army of Santa Anna.

And that was where things began to turn for him.

As an officer, he didn't have to suffer the same rigors as the bulk of the soldiers. He could sleep in a tent, have meals prepared by an aide-de-camp, consult with his fellow officers on strategy and tactics. But still, occasionally, an officer had to fight, and that part he didn't like. It was messy, it was bloody, and sometimes it was downright dangerous. The sight of other people's blood offended him, and the sight of his own was even worse. He began looking forward to nothing so much as the war's end. But when that came, his commission evaporated. General Santa Anna, who had been his only champion in the upper ranks, went into exile, and Dominguez was left lost, jobless, his family's wealth destroyed in the war.

Finally, he went to California, hoping to find easy wealth in the gold fields.

That turned out to be far more work than he wanted to do. After a few months of desultory effort, he turned to outlawry. Then, some miracle put him into the band of Joaquin Murrieta, and he knew his luck had again turned.

Joaquin was every bit the equal of Santa Anna in battle. Yes, his army was considerably smaller—but Joaquin shared in the spoils in a way that Santa Anna never had. Dominguez began to suspect that Joaquin had been sent his way by angels, to rescue him from a life of poverty and anonymity. As one of Joaquin's band, he was *somebody*. And as his wealth increased, so did his waistline.

There was only one trouble with Joaquin, that he could see. The man lacked ambition. With his organizational skills and his understanding of the fact that wealth, spread widely, could do more for a person than piled up in some counting-house, he could become a significant player in California's future. It was true that the state would likely never elect a Mexican governor—but Dominguez knew that behind every politician there were the people who pulled his strings. Those people had wealth to spare, and when they doled it out appropriately, they got to give orders to the speechmakers and elected officials. Dominguez had never seen someone turn down a hefty donation because the giver had been Mexican. He doubted that it would happen, even in California.

He wasn't riding with Joaquin just to get rich, he discovered. As with Santa Anna, it was the proximity to power that attracted him. In the general's case, the power had been real, built on the back of a massive fighting force. In Joaquin's case, it was still mostly theoretical—Joaquin thought of himself as a bandit first and last. Dominguez tried to press him when he could, to help him see what he'd blinded himself to. But he had to be careful with that; Joaquin's temper could flare if he was pressed too hard, and Dominguez had already endured several cold stares and angry scowls.

The next time Joaquin turned to him for military advice, though, he would speak up, and damn the consequences.

• • •

Between robberies, Joaquin had made two more trips to San José. He couldn't get Antonia Molinera off his mind. He went to the bakery, spoke with her parents, and visited with her. But so far, she had declined all his requests to do so much as to walk with him in the plaza.

This time, he returned to the bakery determined to change that. He'd visited the tailor first, and again wore brand-new clothing, with a new hat and shiny new boots. He purchased flowers from a street vendor and carried them in his left hand, to present to her when he saw her. He swept through the door, determined to make an entrance she would remember.

No one was at the front. For a moment, he thought the place was empty. But he inhaled the aroma of fresh-baked breads and sweet treats, and he knew somebody had been there. "Hello?" he said. "Antonia?"

"Coming!" a masculine voice called from behind the corner. Joaquin recognized it as belonging to Diego Molinera, Antonia's father. He emerged shortly, clapping his hands amid a cloud of flour. "Oh, it's you."

"It is," Joaquin said. "Are you alone today?"

"For now," Diego said. "Marisol will be back shortly."

Marisol was his wife, who usually worked the counter, selling the goods that Diego baked. "And Antonia?"

Diego noted the flowers clutched in his fist and offered a wan smile. "She's out today. Those are for her?"

"They were."

"Leave them with me. I'll tell Marisol you brought them for her." He winked. "It's good politics."

Joaquin laid them on the counter. "Put them in water," he said.

"I will, I just don't want to handle them with these dirty hands." Diego leaned forward, elbows on the counter, and lowered his voice. "Let me tell you something, son. Antonia likes you. But she's a grown woman, and you come at her like a little boy. Every time you come to the shop, you spend as much as regular customers do in a month, and you speak with her, and with her mother and me. But that's not what she wants. She wants a man who'll sweep her off her feet. She feels like you're a little bit afraid of her."

"Afraid of her? Does she know who I am?"

"She knows what you are," Diego said. "So she wonders why a man who takes what he wants from others is so cautious with her. Your approach makes her think you're putting on an act, trying to be something you're not."

"Do you know where I can find her today?"

"Today? No. But I know where she'll be tonight." Diego leaned closer still, and lowered his tone further, as though the breads themselves might be listening. "Here's what I'd do . . ."

38

Even from blocks away, the fandango on Second Street was loud; raucous music punctuated by the stomping of feet on the floorboards. As he drew nearer, Joaquin heard laughter as well, and voices singing and shouting. It sounded like a party that everyone in San José had been invited to, except him.

Closer still, he started to see human detritus, drunken men sitting on the side of the dark road, or stumbling along arm-in-arm, cursing or telling crude jokes in slurred voices. On side streets or up alleys, lovers who couldn't wait to get home or who had slipped their chaperones grappled. None of them paid any mind to the man who rode up the street on his own horse, leading a second. The other horse was the best he'd been able to purchase that day, and it sported the finest Mexican tack and saddle—sidesaddle, because that's how Diego had told him Antonia was most comfortable.

Given what she was probably wearing for the fandango, it was also the most sensible. She wouldn't be going home to change.

He remembered his last fandango, in Sawmill Flat, when he had danced the night away with Rosita, then taken her home and made love with her until they finally slept as the sky grew lighter with the dawn. He thought of her now and hoped that she would forgive him. She probably would, he decided; she knew human nature better than he did, after all.

She wouldn't have wanted him to spend the rest of his life alone, missing her.

A tarima had been raised across Second Street, taking up most of the block, with at least a hundred people dancing and half again as many on the sidelines, watching, drinking, talking, or resting. The fandango was a celebration of the end of summer and the coming of autumn, and there was a distinct chill in the air. This close, the racket was almost deafening, and the odors of roasting peppers and tortillas, tobacco smoke, sweat, and liquor battled for dominance.

Joaquin stayed on his horse so he could see over the crowd. Finally, he spotted Antonia, wearing a white dress with red trim and lace, and white and red ribbons in her hair. She was dancing with a tall, broad-shouldered, blond-haired American man, so handsome that God himself must have been envious. She laughed as he drew her close to him, and Joaquin had to suppress an urge to draw a pistol and shoot him on the spot.

But then, another man came up to her, this one a Mexican. Joaquin realized that probably a third of the men in the crowd were Americans, here to dance with any woman they could find. Antonia turned away from the first one with a giggle, and danced with the new man, just as flirtatiously. Joaquin was glad to see it; it meant the first man wasn't a lover, but simply another man who couldn't resist her charms. Joaquin had that in common with him, if little else.

After she started to dance with a third, Joaquin handed his reins to a young boy idling on the edge of the crowd, and gave him a couple of coins to hold them for a few minutes. Then he wove his way through the dancers, smiling and excusing himself when necessary, until he reached Antonia. He reached for her shoulder, but as his hand touched her, she was already turning around. Her face registered something between delight and surprise—better than the dismissal he'd half-feared.

"Oh, it's you!"

"It is," he said, half-shouting to be heard over the racket. "It looks like you're having fun."

"I am, so much fun. I love to dance."

"I like watching you dance. But it's time to go."

"Go?" she asked. "Go where?"

"With me."

"What are you talking about?"

He took her hand and drew her across the platform, toward where he'd left the horses. She didn't resist, but whenever he glanced back at her, he saw puzzlement on her pretty face. He almost lost her once, when a man grabbed her and tried to start dancing with her, but Joaquin swiveled about and gave the man a look that shrank him in his boots, and he released her. Then they broke free of the crowd, and Joaquin showed her the horses. "Our mounts," he said. He slipped the boy another coin and took back the reins. "I heard you prefer sidesaddle."

"From who? Wait, let me guess. My parents."

"Your father. Your mother wasn't there, but I had a long talk with him. Let me help you up."

She studied Joaquin briefly, bemused, then shook her head and put a foot in one stirrup. He hoisted her up, accidentally cupping her behind as he did. She didn't object. When she was positioned, she tugged her skirts out from under her, and sat the horse like a true equestrian.

"It's a lovely saddle," she said.

"The best money can buy. In San José, at least."

"I should have some boots, though." She kicked her feet in the air, still wearing her dancing shoes.

"In the saddlebags," he said. "Along with everything else you'll need."

"My father helped you pack?"

"He did." Joaquin stepped behind her and found her riding boots, handed them over and tucked away the other shoes.

"Are we riding far?"

"A couple of days."

"When will we leave?"

Joaquin checked to make sure she was ready for a long ride. That dress wasn't the most practical thing, but she could change it in a few hours. He hoped to have her undressed by then, anyway. Satisfied, he climbed onto his own horse and turned it away from the ongoing festivities. "Right now," he said, and started at a walk.

"Now?" Antonia asked.

"Keep up," he said over his shoulder. She gave the horse her heels, and followed.

A few blocks away, the noise from the fandango had faded enough that they didn't have to shout.

"So we're riding at night?" Antonia asked. "Out of town?"

"We are. We'll stop and sleep in a while, but I want to put some distance between us and San José before we do." He grinned. "Old habits die hard."

"I don't think I want to know what that means," she said. "But what about bandits in the hills outside of town?"

"I'm not sure you know who I am," Joaquin said.

"You told me. You're Joaquin Murrieta. But what does that mean?"

"It means, the only bandits we'd have to worry about work for me."

"You're *that* Joaquin?" she asked. It was the first time she'd truly sounded surprised by anything he had said.

"I am. I thought you knew."

"I figured you were some kind of criminal. A smuggler, maybe, or a horse thief. I never imagined you were the bandit leader everyone talks about."

"Yes, well, it's safer that way, isn't it? When I want people to fear me, I let them know who I am. When I want to be left alone, I keep my own counsel."

"Not everyone fears you. The Americans do. Our people mostly admire you. Or they lap up the stories about you, anyway, without knowing which ones are true."

"Probably only the worst ones," Joaquin said.

"So, you want me to fear you, too?"

Joaquin laughed. "Not *you*! I want you to love me. As I do you."

"Love you? I hardly know you."

"You said that the first time we met. You know me better now, and soon you'll know me much better still."

"You hardly know me," Antonia argued. "And yet you think you love me."

"I know I do. I can't stop thinking about you. Day and night. It's terrible."

"And being around me day and night will be better?"

"I believe it will."

"I'm not sure you know who *I* am," she said. She was riding beside him, keeping up easily. They had reached the edge of San José, and beyond was only open country, silvery in the moonlight. "If you think I'm some kind of innocent young thing—"

He laughed again. "Innocent? Hardly."

"Well, I'm not sure how to take *that*. But you should know about me, now that you've told me about you. Before they opened the bakery in San José, my family was poor. Dirt poor.

As a young girl, I . . . I earned money to help. The way only a young girl can. Even after the bakery, I kept at it from time to time, when times were hard. Now, the bakery's successful enough, and I haven't had to do that for a few years. I don't miss it, but I don't regret doing what had to be done."

Joaquin hadn't expected anything like that in her background. She was nothing like the prostitutes he had known in the gold camps, the ones who had tormented Rosita. They were hard, cruel women. He sensed some steel in Antonia, too. Perhaps those early experiences had put it there. But he didn't believe she thrived on meanness, the way those other women had.

She would need some steel, to live at Arroyo de Cantua with him and his band. More than ever, he was sure he had made the right choice.

He just hoped it wouldn't take too much time for her to agree.

• • •

As Joaquin had promised, they stopped after a couple of hours, near a creek that he knew about. When she began kissing him, he was anxious. He had only ever made love with Rosita, and together they had learned how to pleasure one another. But Antonia had, she'd indicated, been with many men; perhaps dozens. Or more. His inexperience would be revealed. He tried, as befitted an outlaw and a leader of men, to appear as nearly infallible as possible, perpetually confident and decisive. The idea of exposing his vulnerability to her—a woman he hardly knew, as she kept reminding him—was suddenly terrifying.

She undressed him and then herself. Her touch, her caresses, of both his body and her own relaxed and aroused him at the same time, until no force on earth could have stopped him. She knew some tricks that Rosa hadn't, slowed him down when he was too close to the edge and speeding him up when she wanted more, until finally, spent, he lay gasping for breath in her arms.

After a while, they bathed quickly in the cool water, and slept for a couple of hours. With the sun, they rose and continued on their way.

The sun was high, the day cloudless and warm, when Joaquin spotted a pair of men racing toward them down a grassy slope. Antonia saw them, too, and drew her mount closer to Joaquin. "Is that bad?"

"You wanted to see bandits. There they are."

Her brow furrowed, and she kept glancing at the men, gauging their distance and speed. She looked frightened. "That's not what I said! Are they some of yours?"

He couldn't quite tell until they came closer, but he thought he recognized them. "I believe so."

In another minute, he realized they were shouting his name. Now he could make them out: Juan Gallego and Humberto Mota. Both were relatively new to the gang and had ridden with other bandits before joining him. He halted his mount, and Antonia, riding slightly ahead of him, circled back to stand beside him.

"Joaquin!" Mota said as they came to a stop. "Right before we spotted you, we saw a circuit judge I've seen before. He stays in hotels in every town, and usually carries plenty of money. We were thinking about robbing him, but then saw you and thought you might want to join in."

The men were gaping at Antonia, which reminded Joaquin of the manners that Rosa had often said he lacked. "Men, this is Antonia Molinera. She's with me. These are Juan and Humberto, two of my men."

Both men doffed their hats. Mota's was a big sugarloaf sombrero, and he was a tall man anyway, so with the hat on he looked like a giant. Gallego was shorter, and squat. The two were fast friends and nearly always together. Gallego's hat was small and narrow-brimmed, but he was usually close enough to Mota to stand in his shade. "A pleasure, senorita," Mota said. Gallego just grinned. That was what he did, mostly. He was a happy sort, quiet and not too smart.

"Can we catch this judge?" Joaquin asked.

"He's not in any hurry," Mota said.

Joaquin grinned. Maybe Antonia had far more experience than him at lovemaking, but he trumped her at banditry. "Let's ride, then!"

With a laugh, Mota put the spurs to his mount and tore away. Gallego followed on his heels. Joaquin caught Antonia's eye, touched two fingers to the brim of his hat, and took off after them. Antonia stayed close behind.

Within minutes, they saw the judge crossing a shallow valley at a steady trot and starting up a low hill on the other side. They raced across the valley, and by the time he had crested the hill, they were already climbing it.

The rise dropped into a wide valley, flat and dry for mile after mile, with purple mountains hemming in the far side. The judge happened to glance back, or he heard the hoofbeats behind him. When he saw the outlaws—though the presence of a woman among them might have given him pause—he picked up his pace. As Joaquin and the others hurtled down the hill toward him, the judge drew a pistol. He was no marksman, and trying to ride while shooting over his shoulder meant he did neither particularly well. His shots flew toward the clouds, into the earth, or well wide of their marks.

Likewise, Mota pulled out a pistol. Joaquin shouted to him to put it away. "Watch this!" he said. He took a lariat from its place on his saddle and started spinning it perpendicular to the ground, slow, lazy spins at first, to draw out the loop. Then he spurred the horse, and as he gained on the judge, he brought the lasso over his head. A few faster spins gave it the speed and velocity he wanted, and he let it fly. The rope soared out over the judge, then dropped down around him. Once it had encircled his arms and torso, Joaquin brought his mount to a sudden stop and yanked on the rope, cinching the loop tight around the judge. His horse kept going, which caused it to run right out from under its rider, dropping the judge unceremoniously to the dirt. His gun landed a safe distance away. His arms pinned by the lasso, he sat and waited, scowling, while his four attackers circled him.

"I hear you're a judge," Joaquin said as he dismounted.

"I am, indeed. I am Samuel Loudon, Esquire. An officer of the court, if you will, and not one to be treated in such a shabby manner."

"I apologize," Joaquin said, doffing his hat and bowing deeply. "I thought it the best way to stop you before you hurt yourself. And to disarm you before you hurt one of us. I am Joaquin Murrieta, and this, sir, is a robbery."

The judge had lost his hat in the chase, and his white hair stood up in patches. His black clothes were covered in dust, and a stray bit of cholla cactus had landed in his beard. His brow was knitted, his glare furious.

"You can't rob a judge!" he snapped.

"You might be surprised," Joaquin said. "All manner of people can be robbed, from the most dignified to the most churlish."

"You are no gentleman."

"Perhaps not. But neither am I the one sitting on my behind in the dirt."

His men laughed at that, and Antonia joined in. The judge

seemed not to have noticed her before. "And you? A woman? How can you join in such a nefarious act?"

"It wasn't hard," Antonia said. "Even a little girl could do it, if she could ride."

The judge *humphed* at her.

"You are carrying money, correct?" Joaquin asked. The judge fixed him with an angry stare, but didn't answer.

"Humberto, check his horse," Joaquin said. "Juan and Antonia, undress him. Check his clothing, and anyplace on his person where a man might conceal something."

"Anyplace?" Antonia asked.

"Anyplace at all."

Judge Loudon kicked his feet and tried to rise. "It's in my bags," he said.

"Antonia might check you anyway, just to be sure."

"All right, and in the pockets of my frock coat. And some in my hatband."

"Juan, fetch his hat," Joaquin said. "Sir, Antonia will check your pockets. If you cooperate, she'll leave your clothing on. If you don't, she'll strip you to the skin. That can be a pleasurable experience, to be sure, but if you'd prefer to avoid it, I suggest you not resist."

"Take it. Take it all."

"Oh, we wouldn't dare," Joaquin said. "How would you find lodging tonight? You might be in need of a drink or two, as well, although I suspect that your tale of being robbed by the famous bandit Joaquin might ensure you don't have to pay for your own drinks for some time to come."

"You're planning to let me live, then?"

"Of course!" Joaquin removed his hat and crouched beside the judge. "Take a good look at my face, Judge Loudon, and remember my name. Joaquin Murrieta. If I or any man who swears allegiance to me should ever appear before you in court, I trust that you'll show that man the same mercy I showed you here today. If I hear that you didn't, then I'll have to find you again and have a different kind of conversation. Is my meaning clear?"

"Clear as day, outlaw. You mean not only to humiliate me and to rob me, but to make me violate my oath to do impartial justice."

"Say it any way you like, Judge. Just don't forget it. I hope we never meet again, but if we do, you won't enjoy the reunion."

At that threat, the judge stopped arguing and cooperated fully. Joaquin, as promised, allowed him to keep enough of his money to find lodging for the night and send for more, or perhaps to earn enough through his judicial work to get by. Finally, they removed the rope, unloaded his gun but gave it and his hat back to him, and even caught his horse for him. As he rode off, Antonia broke into gales of laughter.

"What is it, my beloved" Joaquin asked. "What do you find so funny?"

"It's just . . ." she began. She bent over double, clutching at her sides, and came back up with her face red. ". . . it's . . . you never told me how *fun* robbery was! Why didn't you tell me?"

"I suppose I didn't know you would want to know. I wanted to protect you."

"Protect me?" Antonia flew into another fit of laughter. When she could catch her breath, she added, "Joaquin, darling, I think I'm the one who needs to protect you!"

She took him in her arms and kissed him. He felt the eyes of the other men on them, and he realized he didn't care.

Rosita was never meant to be an outlaw's woman, he knew.

But Antonia had been born for the role.

39

Late December 1851, Hangtown, California

Tom Springer turned the wick wheel on his oil lamp and plunged his desk into darkness. His office at the *El Dorado Republican* was spartan, to say the least, but the rest of the facility was overflowing with all the necessary equipment for typesetting and printing, and during the day, the noise was constant. He liked to be able to close his office door and keep some of the chaos at bay.

Now, though, it was late, and he was nervous. He had an appointment, and if he'd been a wagering man, he would have put the odds on surviving it at around forty percent. The building was still, so he sat in the dark, listening for the knock on the front door that would be his signal.

He had put out word in local Mexican communities that he wanted to meet the bandit Joaquin, whose crimes had become so commonplace—and frequently violent—that the very mention of his name was enough to raise gooseflesh on American skin. He wanted to understand the tragedies that drove him, if the rumors could be believed. Mostly, he wanted to confirm that Joaquin was the Mexican Murderer who had terrorized his own town. He hadn't really expected anything to come from it, but he was a journalist, and news didn't usually come to him. He had to get out and find it.

Then yesterday, he'd had a visit from one of the people he had asked to spread the word. The man had been a miner who'd given up when the Foreign Miners' Tax was implemented, and since then had raised sheep and goats on a small plot of land. He sold milk, cheese, and wool, and his wife made tamales and tortillas and sold those in town. Springer had targeted people who seemed to have wide networks of connections in the community, and this couple definitely fit that criterion. The man, whose name was Jose Colon, had come early in the morning, before Springer even unlocked the front door. His message had been brief: "Someone will come here tomorrow night after dark, but before midnight. Be ready to go." He had resisted all of Springer's efforts to tug more information from him, leaving Springer no option but to wait.

Darkness had fallen hours earlier. Springer had worked for a while, finishing up a story for the newspaper and working a little on the history of California that he hoped to write. He wrote when he had time, around his newspaper duties, but that time had been hard to come by since the Mexican Murderer had ravaged the area, followed by the reign of terror wrought by the bandit Joaquin. Everyone else had long since left the offices, which Springer had assumed whoever he was meeting was waiting for.

Midnight was less than an hour away. Even though his office was in the interior of the building, it had windows that looked through the typesetting and printing areas to the street, and he had felt strangely vulnerable in the lamp's glow.

Finally, he heard a tap on the building's front door. He picked up the satchel he'd packed, containing a change of clothing, some paper, pens, and ink, a canteen of water, and a pistol. His hands were trembling. He had interviewed killers before, but he had never put himself entirely at the mercy of one. For all he knew, the man at the door was Joaquin himself, here to kill the man asking questions about him.

He walked between the stacks of paper, racks of type—even in the dark, he could have picked out individual letters of specific fonts, so many times had he handled them—and the big, hand-cranked printing press, and toward the shadowed figure standing outside the glass of the door. He pulled on a buffalo coat and gloves on the way; there'd been snow flurries all day, and he could see the stranger's breath.

When he opened the door, he could see the man outside, partially illuminated by light spilling from nearby businesses. The man wore a sombrero that kept his face in shadow. Springer could see a serape draped over his thin torso, with a gun belt at his waist that held two pistols. Below that, trousers that had been patched a few times were tucked into short-heeled boots. He had a mustache, a beard that looked like it had given up halfway through growing. One gold tooth and some dark gaps.

The man didn't speak, so Springer did. "I'm Tom Springer."

"Come," the man said. His voice was thick, ragged, as if he had a throat full of sand.

Springer locked the door behind him. There were no horses outside, which surprised him. The man turned away and walked quickly, and Springer followed. Around the corner, a wagon waited, with a pair of mules hitched to it. The man headed for it, so Springer started toward the bench. "No," the man said. He jerked a thumb toward the back.

"You want me to ride in the bed?"

"Joaquin wants you to."

Springer started to complain, to insist that a grown man didn't ride in the bed of a stranger's wagon. But he didn't want to lose what was likely his only shot at meeting Joaquin. Reluctantly, he climbed into the back, picking up a splinter in his finger as he gripped the sideboard.

The other man climbed on as well, his weight making the wagon creak and groan. Springer didn't like that, didn't like how any of this was going. But he was committed now, wasn't he? If he tried to bolt, the man might just draw one of those pistols.

But all the man had in his hands now was a piece of burlap and a length of thin rope. "Put this on," he said.

"What is it?"

The man handed him the fabric. It had been stitched into a kind of pouch, and Springer realized with an anxious shiver that it was a hood. Eyeless, just solid expanses of burlap. He would be blind, his breathing restricted. He could still scream, he supposed, if it came to that. Not that there'd be anyone around to hear.

"I don't want to," he said.

"Joaquin wants you to." The second time he'd said that. Springer didn't like it any better this time.

"How do I know that?"

"You want to see Joaquin, you follow his rules."

"For how long?"

"I'll take it off come morning," the man said. "Then put it back on when we're getting close. He don't want you to see which way we're going or how to get there is all."

So, overnight. And then more, later.

"How long is the trip all together?"

"Couple days. Three, maybe, depending."

"Depending on what?" Springer asked.

The man tapped the hood, which Springer was still holding delicately, as if it was a rat he wasn't quite sure was dead.

"Depending on how quick you put this on."

Springer got the message. He pulled the hood on. It smelled rank inside, like it had been used to carry that half-dead rat.

He heard the man step closer, smelled him through the hood. Then he felt the length of rope going around his neck, cinching the hood tight. The man tied a knot that felt like a fist against Springer's throat. He swallowed, but it hurt.

"Are you going to tie my hands, too?"

"No," the man said.

"But you know I'll be able to take this off any time I want."

"You do," the man replied, "you won't see Joaquin. Or anybody else."

It took a few seconds for his meaning to sink in. The man stepped past him, rocking the wagon like a skiff on a still lake, and settled down on the bench, springs creaking under his weight. Springer heard him shake the reins and say something to the mules.

The wagon lurched forward. Springer, off-balance, sprawled on the bed, throwing his arms out to break his fall but misjudging the distance. His head hit the planks with a loud crack.

Up front, the other man chuckled. "Oh, yes," he said. "You'd better sit down."

40

Life at Arroyo de Cantua wasn't all planning for robberies. The men held dances and contests—primarily involving shooting, riding, and drinking, sometimes all at once—and sang songs, told stories of home, laughed and wept and plotted revenges large and small. Because there were few women at the camp, men danced with men, and sometimes more, though for that, they usually stole off into the trees on the canyon's far eastern side, rather than using their tents or shabby homes.

But at Antonia's suggestion, Joaquin planned a real party for Christmas. He sent a couple of men to San Luis Obispo with orders to bring back two wagons of women and several barrels of tequila and wine. Antonia told them which houses to go to, and who to speak to there, to ensure a good selection of ladies.

On Christmas Eve, everyone who owned a musical instrument brought it out. They all played together, mostly poorly but with real enthusiasm, and a huge fire was lit to ward off winter's chill. If Joaquin felt the cold at all, it disappeared when he saw what Antonia had chosen to wear: a white, ruffled blouse, cut low and straight across the bust to show the upper globes of her generous breasts, and a brown skirt slit to the hip on one side. "I've never seen you in those before," he said.

"I save them for special occasions." She gave him a sultry smile. "I'm glad you approve."

"How could I not?"

At one point during the festivities, Antonia got up and performed a slow, sensuous dance, showing off her figure and her supple agility in a way that would have had every man looking for a partner, even if they weren't already. The imported prostitutes whooped and cheered her on. Joaquin could hardly wait for the party to end so he could take her back to the enclosed room of the ramshackle house and make love until dawn. So much liquor was consumed that some of the men passed out before they even had a chance to take advantage of the ladies brought in from the city, but Joaquin had been sipping slowly, trying to make the night last.

He finished one drink and poured a bigger one, but before he even got the cup to his mouth, Gregorio Lopez approached him with a serious look on his face. "What is it, brother?" Joaquin asked.

"Huerta's here, with that man from the newspaper."

"Now? I told him to come tomorrow."

"Well, they're here now. I can tell him to wait."

Joaquin considered only briefly. He hadn't wanted the night to be spoiled by something he considered work, but if that was to be the case, he would minimize the disruption the best he could. "No, the man's a guest. I'll talk to him. Take me there."

Lopez led him to a wagon, stopped near the two that had brought the women. A couple of the younger men were already tending to the mules that had brought it, frothy with sweat and thirsty from the long journey. Felipé Huerta was helping another man—his head enveloped in burlap—climb awkwardly down from the wagon's bed.

"Take that thing off his head," Joaquin ordered as he approached. "This man is an honored guest."

Huerta drew a knife from a scabbard and pointed it at the prisoner's throat. Joaquin tensed, wondering if this was an act of rebellion. But Huerta merely used it to slice through the rope holding the burlap fast. He whisked it off the man's head, dislodging his spectacles. The man caught them, repositioned them on his face, and looked around with a bewildered expression. His gaze flitted from Joaquin to Lopez and back a few times.

"I am Joaquin Murrieta," Joaquin said, stepping forward and offering his hand.

"Oh," the man said. He was still somewhat disoriented from the ride, Joaquin guessed, and trying to get his bearings. "Oh, good. I'm Thomas Springer, of the *El Dorado Republican*."

"I know who you are, Mr. Springer. Welcome to our camp."

Springer's eyes twitched back over to Lopez. "You two gentlemen . . ."

"I know," Joaquin said. He chuckled. "We could be brothers. Not long ago, I was in Volcano, and a man stuck a gun in my belly, demanding the money I owed him. I had never seen him in my life, and I told him so. We spent a few tense moments together before I convinced him that I was not my friend Gregorio here, who really owed him the money."

"Of course, I killed him for his insult to Joaquin," Lopez added, "so I didn't have to pay him, after all."

Springer took a half-step back and glanced at the wagon, as if wishing he were back in it and racing in the other direction. Joaquin threw an arm around his shoulders. "You came on an auspicious night, my friend."

"I could hear the festivities," Springer said. "Your

Christmas celebration?"

"That, and celebrating the joy of being alive and free," Joaquin replied. "La Molinera—my woman—wanted a party, so I gave her one."

"Your woman?" Springer looked confused. "According to the rumors I've heard, your woman was . . ." he let the sentence trail off, as if sorry he had even brought it up.

With his arm still draped around the man's shoulder, he started walking Springer toward the party. "My Rosita was murdered in the foulest manner imaginable. I was destroyed. But she would have wanted me to keep living, and to truly live, one must love. What about you, my friend? You have a woman?" The American was scrawny, pale, bespectacled, with a narrow, pinched face, but he'd seen uglier men who still had women love them.

"No," Springer answered. "I mean, I did, back in Ohio, but . . ."

"Ohio," Joaquin echoed. "And she broke your heart, this woman?"

"Something like that, yes."

"We have women here tonight who would never break your heart. Other parts of your body, perhaps, but only by wearing them out. Feel free to indulge yourself. As for drink, is tequila to your liking?"

"It was a long trip. Some water, possibly?"

"Water we have. Gregorio, fetch water for my new friend. Come, Thomas Springer. Let me show you how outlaws live . . ."

• • •

Springer hadn't known what to expect of Murrieta—even rolling around in the back of the wagon, he hadn't been certain he would ever meet the man, or that he wasn't being taken someplace to be murdered. But whatever he had expected, it hadn't been this. A huge, roaring bonfire, music being played badly but loud, men and women dancing and kissing and more, some making love right out in the open. Liquor everywhere. People smoking, laughing, naked women dealing cards. It was like some Roman bacchanal. If it had been a dream, he would have dismissed it as unrealistic.

And whatever he might have expected hadn't been this. By reputation, the man was a bloodthirsty ruffian, a ruthless thug, some kind of monster. Rumors abounded of his wife's grisly demise, his brother's hanging. But just as many people swore he didn't exist at all, that he was some kind of composite of many Mexican bandits. Joaquin was a common Mexican name, they said, so chances were good that one or more of the villains was named Joaquin. But no one man could be in so many places at once, could rob and kill so many people. He's a myth, a story made up to frighten children.

Yet, here he was, in the flesh. Young, handsome, courteous, friendlier than many people Springer had met, in California or back in the States. Felipé Huerta had been taciturn, but he'd stopped when Springer needed to relieve himself, given him water and sustenance whenever he'd had some for himself, and true to his word, had let him ride most of the time without the hood on, sitting up in the wagon's bed. That Lopez fellow was a little scary, but who knew if his tale about killing the person to whom he'd owed a debt was even true?

"Tell me," Joaquin said, "why did you ask to meet me?"

"I want to interview you for the newspaper," Springer said.

"But I'm nothing important, not some politician or wealthy landowner. I'm a simple man." A drunken man stumbled into Joaquin, knocking him off his stride. Joaquin just grinned and caught the man so he didn't fall over, and the fellow continued on his merry way.

Springer rubbed his chin, which was covered with stiff bristles. He'd brought a shaving kit, but Huerta hadn't given him the opportunity to use it. It reminded him of his early months in California, when his beard had grown as long as any miner's. He preferred being clean-shaven, though, just like he preferred working indoors and living in town instead of a tent. "But you admit you're an outlaw."

"Oh, yes. Why try to hide that? Everybody seems to know already."

"Well, if everybody knows about you, then you're important. But I don't think they do know, not really. They think they know. There are so many stories about you. I want to find out which are true, and which are made up."

"The made-up ones are probably more exciting."

Springer shook his head rapidly. The surreal scene made him feel dizzy, drunk, even though he hadn't had so much as a sip of water for the last couple of hours. As if thinking it had made it happen, Lopez rushed up to him with a tin cup, water sloshing over the side. Springer took it, thanked him, then turned back to Joaquin. "I only print the truth, or as much of the truth as I can find out. And I thought, who would know the truth about Joaquin better than the man himself? Thank you for agreeing to see me."

"I've read some of your articles. You don't like me very much."

Springer had been afraid that would come up, and he had decided the best way to address it was with the truth. "You prey on innocent people."

"I prey on people who've preyed on others. The wealthy who take most of what the workers earn. And I give to the poor, especially to poor Mexicans, who are the most downtrodden of all Californians."

"Some would say that's the Indians."

Joaquin considered briefly. "True. I admit they were here first. We came second, and although we tried to convert them, we didn't try to exterminate them. And they never claimed the land. Mexico did, and you took it from us by force of arms. Having done so, you've since done your best to drive us out. You're the newcomers here, but you seek to hold every bit of California for yourselves. I speak of Americans in general, of course, not you yourself."

"I won't argue," Springer said. He was hesitant to push too far, lest he incur the outlaw's wrath. But the man seemed open to honest discussion, which was more than he could have hoped for. "Our history is full of such acts. We came from Europe to American shores and immediately started wiping out everyone we met. Your people came from Spain and—though you did your share of enslaving and slaughtering—you also brought Christianity to many, and your people intermarried with those who were here before, far more than mine did."

"None of us are truly innocent," Joaquin said. "That is, after all, the Bible's first lesson, isn't it? You're right, my men and I are bandits. We steal. Sometimes we kill. But we also have rules, things we will not do. Those aren't always the things your laws prohibit, but the things my personal code prohibits. We will not steal from the poor. We will not take women against their will. We don't steal from the Church."

"All honorable positions, I suppose."

Joaquin's men parted before them as they passed through the crowd. The din was louder here, the heat from the fire almost unbearable. Around the fire, a bevy of crude habitations had been erected in no discernable order. Near what looked like an old house, a stump of a flagpole—Springer remembered having heard something about a flagpole being chopped down in San Andreas, the American flag left draped over a bush, and supposed he had just located it—flew the green, white, and red Mexican flag. Joaquin noticed his gaze and said, "Welcome to Mexico."

The wagon ride had only been two days long, and Huerta hadn't been racing his mules. "Surely, we're still in California."

Joaquin swept an arm, indicating the rocky heights surrounding them. They were in some kind of canyon, though where in the state it was, Springer had no idea. "Within these walls, it's Mexico," Joaquin said. "A territory, if you will. Soon to be larger still."

Joaquin led him to a spot where cane-bottomed wooden chairs had been set up on the grass. Springer saw a house behind them, or what remained of one, but these chairs were too new and pristine to have come from that wreck. He supposed the bandits had stolen them from some local person's home. A wealthy home, if Joaquin was to be believed. The quality of the chairs gave some credence to that theory.

A stunningly attractive woman sat in one of them. Unlike the women who were obviously prostitutes, this one had all her clothes on and wasn't engaged in some intimate act with an outlaw or two. Her clothes didn't leave much to the imagination, and she didn't appear particularly shy about showing what she had. Her hair was light, her eyes light brown, her smile loaded with promise. Her clothing revealed acres of flesh that made a man think things. Chairs on either side of her were empty, although men stood nearby or sat on the grass. None of them were talking to her, and Springer could tell they were trying not to even look at her, despite the obvious appeal.

Joaquin's woman, then. If he was the chieftain here, as he claimed, then his woman would go unmolested, however inviting she might look.

"Come," Joaquin said, waving a hand toward the chairs. "Sit with me and La Molinera. We can speak freely there."

"If you have other obligations, we can talk tomorrow," Springer said. "If it's all right for me to stay the night, that is."

"Of course. We've set up a special tent for you. Look around; if you see a woman who you'd like to have join you there, just point her out."

Springer had already seen at least a dozen women more enticing than any he'd known in Ohio, including his Beulah. And women were scarce indeed in Hangtown. But he hadn't come here to engage in his carnal desires, and he had a feeling that doing so would not reflect well on his true mission. "Thank you, but no. It really was a long trip. If we can talk more tomorrow, I have many questions to ask."

"Up to you," Joaquin said. "Gregorio, show Mr. Springer to his tent. And make sure he has anything he needs." He put his fingers to his ears. "Except, perhaps, for quiet. That, I'm afraid, will be hard to come by tonight."

Lopez hurried to do his master's bidding, but before he could, Joaquin grabbed Springer's arm in a steely grip. "Two things," he said. "You always misspell my name. It's M-U-R-R-I-E-T-A."

"One T?"

"Correct. Some of my relations spell it with two, but my family has always used just one."

"Noted. And the other thing?"

"You must never tell anyone that you came here, or that you met me. Swear it."

Springer was confused. "But . . . the perceived veracity of

an interview depends upon the reader's certainty that the writer actually questioned the subject. Face to face, as it were."

"It's for your safety as well as my own," Joaquin said. "Either swear it, or be buried here. The choice is yours."

Really, it was no choice at all.

Springer swore.

41

February 1852, San José, California

Antonia liked to visit her parents in San José whenever she could. But the Molinera home was small, so Joaquin, claiming to be Julián Vallejo, an imaginary wealthy rancher from Santa Barbara, purchased a grand house on the corner of Fourth and San Fernando, with stone walls and three stories. They sometimes made the trip alone, just the two of them, but other times Joaquin brought a larger party, and the house had room for all of them.

On this occasion, ten men accompanied them, carrying with them a small arsenal of weapons and ammunition. Joaquin's spies had told him of a large transfer of currency to a bank in San José, and he intended to transfer that currency to himself. The sweetest twist was that he had bought the house from the head of the bank himself, who had recently moved to an even larger one nearby.

Joaquin had gone so far as to confirm the transfer with the banker, one Virgil T. McGee, owner of the Capitol Banking Company. All manner of currency was in use in California, including gold and silver dust and nuggets, but also Mexican reals, double-reals, and dollars, French francs, English shillings, Dutch florins and guilders, even Indian rupees. Occasionally continental currency showed up, though most of it was frayed and ripped into illegibility. McGee's Capitol Bank had printed up its own paper money, to be backed by its reserves of gold and silver, in order to try to standardize the currency of the region. McGee was proud of it, and happy to discuss it with his new neighbor.

He had consulted with Antonia and Pancho Dominguez on the plan, because the man loved plans and considered himself a strategic genius. Joaquin wasn't so sure about the genius part, but he often liked Pancho's ideas. What he didn't like was the fact that Pancho usually didn't want to be around when the plan was put into action. But between his ideas and Antonia's contributions, the plan seemed sound, and simple enough to pull off. Joaquin would ride over a few minutes ahead of his comrades and go into the bank. If McGee was there, he would exchange a few pleasantries and then leave quickly, and the men would wait until another time. If McGee wasn't there, Joaquin would note the positions of any guards, and anything else that might present a problem, then go back outside and tell his men what to expect. So forewarned, they'd go in with guns bristling, disarm the guards, and take the bounty.

The morning was cold but clear, the sky so crisply blue it almost hurt to look at. Joaquin's horse, a gray mare chosen specifically for her speed, emitted clouds of steam with every exhalation. He didn't race her, not yet, just had her walk down the street, around the corner, and over to San Fernando, then up to the bank. The exterior was finished in squared-off stones the same gray as Joaquin's house—apparently McGee's favored building material. A few other horses were tied to the rail outside, and a couple of buggies waited nearby.

He casually looped his horse around the rail, giving the mare a once-over to ensure that none of the various weapons she carried were easily visible to observers. Satisfied, he brushed nonexistent dust from his shoulders and stepped inside.

He didn't see McGee, but what he did see unsettled him. This wouldn't go exactly to plan, after all.

By the time he got outside again, his men had arrived, along with Antonia. She had so enjoyed the first robbery she'd been part of, she had insisted that Joaquin include her in more. At first, he had resisted, but in the end, he had a hard time denying her anything she wanted. She carried an 1848 Colt Baby Dragoon, a pocket-sized revolver suited to her smaller hands. Joaquin had bought it for her and given her lessons at Arroyo de Cantua. She'd never had to use it on a person yet, but she was good at target shooting and seemed to relish the idea of trying it on a man.

They were waiting to one side, out of sight from the bank's door or the one large window facing out onto San Fernando. "Two guards inside," he said as they huddled around. "One to the right of the door, about eight feet away, sitting in a chair. He's older, but he has a shotgun across his lap. The other was leaning on the counter when I was there, flirting with a pretty teller. He has a Colt in a holster on his hip.

"But something else you should know—the pretty teller, and another one, a young man, are both Mexican."

"Working in a gringo bank?" Tres Dedos asked. "They're trusted to handle money?"

"So it seems."

Tres Dedos shook his massive head. "Maybe the world really is changing."

"We should try not to hurt them," Joaquin said. He pointed to Claudio Feliz and Luis Vulvia. "If we have to hurt anyone, it should be those two guards. I want you two to go right as soon as you enter and shoot the one in the chair." Indicating Joaquin Valenzuela and Juan Senate, he added, "And you two go for the younger guard." He tapped three on their chests: Tres Dedos, Gregorio Lopez, and Humberto Mota. "You three take the workers at the counter. I don't think they'll try anything, and I doubt they're armed. Just stand close and make sure they don't interfere." Catching the eyes of Reyes Feliz, Juan Gallego, and Antonia, he added, "You three watch the customers. They might be armed, and they might be foolish. After all, they're in there because they have money. And you, Felipé," he said, addressing Huerta, "You stay close to me. We'll bag any gold, silver, or bank notes we can find and carry them to the door, then as we all leave we can each grab some bags. We'll ride out of town to the east, because from here that's the closest to open country. Does everyone understand?"

No one said otherwise, so Joaquin walked briskly away from them, drew two pistols from his saddlebags, hid them under his coat and went back into the bank. The others would follow a few seconds later, but the extra time would allow him to see if anything had changed in the last few minutes.

Once again assuming the guise of an ordinary citizen, he got in line behind the other customers waiting their turns. The three tellers were all busy. The inside floor was tiled, the counter made of a rich, dark wood, and it appeared that McGee was already a wealthy man. Joaquin supposed that only wealthy men opened banks in the first place—and that the goal of doing so was to become wealthier still.

He guessed they had that in common.

The others came in behind him, in the order that he had suggested. Rough-looking Mexicans all: towering Mota with his sombrero, ugly Huerta, savage Tres Dedos, even the lovely

La Molinera, each one armed; no one could fail to understand what was happening. Claudio and Vulvia turned toward the seated guard before he could even react, and with two shots to the head, dropped him to the floor. A puddle of blood behind his head quickly turned into a pond and would soon be a lake. Claudio snatched up the man's shotgun.

The younger guard came away from the counter, pawing at his hip for the gun holstered there, but Valenzuela and Senate blocked his path. "See here!" the guard said. "You've hurt Brett!"

"He's not hurt," Senate said, "he's dead. Calm down before you get the same." The guard stood still while Valenzuela relieved him of his weapon.

The guards dealt with, Joaquin loudly announced the obvious. "This is a robbery! Everyone cooperate and no one will be hurt. We only want the bank's money, not yours!"

A couple of the customers in line shouted. One snatched a pistol from under his coat, an old single-shot flintlock model. As he tried to ready it to fire, Gallego smacked it from his hands. It clattered on the floor and Gallego kicked it away. It spun and slid to a halt against the wooden counter, where Tres Dedos, Lopez, and Reyes leaned, letting the employees know not to interfere.

Joaquin shoved the barrel of his Navy Colt into the gut of the younger guard. "Take us to the safe," he said.

The guard's face was pale, his lower lip trembling. Joaquin was afraid he was going to vomit. "This way," the fellow managed.

He led them toward a door at the end of the counter. It swung open as they approached, and Virgil McGee stood on the other side in a vest and shirtsleeves, with a rifle in his hands. Beads of sweat dotted his brow. "Vallejo!" he said—

the name under which Joaquin had purchased the house. "What's the meaning of this?"

Recognized, even under a false identity, Joaquin had no other option. He fired three times, catching McGee once in the chest and once in the neck. His third shot shattered the older man's jaw, spraying teeth, bone, and blood. McGee crumpled, and Huerta snatched away his rifle as he fell.

Behind Joaquin, another man had started to step into the bank. Hearing the shots and seeing what was going on, he backed out the door, shouting, "Robbery! To arms! Murder!"

Gallego spun around and fired a shot through the glass of the door, shattering it and hitting the man in the back. He reeled, but caught himself on the side of the building, out of view, and continued screaming. Other shouts came then, and the sounds of men running.

"Let's go," Joaquin said. "Quickly, now."

"But the money . . ." Huerta began.

"Forget the money. It's our lives I'm worried about. Go!"

They barreled out the door, boots grinding broken glass underneath. Tres Dedos didn't like to let Joaquin go first through any door behind which danger might lurk, so he shoved ahead and charged out in front, Joaquin right behind.

Outside, local men had tried to find safe positions, but it appeared that few of them had real experience in a gunfight. One crouched behind a trough full of water, across the street from the bank. Another stood in a shadowed doorway, as if the shade itself offered him protection. Two more were in second-story windows, and three others stood right out in the street.

They opened fire as the Mexicans poured out of the bank, and their first rounds had some impact. A shot from a window hit Tres Dedos in the meat of his upper left arm, but he returned the fire with three quick shots that felled his attacker. Two of their horses were hit, along with one horse belonging to a bank customer. A lucky shot hit Gallego in the belly; he dropped his gun and clapped both hands over it, but already blood oozed between his fingers, and Joaquin expected the wound to be fatal.

Joaquin dropped to one knee and aimed at the man who'd shot Gallego—one of those standing in the street. His first shot was low, but he raised the barrel and fired again, and this one hit the man square in the chest. The man took a step back, looked down at his chest, then fired again, his shot ricocheting harmlessly off the stone of the bank's outer wall. Antonia and Tres Dedos got him in their sights, and they and Joaquin all fired within an instant of one another. All three rounds hit home, and the man pitched forward.

Claudio unloaded the shotgun at the man hiding behind the wooden trough. The distance was too great for the shot to have maximum impact, but it still shredded his face and tore up the edge of the trough, splashing water everywhere. Some of the shot must have hit his left eye, because he threw his gun down and clamped a hand over it, screaming. Huerta ended his pain with a shot from McGee's rifle. He levered another bullet from the rotating cylinder and fired again, removing the threat from the other window.

All was acrid smoke and noise and chaos now, as the outlaws exchanged shots with the last of the locals—two in the street and the one in the shadows of a doorway. One more horse was hit, and then Huerta took a round at the inner edge of his right eye. He dropped the rifle and his arms and legs went limp, like a puppet with its strings cut. He collapsed where he'd stood. Lopez fired five shots at the man who'd shot him, one of those in the street, and he fell with half his head chewed away by Lopez's bullets. The man in the doorway threw his gun out into the street and curled up in a ball, trying to make himself as small as possible. The last one in the street ran into an alley between two buildings, and Joaquin's last shot creased his shirt as he disappeared.

In the quiet brought about by the end of the gunfire—though it still echoed in Joaquin's ears—he could hear shouts and horses in the near distance. The immediate threat might have passed, but things were about to get considerably worse. "Mount up!" he cried. "Ride like your lives depend on it!" Even as he said it, he scrambled onto his gray mare, thankfully unhurt and glad to see that Antonia was similarly unscathed.

Gallego and Huerta weren't dead yet, but they would be soon. Tres Dedos's arm hung uselessly at his side, but he could ride. Three horses were down, so skinny Mota climbed up behind Lopez, and they all raced toward the eastern edge of San José, as Joaquin had declared at the start. Riding west would put them into the coastal hills too soon, and the open space of the valley would allow them more speed.

Once they were out there, Joaquin would figure out what to do next. For now, the only plan was to put distance between himself and any potential pursuers.

It would prove to be more difficult than he'd thought.

42

They rode until the horses were covered with froth and Joaquin feared their hearts would burst. Finally, they stopped near a stream, access to which was largely choked off by western sycamores and heavy underbrush armed with thorns, and gingerly made their way through to let the horses drink and to fill their own canteens. The water was cold, as was the air, but Joaquin was glad to be off the horse, and was certain she felt the same way about her rider.

He was crouched near the stream, holding his canteen in the flow, when Mota came up beside him. "Hey, boss," he said.

Joaquin pulled the canteen, dripping, from the water and turned around. Mota wore a hangdog expression at the best of times, but now he looked on the verge of a breakdown. "Humberto. I'm sorry about Juan. I know he was your friend, but he wasn't going to make it."

"I know, I could see that. I just wanted to say, I thought I saw someone on our backtrail."

"Like who?"

"You know, like horses. A cloud of dust."

"Following us?"

"Seemed like maybe. I thought I'd climb one of these trees, see what I can see."

"If you want. Just be careful you don't fall out. If you do, land on Tres Dedos, not me."

"I'll try to. Does anybody have a spyglass?"

Joaquin didn't know the answer to that, so he repeated Mota's question, louder. It turned out that Vulvia, who seemed always to have one of anything someone might need on him at all times, had one in a saddlebag. He fetched it and handed it to Mota.

Joaquin was amazed by how fast Mota went up the tree. The lowest branches were easily reached, and Mota, all arms and legs anyway, scampered up it as if he had monkeys in his family tree. In a few minutes, he was so high Joaquin could barely make him out. If it hadn't been winter and the sycamore largely bare of leaves, the man would have been hidden entirely.

He stayed up for a short while. The sun glinted off the spyglass two or three times, and then the tree rustled again as Mota descended.

"Well?"

"Twenty men, maybe twenty-five," Mota said. "I couldn't count for sure."

"Twenty men? On our trail?"

"Dead on it."

"How far back?"

"Not far enough."

"Mount up!" Joaquin shouted, without waiting for more detail. "We're being followed!"

"By who?" someone asked.

"I don't know. Who's sheriff in Santa Clara County?"

"John Yontz," Antonia said. "But I don't think he would leave the county. He'd send a deputy."

"Who would he send?"

"Probably Robert Clark. He's a big man, with a huge belly

and a barrel chest. Bright red hair and a mustache that hangs down past his chin. There's usually some food in it from his last meal."

"I couldn't make out that much detail," Mota said.

"Is he any good?" Joaquin asked.

"Clark? He's stubborn as hell, is what I've heard," Antonia answered. "Like a dog after a juicy bone."

"Just what we don't need, a stubborn lawman. Let's get out of here, men."

The horses objected but gave in, as horses tended to do, to the insistence of the humans who had bits and bridles and spurs with which to encourage them. They rode upstream for a mile or so, hoping it would hide their tracks and make them harder to follow, then scrambled up the far bank and struck off in a northeasterly direction, up the valley and toward the Sierra Nevada.

Clark was stubborn? Joaquin could be stubborn, too.

Especially where evading the law was concerned.

• • •

They had only expected to be away from Arroyo de Cantua for a day or two, so hadn't packed many supplies. But with the posse after them, they couldn't risk going back there, nor could they return to San José. Instead, they headed north, stopping at the homes and ranches of friends who would hide and feed them for a few hours. They didn't dare stop anyplace for longer than that. Always, they moved on before Clark's posse arrived, knowing the lawman would have hard questions for their supporters.

A few times, the pursuers came dangerously close. Knowing they were out there, Joaquin and his men tried to keep tabs on their movements, while also looking for opportunities to hide their own tracks or, if necessary, to lay an ambush.

The days and nights were colder in the north, with snow on the ground in some spots, smaller creeks and ponds frozen over. This was another problem not planned for, as they'd expected to ride from temperate San José straight to Arroyo de Cantua. If they had successfully filled their pockets at the bank there, they could have bought heavier coats or warm woolen shirts. But because their plan had been to be leaving with the bank's riches, they hadn't carried much of their own. He worried about Antonia, who'd been quiet and withdrawn for several days, and had started to wish he'd never allowed her to take part. As the days dragged on, hungry and cold and so very tired, Joaquin's mood grew bitter and angry.

So he felt as he sat one night, shivering beside a wind-whipped fire that caution wouldn't allow them to build any larger, for fear of giving away their position. He sipped coffee from a tin cup, but even with that, he felt like he would never be warm again. It was as if California had descended into eternal winter. When Reyes Feliz approached him with a newspaper in his hands, he almost snapped at the young man. Instead, he fixed Reyes with a weary glare.

"I grabbed this back in Centerville to use in the fire," Reyes said, holding the newspaper toward him. He had folded it to a particular page. Like Joaquin and Rosita, he'd been educated in the mission school. "But I decided to read it first. You should look at this."

"What is it?"

"I can't even explain it. Just read it."

Joaquin snatched the paper from the young man's hands. He nearly threw it straight into the fire, hoping it would catch quickly and produce a blast of heat. But the headline Reyes had folded it to caught his eye. "I DREAMED I MET THE BANDIT JOAQUIN," it said.

He looked more closely and saw that he was holding the *El Dorado Republican*, and Thomas Springer's name was under the story. He began to read.

> Some readers of this newspaper, particularly our Cornish friends, may recall the Charles Dickens tale of 1843, entitled *A Christmas Carol. In Prose. Being a Ghost Story of Christmas*. The story tells of the miserly Ebenezer Scrooge, who finds himself visited by three ghosts on Christmas Eve. This writer was not visited by ghosts, but perhaps visited one—or was it all a dream?—on Christmas Eve last. That ghost, or dream personage, was the bandit Joaquin Murrieta. And the place was an outlaw camp somewhere in California, at which a giant bonfire roared but a wild Christmas bacchanalia roared louder still.
>
> I arrived there, hooded, after a ride of many hours in the back of a wagon. Where in the state I was, I have no idea. When the hood was removed, I was in a canyon surrounded by steep walls. Night had fallen, and I never saw the landscape within the canyon until the following morn. It was indistinguishable from many other places within the state.
>
> The bandit himself, contrary to expectations, was a perfect gentleman—or so I dreamed him. He is fair-skinned, with dark

hair and mustache and eyes that remind one of burning coals, full of fire but black as night. He was polite, well-spoken, and his English, although accented, was impeccable. I never heard him speak Spanish, although some of his banditos spoke it amongst themselves.

Authorities in numerous districts hold him responsible for robberies, murders, and more. I could not say whether this dream-Joaquin is guilty of those crimes, or innocent. But I can say that, be his story true, he would have as much reason as any man for such actions. He came to our state like so many others, in search of gold. Unlike many, he worked a rich claim, until it was stolen by American miners. In the process of so doing, those miners beat him senseless, then ravaged and killed his young bride. Not long after, his brother was lynched by Americans on trumped-up charges of horse theft. Murrieta himself was whipped by those same stout citizens and left for dead.

If it sounds as if this writer feels sympathy for the dream-bandit, it should not. Any killings he may have committed simply layer more deaths upon the too-many already experienced. Robbery is a scourge of our area, which, in the early days of the Gold Rush, was known as a safe place where a man might leave his gold unattended in his cabin, knowing it would be there when he returned from his claim. Those days, sadly, are gone.

For his crimes, Joaquin Murrieta deserves whatever punishment the law provides. It is difficult, however, for this writer to reconcile the ghost-bandit he met in a dream with the brutal killer described by so many. Having enjoyed his hospitality and his wide-ranging conversation the next morning (in my dream, which seemed of considerable length), he seems to be the sort of man California ought to welcome, rather than to harass and assault. California has, I fear, brought any predations he has committed on itself.

As a people, we ought to look upon Mexicans as neighbors and friends, not enemies and not victims. This state was, after all, theirs as of quite recently. To many, it should have remained so. And regardless of the change in the landscape's legal status—about which, one might argue, the Indians who were here even before the Mexicans or the Americans might be entitled to a different opinion altogether—the Gospels beseech us to treat one another as brothers. Perhaps those who victimized Murrieta, his brother, and his bride should have remembered that from the start.

By the time Joaquin finished the article, his hands were

shaking so furiously that the paper was rustling in them. "Is everyone awake?" he asked.

"Some are sleeping," Antonia said. "Like I wish I was."

"We need to wake them. I want to be in Hangtown by morning."

43

In the pre-dawn half-light, Joaquin watched Springer approach the door to the *El Dorado Republican* offices. He had a key in his hand, but when he slid it into the lock, the door bobbled open a little. Springer's face was shadowed, but Joaquin could tell that he instantly tensed. Shoulders tight, he pushed the door open slowly, as if expecting trouble. "Hello?" he said. "Is somebody here already?"

He paused just inside the doorway and scanned the offices. Joaquin decided to give him a break, and he lifted Mota's sugarloaf sombrero away from the glass chimney of the oil lamp he'd lit. Just in time; the inside was blackened, and it might have caught fire if he'd held it any closer or much longer.

Springer noticed the sudden glow. "Who's there?" he demanded.

"Come in, Mr. Springer," Joaquin said.

If Springer had been tense before, at the sound of Joaquin's voice he looked almost panicked, as if he might turn and run rather than continuing into his own office. Hesitant, eyes locked on that pool of light, he made his way through the printing area, bumping into things along the way. When he reached the door to his inner office, he stopped again and peered through the glass.

Joaquin moved the lamp closer to his face and beckoned

with his fingers.

Springer swallowed hard and opened the door. "Señor Murrieta," he said. "This is private property, sir. May I ask what you're doing in my office?"

Joaquin was sitting in a wooden guest chair with a slatted back and a cushioned seat. Springer's desk chair was empty. Joaquin waved him toward it. "Sit, Mr. Springer. No need to stand on my account."

Springer hesitated again, as if unwilling to obey the outlaw's instructions. But common sense and practicality left him little choice. The office was small and crowded. The only other chair, another guest chair like the one Joaquin occupied, was stacked high with books and papers. He sat in the desk chair and held his arms close to his sides. "Again, I ask you what you're doing here."

Joaquin caught his gaze and held it. "I specifically instructed you not to say that you'd met me," he said flatly.

"And I didn't," Springer protested. "If you read my piece—"

"I read it."

"Then . . . then you know I . . . I mean, I . . ." Springer stammered.

"Ha!" Joaquin broke into laughter. He continued for more than a minute, bending over, slapping his own thighs, unable to speak. Finally, he was able to bring himself under control, though his eyes watered. Rubbing them with his fists, he managed, "Your face! You expected me to gut you like a fish!"

"I . . ." Springer began, but he had nowhere to go with the sentence, and left the single word hanging there.

"I wanted to tell you that I thought your idea was ingenious," Joaquin said. "A dream. You met me in a dream. Brilliant!"

"Really?" Springer asked.

"Of course. Any reader with a working mind will know that of course, you met me. It's obvious. But should anyone demand more information from you than what your article provides, you can deny the whole thing. Say you never met me, and you made the whole thing up. Or that it truly was a dream."

Springer allowed himself a satisfied smile, and his chest seemed to swell a bit. "Well, that was the idea."

"And it was a good one. I wish I'd thought of it myself."

"So you're not angry?"

"I was," Joaquin admitted. "When I first read it, if you'd been standing there, I might have shot you. I woke those I've been riding with and we came straight here, riding through the night. But the more I thought about it, the more I realized how clever you were. When I came in here my intent was to punish you, but now I'm left only wanting to congratulate you."

He reached under his coat and withdrew a bag of gold dust, placing it firmly on the desk. "And to give you this, for your trouble. I'm sure running a newspaper is no way for a man to get rich."

Springer chuckled. "It's often said that the best way for a man to make a small fortune in the publishing business is to start with a large one. But sir, I cannot accept your generous offer."

"Why not? Do you indeed have a large fortune?"

"I do not. As I've told you, I came from Ohio, like so many others, hoping to make it in mining. And like so many others, I met only disappointment and bare diggings. I had a trade, which I'd practiced at home, and I saw that a responsible newspaper was needed more here than there, where there were already journalists aplenty. So I stayed. But accepting money from the subject of so many stories is inherently wrong. It might affect the way I wrote about you henceforth, after all. Or even if it didn't, the argument could be made—should anyone become aware of it—that it would. And I daresay, if you're intending to continue your banditry, I'm certain I'll be writing more about your exploits."

The man's reluctance to accept treasure seemed odd to Joaquin, but he thought he understood Springer's reasoning. He wanted to appear even-handed, not to be swayed by those about whom he wrote. "So, if the Governor of California wanted a favorable story about him, come election time, and offered you money to print one, you'd refuse him as well?"

"Not only refuse him, but publish a piece describing his offer," Springer said.

"Will you then write something about my offer?"

"You're not the governor. Besides, I've never met you, except in a dream."

Joaquin laughed again, and this time, Springer joined in. When both men composed themselves, Springer said, "I'm surprised you made time to come here. Are you not on the run from Deputy Clark's posse?"

"I am," Joaquin said, his mood suddenly souring. "That man's the worst sort of pest. I've hardly slept these last two weeks. Hardly had a decent meal. My guts are in an uproar, and the same goes for my comrades. Worse, La Molinera rides with us."

"I may have some good news for you, then. Clark's posse has been shrinking by the day. Those men thought they were signing on for a chase of a day or two. When it turned into a week, then ten days, some needed to get home, back to their families and their businesses. As some abandoned the effort, others started to feel less confident about their chances of surviving an encounter with you, should they in fact catch you."

"As they should. My men are angry enough to tear them apart by hand and feed the pieces to the wolves."

"So those men also left the posse," Springer continued. "Clark's left with less than a handful. He needs to get back to San José, too, and he knows that if he actually encountered you with the minimal force remaining, it would be a slaughter. My sources say he'll claim victory later today—not that he's killed you, but that he's obviously driven you from the state, since you can't be found and you haven't robbed anyone in many days. Having so declared, he'll call off the chase and go home."

A thrill of hope rushed through Joaquin—an emotion he hadn't experienced in what seemed like ages. "Is this true?"

"From all that I've heard. I can't swear to it, but I have good sources in San José."

"That's the best news I've heard in weeks, Mr. Springer. I must go and tell the others. Are you sure I can't leave you a little something in return?"

"All I ask, Señor Murrieta, is that whenever you see the newspaper for sale, you buy a copy. Don't steal it."

Joaquin felt a flash of anger at the accusation, but then he saw that Springer's eyes were twinkling behind his spectacles, and he was working to keep a grin from his lips. He laughed once more and shook Springer's hand before departing. On his way out into morning sunshine, his step was as light as his spirits.

44

With the threat of the posse removed, Joaquin let most of his men travel from Hangtown back to Arroyo de Cantua. He, Antonia, and Tres Dedos followed Clark's trail to San José—not intentionally, but because it was the quickest route to the former capital city—so she could reassure her parents that she was alive and unhurt. They went first to the house Joaquin had bought, approaching it cautiously in case anyone had connected it with the "Vallejo" who'd tried to rob the bank and killed McGee in the process. Seeing no one watching it, they went in and found it empty, with that particular, hollow feeling of a house that's been standing vacant for some time.

They were all tired from the long days and nights in the saddle. Joaquin suggested that Antonia make them a meal while he and Tres Dedos rested. "This city has plenty of restaurants," she snapped. "I'm not your cook." She spun around and left the room, clomping upstairs with deliberately exaggerated footsteps.

"That was the wrong thing to say, Joaquin," Tres Dedos said with a laugh. "She's mad at you, cousin."

"She's the best cook among us," Joaquin argued. "All those years in the bakery. She knows that."

"Knowing it and liking it aren't always the same."

"And what makes you the expert on women?" Joaquin asked. He knew Tres Dedos was joking with him. But he also knew that his friend was probably right. He'd seen flashes of La Molinera's fiery temper, but he'd rarely seen it directed at him. He thought the muzzle of a shotgun might be less frightening. "When was the last time you had one you didn't pay for?"

"I know better than that," Tres Dedos answered. "When you pay them, it's a business arrangement. You get what you want, and they get what they want. Your way, you never know for sure what they want until they don't get it, and then they blame you."

"I'm starting to see why you have to pay for it. Between that attitude and your homely face, I mean."

Tres Dedos put on an exaggerated frown. "I told you, my mother loves my face. Well, she did when she was alive, anyway."

"Did looking at you kill her?"

"Looking in the mirror did. She looked just like me."

"Poor woman."

They laughed, but Joaquin still had a knot in his stomach. Antonia was upstairs, probably waiting for him to come up and apologize. He would do that, but he had something else to discuss with her, and he didn't expect her to like it.

Tres Dedos chose to stay downstairs, which Joaquin guessed was the wisest course of action. Alone and anxious, Joaquin climbed the staircase with the somber steps of a man heading toward the gallows.

Antonia was in their room, sitting on the edge of the bed. She'd taken off her boots, but otherwise looked the same as she had downstairs. Joaquin found himself hoping she hadn't brought the revolver up with her.

"I'm sorry," he said as he entered. "I know you're tired, too. We can go to a restaurant."

"Are you sure you don't want to go with Manuel? If I didn't know better, I'd think you two were married."

"He's my cousin, and a loyal lieutenant."

"And I'm your woman. Doesn't that matter?"

"It does, Antonia." He sat beside her on the bed, put a hand on her leg. At first, she froze, and he was afraid she would swipe it off, but she didn't. "So much more."

"How much more?"

"More than I know how to put into words."

"Do you love me?"

"You know I do."

"You haven't said it in days."

He had hoped she wouldn't notice, but he should have known she would. "It's . . . awkward. In front of the men."

"Awkward."

"Antonia, my love, I . . ." He let the sentence hang there, while he tried to find the right words. The safest words, he realized—what he wanted to avoid most of all was angering her further. "I don't think you should go with us anymore. When we're . . . working."

"Working? You mean robbing."

"Yes," he said.

"You think I should stay behind in camp and get lazy and fat, like the other women there?"

"No," he said quickly. "It's nothing like that, and I know you wouldn't. But it's too dangerous. We lost Gallego and Huerta, and others were wounded. I couldn't bear it if something happened to you."

"Am I not helpful? You seemed to appreciate my suggestions."

"I do. And you are! But perhaps you could help me plan, then stay behind where it's safe."

"Because I'm a woman," she said flatly.

"Because you're the woman I love."

"You love Manuel."

"That's not the same. And if he was killed, I wouldn't grieve in the same way."

He couldn't speak what he really felt. She was sometimes jealous when he mentioned Rosita. But he couldn't bear the thought of losing a second woman to violence. Just the thought of it sent spasms of terror through him. He didn't want to say that to her, didn't want to remind her that he still missed Rosita and always would.

She turned her head slightly, meeting his gaze directly. "If you're asking me to—" she began.

"I'm not asking you. I'm telling you. You can't be put in harm's way. I won't allow it."

"You're the leader of our band, Joaquin," she said. Her voice was cold enough to freeze the American River. "You make the rules. But remember one thing."

"What is that, my love?" If he hoped that endearment would thaw her, he was disappointed.

"You don't own me. I love you, but I am my own woman."

"I . . ." he began. He didn't know what came next, so he just closed his mouth.

"Now, where are you taking me for dinner?" she asked. "Someplace expensive."

• • •

The next evening, Joaquin had another task he meant to carry out before leaving San José behind. He had met briefly with a few of his local contacts during the day and found that Deputy Clark's favorite nighttime spot was a restaurant and saloon called Weber's, just off Market Plaza. He directed one of them to watch Weber's and to let him know if Clark showed up, and around eleven that night, the spy rapped on Joaquin's front door with the news.

"Do you want me to go with you?" Tres Dedos asked. "The way Antonia pushes you around, you might have lost your manhood."

Joaquin was momentarily offended, until he saw the grin on his cousin's lips. "You're too easily recognized," he said. "I'll do this alone."

He dressed in a dark suit—the clothing of the wealthy and imaginary Vallejo—and didn't even take a gun. Market Plaza was close enough to walk, but he realized he might need to get away quickly, so he took the gray and tied her near Weber's.

The place proved to be more than his spy had suggested. Weber had a row of businesses standing side by side: a general store, a bakery—which did not look as enticing as Molinera's, but then, it was closed, the windows dark—the restaurant, and the saloon. A board nailed to the façade of the general store gave the locations of other businesses, including a blacksmithing shop, a soap and candle factory, and a flour mill. It was signed CHAS WEBER at the bottom. He must have been quite the businessman, Joaquin thought.

A few people were eating in the restaurant, despite the lateness of the hour, but only the saloon was thriving. Joaquin entered through the open door and found himself in the usual buzz of noise and activity, slightly more sedate than a gold country saloon at high fever, but not by much. The clientele was a mixture of white Americans, a few Mexicans or Chileños, and others who might have been Germans, Swedes, Frenchmen, and even a couple of blacks who might have been freed slaves or Africans. It was a surprisingly international gathering for a city that wasn't even a port city, though there was access to the ocean through the San Francisco Bay.

Standing at the bar, facing the door with his back to the barman, was the man Joaquin had come looking for. He had only seen Clark through the telescope, on one of the occasions that the posse had come uncomfortably close, but still the distance had been too great to make out much detail. He knew who Clark was as soon as he spotted him inside, though. He was heavyset, with a barrel chest and a gut to match. His nose was bulbous and threaded with red veins, and it jutted out over the red handlebar mustache that Antonia had described. To confirm Joaquin's suspicion, his badge was prominently displayed on his shirt.

Once he had identified the man, Joaquin pointedly didn't look at him as he crossed the room and bellied up to the bar. He ordered a tequila, downed it, and ordered another. After the first few, he began to surreptitiously spill some of each drink onto the floor, his sleight-of-hand covered by the shadow of the bar top itself and the general noise level of the establishment. He wasn't there to get drunk, after all, but he wanted to run up a big tab.

After more than a dozen drinks—and a few "bought" for the drinkers on either side of him, with whom he'd struck up conversations and shared entirely imaginary details of his life, using the name "Sancho Panza," which neither of the Americans he spoke with recognized as the squire from the Spanish novel *Don Quixote*—he declared that he'd had enough. "That'll be twelve dollars, sir," the barkeep said. He was a burly fellow, his forearms exposed by rolled-up sleeves knotted with muscle.

Joaquin patted his pockets, then shrugged. "I seem to have forgotten my money. I can bring it to you tomorrow."

"Tomorrow? That ain't how it works, pal. You don't got

any money or gold, you don't drink."

Joaquin reached for his own waistband. "I could give your liquor back right here, but I don't think you want that."

The barkeep's bushy eyebrows arched, pushing a series of furrows up his bald head, and his thick mustache twitched. "Don't get wise, mister."

"What do you suggest, then? It's an honest mistake."

"I tell you what I suggest." He turned toward the deputy. "Hey, Deputy. This feller, here, run up a twelve-buck tab, and now he's claimin' he ain't got the money. You want to show him what happens to guys try to stiff me?"

Clark, who'd been drinking since before Joaquin had arrived, seemed to have some difficulty straightening up, as if his back had been glued to the edge of the bar while he was leaning there. But he managed, then stepped unsteadily to confront Joaquin, smoothing down his clothes and making a point of displaying his badge. Joaquin found the thing unnecessarily gaudy, a seven-pointed star, each point blunted by a circle, and "Deputy Sheriff Santa Clara County" stamped into the metal.

"What seems to be the trouble?" Clark asked.

"I'm afraid I didn't bring any money," Joaquin explained, intentionally slurring his words. "It's so dangerous out there these days, what with all the bandits and the law doing nothing about them, I've fallen out of the habit of carrying any valuables when I leave the house."

Clark's expression shifted from mildly bemused to furious at Joaquin's comment. "Doing nothing? I guess you didn't hear about the fortnight I just spent on the trail of the bandit Joaquin. Drove him clean out of the state, didn't I, boys?"

Some of the men around him roared their agreement.

"I apologize, sir, I hadn't heard. You must be quite the

lawman, indeed."

Clark leaned in closer. "Remember that, come election time, if you're a citizen."

"Oh, I am," Joaquin assured him. "Sancho Panza, at your service."

"Well, Panza, what are we gonna do about this situation? I oughtta run you in for vagrancy."

"I have money at home, Sheriff. It's only a couple of blocks. I can go get it."

Clark ticked his big head toward the barkeep, who glowered from his post, hands gripping the edge of the bar. "I don't think Sam wants to let you out of his sight."

"He can accompany me."

"I got a saloon to run," the barkeep objected. "I can't go nowhere for hours yet."

Joaquin blinked and looked up, as if he'd just had a brilliant idea. "How about you, sir? A couple of blocks, a few minutes in the fresh air, and I can give you the money for my tab. And perhaps a little something extra, for your trouble."

"I guess Sam wouldn't complain about that," Clark said.

"I trust you, Rob."

Clark nodded. "It's settled, then. Couple blocks, you say?"

"That's right. A quick trip."

"Lead on, Mr. Panza."

The crowd parted for the deputy and his new charge. Joaquin kept up a running patter, telling Clark some of the same stories he'd told the men at the bar. Many of the details came straight from the novel. He'd been born in Spain and had been a squire to a knight—yes, they still had knights in Spain, they just didn't wear as much armor as they once did, and they used guns as well as swords and spears. Clark swallowed every lie and asked for more.

At the end of the first block Joaquin turned to the right. The street here was dark, quiet, out of sight from the door of Weber's and anyone who might be lingering on the Market Plaza. He didn't see anyone in either direction.

Joaquin faked a stumble, and caught himself on Clark's shoulder, pressing the deputy against the wall of the nearest building. "Excuse me," Joaquin said. "I think I'm a tiny bit drunk."

"That makes the both of us," Clark said. "But what's a saloon for, otherwise?"

Laughing, Joaquin said, "An excellent point, my man." He kept a hand on the other man's shoulder and pushed him more firmly against the wall, sliding his knife from its sheath as he did. "Also, I have a surprise for you."

"A surprise?"

No longer feigning drunkenness, Joaquin looked directly into Clark's eyes. "I am Joaquin Murrieta. And I've brought you here to kill you."

Clark blinked twice as the words sank through his inebriated state and settled in his mind. He reached for his gun, but Joaquin was faster. He rammed the knife guard-deep into Clark's midsection, twisted it, and wrenched it to the side. The smell of blood and innards hit his nose even before blood and fluid splashed on the street. Clark made a gurgling noise and tried to get his arms working, still pawing for the gun on his hip, but his legs were already going slack and Joaquin knew if he let go, the deputy would fall.

Instead, he withdrew the knife and drew the blade across Clark's throat. More blood shot forth, though not as much as there would've been had he started there. Clark's eyes rolled back in his head and his jaw dropped, mouth open, as he tried to breathe his last.

Joaquin—drenched and trembling—lowered the big man to the ground, facedown. Tres Dedos had told him how to cut off a man's head. It wasn't easy, mostly because of the spine, Tres Dedos had said, but it can be done if you've got the will. Joaquin knelt on Clark's back, feeling the uneven hammering of the deputy's heart against his knees. Wiping his hands on his pants to get a better grip on the bloody knife, he grabbed a fistful of Clark's hair to hold his head still and sawed on the muscles at the sides of the neck, first on the right, then the left. Finally, he sliced through the flesh at the back of the neck and put his knife blade against the spine, between two of the bones, and leaned into it with all his weight. The steel held and popped through the spine. Joaquin almost fell when the resistance was suddenly gone, but he caught himself and rolled off the body.

Head in one hand, knife in the other, as blood-drenched now as if he'd cut his own throat, he retraced his steps to Weber's. He opened the door just wide enough to reach through, using it to shield his body from view, and hurled Clark's head into the saloon. He heard it crash into glasses on a table, and then the screams of terror that followed, but he was already running.

He'd have to bathe the gray, later, and the saddle might be ruined, but he jumped onto the horse, and galloped off into the night.

45

"Throwing his head into the saloon? What was that meant to accomplish?"

Joaquin was holding a war conference in the unroofed section of his house in Arroyo de Cantua. Tres Dedos was there, of course, along with Gregorio Lopez, Reyes Feliz, and Pancho Dominguez. And Antonia Molinera, who was the one asking the most difficult questions, and with the least deference to Joaquin's status as leader.

He would talk to La Molinera later about her tone. That would turn into an argument—the lady's temper was ferocious—but arguments with her usually prompted their most passionate lovemaking, so that was a saving grace.

"I wanted to send a message to the other lawmen in California," he said.

"And that message was?"

"To leave us alone or suffer the consequences."

"I'm not sure they got that message the way you intended it."

She was right about that. In the three weeks since Deputy Clark's killing, lawmen might have trembled in their boots, but the towns and cities they worked for had taken a more aggressive stance. Up and down the state, they'd posted rewards for the capture or killing of Joaquin. The first ones, Stockton and San José, each offered five thousand dollars. Los

Angeles, San Francisco, and Sacramento City matched that. Smaller towns put up a few hundred dollars. Instead of making them all safer, he'd managed to get a price put on his own head. And his men would, doubtless, be targeted as well.

"True," he said. "We might well have amateurs after us for the reward. Bounty hunters. I say that any lawmen who come for us have to suffer, painfully and publicly. If we keep the professionals frightened, the amateurs will tread carefully."

"What about the other Joaquins?" Reyes asked. "Should we do anything about them?"

Over the past few months, at least four other bandit leaders in California had started calling themselves Joaquin, whether or not that was their true given name. Each seemed to be trying to achieve some level of notoriety, perhaps to become known as the fiercest of the Joaquins. "They only help us," Joaquin said. "If one strikes in Santa Barbara on the same day that I strike in Volcano, then people think I'm a phantom, able to be in two places at once. And if some lawmen or bounty hunter kills any of the Joaquins, people may believe he's killed me, so when I strike again, I'll seem to have risen from the dead. The more afraid of us there are, the better."

"So, business as usual?"

"More or less. I'd like to step up the pace. More robberies. More horses stolen. Let's amass as much wealth as we can, while showing the authorities that they can't frighten us. I've heard about a place called Garlin's Draw, a camp in the northern mines, that's discovered a rich vein. By all accounts, everybody there is stockpiling gold by the pound. I want to raid the camp with a dozen men or more and scoop up as much gold as we can carry. But it's going to be a complex operation, and dangerous, and I wanted to get everybody's thoughts on how best to carry it off."

Pancho Dominguez cleared his throat. Joaquin planted his feet on the floor and turned his attention to the man. "You have something to say, Lieutenant Dominguez?" Using his old army rank was intentional, meant to put the man off guard, to diminish the import anything he might say. His tactical advice was usually sound, but because Joaquin relied on it from time to time, he seemed to consider himself more important to the operation than he really was.

"I'd like to know, Joaquin, what is the strategic purpose of this?"

"Strategic purpose?" What the hell was the man talking about? "We're bandits. We steal. These people have found lots of gold. The purpose is to take their gold and make it ours."

But instead of quieting Pancho, the answer just seemed to annoy him. "But to what end?"

"I don't know what you're talking about, Pancho. To get rich. That's obvious."

"We're already rich," Pancho said. "I've got more treasure in my tent than I've ever had in my life. But if you'll look around Arroyo de Cantua, you'll see there are very few places to spend it."

"You can go to Sacramento City, or San Francisco, or someplace. Even the mining camps have cantinas and gambling parlors and whorehouses, as well as shops and restaurants. If you want to spend some, take a few days and pick one."

The others sat quietly, listening to the debate. They'd better not be getting any foolish ideas in their heads.

"That's not my point. The point is that we're amassing all this wealth and hoarding it away. Meanwhile, most Mexicans in California are dirt-poor, scraping to get by. Children going hungry."

"We share our wealth with them whenever we can!"

"A little here, a little there. We improve the lots of people we happen to run across, and that's fine. But it's not a plan. It's not, as I said, a strategy. We could use our wealth to help *all* our people, if we put some thought into it."

This was aggravating. What would the others think if he just pulled out a gun and shot Dominguez in front of them? Relax, he told himself. Pancho's got a wild hair, but he'll get past it. "How would we do that?"

"I'm not sure. But I know that with wealth comes power, and with power comes the ability to do good for people."

"Now you're sounding like a politician, Pancho. We aren't politicians! We're bandits!"

"I just know that in the army—" Joaquin had known this was coming. It always did, with this guy. "—in the army, the enlisted men were far more numerous, but the officers had the power. They told us where to go, what to do, who to shoot. Sometimes, they sent us forward to die. And we did it. Because we had to believe that the officers had a strategy in mind. I don't think you do, Joaquin. I think you're only interested in amassing more wealth, but not in doing anything useful for our people with that wealth."

"I'll tell you what, Pancho. When I want your opinion from now on, I'll ask you for it. Otherwise, I don't want to hear your voice. Is that clear?"

Dominguez crossed his arms over his expansive gut and studied Joaquin with narrowed eyes. He wanted to keep arguing, that was clear, but he didn't dare.

Joaquin let his gaze travel across the others, to see how they were reacting.

But when his eyes met Antonia's, she said, "Pancho has a point. If we put some effort into it, we could gain real power in this state."

"We do have real power," Joaquin insisted. "We're getting more all the time. Right now, I'm mostly concerned about keeping the law off our backs and continuing to make Mexicans richer and gringos poorer. If anybody has a problem with that—" He paused, then, and let his gaze rest on Dominguez. "—he can feel free to leave at any time."

Pancho held his gaze for a few seconds, then looked away. Later, Joaquin would talk to him directly, making sure that he understood the message. His people could disagree with him, but they couldn't threaten his authority like that. Pancho's career in Joaquin's band had just come to an end, whether he knew it yet or not.

• • •

The meeting broke up a few minutes later. After taking turns at the latrine and washing up in the basin of water that Reyes filled three times a day from the creek, Joaquin and Antonia retired to their room and closed the door. Joaquin had a nightly ritual: rifle—a brand-new Sharps carbine—by the window, which Carrillo, who'd been a skilled carpenter, had covered with a heavy wooden shutter that he had stolen from a home near Monterey and affixed to the outer wall. An ammunition pouch close by. Colt revolver on a small table by the door, with two spare cylinders, already loaded. Bowie knife beside the bed, and a cavalry saber under it.

Those things done, he turned to Antonia, who was half-undressed. "You can't talk to me like that in front of the men," he said, working to keep the anger from his voice. "They need to know that I'm the boss—not you, or anybody else. It undermines me."

"I'm not one of your men," she said, not even trying to hide her anger. She'd known this was coming. Her eyes narrowed as she cupped her breasts. "See? I'm your woman, and if I can't speak honestly then there's no reason for me to be here."

"Can't you speak honestly but with more consideration for my position? It's not easy to lead such a large band. We're almost a small army now, and in any army, some men look for any chance to replace the generals."

Antonia shed the rest of her clothing. Her body never failed to stir Joaquin, but the look she gave him was cold, appraising, and not necessarily liking what she saw. "What do you know about armies? You never fought in the war."

"My father and brother did. So did Tres Dedos, but I was too young."

"Boys fought. Pancho fought."

"Don't mention his name! He's finished here. Anyway, you know my father made me stay home to take care of the women. Somebody had to."

Antonia pulled on a nightgown that clung to her curves. "Joaquin, you knew before you took me away that I speak my mind. Do you want me to be more like your Rosa, is that it? Young, shy, depending on you for everything?"

He hated it when she used that name. She asked sometimes about the frayed scrap of red silk he always carried in a pocket, but he had never told her what it was. He knew it would have ignited her jealousy, and she probably would have demanded he get rid of it. Or destroyed it herself.

That, he could never allow. "You have no idea what Rosita was like, Antonia. There was only one of her, and there'll never be another. I don't even compare you to her."

"I've heard your stories. If what you want in a woman is a decoration instead of a full partner, and an honest one, then perhaps I should go home. Is that what you want? To get rid of me?"

"You know it's not. You've seemed . . . I don't know, far

away sometimes, even when we're together. Like there are other things on your mind, weighing on you."

"Is that a surprise? You're gone so much, and now, you won't even take me with you when you go. Of course there are other things on my mind. I'm not a doll you can pick up and play with, and then I just sit on a shelf while you're away. I'm a person, with a mind. When you're gone I have to amuse myself, and there's not much to do around here but think. Most of your men aren't intelligent enough to have a conversation with, and their women are even worse."

She'd never spoken to him about these concerns. He knew she was still angry about being left behind, but he had thought she would be as happy here as he was—not that he had given much consideration to her feelings about it. When he was here, she seemed content enough, but when he was gone, he was usually too busy to wonder how she was faring. She complained occasionally, but he had too much on his mind to pay much attention. "I'm sorry it's so boring for you."

"You know what my life was like before. I was busy, working in the bakery. At night there were parties, dances, restaurants. People around. Then you let me go along on robberies, and I loved that. Then you took that from me, too. Of course this is strange and different."

He sat on the bed, pulled off his boots and dropped them one by one to the plank floor. "I guess I never thought about it that way."

"Of course not." She climbed into the bed on the other side and sat up with her back against the wall. He undressed, but she didn't look at him. Maybe there would be no lovemaking tonight, after all.

"What does that mean?"

"You put me on a horse and took me away from the life

that I had. You didn't think about what that would mean to me. Men never think about things like that."

"So now it's not just me, it's all men?"

She crossed her arms over her chest. "You said it, not me."

"But it's true?"

"I wouldn't argue with it."

He sat beside her on the bed, took her hand in his. She didn't resist, but she didn't squeeze his hand. Hers was so limp he might as well have been holding a dead fish. "What do you want, Antonia?"

"You're going to go raid this rich camp you've been talking about. I don't want to be stuck here while you're being chased, if you are. And you won't allow me to go along, even though most of the plan was mine. It's better if I go home. At least I can see my parents and my friends. I miss them."

"I don't have time to take you back to San José," he said. "We have to leave for the north right away, before they transfer out any of the gold."

"You asked what I want. I don't want to wait here, where there's nothing to do. Either take me along, or—"

"No!" They'd been over this. Why didn't she understand? It was for her own good. "I told you before, you can't go out with us anymore. It's too dangerous."

"I don't get to decide what danger is too much?"

"No. I'm the leader of this band. What I say, goes, and I say you stay back."

"At least let me visit my family, then. Or is that too dangerous, too?"

In San José, at least she would be safe. And letting her go would make her feel like she'd had a victory. Or, at least, he hoped so.

"All right," he said. "I'll send a couple of men along, to see

you safely there. They'll stay in the house so if there's anything you need while you're there, they can provide it. You
can stay there, too, or—"

She cut him off. "I'll stay with my parents. I don't trust your
men, when you're not around."

"Antonia, I love you. I wouldn't let anything happen to
you."

"You love me?"

"Of course I do."

She squeezed the hand holding hers, and he felt her other
hand on his thigh. When he looked at her, her expression had
changed, the anger gone or at least dimmed. Instead, her eyes
were wide, her lips parted. "Prove it."

He shifted position, put his arms around her, and drew her
in for a kiss. That led to other things.

By the time they slept, dawn was breaking, light slipping
in through the slats in the shutter.

46

April 1853, Garlin's Draw, California

Some aspects of life in the camps had changed since Joaquin's mining days, but not this one: Sunday was a day of rest. Monday through Saturday were for backbreaking labor, working to eke out every flake of gold that could be torn from the earth. Sundays, miners patched their clothing, mended their boots, fixed their tools, hunted game. They wrote letters home and reread the ones they'd received. Some of the larger towns had Democratic or Republican clubs, or cultural organizations where those of a mind to could discuss the arts, watch plays, read books, and talk about philosophy. If there was a church nearby, some attended services. Those with different inclinations might visit brothels or saloons, but even those were quieter on Sundays than on evenings during the week.

Thinking about church brought a lump to Joaquin's throat. He hadn't attended Mass since Rosita's murder, and if he ever again set foot in a confessional, he would likely be there for a month.

Garlin's Draw wasn't one of the bigger towns. When he spied it from a nearby hillside, Joaquin was reminded of the rough-and-ready camps he had found upon first arriving from Mexico. People lived in tents and hastily erected shacks set among boulders bigger than any of the homes, not buildings of stone or brick. Mature trees, widely spaced, stood among the dwellings, but if there had been underbrush, it had been cleared away. The ground was dirt, well-trod but not completely packed. The strike here was recent, and men—as they had always done—were still in the process of abandoning their existing claims to race to this new one.

Joaquin knew how that would go. Those who were here first—the ones who'd discovered gold in the rivers or streams or, as in this case, in a ditch they'd been digging to divert water from a stream, only to find that the earth was richer than the water—would become wealthy. Latecomers would arrive to find the best claims taken, the vein tapped out. They would move on, most of them, chasing the next rumor. A few would give up, finally coming to grips with the fact that California's riches weren't for everyone. Some of those would go to the cities—San Francisco, Stockton, even Los Angeles—and look for work. Others would go back to Virginia or Pennsylvania or Georgia, wherever their homes and families were. Still others, unable to face defeat or the embarrassment of returning empty-handed, would end their lives with a bullet or a leap from a mountain path, or the slow way, with liquor or laudanum or opium. There were plenty of ways to die in California—more than there were ways to grow wealthy, anyway.

Then, there were the bandits.

Fourteen mounted men surrounded Joaquin. Spring in northern California was edging toward summer. Mexican poppies carpeted the hillside beneath them in a brilliant orange, fairly glowing in the early-morning sun.

"It's a little larger than I expected," Joaquin said. "More tents."

"It's been a few weeks," Tres Dedos said. That was true; the message from one of Joaquin's contacts in this part of the state had taken some time to filter through channels to him. Then, more time had passed while they'd made the plan, chosen the men, and reached this point. During that time, the ranks of gold-seekers must have grown dramatically.

"We should have brought more men. All of them."

"And leave Arroyo de Cantua unguarded? Just the women there?"

"We don't have enough."

"We have what we have, Joaquin. Do you want to call it off? Go back home?"

Joaquin shook his head. He rubbed his forehead with his fingers, trying to think. He'd imagined a sparsely populated camp, with maybe two dozen miners and piles of gold. From the looks of the place, there must be at least fifty or sixty men living here—how many he couldn't say for sure, because some of the tents and structures might hold two or ten. His original plan had been to ride in with guns blazing, to intimidate the outgunned miners into giving up their hoards.

That wasn't going to work. Without knowing how many men were in those shelters, they might find themselves vastly outnumbered. He wished he had brought Antonia after all. The initial idea had been hers; she might have been able to see how to alter the plan to fit the circumstances.

Pancho would've been helpful, too; he was good at military tactics, and this looked more like a battle than a robbery. But the last time he'd seen Pancho, after the meeting, he had redressed the man for speaking out of turn. The conversation had deteriorated into a shouting match. Pancho had taken refuge in his tent, and hadn't emerged when Joaquin had called the men together. It was for the best, anyway. The sight of him drove Joaquin to fury, and if he had been here, Joaquin might have looked for an excuse to put a bullet in his head.

But he wished he knew some of what Pancho did about how to attack a greater force with a smaller one. He pondered a while, then announced his decision. "We can't go in the way we talked about. We'll have to be quiet, go house to house and try not to let anyone sound an alarm."

"You mean kill everyone in the first place, then move on to the next one and kill them?" The glint in Tres Dedos's eye suggested that he liked the idea.

"That's not exactly what I was thinking."

"You think when we rob the first place, the people inside will sit quietly while we go to the next?"

"We can tie them up, gag them. Knock them out. Something."

"Some will have to die."

Joaquin shrugged. "Perhaps some. But not all. We didn't come here for a massacre."

"You're the boss."

"Don't forget it."

• • •

They discussed the new plan with the other men, and when everybody was informed, they rode down the hill. A few of the men stayed behind the huge boulders with the horses, out of sight of the small settlement, with orders to quietly deal with anyone who might happen across them. Joaquin, Tres Dedos, and Florencio Cruz, who was two heads taller than Joaquin and heavily muscled, with a wicked scar bisecting his face from brow to upper lip, went alone to the nearest dwelling, while others waited outside. The first few shelters went off without a hitch. They encountered two men in a shack, and one each in a few tents. Whether intimidated by the guns, Tres Dedos's knives, or Cruz's sheer size, the men gave up their gold without a fight. In each case, Joaquin called two of the other men up at the end, one to carry the gold to the horses and the other to ensure the occupant's silence one way or another.

The fifth place they approached was somewhat sturdier than most of the others, and Joaquin suspected its resident was probably one of the original miners who'd happened upon the rich vein. When they reached the door, Joaquin tried it. Bolted from the inside. He stood aside and told Cruz to kick it open.

Cruz reared back and kicked so hard the door flew off its hinges and crashed to the floor. "So much for doing this quietly," Tres Dedos said.

Joaquin shot him an angry glare and stepped inside, walking on the broken door. Two men had been sleeping side by side on blankets spread on the floor, but they woke at the rude entrance. One reached for a musket leaning against the wall nearby. Joaquin was faster and snatched it away.

"We aren't here to hurt you," he said. He did his best to sound reassuring, although the revolver in his hand and the appearance of Tres Dedos and Cruz behind him made the statement's credibility questionable. "We just want your gold. Show us where it is, and we'll be gone."

The inside resembled many miner's cabins he'd been in. A potbelly stove, some pans hanging on the wall, a rack of dishes and a crude wooden table marked the kitchen area. The aforementioned blankets constituted the bed. Clothing, personal items, and other belongings were piled in another corner. The place smelled of sweat and unwashed bodies. If there was gold, he didn't see it.

"We got no gold," the older of the two said. He might have been in his thirties, his companion barely in his twenties. Mining was no business for old men, but it quickly aged the young.

"You live here, in the best cabin on the draw, and have no gold?" Joaquin said. "Why don't I believe you?"

"If you can find any," the younger man put in, "then take it."

"We don't have time to hunt. Florencio, the younger one, if you please."

Cruz started forward, flexing his huge hands. Before he even reached the young man, the older shot to his feet. "No! Don't hurt him! I'll show you."

"Be quick," Joaquin urged. "Florencio's not a patient man."

The older man stepped off the blankets and to a pair of floorboards uncovered by the general clutter. Stooping over, he gripped the slightly raised corner of one board and lifted it up, setting it aside. Then he shoved the other one over, revealing a hidey-hole under the floor that brimmed with sacks of what looked like nuggets, and jars of dust. "Hand it over," Joaquin said, wary of a boobytrap inside.

But the men must have thought their hiding place ensured the treasure's safety. The young one joined his partner and together they hauled the gold up, placing it into the hands of the three men. Joaquin carried some to the door and summoned help.

When he reached the doorway, Mota said, "People heard the sound of that door falling in. You'd better come out here."

"What is it?" Joaquin asked.

"Miners. Coming this way."

"Armed?"

"Some, yes."

"Hurry up!" Joaquin snapped, waving the rest of the men over. He handed some of the gold to the first to arrive. "Get this to the horses and prepare to hold off the miners!"

Seven men managed to carry the gold away. Joaquin quickly scanned for other weapons, seeing nothing but some mining tools—a pick and a couple of shovels—that could be used for mayhem if necessary. He kept the musket in his left hand, thanked the miners inside, and stepped out over the remains of the door.

Mota had been right. Other men from around the draw were converging, most carrying weapons of some kind. At a quick glance, Joaquin estimated twenty, but others were still emerging from their dwellings and starting down a gentle slope toward them.

"They seem nice," Tres Dedos said, his tone heavily laced with sarcasm.

"Maybe they'll let us go without a fight."

"Maybe they came to offer us the rest of their gold."

Joaquin transferred the musket to his right hand, with the pistol, making it clear that he couldn't use either. He held up his left and, palm out. "Stop there," he said. "This has nothing to do with you. We're leaving."

Then the younger man burst from the cabin, shouting, "They took it all! Every flake!"

"Should've killed them," Tres Dedos muttered.

"When you're right, you're right," Joaquin said. He dropped the musket and raised the Colt.

The miners had stopped at his command, but the young man's words had inflamed them. The man who had advanced the farthest was a hard-bitten sort, with muscular forearms holding a musket of his own. His nose had been broken at least once, and the scars on his face and exposed arms suggested a history of brawling. "We don't much like Mex thieves here," he said.

"But gringo ones are all right?" Tres Dedos asked him.

"Any kind o' thieves. Or any kind o' Mexes, for that matter."

Joaquin lowered his left hand, slowly, and curled his finger around the Colt's trigger. "Like I said, we're leaving."

"Not with American gold."

"Do you see any gold? Are we carrying any?"

"They already put it on their horses!" the young miner shouted.

These men wanted a fight, and they wouldn't stop until they got one. Joaquin didn't care for the odds, but a person had to play the cards he'd been dealt. He turned toward the young miner with the big mouth and fired a shot that caught him in the belly. Then he whirled back toward the armed miners and snapped off another at the mouthy one with the musket. This round struck the man just below his right eye, and he crumpled instantly.

The other miners armed with tools charged, screaming raw, wordless cries. Most of those with guns hesitated, afraid of shooting their own, but a few got off shots that flew more or less toward Joaquin and his men, kicking up dirt and shredding leaves on trees overhead.

Joaquin's men had it easier. The approaching throng made for easy targets, and the miners ran headlong into a fusillade of lead. Some were struck two or three times and went down before they reached the outlaws. Others kept coming.

Through the haze of white smoke Joaquin saw a man wearing the tattered remnants of an American army uniform shirt drop to one knee and sight down the barrel of a musket at him. Joaquin didn't have time to deal with him, though, as another was rushing at him with an upraised ax, seemingly heedless of the three shots he'd already taken, from which blood blossomed on his shirt and vest like wildflowers in spring. Joaquin squeezed off one more, but the man ignored that as he had the others.

Instead of wasting another bullet, Joaquin shoved up from a crouch, lunging in too close for the ax to strike him. He slammed his skull into the man's chin, stopping his advance, and grabbed the ax handle. Using it as leverage, he turned his attacker so that he was between Joaquin and the sharpshooter with the musket. As the two wrestled, the musket ball crashed into the ax-wielder's head, showering Joaquin in blood and bone fragments. Finally, the man collapsed.

Joaquin snatched the ax from the dead man's hand and swung it into the nearest miner. The sharp edge tore into the man's midsection and innards and fluids spilled onto the earth. The injured man stood there for long moments, looking at the wound, his hands seeming to try to reach down to hold himself together but unable to move, and then he fell forward and landed with a thud.

As if that took the steam out of the miners, the attack stopped as suddenly as it had begun. The people farther away from the bandits simply turned and left the scene, heading for their homes or the shelter of the big rocks and trees. The ones who were closer or locked in battle lowered their weapons. Some gave brief nods, as if acknowledging defeat. A couple of his men seemed like they wanted to give chase or continue the fight, but Joaquin ended that with a gesture.

"Let them go," he added. "We're finished here. Let's mount up."

He took a last look at the battlefield. Two of his own men were down, but at least nine of the miners had fallen, either dead or soon to be. Blood trickled downslope, and soft moaning could be heard, as could weeping and grumbling from some distant tents. Soon enough, anger would force some of the men out again, better armed if they had the option. It was time to go.

As he mounted his horse, he thought about the man with the musket. He'd appeared to have combat experience. He had identified Joaquin as the leader and decided that if he fell, the others would lose their spirit. He had taken careful aim, and he'd handled the weapon like he knew what he was doing. He'd had Joaquin dead to rights, and by rights, Joaquin should be dead right now. But by the time he'd pulled the trigger, Joaquin had managed to position one of the man's own neighbors to block his shot.

Was he, in fact, indestructible? He had heard about a man in southern Mexico who could fly over the mountains and forests. He didn't know if it was true, but he had no reason to doubt it. The Church preferred that the only acknowledged supernatural feats were those it described, but however devoutly Catholic a man was, Joaquin was still a Mexican, and every Mexican knew that magic was all around him.

Once more, he'd escaped almost certain death. What if he hadn't simply come to California, but been called here? Pancho had suggested as much from time to time.

Perhaps the part he had to play had been ordained from the start.

He couldn't know for sure, but riding away with pounds and pounds of gold distributed between his saddlebags and those of his comrades, and only two men left behind on the field, he couldn't deny the possibility.

He had always felt that he was destined for greatness. The longer he lived when everyone seemed to want him dead, the more convinced he became.

47

Lucas Rhodes sat in the office of Benjamin Franklin Marshall in Carson's Creek, describing the atrocity that had occurred at Garlin's Draw. Both men were veterans of the Mexican War, but they hadn't known each other then. Rhodes had seen combat at Monterrey and Buena Vista, where he'd been grievously wounded by Santa Anna's lancers and forced to give up the fight. He wasn't sure where Marshall had fought, but he was from Indiana, so might've been with the Indiana Volunteers, which also would've placed him on the bloody ground of Monterrey. Rhodes was twenty-seven years old but felt considerably older. At Buena Vista, he'd been barely out of his teens.

"And you think the leader was the outlaw Joaquin?" Marshall asked. Rhodes thought he'd already made that clear.

"I'm certain of it."

"How can you be so sure? Do you know him?"

"Only through stories. But from all of those, I have an idea of what he looks like. Another of his men was missing a finger on one hand, so I took him to be Three-Fingered Jack."

Marshall rubbed his narrow jaw. He was a slender man, unprepossessing at first glance, but with a wiry strength to him. A full head of brown hair and piercing blue eyes were his most noteworthy features. He'd been elected in 1851, using the slogan "Time for Marshall Law," but his position had been in question until this year. After the election, the county clerk had certified W.H. Nelson, not Marshall, as the winner. While Nelson and Marshall fought it out in district court, another fellow, Albert La Forge, had taken it upon himself to collect taxes in Calaveras County, and had done so, keeping the sheriff's standard share for himself. Finally, Marshall had been ruled sheriff and been officially recognized.

"And how many men did he command?" Marshall finally asked.

"More than ten. I'd say between twelve and eighteen, but I'm not certain. Two of them were killed in the fight, as I said. They haven't been buried yet, so if you'd like to see them—"

Marshall's face wrinkled at the idea, causing Rhodes to wonder briefly if the man had seen combat at all. The sight of corpses was surely a familiar one to anyone who'd been at Monterrey.

"That won't be necessary. I'm sure I wouldn't recognize them."

"Just the same, the tracking will have to begin at the Draw."

"Of course."

"So, you'll raise a posse? Several of us from Garlin's Draw will volunteer. They murdered our friends, our neighbors."

The sheriff's right eyebrow arched. "How many volunteers, would you say?"

"Nine men told me they'd go, if we can raise a reasonable number force."

"To kill the outlaw Joaquin?" Rhodes caught the gleam in Marshall's eyes. He was either thinking about the rewards that had been offered, or about the glory of being the man to bring in the infamous bandit. Rhodes didn't care which, as long as the lawman was handy with a gun. He had missed his only shot at the outlaw leader, back at Garlin's Draw, and he wanted another one. But this time, he wanted more men behind him. "I think I can pull together a right smart posse for that."

"When will you start?" Rhodes asked.

Marshall pushed back his chair and rose to his feet, hands flat on his desk. "How about now?"

• • •

Worried about possible pursuit, the bandits had once again steered clear of Arroyo de Cantua until they knew they were in the clear. Instead, they'd traveled north and east, into El Dorado County and the foothills of the Sierra Nevada. Arriving one night at the remote ranch of a contact named Elfuego Torrejon, he fed them beef from his own stock and brought them news that had been sent through the Mexican grapevine.

"Sheriff Marshall is on your trail, maybe two days behind," Torrejon said.

Joaquin nodded. "Not surprising. Thirteen men and fifteen horses leave an easy trail."

Torrejon frowned. "People are saying he's not just following your tracks. He's torturing Mexicans to find out if anybody knows where you are."

"Torturing?"

"He and some of the other men have beaten men, choked them, cut them, made them stand naked in the cold. I heard a few have even raped women in front of their men, or begun to, unless the men said what they knew."

The news tore at Joaquin's insides. He had thought himself steeled against any new outrages from California's white community, but this was a new low. Individuals brutalizing others. "And have those men told them anything useful?"

"Hard to say," Torrejon replied, shrugging his shoulders. "What seems minor or obvious to us might be helpful to the law. Possibly any little fact they can learn could help them find you."

"So, we have to make sure we can't be found," Tres Dedos offered. "Avoid our usual spots."

"Yes," Joaquin said. "I'm sorry we came here, Elfuego. I hope we haven't brought you trouble."

"There's nothing they can do to me that hasn't already been done." One look at Torrejon proved the truth of that. He was perhaps in his mid-forties but looked decades older, his face lined and worn, his dark hair streaked with silver, shoulders stooped from a lifetime's hard labor. "I have no woman for them to threaten, and my ranch hands would fight like wolves if they came near me."

The mention of wolves gave Joaquin an idea, but he didn't want to discuss it in front of Torrejon, in case he was indeed tortured and proved weaker than he thought. They spent the night in the man's barn, and there, Joaquin discussed it with the men. In the morning, after an early breakfast of eggs from Torrejon's chickens and pork from his swine, they started out again, this time with a specific destination in mind.

• • •

Bear Mountain had changed little since Joaquin's last visit. It was far enough from any settlements that people seldom visited. No gold had been found there, and the presence of the numerous bears, wolves, and other wild predators helped dissuade the merely curious. The cavern below the summit would offer safe refuge for his men, and the rocky slopes would make tracking difficult. If they took care to cover their back trail, finding them would be close to impossible.

They took care. After circling around the base of the mountain and climbing about a third of the way up, they dismounted, left the horses in the care of one man, and walked back over their own tracks for an hour. From that point, they worked to restore the land to the condition it had been in originally, brushing away hoofprints, straightening branches, replacing upturned stones and the like. They continued disguising their tracks until they reached the horses again. Hours had passed during which they hadn't put space between themselves and the posse, but the hope was that the posse would lose their trail altogether at that point.

Having done that, they continued up the mountain to the cave. From there, they could see the posse's approach, and follow their progress—if any—once they reached the spot where the bandits had covered their tracks.

The posse members arrived at that point late that afternoon. Joaquin watched through a spyglass as trackers climbed down from their mounts and studied the ground. He couldn't hear from this distance, but they were obviously discussing the impossibility of fifteen horses simply disappearing. They started off on foot this way and that, but couldn't find a clear trail in any direction. Joaquin doubted the skills of their trackers—despite the efforts of his men, a good tracker should have been able to pick up some sign of passage. But their confusion lifted his spirits. When the sun sank behind the mountains and they still hadn't found the trail, the posse members pitched tents and lit a small fire for cooking.

Marshall was there, all right. A thin man, brown-haired, with no mustache. He didn't look like a dangerous type. Joaquin had seen him a time or two in his mining days, before he was sheriff, and never had a problem with him.

But he had a problem with him now.

Standing near the sheriff was another man who looked familiar, though it was hard to be certain through the little telescope. But he wore the sky-blue of the American army, and

Joaquin believed him to be the man who'd nearly shot him back at Garlin's Draw.

"All right, men," Joaquin said. "Time to go back down the mountain. Those fellows are in for a surprise."

• • •

The outlaws were in no hurry. Making one's way down Bear Mountain on foot was a dangerous pursuit, especially if one rushed and took foolish chances. The moon was just a sliver behind high, wispy clouds, and it had risen in mid-afternoon, so would soon be gone altogether. With Joaquin leading the way down game trails he knew, they moved slowly and quietly, helping one another through difficult stretches. They wanted to give the posse time to eat, perhaps drink some liquor, and fall asleep.

The descent took hours. Joaquin spotted only one bear, and it kept its distance because of the number of men. He figured there was probably a cougar or two watching their efforts, but the big cats were stealth itself, and most people never spotted one, though the beasts always knew what was happening in their territory. Wolves, too, kept their distance when so many men were about, but other creatures of the night—owls, bats, snakes, rabbits, rats, and more—were everywhere.

As they neared the camp—the fire had dwindled to bright coals, but its smoke could be seen rising into the air, and the snores of two dozen men or more heard for some considerable distance—they slowed even more. Silence became the order of the moment. The posse had surely posted guards, and it wouldn't do to alert them and have the rest of the camp aroused.

Finally, they were close enough to look down upon the camp. Some men slept in the open, others in tents. Joaquin turned to Tres Dedos, at his side as always, and whispered,

"There they are. You see any guards awake?"

"I see one sleeping at his post," Tres Dedos said, pointing out a man sitting upright with a rifle in his hands, but with his chin against a chest that rose and fell in the regular rhythm of slumber.

"I'd post more than one, if it was me." Joaquin let his gaze travel across the camp and its surroundings, until it landed on a man walking toward the camp, adjusting his pants.

"There," he said, directing Tres Dedos's attention toward the man. "He was pissing."

"I hope he had a good piss," Tres Dedos said. "When I die, I want to have had a good piss first, so I don't soak my pants. Outdoors, against a tree or into a river, that's the way to do it. The way God intended. If they ever put me in jail, I won't piss inside. I'll just hold it in until I explode."

"I'm not sure that's possible," Joaquin countered.

"Well, I'll try, anyway. I'm glad this fellow did it away from the camp," Tres Dedos said. "That's decent of him. I hate it when a man can't bring himself to walk far enough away that the smell doesn't drift back before he does."

"Don't admire him too much to kill him."

"Never."

"So, two. Any more?"

Tres Dedos tapped his arm and pointed to a man lying down, but rolling and twitching in obvious discomfort. "He's no guard, but he's not sleeping soundly, that's for sure. Stomach troubles, maybe." He sniffed the air. "Smells like they had vulture for dinner. Or skunk. Something that shouldn't be eaten, anyway."

Joaquin kept studying the layout. He'd heard there were thirty-two men at the outset, but rumor had it that some had already dropped out and headed home, and that was obviously true. He couldn't get a definite count, with some ensconced in tents, but with the spyglass earlier he had counted fourteen. Even that was uncertain, though, as they'd been moving around and he might have missed a couple, or double-counted some. Around that, though.

And he had thirteen. Not only were the numbers close, but he had the advantages of surprise and elevation. And his men were wide awake.

He gathered the men around him and pointed out the camp, the tents, the fire, and the guards. The one who'd just returned had found the sleeping one and shaken him by the shoulder, rousing him. Two awake, for sure. That one on the ground who might or might not be sleeping. No way to know the status of anyone in the tents. The guards had moved away from the fire and taken up positions on opposite sides of the camp, looking outward. Every few minutes, they got up and moved around, keeping themselves alert and sweeping the whole perimeter.

They'd chosen a good spot to make camp. Most of it was ringed by large rocks that would block the wind and could provide cover in a fight. The ground was fairly flat, but on a very slight slope, so in the event of a sudden storm, the water would move through instead of building up. Their horses were picketed a short distance away, within sight of the camp.

He outlined his proposal, and the men nodded their agreement. At his direction, some of the biggest of them put their backs to a massive boulder, seemingly well-rooted in the mountainside. Heaving and grunting, they pushed and pushed, and finally it broke free from its resting place. Suddenly, loose dirt cascaded down the slope, and Joaquin worried that it might alert the posse below. If any fell that far, though, nobody reacted in a way that he could see.

Then the men stopped, with Florencio Cruz and Atanacio Moreno straining to hold the big stone from beneath. "Are we ready, Joaquin?" Cruz asked.

Recognizing the urgency of the moment, Joaquin took a quick, last look at the path. "This should wake them," he said. "Let it go!"

Cruz and Moreno moved and the men holding the stone from above released it at the same moment. It shifted, then leaned, and seemed like it might stay in one position forever. Then, without any apparent reason, it decided to let go, and it toppled from the spot it had rested for what might have been decades, or centuries.

On the way down, it struck the mountainside a couple of times, breaking other, lesser rocks free. The noise was thunderous, and the men camped below heard it, too. Screams of terror reached Joaquin's ears. He leaned far over the side for a better view, and almost slipped, but Gustavo Zaragoza caught his waistband and held on.

Then the boulder crashed to earth, accompanied by a storm of smaller stones, in the center of the camp. Joaquin couldn't see how many men were killed instantly, though some certainly were. Others scrambled away from the rain of stone.

"All right, men," Joaquin said. "Pick your targets and let go." He selected a man who'd been hit by a good-sized rock and was bleeding from the scalp and stumbling around senselessly and fired his revolver. The range wasn't ideal, but he was shooting almost straight down, so the bullet would strike with sufficient force, he thought. His first shots missed, but he hit the man on the fourth try. The others were all shooting by then, too, and most of the posse members who'd escaped the initial landslide had fallen. Some, though, had escaped both, and were trying to return fire.

After several minutes, nobody fired guns from below, and he could no longer see movement from the camp. "Let's go," he said. He led them back to a game trail he knew, and within a few minutes, they'd passed through a choking cloud of dust rising from below and arrived at the scene of the carnage.

Dead and dying Americans were everywhere: one beside the fire, face down, another with his lower half sticking out of a bloody tent flap, two who'd never made it out of their bedrolls. Parts of what might have been several different people showed at the edges of the great boulder.

He didn't see Marshall anywhere.

As the odor of burnt powder cleared, he smelled piss and shit, blood and vomit and sweat; the scents of men under fire. Only two of the bodies wore badges. Most of these men were merchants, miners, farmers, husbands and fathers, not deputies. They'd been conscripted or volunteered for a task to which they were unsuited, and they'd paid the highest price. The things they carried, for the most part, weren't even worth the taking. Joaquin felt sorry for them, for having been put in danger by a lawman who should've known better.

Inside a tent, someone whimpered in obvious agony. Joaquin bent over, stuck his head and arm inside the tent, and ended the young man's pain with one shot. He went from there to the other tent, on the eastern edge, and saw a slash at the back of it where the occupants had cut their way out and run out into the night.

"I count ten," Tres Dedos said. "Hard to tell how many are under the rock, though."

"Mota, count!" Joaquin called.

Mota nodded and raced around the camp, poking his head into tents and kicking at bunched blankets. "Ten!" he reported.

"So four escaped, if my count was right. Four, more or less."

"Do you want to try to find them now?" Tres Dedos asked. "Could be dangerous in the dark."

Joaquin knew that to Tres Dedos, danger wasn't a drawback. It was the attraction. "No, let's get some rest and wait until dawn."

"They could get pretty far by then."

"They won't. They don't know where they are, or what they're facing. And besides..." He paused, smiled.

"Besides?"

"They're on my mountain."

48

When the attack began, Lucas Rhodes was already awake. He'd slept little since Sheriff Marshall had agree to form a posse to pursue the murderers from Garlin's Draw. None of it had gone as he'd expected. He'd thought Marshall a righteous man and had guessed that the posse would simply follow the tracks left by the Mexican bandits' horses until they found the men.

But Marshall had a different idea. He had a reasonably skilled tracker on his payroll, a deputy named Link Jacobson, and the trail was easy enough to follow at first. But each time it became slightly more difficult—when, for example, it crossed a heavily traveled road, or in one case a path made by dozens or hundreds of sheep being driven from one pasture to another—Marshall didn't want to rely solely on Jacobson's skills. Instead, he found the nearest greaser and tried to pull information from him by brute force. A few Mexicans might have known something about Joaquin's whereabouts, but many didn't. It seemed to matter little to Marshall, Jacobson, and some of the other posse members, either way. Rhodes had the impression that the brutality was the point, and not the information that might or might not be gleaned.

He could have interfered, but the truth was, he didn't care much one way or the other. Ben Marshall felt the Mexicans were a scourge, almost as bad as the Miwoks, and that California rightfully belonged to white Americans now. Rhodes didn't have strong feelings about it. No, that wasn't true—the bloody massacre on Garlin's Draw haunted his dreams and his waking hours. He'd tried for years to convince himself that the Mexican War was about territory, not about hatred for another race of people. But the raid at the draw had changed that. He felt that Joaquin's band had targeted the draw specifically because those digging up gold were white. Only evil men would rob and murder for that reason. That made people with knowledge of their whereabouts who refused to cooperate equally suspect, and justified Marshall's treatment of them.

Some of the posse members couldn't take the brutality and abandoned the quest. Others left for reasons of their own. Marshall threatened a couple, but he couldn't scare people into staying. By the time they reached this mountain, Rhodes had started to doubt their chances even if they did find their quarry.

When they'd mysteriously lost the trail and looked for it until the sun was too low in the sky to continue, they'd made camp in a little hollow on the mountainside. Provisions were growing short, but they'd managed to bag a handful of rabbits, so everyone ate that night, and there was still plenty of liquor spread throughout various saddlebags. Because Marshall's tent was big enough for four men, he'd invited Rhodes, another war veteran named Charley Kroloff, and Jacobson to share it.

Lying awake, Rhodes heard something that didn't sound quite right—almost like rain, but not quite. He climbed out from under his blankets and crawled to Marshall's side. There he clamped a hand over the sheriff's mouth, waking him. "I think we're—" was all he got out when the big rock landed with enough force to shake the earth underfoot.

The other men woke at once, grabbing for their guns. They'd all slept in their clothes, with their boots on, as they had every night, half-expecting Joaquin's gang to double back on them. But instead of stepping out of the tent and into the line of fire—already, stones were ripping through the tent's roof—Marshall unsheathed a big knife and sliced an opening in its rear wall. He said, "Join me or not, up to you. But staying here is suicide." Jacobson pulled on his bowler hat and ducked through the opening as Marshall held it. Kroloff followed close behind. Rhodes and Marshall looked at each other, shrugged, and did the same. Rhodes grabbed a rifle and a canteen on his way out.

But by the time Marshall and Rhodes were out of harm's way, Kroloff and Jacobson were gone. They couldn't call out for the others, or risk circling around to where the horses were picketed. They were on their own, on foot in unknown country, with their comrades being murdered behind them.

It was a hell of a fix.

• • •

The only casualty among the bandits was Gregorio Lopez, who had a scrape on his right cheek—not from a bullet or a rifle ball, but from fragments of the rock he'd been leaning on to steady his gun that were thrown up by a bullet hitting the stone. It would leave a scar, likely, but it was far from life-threatening.

Joaquin had his men gather up the posse's weapons and ammunition. They deposited those near the horses—fourteen of them, so his long-distance count had been correct. One for each of his men, and a spare besides. He posted three guards, and the rest of the men settled down—just far enough away from the posse's camp to avoid the stench—to sleep until daybreak.

They didn't bury the bodies; already, vultures kettled overhead. Once the pack of human beings had left, wolves and coyotes and possibly bears would move in looking for the meat they'd smelled for hours, filling their bellies and then squabbling for the scraps. Finally, insects would clean the scattered bones. Burial was a ceremony for the living, but the dead didn't care, and nature dealt with the mess.

When the sun cleared the mountains to the east, they returned to the camp and scoured the eastern edge for signs of the men who'd escaped through the tent wall. Finding some broken branches in the brush, and prints from a few different boots, Joaquin put a man in charge of watching the extra horses they'd just acquired, while the other eleven mounted up and set off in pursuit. Joaquin wasn't worried about losing them—even if the men made it off the mountain, they were on foot, and the bandits had their horses.

For the first stretch, all four pairs of boots had gone in the same general direction. But then two pairs had taken a game trail that led farther up the mountain, and the other two had seemingly missed the trail in the dark and continued in a more-or-less straight line, cutting through thick underbrush. Mota, who was the best tracker among them, turned to Joaquin. "Should we split up?"

"No," Joaquin replied. "That trail is only going to take those men higher up, so we'll have more time to catch up to them. Let's stay with these two for now."

After another mile or so, the line the two men took

intersected another game trail. They had taken this one, turning downslope. Joaquin guessed that because they'd become separated and realized they'd lost the tracks of their comrades, they had decided their best course of action was to get off the mountain. This down-trending but winding path would run into dozens of other trails. Even if they made the correct choice every time, they still had hours to travel before reaching the bottom.

But the trail was easier on the horses, and the men had made no effort to hide their tracks. In less than an hour, Vulvia caught a glimpse of them and pointed them out to the others. Only one wore a hat, a dusty black bowler; the other was bareheaded, and had a long gun resting on one shoulder.

"We can take them from here," Lopez suggested. He was, perhaps, marksman enough to do it, but the distance was still great.

"Let's get closer," Joaquin said. "I want to see if one of them is that sheriff."

Lopez shrugged, but Joaquin could see the disappointment in his eyes. He liked to show off his sharpshooting skills.

Within a few minutes, the two Americans knew they were being followed. They took off at a run. Joaquin put his heels to the horse and sped up to a trot. The other men did the same. The men on foot reached a level spot with rocky soil, sparse vegetation, and a few larger boulders that had fallen from the heights over the centuries. Once they had a clear view of the mounted outlaws chasing them, they started sprinting, either hoping to find cover where it was scant or somehow, impossibly, to outrun the horses.

Finally realizing the latter was hopeless, they ducked behind one of the largest of the fallen boulders. The one with a long gun loaded it quickly and rested it on the boulder. He aimed and fired, but in his rush, he shot high, his ball soaring far over the heads of the riders. The other man had a revolver, which he fired several times. Two of his shots hit Tres Dedos's horse. The animal stumbled and fell, pitching Tres Dedos into the dirt.

"Goddamnit, not another horse!" he shouted, rising and dusting himself off. His face was bloody from scraping against the earth. He stormed toward the rock, seemingly oblivious to the fact that the men there still had guns. "They're mine!" he cried.

"Wait!" Joaquin called. He raised his hand and brought the other riders to a halt. "You men, throw down those guns. You have no chance against all of us."

"What kinda chance do we got without 'em?" the bare-headed one asked.

"I admit, that's a fair question," Joaquin said. "But the truth is, you men aren't very good shots. And you've made my friend very angry. At this point, I suspect he'd take you both on at once, without any guns. Is that right, Jack?"

He rarely used the name the Americans had given to Tres Dedos, but at this moment, it had the desired effect. The men's eyes widened, and their mouths dropped open. They were being asked to confront the dreaded Three-Fingered Jack, two-to-one, but with no firearms in play.

"Look, I ain't no fightin' man," the bareheaded one said. "I came out here to work the diggings. I went bust, and now I work in a store. I never hurt nobody."

"But you were willing to kill us, if you could have."

"You killed a bunch of Americans! Took their gold!"

"So, to punish killing, you would kill others?"

"An eye for an eye. It's in the Bible."

"Then if you would kill us, what's wrong with us killing you?"

By now, Tres Dedos was almost upon them. They hadn't given up their guns or come out from behind the big rock. Every few seconds, the one in the hat looked over at Tres Dedos like he was some malevolent demon from Hell.

"I just . . . look, I don't want no trouble," the bareheaded man said. The man in the bowler still hadn't spoken.

"You were just *shooting* at us," Joaquin pointed out. "We could have been anybody, and the first thing you did was start shooting. That sounds like trouble to me. And your friend killed my friend's horse. There has to be some payback, don't you think?"

The bareheaded one snatched the revolver from the other man's grip and threw it toward the outlaws. "He's the one shot the horse. I only fired the one shot, over your heads, like to scare you is all. You want to fight somebody, fight him!"

"Charley," the bowler-hatted man said, a look of rage on his face. "What the hell you doing?"

"I'm just sayin', you're the one shot that feller's horse. Anybody got to answer for that, should be you."

"Damn you, Charley, you lily-livered son of a—"

"Gentlemen!" Joaquin barked, cutting the man off. "That was an interesting choice you made, Charley. But that's not the decision you face right now. The only decision you have is, two against one? Or eleven against two? And I assure you, unlike my friend Three-Fingered Jack, we won't hesitate to use our guns. The only reason you're not dead yet is that Jack wants to do it himself."

Charley and the man in the bowler faced each other, fear

and fury warring within them both. Finally, Bowler nodded, and Charley did the same. "Two against one," Charley said.

"Are you sure?"

"We beat him, what happens?"

"If you beat him, we give you two horses and send you on your way."

"Honest?"

"Yes," Joaquin assured him. "But you won't beat him."

"We'll die tryin'."

"Yes," Joaquin said. "Yes, that's exactly what you'll do."

49

Tres Dedos took off his serape and his sombrero and handed them to Lopez. He removed two pistols from his belt and handed those over, as well.

For their part, Charley and the man in the bowler followed through on their agreement. Charley tossed his rifle down, and both men stepped out from behind the rock. Without being told to, Joaquin's men spread out, making a circle around the combatants.

Tres Dedos paused briefly beside Joaquin and looked up at him, his anger undiminished. "When this is over, if I'm dead, let those men live."

"That's the agreement."

"But before you send them on their way," Tres Dedos added, "cut off their balls!" He let out a low growl, sounding more like an angry bear than a human being, and charged Bowler.

That man had stayed largely quiet throughout the confrontation, so although Joaquin knew Charley's name and story, he knew nothing of the other's background. The man met Tres Dedos's charge with feet planted, widespread, giving him balance and stability. As Tres Dedos neared him, he threw an awkward punch while still on the move. Bowler dodged it easily and let Tres Dedos's forward momentum carry him too close to throw another. He grabbed Tres Dedos's out-flung arm and yanked on it. Off-balance, Tres Dedos stumbled, and Bowler slammed a knee into his chest. Air blew out of him in a huff.

Bowler pressed his advantage. He lashed out with his fists, landing a flurry of blows against Tres Dedos's face and neck, staggering him. Charley joined in, positioning himself behind Tres Dedos and kicking, his boot crashing into Tres Dedos's lower back. When Tres Dedos whipped his head around to see this new assailant, Bowler doubled his fists together and swung them against Tres Dedos's jaw.

For the first time, Joaquin considered the possibility that his friend might lose. Against Charley alone, Tres Dedos would already be done, wiping his hands of the other man's blood. But the man in the bowler proved to be a challenge of a more serious nature. Already, blood flowed from Tres Dedos's nose and mouth like water from a pump. He looked dizzy, reeling as he fought for balance.

Then Bowler made his first mistake. Apparently believing Tres Dedos had already lost, he wrapped his hands around Tres Dedos's throat and started to squeeze. But Tres Dedos managed to lower his head, and he bit down on Bowler's upper forearm. Bowler screamed as the teeth sunk in and tore. After a moment, Tres Dedos whipped his head up again, a chunk of bloody flesh clenched between his teeth. He spat it in Bowler's face, and Bowler released Tres Dedos's throat. Tres Dedos roared and lunged at him.

This time, the advantage was his. Bowler's ruined arm gushed blood. His face had been red with anger when he'd met Tres Dedos's attack, but now it had paled, and he was unsteady on his feet, his weight back on his heels. When Tres Dedos plowed into him, he went down, Tres Dedos straddling him. Tres Dedos rained punches down, pulping Bowler's face—his hat had finally flown off as he'd fallen—and driving one knee into the man's midsection at the same time. Bowler writhed under the attack, but the fight had gone out of him. When Tres Dedos realized his opponent was no longer striking back, he gripped Bowler's throat, pressing his thumbs against either side of his windpipe. Bowler fought for breath, his feet kicking, but after a few minutes, he was still.

Apparently remembering Charley, Tres Dedos rose quickly, smashed a boot against Bowler's face for good measure, and looked for the second man. But Charley had curled up in a ball, sobbing, his back against the boulder like he wanted to sink into it. When Tres Dedos took a step toward him, Charley let out a panicked cry.

Joaquin didn't really blame him. Tres Dedos looked more monster than man: blood-soaked, barrel chest heaving, face a rictus of rage and bloodlust.

Surprisingly, instead of attacking, Tres Dedos went to one knee beside Charley. Charley, still sobbing and quaking in fear, tried to edge away, but Tres Dedos put a hand on one leg and spoke in quiet, calm tones. "I have to do this, but I'll make it fast. All right? It won't hurt."

Charley tried to answer, but he could only sputter. Instead, he nodded his head, then tilted it back and looked at the sky, as if beseeching the heavens to intercede. Tres Dedos reached up his sleeve and brought out a long-bladed knife. With a smooth, swift motion, he drew it across Charley's exposed neck. Blood jetted from the wound, splashing Tres Dedos and the dirt beneath him in more or less equal measures. Charley's body spasmed a few times, each one spraying out more blood, his boots rapping against the earth like a dancer at a fandango, and then he slumped over sideways. The flow of blood from the gaping wound at his neck slowed to a trickle.

Tres Dedos turned back to Joaquin. There seemed to be as much blood outside him as inside, but most of it had belonged to his foes. When he grinned—showing blood-spattered teeth, one eye already swelling shut—the sight was horrifying. "That was fun!" he said. "Let's find those other two and do it again!"

• • •

The group backtracked to where the other two escapees had started on the path that would lead them up the mountain. In the soft earth of the game trail, their tracks were easy to follow. The horses shied at the scent of bear droppings, but the men urged them on, and the beasts relented. Joaquin also spotted the uniform pellets of deer and the mid-trail spoor of coyotes—all of it to be eclipsed, after this ride, by the grassy road-apples their horses left behind.

The men had been covering considerable distance, but they still hadn't seemed to figure out that their route took them farther into the wilderness and gradually toward ever higher elevations. Or their only goal was to escape the outlaws, and they would figure out the rest later. Joaquin wondered why they stayed on the trail, where their boots left the only remotely human tracks.

His inclination was to just let the men go—let them battle the elements on foot, without supplies, and see how they did—but one of them was the sheriff, and he had decreed that any lawman who harassed him or his band would have to suffer. Now he was locked into that rash pronouncement, lest his men see him as indecisive and weak. He was feeling sick from the sight of watching his cousin brutalize the first two, but he couldn't show that, either. He'd known that Tres Dedos enjoyed killing—he'd never made a secret of that.

But in the midst of that fight, his friend had turned into

something not even human, some monster from ancient myths, blood-soaked and craving destruction. Certainly, there had been times when Joaquin wanted to kill. Ending the lives of the murderers of Rosita and Jesús had seemed right and proper, and he'd been glad to do it. But most of the killings he had done since were matters of necessity. He was defending himself or others of his band, or fighting those who would stop him from taking what he wanted to take. He had never killed with the ferocity that Tres Dedos had shown there, and he hoped never to see that side of the man again.

But he knew what the sheriff and his companion didn't. He brought the group to a halt. Mounted and traveling on a well-established trail, Joaquin's band had made better time than their quarry, and the tracks here were fresh. Very soon now, the game trail would split, and they would have a decision to make. One route would take them onto a narrow path with mountain on one side and a drop of several hundred feet on the other. They'd have to sidestep, hugging the rock wall all the way, or risk falling. When the wind blew it was an almost impossible route for humans.

The other path would look much more promising. It was a winding route, though, and there was a quicker way to its end if one knew the area.

He hoped they would see that promise, choose that path. Because it would mean he was almost done here, and he and his men could soon return to Arroyo de Cantua.

He told Vulvia to stay with the horses and ordered the others to dismount. They hiked at a quick pace, away from the game trail and into the scrub.

50

"I don't like this," Lucas Rhodes said.

"Don't like what?" Marshall asked.

"That trail."

They were standing at a point where the trail forked. Marshall wanted to take the path with the most animal tracks, but it felt wrong to Rhodes.

"What's wrong with it? Plenty of game taking it, looks like."

"Those walls are pretty steep." The trail led into a canyon. Rhodes couldn't see the end of it. The sun was high in the sky, shadows straight up and down. He could only see a dozen yards or so, then there appeared to be a sharp turn, but he couldn't even tell from here in which direction. "I don't like the idea of walking into someplace where we don't know where we'll end up."

Marshall laughed. "Hell, we haven't knowed where we'd end up all the damn day. Why's this any different?"

"I don't know," Rhodes said. "I just don't like the feel of it."

Marshall wasn't a tall man, but he hitched himself up to his full height, faced Rhodes, and held his gaze. "You might've outranked me in the war, *Lieutenant*. That's why I invited you to share my tent. But I'm in charge of this outfit."

"Not much of an outfit left, is it, Ben? Two of us? Two more maybe alive, and maybe not. That was gunfire we heard earlier, after all." He'd avoided the topic of Marshall's cowardice so far—running as soon as the trouble started, instead of staying near and fighting what were likely the bandits the posse had been chasing. Presumably, it had been weighing on the sheriff, too, because he seemed to know what Rhodes was inching around.

"I didn't have to ask you twice to come with me. You could've stayed there and died with the rest of 'em. I knew we didn't have a chance if we stayed. But I sure didn't have to force you out that hole I cut."

Eight men from Garlin's Draw had joined the posse, out of burning rage at the bandits who'd robbed and killed their comrades. Seven were doubtless dead by now, and only Rhodes yet lived. He faced a new choice, now—stay with Sheriff Marshall, or split from him?

He didn't, after all, have any sound reason for not liking the canyon route. He couldn't tell where it led, but he didn't know where the other path went, either. All he knew for sure was that from here, the other path looked more open, and he didn't cotton to the idea of being hemmed in. Maybe the canyon was short, though, and they'd be out the other side in a few minutes.

And if they should run into the bandits—or some other threat, like an angry mother bear or a hungry mountain lion—two armed men would be better than one. Finally, he shrugged. "Have it your way."

Marshall couldn't help letting a smirk cross his face. "I intend to."

He started up the canyon. Rhodes followed. It seemed

peaceful within. Birds called, unseen, just occasional shadows flitting by. The air smelled almost sweet, and Rhodes thought maybe he caught a hint of water somewhere ahead.

Marshall trudged on, not looking back. Rhodes followed. A couple of times, he eyed Marshall's spine, thinking about where it would be best to place a bullet to drop him in his tracks. He had no intention of doing that, of course—it'd be pointless, for one thing, and the sound of the shot might summon the bandits. It was just his simmering anger at the sheriff's attitude. The man had put together a posse and led them into a trap that had gotten most of them killed, but even so, he thought he had all the answers.

The canyon took a sharp left turn, toward the bulk of the mountain. For a moment, Rhodes thought it dead-ended there, but then he saw a bird dart out from somewhere on the right and realized it was just another turn, not quite as severe as the last.

When he reached that next turn, Marshall cried out, "I knew it!"

"What?" Rhodes asked. He picked up his pace, but Marshall was already racing out of sight.

"Water!" Marshall called.

"Careful!" Rhodes shouted. "It could be poisoned."

But he reached the turn as well, and saw the sheriff rushing toward the far wall—the true end of this box canyon. A spring high up on the rock face dribbled water down the wall, and where it landed, a small pool had formed. The rocks behind the pool were green with moss. From here there was no way to know how deep the pool was, but it was surrounded by animal tracks. The creatures who came into this canyon did so because they knew there was water here, and it was fresh and drinkable. The earth around the little pool was completely churned up by its many visitors.

Rhodes had taken a canteen when they left the tent, and Marshall hadn't. He'd shared with the sheriff, but he'd been stingy about it, because neither man knew when they'd find fresh water again. Marshall reached the pool ahead of him, dropped to his belly, and plunged his head in. He splashed with his arms and drank deep. When he caught up, Rhodes lay down the rifle, dipped the canteen, filled it, and allowed himself a few big swallows.

"I'm glad we found water," he said when Marshall pulled his dripping head out. "But I still don't like it here. There's no way out but the way we came in."

Marshall pointed to the rock wall. On either side of where the spring water seeped down, the rocks were jagged. "A man could climb there, he had to."

"Could, I reckon," Rhodes admitted. "Wouldn't be easy, though."

"You in a hurry to leave?"

"All kinds of critters drink here," Rhodes pointed out. "You want to be here when Mama Bear comes in with her cubs?"

"We got guns."

"And precious little ammunition. Let's take what we can carry and get out of here."

Marshall hadn't budged, and he had a sullen look on his face. Rhodes feared another argument was brewing. Would the sheriff want to stay here all night? It was barely past noon; they had hours of daylight in which they could be putting space between themselves and the bandits. For starters, they still had to get off this mountain, but every path Marshall chose either kept them at the same elevation or took them higher, not lower.

"Easy for you to say," Marshall shot back. "You got a canteen."

"You want to carry it? You want to carry the long gun? I don't mind giving up some of the weight I'm dragging around. You just got to share with me, like I done for you."

Marshall stuck out a hand. "Give it here, then."

Rhodes started to hand it over, but a noise behind them made him stop. It sounded like a big, heavy animal. Deer, maybe, or elk? He hoped it wasn't the bears he'd been worried about.

But when he turned, he saw five Mexican men. Bandits, from the look of them. Their pants legs were tucked into their boots. Three of them wore wide-brimmed sombreros. All had mustaches, ammunition belts, and carbines.

"Ben," he said. "Easy, now. Don't start. We got company. Don't give 'em any reason to shoot."

Marshall scowled, sat up quickly, and turned around. When he saw the men, his face blanched. "Think we could climb that wall?"

"And get backshot?"

"Back or front don't make much difference."

That was true. If there was a slight chance of escaping that way, it might be a better option than trying to shoot it out with these men. His rifle was on the ground, and by the time he could draw his pistol, they could shoot. He glanced back at the wall again.

And this time, he saw four men standing atop it, looking down.

One of them was the man he'd had in his sights, back at

Garlin's Draw. The leader of the bandits, the one they called Joaquin.

And Joaquin was smiling.

"That's good water, isn't it?" Joaquin asked. "Sometimes I drink from there. Other times there are too many animals, and the smell of their shit keeps me away. You're lucky it rained hard the other day, washed some of it away."

Rhodes stood perfectly still, but Marshall's right hand inched toward the gun at his hip. Joaquin saw it and pointed a rifle at him, and the other men around him did the same. Rhodes heard the men behind them, and could tell from the sound that they'd raised their guns as well. "I wouldn't do that, Sheriff," Joaquin said. "Unless you're reaching for that gun so you can drop it into the spring."

"Actually, I had a mind to put a bullet in your head, mister."

"Trying that would just get you killed. And if you fell into the water, you'd spoil it for those who depend on it. We can't have that. How about if you raise your hands and back away?"

"How about if you fuck your Mexican whore mother?"

Joaquin's smile vanished and his face darkened, as if a cloud had crossed over the sun. "Ben . . ." Rhodes began, but he left the warning unstated.

"That isn't very neighborly," Joaquin said.

"We ain't neighbors," Marshall snapped.

"We are now. Only you're in *my* neighborhood. You might have noticed that you're surrounded."

"I did."

"I would like you to drop your guns on the ground. Easy—pluck them with two fingers and put them down where I can see them."

"Or what?"

"Or you'll die where you stand."

"You expect us to believe you won't kill us anyway?"

"That is not my goal," Joaquin said. "I want you to live. I want you to carry a message to other lawmen around California."

"Fat chance I'll carry anything for you."

"I think you will. The guns, please."

"Best do as he says," Rhodes whispered. "They wanted us dead, we'd already be there."

Marshall hesitated, but ultimately, he agreed. He pulled his pistol free with two fingers and dropped it onto the churned-up earth. Rhodes followed suit.

"I'm coming down," Joaquin said. "Remember, if you go for those guns, you're both dead."

"We get it," Rhodes said. "Whatever you've got in mind, just get it done."

Joaquin climbed down beside the spring water, just where Rhodes had thought it might be possible to go up. The man knew where to put his feet; he'd obviously done this before. In moments, he was down where they were.

The men on ground level behind them had moved in closer, still keeping their long guns trained on the two Americans. Rhodes tried not to show fear, but he didn't like where this was going. The bandit leader said he didn't want them killed, but he wasn't sure how they'd get out alive. His guts had turned to ice water and he had to clench his muscles to keep it from leaking out.

Joaquin walked up to Marshall. He was slightly taller than the sheriff, but not by much. He didn't seem afraid that

Marshall would try to tackle him or throw a punch. On the contrary, he appeared supremely confident that Marshall would do just as he was told. "Take off your boots," he said.

"My boots?"

"Did you get water in your ears? Yes, your boots."

"Why should I?"

"Because I told you to. If you want to live another minute, take them off."

Marshall grumbled, but he sat down in the dirt and pulled off his boots. "Now what?"

"This will hurt," Joaquin said. He crouched beside the sheriff and took one stockinged foot in his hand. Gripping it tightly, he snatched a knife from his belt and slashed the bottom of Marshall's foot before the other man could react. Marshall screamed and yanked his foot back, leaving a trail of blood on the ground.

"Now the other one," Joaquin said.

"Are you fucking crazy?"

Instead of answering, Joaquin grabbed the other foot and wrenched it toward him. He sliced that one, too. Marshall screamed again. Joaquin released him and stood.

"That's the message," he said. "You might be able to walk, but it'll hurt like hell. You might never walk right again, I don't know. I'll send men back with a horse for each of you, canteens, bedrolls, everything you'll need to get home. When you do, let all the lawmen know what happened. Let them know that any man who comes after me is going to regret it, as long as he lives. And in many cases, that might not be long at all."

"You're a lunatic," Marshall said bitterly.

"But you're the one who's bleeding. You might want to

wash those in the spring while you're waiting for the horses."

He picked up the dropped pistols and Rhodes's rifle and walked over to join the other men at ground level. The men at the top of the cliff drifted out of sight. In just minutes, Rhodes and Marshall were alone again, Marshall crying and cursing and pounding the dirt with his fists.

It seemed like a long wait for those horses, and the ride back to Carson's Creek would be longer still. Lucas Rhodes decided that if he ever got Joaquin in his sights again, he would make sure he killed the bandit. Never again would he leave that task undone.

Joaquin was a stain on the state and the nation, and he had to go.

51

Something had gone wrong.

Joaquin and the others had only planned to be away from Arroyo de Cantua for a few days. A quick ride to Garlin's Draw, a surprise attack. Possibly a day or two of circling around, trying to lose any pursuers, cover their tracks, then home. But six days had passed, and there had been no word from them. Antonia had left for San José, accompanied by Antonio Severino and Gustavo Zaragoza.

Pancho Dominguez had nursed his anger for days. He'd wanted Joaquin to return, so he could have it out with him, express all the rage and frustration he felt. Someone needed to tell Joaquin that he was betraying his own destiny, failing to live up to the promise he had shown. Pancho had intended to be that someone. None of the others seemed to recognize it— or if they did, they were afraid to say it.

Pancho wasn't afraid. He would say what was on his mind, and the outlaw leader would respond with weak excuses. He would say it was too soon, or that he had never had such an inflated sense of his own importance. That was a lie—anybody who knew him could see that. What held Joaquin back was a failure of imagination, an inability to grasp what everybody else could see. He was not just a man, not just a bandit. He was rarer than he thought, more special than he believed. He alone could restore California to the Mexicans. He was the leader the Mexican people could rally behind.

But he had turned away from all that. He refused to accept it, and when Pancho tried to press him, he responded with fury and threats of violence. No matter how Pancho played out the conversation in his head, it always came out the same way. If he confronted Joaquin now, feeling the way he did, it would end in bloodshed. Joaquin would likely kill him—he was younger, stronger, a better shot with a pistol. But it wouldn't matter, because even if Pancho won, the others would turn on him for having killed Joaquin. The bandit leader claimed that anyone could challenge him and take over the band, but that was just another lie. The truth was, at this point nobody who killed Joaquin Murrieta would live for more than a few minutes.

Anyway, Antonia's absence gave him a better idea. He couldn't kill Joaquin in front of the band. Probably couldn't kill him in a fair fight.

But there were other ways, weren't there?

He packed his kit and slipped away from the arroyo while most people were sleeping. If anyone noticed his absence, they would put it down to the public argument he'd had with Joaquin.

And that was just fine.

• • •

Joaquin had fully intended to kill Marshall and the other man, the one who'd tried to kill him back at Garlin's Draw. That had been the idea, anyway, up until he watched Tres Dedos beat two men to death with his hands and a knife. That had turned his stomach, and he'd lost all taste for more killing.

His earlier proclamation, that lawmen should be spared but injured so they could serve as examples, had given him a way out of it. What he'd done to Marshall had been cruel, and the man would live with pain for a long time, possibly for the rest of his life, if too much damage had been done. But he would live. He would be able to get back home. With luck, the story would spread, and other lawmen would think twice about trying to chase Joaquin Murrieta.

He didn't know if his disgust at killing would fade, or grow stronger, with time. He knew it might still be necessary from time to time. He was the leader of an outlaw band, and that wasn't something from which one could simply walk away.

For Joaquin, wealth was no longer the point of robbery. He had everything he needed: plenty to eat and drink, tailored clothing of the finest fabrics, the newest advances in guns and ammunition, a roof over his head, and the love of La Molinera to warm his heart. Having grown up poor, he had little interest in rare works of art or ornate furnishings, and no idea how to acquire those if he had cared to. Instead, the point was to terrorize the white communities, as repayment for the indignities he and every other Mexican had suffered at their hands.

He buried some of the gold from Garlin's Draw in the floor of the Bear Mountain cave, in case he might need it later. More of it he spread throughout poor Mexican neighborhoods as the men headed for Arroyo de Cantua, ensuring future cooperation from those benefiting from his largesse. Joaquin and his men were heroes in those places. Families hung crude paintings or drawings of him on the walls, and shared news of his exploits at the table. When they didn't refer to him by name, they called him *el patrio*—the patriot—remembered him in their prayers, and considered him a kind of unofficial patron saint of the Mexican people.

He didn't plan to stay at the arroyo for long, but he wanted to drop off the horses taken from the posse. Horseflesh continued to be a valuable commodity, here and across the border in Mexico, where he worked with brokers who would sell the horses in Sonora and farther south in exchange for a generous cut. Antonia was already gone, so he didn't even have that reason to linger. After leaving the horses there to graze on the arroyo's healthy grass, he and a group of twenty headed south to raid wealthy ranches in the Santa Ynez Valley. The horses they took there would be delivered across the border immediately.

Along the way, Joaquin handed heavy purses to Hector Gonzalez and Juan Cardoza to carry to his parents and sister in Sonora, with orders to report back on their health and general wellbeing. Those two split off from the band and rode hard for the border, with the intention of meeting up with the others in a little valley outside La Cañada de los Berros, near the La Purisima Mission, in a week's time. Meanwhile, Joaquin and the others set to work cutting out the best fifteen or twenty horses in each herd they found and penning them in a nearby valley until they could be driven to Mexico.

• • •

Santa Barbara deputy Harry Love rode alone, which was the way he liked it. No underlings asked him stupid questions; no sheriff told him what to do. He went where he wanted, when he wanted. He ate when he was hungry, slept when he was tired, and drank, smoked, spat, and scratched on his own say-so.

Ranchers in the hills had been reporting horse thefts, and he had volunteered to ride out and check the reports. The thieves had been careful. They'd closed gates behind themselves, and only thinned the herds they targeted, rather than emptying them out. Most of the ranchers hadn't noticed at first that they'd lost any, until they went looking for their most prized animals. These horse thieves knew what they were doing. Some said it was a band led by one of the Joaquins, though Love didn't know which Joaquin it might be. Some even said it was Joaquin Murrieta, who had worked Love's claim along with his brother and cousin years ago. It didn't sound like the Joaquin he'd known—but much had happened to the young man since then, if the rumors could be believed.

The day was cool, though dwindling waters in mountain-fed creeks and the wildflowers blanketing grassy slopes hinted that summer wasn't far off. Spring had been a relief after the hard winter, with its floods in the south and blizzards in the north, and he would miss it when the fullness of summer was upon them. The sun was high, midday of his third day on the trail, and although he'd found plenty of tracks leading away from the affected ranches, he hadn't been able to follow any to the stolen horses. Nor had he seen any sign of a Joaquin, unless some of the hands working the ranches also carried that name.

Some of the tracks he followed headed north, and he kept after them even though he'd crossed the county line. After a while, he stopped at a nameless saloon in La Gaviota to wet down some of the trail dust caking his throat. There wasn't much to the place: a wooden bar with a tiny mirror behind it, some bottles of liquor on a shelf beneath that. A few men stood around silently drinking, but there were no chairs or stools to sit on. The bartender was young and pudgy, on his way to downright fat before too long. He had thin hair combed over his scalp and a long mustache that looked like he'd been chewing on it.

As Harry stood at the bar and drank, he talked to the barkeep and a couple of the other men around, asking them about horse thieves. When he mentioned that they were Mexican, the bartender spoke up.

"There was a pair of greasers in town for a couple of days. Left not twenty minutes before you got here. I don't speak no Mexican, and they wasn't speakin' English when they come in here, but they looked like hard types. Guns, ammunition belts crisscrossing their chests. They spent plenty of money on booze and women and card games while they stayed."

"Do you know where they were headed?"

"I seen 'em," another man offered. "They was headin' north when they left."

"Toward Mission Santa Inés?"

"Could be."

"Can you describe them?"

"What he said." The man nodded toward the barkeep. "Mexicans. Dark skin, dark eyes, uglier'n stray dogs that somebody's kicked. Them big hats, too."

"Anything more specific you can think of?"

"One of them wore a eyepatch," the barkeep said. "He had a scar runnin' down his cheek, Made his lip curl up on that side, and there was a gold tooth under the curl. The eyepatch was on that side, too, so I expect he lost the eye when he got the scar."

That sounded to Love like Hector Gonzalez. He'd been a small-time thief and gambler in Santa Barbara, before he up and disappeared. The rumors were that he'd left town to join up with one of the Joaquins. The scar had come from a poker game three years earlier, when he'd been found with two aces in his hand and three more up his sleeve. He had survived the fight, but lost an eye and been left even more hideous-looking than before.

"Twenty minutes, you say?"

"Twenty-five or thirty, now you been settin' here drinkin' and talkin'."

"Riding fast?"

"Not as they rode out," the other man said. "Didn't seem like a big hurry to me."

"Then I can still catch 'em." Loved downed his drink and slammed the glass down on the bar top. "Thanks."

He was out the door before the barkeep even remembered to ask for payment for the drink. That, too, was the way Love liked it.

He'd been discouraged, but with this new information, he felt revitalized. He rode hard, his horse working up a sweat that dampened Love's legs where he gripped the beast. Off to his left, when he could see it between the trees, the ocean pounded at the shore. He could hear the surf sometimes, over the drumming of his horse's hooves and his own blood rushing in his ears.

A few hours later, he rounded a wooded bend and spotted two Mexican men climbing down from horses and heading into a roadside tavern. He couldn't tell from this distance who they were; only their sombreros gave them away. He rode a little closer, dismounted, tied his horse to a tree and walked up to a window.

Inside, the two men stood at a bar in the back of the room, on the other side of tables at which people were eating lunch. The aroma of the food set Love's mouth to watering, but he tried to ignore it as he studied the men. Finally, one of them turned around enough for him to recognize Hector Gonzalez. The eyepatch was a dead giveaway. He didn't know the other man, but if he was riding with Gonzalez, he was up to no good.

He drew a pistol and stepped inside. As he did, he announced loudly, "Nobody move! I'm Santa Barbara County Sheriff's Deputy Harry Love. Hector Gonzalez, you and your friend are under arrest!"

Gonzalez froze, a glass in his hand six inches above the bar.

The other man didn't. He dropped into a crouch, slapped leather, and fired, all in the same motion. His shot went wide, slamming into the wall two feet from Love. Love fired back, but he hit the wall behind the bar. The barkeep ducked down. The outlaw was already bolting for a back door, and Gonzalez, slower than his companion, was finally reaching for his pistol. Love decided one live outlaw was better than none, so instead of firing at the escaping one, he lunged for Gonzalez and caught him before he freed the weapon from its holster.

"I'll take that, Hector," he said.

Gonzalez didn't argue. Love snatched the pistol from him and tucked it into his belt at his back.

"I don't think we're in Santa Barbara, Deputy," Gonzalez said with a grin.

"My jurisdiction is the whole county, Hector."

Gonzalez shrugged. "I don't know the law so well."

Love knew the law, and he knew Gonzales walked the wrong side of it. "Your criminal record is well documented, Hector, in both Los Angeles and Santa Barbara." he said. "I had reason to believe you were headed north, and further reason to believe you and your amigo were mixed up with a gang of horse thieves."

"I'm only here to have a drink," Gonzalez protested.

"You're a long way from home."

"Maybe so."

"And your friend shot at me when I announced myself. That don't seem like the act of an innocent man."

"I don't know that man. He was just standing here when I came in."

"I watched you ride up together, leave your horses out

front, and walk inside together. I also know you both spent a lot of money in La Gaviota over the past few days. So I know he's not just some greaser you happened to run into here. What's his name?"

Gonzalez shrugged again. "All right. He's Juan Cardoza. I do know him."

"I knew you did. You riding with Joaquin's band now? Haven't seen you in town lately."

"What if I have been?"

"You mind telling me where they are?"

"I don't know. Honest."

"But you were going to meet up with them, right?"

"I can't say."

"Can't, or won't?"

"I can't say." Another shrug. "You taking me back to Los Angeles?"

"There's a rope waiting with your name on it."

"A rope? For what?"

"Stealing horses. Trying to kill an officer of the law. General misbehavior and a bad attitude."

"There's nothing wrong with my attitude that another drink won't fix, Deputy."

Love saw the wisdom of this idea. "Then drink up. We got a long ride ahead of us, most of it in the dark. I believe I'll have one, too."

52

Cardoza—somewhat astonished that the lawman hadn't chased him outside, but instead seemed to be taking his time arresting Gonzalez—circled around the building, retrieved his horse, and walked it away from the tavern's window. When he couldn't be seen from there, he mounted up and rode for La Purisima. They were barely going to make it on schedule, but the last few days of celebrating had left them parched, and they'd both needed a drink before continuing on.

Now his drink had been rudely interrupted, and he had to continue alone and thirstier than ever. The sun sank toward the Pacific as he followed the coastline northwest until shortly before it made its sharp northern turn. When he saw the pink walls of La Purisima, he made another turn, curving away from La Cañada de los Berros to a Mexican-owned ranch he'd visited with the band before, nestled in a grassy valley. Joaquin and the others were already there.

Cardoza jumped off the horse, threw the reins to a man standing nearby, and raced to Joaquin's side. "Joaquin, Hector's been arrested! Some deputy named Love cornered us on the road, when we stopped for a drink. I got away, but he took Hector."

"Love?" "Could it be his old friend from Sawmill Flat? "The deputy from Santa Barbara?"

"That's right. He's probably taking Hector back there."

"How long ago did this happen?"

Cardoza glanced at the western sky, painted in peach and gold tones. "About an hour. Little less."

"So we could still catch them, if we hurried?"

"Maybe. I don't know if they'll ride all night or stop somewhere after it gets dark."

"Did you deliver the purses to my family?"

"Of course, Joaquin. They were most appreciative, and glad to know that you're still alive. They seem in good health for their ages. Your sister is thriving, too. She's the most beautiful woman in town, people say."

"Good, thank you," Joaquin said. "I've always liked Hector. And you, of course. You've both become trusted lieutenants, otherwise I wouldn't have had you two make that trip to my home. We should free him, if we can."

"My horse is exhausted," Cardoza said. He had run the beast half to death. The truth was, he was exhausted, too. He and Hector hadn't slept much for the last several days.

Joaquin shook his head. "You don't have to go. I know what Love looks like, and of course I know Hector. Thank you for bringing me the news, and again, for carrying wealth to my poor family."

• • •

Joaquin took a few minutes to choose nine men to go with him, and another few to get horses and weapons ready for the chase. Within thirty minutes of Cardoza's arrival, they were on the trail, covering the same ground Cardoza had in his mad dash toward the mission.

They'd arrived at the ranch around noontime and been fed a big meal. After that, many of them had taken siestas, so they were rested and ready to ride when Joaquin picked them.

While they traveled south, the last of the sun's rays vanished behind the ocean and stars winked to life in the sky. The moon was high overhead, half-full.

Joaquin knew that Love could take any of several routes back to Santa Barbara. If he was in a hurry, though, he would take the same road that Cardoza and Gonzalez had taken north today. He was on that road when he'd caught up to them, so the chances were good that he would use that one to return.

Joaquin urged his men on with shouts and jokes and threats. Mostly, they kept up the pace because they all liked Gonzalez, and nobody wanted to see him rot in jail, or worse.

After a couple of hours in the saddle, his mount heaving for air but still pushing itself forward, they still had seen no sign of Love and Gonzalez. Joaquin was beginning to despair. Between the time Cardoza had spent riding to find them, then to explain the situation, and the time to gather his force and get on the road, an hour had elapsed. Perhaps more. Love had a big head start, and he had used it wisely. They could kill their horses, riding them at a fast gallop all the way to Santa Barbara, and never catch him.

But before he had a chance to bring the party to a stop, moonlight showed him two riders heading up a long slope near Gaviota, going south. They weren't moving fast or slow, just maintaining a steady pace that would eat up the distance without straining their mounts. He couldn't make out much detail from here—but one of them wore a sombrero, that much he could tell. And the other one looked almost as wide as his mount—Harry Love, he was certain.

"I think we've got them, boys!" he cried. "Don't let up now!"

• • •

For hours, the only sounds Love had heard had been night birds, crickets, the occasional attempt at conversation from his prisoner, and the steady clopping of their horses' hooves. But now another sound broke the night's stillness, a kind of thunder—still distant, but approaching quickly. Still short of the hill's summit, he turned in the saddle and saw riders racing toward them like a tiny cavalry at the charge. Gonzalez had heard them, too. Though his wrists were tied together in front of him, he was twisted around in the saddle and furiously waving a bandana, his reins abandoned around his horse's neck.

"What are you doing, signaling to your friends?" Love asked. "Pick up your reins, damn you. We've got to ride!" He punched Gonzalez hard in the shoulder to further suggest the gravity of the situation.

The bandana fluttered out of Gonzalez's hands. At the same time, Love snatched up the other man's reins and put spurs to his own horse. The two animals broke into a run, dangerously close together, until Gonzalez got serious about riding, retrieved his reins, and leaned over his mount's neck.

The summit was still several minutes away. Behind them—out of range still—the outlaws had begun to fire pistols on the run. Love thought they were crazy—mounted, shooting from a distance, if they did hit anyone it could just as easily be the friend they were trying to rescue as the lawman. But it impressed upon him the danger they were both in. He couldn't count the bandits from here, but it looked like a dozen or so.

A new question arose. Try to outrun them? Or hunker down somewhere and fight? There was no cover on this side of the hill, and under the circumstances, his mind was blank when it came to the downslope side.

A third solution came to him. Still riding alongside his captive, he drew a pistol and said, "Hey, Hector."

Gonzalez turned his head and Love fired, his bullet tunneling through the inner corner of his left eye. Gonzalez went limp. He dropped from the confused horse like an oversized sack of flour and hit the trail with a thump.

Love spurred his horse again, and the beast charged up the hill.

• • •

Joaquin saw the muzzle flash ahead and knew immediately what Love had done. He slowed the pace as they approached the fallen Gonzalez, then came to a halt just before the body. Joaquin jumped down and rushed to his friend's side. He lay on his back, now without any good eyes. A puddle of blood, black in the moonlight, soaked the earth.

"He's dead," Joaquin said. He returned to his horse, climbed into the saddle, and set off at a furious pace, more determined than ever to catch the lawman.

But Love had gained the summit and started down the other side. By the time the bandits reached the top, their mounts, having run full out since the chase began, were faltering. Love had been maintaining an easy pace, and on the downslope his horse was practically flying. Anyway, he didn't like the idea of confronting Love. If they faced each other now, only one of them would live through the encounter. He still retained warm feelings toward the man who'd been his friend, though Love's casual murder of Gonzalez had tempered that.

Again, Joaquin reined to a halt, and the others clustered around. "Never mind," he said. "Love will pay for that, but at another time. Hector's our friend. Let's get him and give him the burial he deserves. I think we passed a church not too far back."

"We did," Juan Senate said. "The priest there is a friend of ours." That meant he was Mexican, and so were his parishioners. Joaquin knew who Senate meant, and also that he had dropped off piles of gold there on a couple of occasions. The padre would find room for Gonzalez in the churchyard and deliver a fine sendoff.

He looked at Gonzalez's still form and tears rolled down his cheeks. Were they for Hector, though? Or for two friendships, ended by a single bullet? He wasn't sure, and couldn't take the time to figure it out now. Joaquin turned his horse around and started back the way he'd come.

53

A week later, having disposed of the stolen horses except for those exceptional specimens they kept for themselves, Joaquin and his men arrived back at Arroyo de Cantua. In the midst of the crowd gathered to welcome them back, Joaquin spotted Antonio Severino and Gustavo Zaragoza. Both men stood together, near the back of the throng.

Both men looked uncomfortable.

Before dismounting, Joaquin scanned the assembly for Antonia. He appreciated the warm welcome, as he was sure his men did, but the person he wanted most to see—to hold, and before long, to make love with—was La Molinera.

She was nowhere to be seen.

The fact sent a chill through him. If Severino and López—the two men who'd escorted her to San José, and who were to stay in the house to ensure her safety on any nights she spent there—were here, she should be, too. And if she were here, certainly she'd have heard the commotion and come out.

He dropped down from the horse. Men rushed to shake his hands or to clap him on the back, but his stern expression discouraged overly effusive praise. The crowd parted for him as he made his way toward Severino and López. Reaching them, rather than make a scene here, he put a hand on each man's shoulder and walked them several paces away from the others.

"Where's Antonia?" he asked.

They both seemed hesitant to answer, but finally Severino spoke up. He was a gangly fellow, with the worst teeth Joaquin had ever seen. They looked like they had been glued into his mouth randomly, with no overall plan in mind. Once in place, but before the glue had set, Severino must have bit down on something like an apple that was rapidly withdrawn. Teeth stuck out at odd angles, many reaching toward the opening of his mouth—and beyond—as if in an escape attempt. He was brave and had a good heart, but Joaquin had a hard time looking past the teeth.

"We don't know," Severino said. "We took her to San José, as you directed. We stayed in the house for eight days and nights. She visited with some friends, and spent time working in her family's bakery. But then one night, she never came back to the house. We went to the bakery, asked all of her friends that we could find, but no one knew where she'd gone."

"No one knew, or no one admitted to knowing?"

López answered. "No one knew. We didn't always ask nicely."

"You didn't harm her parents?" If they had so much as laid a finger on the Molineras, he would have to kill them on the spot.

"No," Severino said quickly. "Of course not."

"We didn't know where to find you," López added, "so we came back here, knowing you would, as well."

Joaquin's mind was in an uproar. Antonia missing? These fools let her out of their sight and now she was gone?

He paced, rubbing his unshaven chin. Of course, they didn't watch her every moment of the day. That wasn't their job. She had lived in San José most of her life and had many friends there. She wouldn't want these two following her around all the time. And she'd always been safe there before.

Was this some kind of revenge for his murder of the lawman, Clark? Had someone figured out that she was Joaquin's woman?

No, if that were the case, she wouldn't be missing. Her body would have turned up somewhere public, to make the same kind of statement he'd made when he'd tossed Clark's head into the saloon. And if she were being held against her will, there would have been some kind of ransom demand.

She was out there. She was alive. He just had to find her.

He pulled his pistol and fired three times into the air. The camp went quiet, all eyes on him. "La Molinera is missing!" he shouted. "She was last seen in San José, but she could be anywhere. I need twenty of you to ride out, check with all our contacts, all our spies, and tell them to look for her and report back. Choose among yourselves who goes, but be on the road tonight. Finding her is now your most important job!"

He turned away from the hubbub that followed. The men would figure things out. They would find her. She was certainly still in California, and she wouldn't have gravitated far from the Mexican communities she knew.

Without another word to anyone, he headed into the old house, into his room. He closed the door and wondered if he would be able to sleep.

• • •

The next few days passed slowly. Life continued around him. Josefina, Luis Vulvia's woman, had a baby, the first one born in camp, and all the other women fussed over her and the boy. He paid a visit to meet the infant his parents had named Joaquin Murrieta Vulvia del Montillo. The child was ugly, but Joaquin proclaimed him the most handsome boy he had ever seen, and Josefina wept with gratitude. Spending time with the women just made him worry about Antonia all the more, so he cut the visit short.

The men who'd stayed behind busied themselves, some working on the more substantial structures they'd begun building once they'd realized Joaquin meant the arroyo to be a long-term base, others practicing marksmanship or their roping and horsemanship skills. Joaquin observed and encouraged from a distance, but didn't join in. Most of his time he spent alone in his room or walking in the unpopulated part of the canyon.

At night, he sat and listened to the soft burble of water in the creek, and the songs of the toads. They reminded him of the spadefoot toads back home who emerged from underground only after a pummeling summer storm and spent a night or two crying out for mates, sounding like nothing so much as a cross between a herd of sheep and a lake full of ducks. Homesick, he found himself missing his parents and sister, their little house, the sleepy ways of Trincheras, and Rosita. What kind of life might he have had if they had stayed? An honest one marked by hard work and poverty, he guessed. Rosita would have been married off, and he would still be working for her father, catching glimpses of her once in a while, most likely continually pregnant with one child after another.

It had seemed, for a little while, like he would have been able to survive a life like that. But the longer he thought about it, the less he believed it. Seeing Rosita married to another would have driven him insane. He had never thought of himself as a killer, in those days, but he knew better now. He might have been driven to murder her husband and take her away.

He couldn't see the hand of God in his life—the God he had studied and believed in wouldn't deliberately turn a man into a killer. But the universe had somehow conspired to do so, and, he had come to believe, would have under any circumstances. It was fated from the start, and now he saw that he couldn't have avoided it.

Men started returning to the camp with reports of failure. Nobody had seen Antonia; nobody knew where she was. Then Atanacio Moreno rode in and handed off his reins, walking directly to Joaquin's house. He knocked on the frame of the outer door and called "*Jefe*?"

Joaquin was polishing some boots in his room. Sitting on the floor with a polishing rag in one hand and a boot over the other arm, he didn't want to stand. "Back here!" he shouted.

Moreno came to the inner door and tapped on the rough wood. "Inside," Joaquin said. "I can't get up."

The door creaked open and Moreno entered. He was a handsome fellow, with a medium build, but muscular. His hair was dark brown, his eyes light, the color of coffee with plenty of milk, but his skin was so dark as to be almost black. It made for an interesting contrast. Joaquin understood why women were drawn to him. But what they couldn't see from his exterior was that he was as ruthless as any man Joaquin had ever known, willing to hurt or kill anyone who offended him in the slightest or who stood between him and whatever he wanted in that moment.

"Joaquin," he began, then paused. Joaquin had never seen him so hesitant. He'd thought the man incapable of appearing nervous, but he was practically trembling in his boots.

"What is it, Atanacio?"

"She . . . she's in Los Angeles."

"Los Angeles? You're sure?"

"I didn't believe it when it was told to me, so I went there myself. I saw her. She's there."

"You didn't bring her back?"

"I . . . I didn't want to reveal myself. She seems to have gone there willingly. I thought you might want to be the one to discuss things with her."

"Discuss? What's to discuss? She belongs here with me."

"Yes, but . . ." Moreno paused. Joaquin waited for him to continue, but he didn't.

"But what? Out with it, man!"

"She's not alone."

The words struck like a dagger in Joaquin's heart. "What do you mean?"

Moreno looked at the floor, then at the ceiling. Back at the floor. Anywhere he didn't have to meet Joaquin's steady gaze. "She's with Pancho Dominguez."

"Pancho? You're sure?"

"I saw them together. They were drinking in a cantina, sitting close together. Like lovers."

Joaquin couldn't believe it. Pancho Dominguez had once been a soldier in the Mexican army. Since then, he had gone to fat, and was now the heaviest man in the band. He seemed more interested in wearing fine clothes and eating expensive meals than in participating in the crimes it took to acquire those things, so Joaquin had taken to leaving him out of most raids. His military experience made him valuable in planning big operations, but he never volunteered to take part in the ones he helped organize. Joaquin couldn't imagine what Antonia liked about him.

Worse still, the images flooding his mind disgusted him. That fat slob making love to his beautiful Antonia? Probably drooling on her? He shook his head, hard, trying to chase them away, and focused instead on Moreno. If it had been him, at least Joaquin would have understood it. But Pancho?

"Did you confront them?"

Moreno hesitated. Scared. He visibly trembled as he answered.

"I didn't want them to see me. After I saw them, I went outside and waited in a doorway until they left."

"How did you happen to see them?"

"I have two brothers in Los Angeles, and a cousin at Rancho Santa Manuela. They all know I ride with you, and my brothers know Pancho, from old times. They saw Pancho with a beautiful woman. When they described her, I knew it had to be her."

"Do you know where they're staying?"

"I think I do," Moreno replied. "I followed them. They went to a hotel. Later, Antonia came out by herself and went to another place."

He stopped there. His lips were quivering, and he couldn't meet Joaquin's gaze.

"What kind of place?"

Moreno looked at the floor. "I don't want to say."

"Atanacio…" It came out as a kind of growl.

"I'm sorry, boss."

"Tell me, damn you!"

Moreno's gaze shifted skyward, as if wishing a lightning bolt would strike him dead before he had to answer.

No bolt came. Finally, he whispered it. "A brothel."

Joaquin exploded. "A brothel? Pancho has her working in a brothel!"

"I don't know," Moreno said quickly. "I don't know if he met her there, or what."

"But he stayed at the hotel?"

"Yes, I asked the clerk about him. He's been living there for weeks and weeks."

"And you know where these places are? The hotel and the brothel?"

"Yes. The hotel is called the Harper House. He has room two-oh-one. The brothel is nearby. I can write it all down for you. Los Angeles has grown since I was there last. It's getting crowded."

Joaquin scrounged around the room for a pencil and a scrap of paper. Sometimes Antonia liked to draw, so she kept both handy. As Moreno wrote, his hand was shaking so badly he could barely keep the pencil on the paper.

Early on, Joaquin had believed that the best way to keep his men loyal was to make them fear him. Now they did, and he thought maybe he'd been too successful at it. Maybe it was better, after all, for them to respect him. Men who were afraid of their leader might be more likely to abandon him in a crisis, seeking some safer alternative. But if they respected him, they'd gather around in the face of trouble, to protect the leader they loved.

It was, he guessed, too late to reverse the approach he'd taken. He could, perhaps, take some baby steps in that direction, though.

"Easy, Atanacio," he said, his voice gentle. "If you'd rather, I can write it down."

"No, I have it," Moreno said. He slid the paper toward Joaquin. The addresses he'd written down were near Calle de los Negros. Joaquin knew the area well.

Honor demanded that he take care of the next part himself, but he didn't think he could bear it. Instead, he thanked Moreno, sent him on his way, and pondered who among his band would be best suited to the grim task ahead.

54

Joaquin found Pedro Vergara in the tent he shared with Sophia Gordo. They were arguing about something having to do with Sophia's weight, which tended to match her name. Joaquin didn't want to be dragged into it, so he just pounded on the tent wall—it was an American officer's tent from the war, but patched over in dozens of spots with various scraps of fabric, so colorful and probably not as water-resistant as it might have been—and shouted Pedro's name.

Vergara ducked out through the flaps a few moments later, waving a hand at Sophia as if to shush her. She wasn't an easy woman to shush—her voice was loud and her temper fierce. Joaquin and Vergara walked away from the tent, and her shouts eventually dimmed to a level they could ignore.

"Thanks for pulling me out of there, boss," Vergara said. "I thought she was going to deafen me with her shouting."

"I need you to kill somebody, Pedro. You might not want to do it, but you have to."

"All right."

"Don't you want to know who they are before you agree?"

"Why?" Vergara appeared genuinely confused. Killing came almost as naturally to him as it did to Tres Dedos, which was why Joaquin had picked him. But he had expected some show of curiosity, at least.

Vergara was not a handsome man, but he had a certain

rugged quality that Joaquin supposed was attractive to some. His face looked like it had been hewn from mahogany by a halfway talented carver with a dull axe. He was tall and muscular, but scars crisscrossed his arms and the exposed part of his chest and even much of his face, from all the fights he'd had, like so many worms writhing under his flesh. Violence had been a way of life for him, probably from the very start. If he'd been more intelligent, he might have made something of his life, but Joaquin had known goats back in Trincheras that were probably smarter than Vergara.

Instead of answering his question directly, Joaquin simply told him who his targets would be. "La Molinera has taken up with Pancho Dominguez, in Los Angeles. I think he's got her working in a brothel. He has to die. But before he does, I want him to know why. Nobody can betray me like that and be allowed to live."

Vergara's face registered surprise. "Of course not. I never expected he would do anything so foolish."

"Neither did I. And Antonia must've known how I'd react, too, which is why they went so far away. They should know I have spies everywhere, though."

"Who understands how the heart compels people to forget all reason?" Vergara asked. He could occasionally put together a clever turn of phrase, unexpected from one so seemingly simple-minded.

Joaquin had underestimated Antonia. He had thought she'd understand that when he told her she couldn't be part of their crimes, it was out of love and concern for her safety. Too many people had died. It was too dangerous for her. He couldn't bear to lose her.

But he'd lost her anyway. Worse, driven her back to her old life, the one she'd left behind so long ago. If only he had explained better, she might still be safe in San José, with her parents.

He was as much to blame as anyone.

Well, almost. If Pancho had indeed set her up in the brothel, then he was more to blame. He'd always been a smooth talker, and for reasons Joaquin couldn't understand, Antonia had enjoyed his company.

He had to pay. After that was done, Vergara could find her, convince her to come back.

He handed Vergara the slip of paper on which Moreno had written the address and explained the tasks ahead. Vergara studied the paper, nodding.

"Do you know where that is?" Joaquin asked.

"I know the alley. I can find it. When do you want me to leave?"

"Right away."

Vergara glanced back at the tent. "Sophia won't be happy. But I will."

"Why do you keep her around, then?"

"She's a magnificent cook, and skilled in bed. But to tell you to truth, boss, even those attractions are starting to fade. She's as stubborn as a burro and twice as ill-tempered. I think the real question is why she stays, when she clearly despises me. Honestly, I don't mind leaving the camp for a few days."

"Do you want me to send her away while you're gone?" Joaquin asked.

"I don't want her hurt."

"That's not what I'm saying."

"She kind of likes Juan Senate. Maybe you could encourage them to spend some time together."

Joaquin chuckled. "I didn't know you hated Juan so much."

"Well," Vergara said, shrugging his shoulders, "he's not my favorite person, I admit."

"I'll take care of it," Joaquin promised. "Go to Los Angeles. Find them."

"I will."

"And, Pedro? Make it hurt."

• • •

Harry Love had to cool his heels outside Governor Bigler's office for almost an hour, which he considered insulting. Bigler had called him to Benicia in the first place. The capital was a long ride from Santa Barbara, and who knew what trouble might be cropping up in his absence? Sheriff Twist was a good man, and brave—he had comported himself well in the war—but he was more suited to the military life than to law enforcement. He needed Love at his side to keep the peace in the growing city.

Finally, the door to Bigler's office opened and he shooed out what appeared to be a bunch of useless functionaries, men in suits who, to a one, didn't look as if they'd ever dirtied their hands with real labor. They disappeared down a hallway in a pack, and Bigler noted Love sitting there. A smile spread on his face.

"It's a pleasure to meet you, Deputy Love," he said. "I've heard so much about you. Come in, please. Sorry you had to wait. A governor's work is never done, it seems."

Bigler turned sideways to let Love in the door, but the deputy's broad shoulders still brushed the man's chest. "Way I heard it, you wanted the job."

"Indeed, I did. I still do. It's a place where I can make a difference. That doesn't make it easy."

"Neither is mine, but it has to be done," Love said. Love didn't mention that it paid decent money, which he needed.

Between his drinking and his gambling, he'd found himself in debt to some bad men. He was paying it back little by little, but still had some distance to go.

Bigler's office wasn't as fancy as Love had expected. He guessed his expectations had been based on his ideas of how governors back east lived and worked, like the feudal lords of Europe. There was no marble in Bigler's office, no fancy sculptures or artwork. His desk was pinewood, as plain as a schoolteacher's. On it were an inkwell and a blotter and a cup that held various pens and pencils. A pair of chairs stood opposite Bigler's seat behind the desk, so some of those functionaries who'd just left must have been standing. The planks of his floor were bare, as were the walls. A bookcase held dozens of volumes, law books and ledgers, but those were the only items Love could see that might not be purely functional—and perhaps they were. He had no idea.

"You say you've heard about me? From who?"

Bigler looked at the ceiling, as if the answer might be written there. "Initially, from a deputy in Los Angeles. Schmitt, I think his name was. I've lost track of him; he headed north for the winter, is what I've heard, and never bothered to return. Since then, I've asked others about you. Your name seems to be known all over the state, and your reputation is sterling. A good soldier and a good lawman, is what I've heard."

"I reckon them as obeys the law might say so," Love offered. "The others are hardly so generous, I'm sure."

"Well, I wouldn't know about that." Bigler smiled. "I don't tend to solicit the opinions of ruffians and renegades."

"Seems reasonable," Love said. He looked around the office. He'd done some asking around, as well. "I reckon your brother has fancier digs than you," Love said.

"Indeed, he does." Bigler's younger brother William was

currently serving as governor of Pennsylvania—one of those back-east states Love had been thinking of. "But I don't need luxurious surroundings. He's dealing with a rigid bureaucracy there—parties that have hardened positions that no force on heaven or Earth could move. Here in California, everything's brand-new. Here, we can create America's future. *That's* the challenge before me, and I embrace it willingly."

Bigler sounded like a politician giving a campaign speech, and looked like one, too, soft and pudgy. His second chin bobbed beneath his first when he spoke. His hairline was receding, leaving a balding semicircle that made his face almost exactly egg-shaped.

"Take a seat, Harry. I appreciate you making the trip up here—believe me, I'd rather have gone to Santa Barbara, but the burdens of this position don't allow me that freedom anymore."

Love pulled one of the plain wooden chairs away from the desk and planted himself, placing his left ankle across his right knee.

"Your letter said something about an opportunity, Governor."

Bigler chortled. "Indeed, Harry. As you so acutely observed, we're not back East. And yes, I do have an opportunity to offer you. I think you'll find it appealing." He sat in his own chair and pressed his palms against the surface of his desk. "As you know, we have a Mexican problem in this state."

"Have had since it became a state," Love agreed.

"Indeed. Difference is, the Mexican problem has largely become a Murrieta problem. Or a Joaquin problem, I suppose we can say, since there appear to be Joaquins behind every tree and rock. Not only are these bandits growing bolder all the time, but with them running unmolested across the countryside, attacking our lawmen and our innocent civilians at will, they're having a deleterious effect on the Mexican populace. To put it simply, the greasers are feeling their oats, Harry. They're thinking themselves high and mighty, and becoming harder than ever to put in their place."

"I had my own run-in with him just a few days ago." He described how he'd dealt with Gonzalez and escaped the outlaw band, earning a grin from the governor. He ended with, "You ask me, their place is south of the border."

"You'll get no argument from me. But that's not so easily accomplished, I'm afraid. We can't scoop them up and move them individually, so our best bet is to make them want to move. And with Murrieta and those other Joaquins running around, we can't get that done.

"To make things worse, the newspapers are having a field day, running stories constantly about Murrieta and his ilk. The Republican-leaning papers are playing up the sob story—how he was supposedly betrayed and brutalized, turning him from an innocent, hard-working man into a hardened killer. The Democratic papers have been more reasonable, but they're putting a lot of pressure on the legislature to get something done. And I mean to do just that."

"And your plan is?" Love was a straightforward man. He liked to get to the point, and Bigler was a typical politician, in love with the sound of his own voice.

"Joaquin Murrieta has to be reined in," Bigler said. "Captured, if at all possible. That's how the act will be written, at least. But if he has to be killed, that'll do as well. I'd like you to do it."

Love sat back and folded his hands across his breast. "I think I know this Murrieta fellow," he said. "I had a young man working for me, for a spell. Up in the mines. He was a right good sort, hard-working and honest. But he met with some dirty doings. If he is the bandit, it's not hard to see what led him onto the outlaw path."

"I leave that sort of thing to others to worry over," Bigler replied. "I don't care if his mother dropped him on his head or any of that. For me it's all about preserving the peace and safety of honest Californians." He let his gaze drift toward the ceiling for a moment, then fixed it on Love again. "Would that be a problem? You knowing him?"

"Not as I see it. He might have been honest once, but he's a killer now. Even a good dog's got to be put down if it goes mad, right? But it'll take some doing. No lawman's been able to get the drop on him yet."

"No lawman has been given the resources you'll have, Harry. I want you to pull together a force of twenty men, loyal to you. You'll have the title of California Rangers. You'll have a salary of one hundred and fifty dollars each, for three months. That's all I've been able to get the legislature to agree to, though if it goes longer, I can go back for an extension. Your men will have to supply their own horses, guns and ammunition, provisions and the like. But you'll have absolute freedom of movement. Carte blanche. You alone will decide where and how to hunt, and no lawman will try to enforce any laws you might happen to break along the way. You understand me, don't you, Harry? *Nothing* will prevent you from doing *whatever* is necessary to bring in that Mexican bastard."

"I understand, Governor. And one-fifty per man ain't bad. But I'll have to pull these men away from their regular lives, for maybe just three months, and—"

Bigler stopped him with a raised palm. "I see what you're driving at, Harry. I'm a man of not inconsiderable means myself, so trust me when I say that even though the legislature won't appropriate the money, I will personally pay what I'm sure you'll find is a very substantial reward for Murrieta. Incidentally, the act—it's already written, and will be signed within days—will not just name Murrieta, but all five Joaquins. Should you happen to locate and capture or otherwise dispose of the others, I'll increase the reward. But Murrieta is the one who's agitating the Mexicans, and the one our white citizens fear the most. So he's the one I want you to go after."

That kind of money could make a serious dent in Love's obligations. He tried to keep a straight face while he continued the discussion, but he was already on board. "So, twenty rangers, to do a job that posses of twenty-five or thirty haven't been able to?" Harry asked.

"Those posses weren't made up of hardened lawmen and soldiers. I trust you to pick men who can get the job done."

"I reckon I've got a few ideas on that count."

"I knew you would. Will you do it, Harry? Will you bring in Joaquin Murrieta, so honest folks can sleep at night?"

Love stuck out his big hand. Bigler leaned across the desk and clasped it. "Governor," Love said, "You got yourself a ranger. I'm going to kick some greaser asses, and they'll all feel the hurt before I'm done."

Bigler laughed again. "Harry, my man," he said, "that's what I'm counting on."

55

Pedro Vergara arrived in Los Angeles as the sun was sinking into the ocean, and by the time he reached Calle de los Negros, dusk had come. The Harper House was just past the end of the alley, on the corner of Aliso and Los Angeles streets. As he made his way there, he kept his hat pulled low over his eyes, because he wanted to be sure that he saw La Molinera and Pancho Dominguez before they saw him.

The street was crowded with people eating and drinking and generally carrying on. He smelled burning mesquite wood and roasted meats, liquor and sweat and smoke. As the name suggested, the area was mostly populated by blacks, California being a free state, but there were plenty of Mexicans and poor whites out as well. Pedro tried to eyeball everyone. But people came here, some of them, to engage in activities that might not be acceptable behavior in more sedate neighborhoods. Saloons were plentiful, and some people served liquor or opium right in their homes. Prostitutes were available any time of the day or night. Vergara saw young girls, young boys, old women, and everything in between, out on the street or beckoning trade from windows. That being the case, he knew that many would react poorly to being observed too closely.

It seemed the only things he wasn't seeing were La Molinera and Dominguez. Still, he had only just arrived, and he knew where Pancho slept, if he was still there.

He passed through the crowds one more time, making his way to the end of the alley. Drunks stumbled into him as he walked, and a prostitute, curvaceous and quite lovely, threw her arms around him and kissed him. "I can make you forget all about her," she whispered.

"About who?"

"About anyone!"

Vergara disentangled himself and shoved her away. She pouted, but then laughed and made a half-hearted attempt to grab his crotch. He walked away from her, and she was already turning her attentions toward another passerby.

At the end of the alley, he stopped and looked across the way at the Harper House. It was a three-story building, right on the corner. Lamp light illuminated three of the second-floor rooms that he could see, and in one a shadowed figure seemed to be sitting at a table or desk. The shape of the figure's hat looked like the sombrero Pancho favored, with a tall crown and a brim almost wide enough to keep even his belly dry in a storm.

He waited for several minutes, hoping that the figure would move, maybe look out the window, so he could determine that it was indeed Pancho. When it didn't budge, he gave up and crossed the street.

He admired Joaquin, and felt honored that the leader of their band had picked him for this mission. He knew it was because killing was easy for him, but he appreciated the man's faith in him. Joaquin's biggest problem was that he was too generous—handing their riches over to poor Mexicans, and sometimes even Chinese, when they could split it among themselves and become even richer. Joaquin claimed there was strategy behind it, and maybe he was right. Vergara didn't know anything about strategy. He did what he was told, and what he was told usually involved taking lives. Now he would do it again, and, he expected, earn some kind of bonus when he returned to the camp.

The Harper House lobby was crowded with people playing faro at a table, chatting, laughing. One man sat in a plush chair in a corner, reading a book—Vergara didn't know how he could concentrate with all the racket, but the man seemed utterly captivated. At the back of the lobby a clerk sat behind a desk, fiddling with paperwork and trying to ignore the bustle around him. Behind him was a board with neatly painted numbers and keys hanging on brass hooks, and below that, a steam radiator. He was a rat-faced man with short hair parted in the middle, a little waxed mustache, and garters on the sleeves of his white shirt. As Vergara approached him, he looked up with the look of a broken man.

"We're full up," he said.

Vergara was ready for this. He reached over the counter and placed a stack of coins on the desk behind it. "I'm not looking for a room. I'm looking for a friend. His name's Dominguez." He turned sideways and held his hand out from his stomach, indicating's Pancho's girth. "Is he still in two-oh-one?"

The clerk swiped the coins off the desk and pocketed them with a smooth, practiced motion. "He is, at that."

"Is he there now?"

"I saw him come in a while back," the clerk replied. "Ain't seen him leave again."

"Thanks," Vergara said, grinning. "He'll be surprised to see me. It's been weeks."

The clerk nodded and went back to his paperwork. Vergara started up the stairs. As he rounded a turn, he heard something like three bangs on a pipe, echoing through the building. The radiator system, he figured, thinking nothing else of it.

When he reached the door of room 201—it was the room facing the street, where he'd seen the figure near the window, so he was sure he knew about where to find Pancho when he went in—something tickled at the back of his mind. He ignored it and drew his pistol, which he had already checked three times since arriving in Los Angeles. Fully loaded.

He turned the knob and threw open the door, stepped inside, pistol aimed at where he'd seen the figure.

It wasn't Pancho. It was only some pillows, stacked in a chair, with Pancho's sombrero resting on top. Confused, Vergara lowered the weapon, looking around the room for Pancho. But the small room was empty.

Then the door opened behind him, and he heard a familiar voice. "You're not Joaquin!"

Vergara spun around. "Pancho! There you are."

Pancho Dominguez held a shotgun in his hands, its barrels cut short. The weapon could cut Vergara in half. He raised his hands, the pistol still clutched in his right. "I was looking for you, old friend."

"With a gun in your hand."

"I wasn't sure you were in here." The thought that had been tickling at him came back, and he suddenly understood. "The knocks on the pipe. It's springtime in Los Angeles. No radiator."

"Clever," Pancho said. "I expected Joaquin to come himself, to defend his beloved's honor. I guess the fact that he chose to send a flunky is all we need to know about his devotion to Antonia."

"So you set a trap for him? To kill Joaquin? Why?"

"Have you ever worshipped someone? Thought more highly of him than he did of himself? Believed he could do almost anything?"

Vergara shook his head. He didn't know what Pancho was driving at, and didn't want to agree with anything while that scattergun was pointed at him.

"Not even Joaquin?"

"I suppose, a little."

"I put all my faith in him, and he refused to live up to it. I expected miracles. All I got was a man—and one who belittled and humiliated me, then cast me out."

"He wasn't even in camp when you left."

"He let me know that I should be gone before he returned," Pancho said. "He betrayed my faith in him. That's something I can't live down."

"You've been planning this for a while."

"Ever since I left. I took this room, and the one across the hall, and I let everyone know about this one. I have an arrangement with the day clerk and the night one—if anyone came asking for me, they'd signal."

"So you thought Joaquin would come to kill you?"

"That's the only part of my plan that failed. Once again, I thought more highly of him than he did of himself. Instead, he sent you to do it."

"You misunderstand, Pancho." Vergara's arms were getting tired, trembling with the effort of holding them up. But if he tried to lower them, Pancho might just squeeze that trigger. He had to figure something out, and fast. "I left him, too. I heard you were here, and thought perhaps you and I could start a new gang."

"We've never been close friends, Pedro. I don't believe you. He sent you here to kill me. But you failed, and now you'll pay the price."

Vergara knew he had only one chance, and he had to act soon, before Pancho decided to shoot. It might not work, and if it didn't, he would be a dead man. But if he didn't at least try, Pancho would kill him, anyway.

"Haven't failed yet," he said. He added a shrug to that, and at the end of the motion, he pulled the pistol's trigger without aiming. The bullet crashed through the wall into another room, and somebody in there screamed.

Startled, Pancho's head whipped around to see where the round had hit the wall. In that instant, Vergara lowered the pistol and fired again, twice in Pancho's gut and once in the face. Pancho crumpled to the floor, blood jetting out around him.

Vergara heard footfalls pounding up the stairs and people shouting below. He wasn't going to make it back through that lobby. Instead, he threw open the window, holstered his gun, and climbed out. He lowered himself as far as he could, then released and fell to the street. Passersby stared at him, but inside the hotel, everybody's attention was riveted to the staircase and the ceiling. Vergara ran into Calle de Los Negros and lost himself in the crowd. He needed to find Antonia. But first, he needed to find a drink.

• • •

An insistent rapping at the door disturbed Antonia Molinera's reading. She had planned to stay in for the night, and she'd curled up with a blanket wrapped around her, a glass of wine close by, and a copy of *Uncle Tom's Cabin*, the new book that had attracted so much attention back East, in her hands. She read English almost as easily as she did Spanish, but some of the words and phrases Stowe used were unfamiliar, and she had to concentrate on context to understand them.

But whoever was knocking wasn't going away. Instead, the knocks grew louder, more urgent. With a weary sigh, she set the book aside and rose from her chair, adjusting the blanket on her shoulders. When she opened the door, a young man she didn't know was standing there. He looked barely out of his teens, and the fuzz that passed for his mustache suggested that perhaps he hadn't even reached that age.

"What is it?" she asked.

"Señorita Molinera, forgive my intrusion," he said, anxiety evident in the tightness of his voice. "I've just come from Castro's Cantina. On Calle Principal, near the church?"

"I know the place. Please, what's your problem? Spit it out."

"There's a man in there, a big man, cruel looking. He's drunk, and he's bragging that he killed Señor Dominguez."

"He did?"

"Somebody did, a little while ago. You haven't heard?"

She put a hand on the door jamb to steady herself. "I've been inside all day. Nobody told me."

"I'm so sorry. I thought you would have known by now."

"It's all right. So, this man is saying he did it?"

"Yes. And that you're next. He's even offering to pay anyone who'll tell him how to find you. He's so drunk, I doubt that he could raise a hand to you even if he knew where to look."

"Let me get dressed," she said. "Wait here. I'll be out in a few minutes, and you can show me."

She dressed quickly. Castro's was a short walk away, less than ten minutes through the warm night air. By the time she and the young man reached it, perspiration glazed her forehead. As soon as she passed through the door, she knew who the braggart was, and who had sent him. Although she hadn't heard anything about Pancho's death, considering who she saw leaning against the bar, hardly able to hold himself upright, she believed the story. Pedro Vergara could kill anybody.

Almost anybody, she mentally corrected herself.

She made her way through the crowded cantina and stopped in front of him, composing her face into a gracious smile. "Pedro!" she said. "What a delightful surprise! I didn't know you were in town."

He looked at her cross-eyed, then shook his head, and finally seemed able to see her. "Antonia!" he cried. "It's you!"

"Of course it's me. Who else did you expect to see?"

"I've been looking for you!"

"And here I am. My beloved Joaquin sent you, didn't he?"

"He's very angry with you."

"He's an angry sort sometimes. I don't take it personally."

"I killed Pancho!" He almost shouted it out, as if it had slipped his mind and he'd just remembered.

"I heard. That's no great loss. He always was five times too full of himself."

Vergara burst out laughing at that. Once he was able to halfway control himself, he said, "And I have to kill you, too!"

"Of course," Antonia said. "But that can wait until morning. You're drunk, Pedro. You need to come home with me and sleep it off. When you're feeling better tomorrow, we can talk about killing me."

"You really are a thoughtful woman," Vergara said. "No wonder Joaquin likes you so much."

"He likes me enough to have me murdered."

"Exactly!" He was so enthusiastic about his task, Antonia couldn't help smiling.

She tipped her head toward the bartender, and he came

over to her. She ordered another drink for Vergara, and one for herself. When he set the glasses down on the polished bar top, Vergara eyed his suspiciously.

"Should I have more?" he asked.

"You're already drunk," Antonia said. "You might as well be a little more drunk."

"That's a good point. You're very smart."

She took a sip of hers, and put the glass back down. "Did Joaquin even wonder why I was in Los Angeles?" she asked.

Vergara stared off into space for several seconds, then tried to focus on her again. "I don't remember. Somebody told him you were with Pancho."

Antonia laughed. "Pancho is a good storyteller. He's funny. But 'with' him in any sense other than having a few drinks? Don't be ridiculous. Did Joaquin believe that?"

"I think so," Vergara said. "That's part of why I'm supposed to kill you."

"Only part?"

"Also because you're working in a brothel, he said."

Antonia just smiled at that. Now it was starting to make sense. Whoever had seen her here must have spotted her going into Elsa's Place. "I did my share of that when I was much younger," she explained. "But I have a friend who is still in that line of work. She had some problems with Elsa, the madam, and I told her I'd help her out. I had to visit her a few times, where she worked, to make sure that the conversations I had with Elsa had the desired effect. For Joaquin to believe that of me . . . he must not trust me very much. After all he said I meant to him, that hurts."

"I'm sorry, Antonia. I shouldn't have told you. I should have killed you first, then told you."

She downed the rest of her drink, surprisingly saddened

by this revelation. "Come outside with me," she said, offering a hand. Vergara hesitated only briefly, then took it. His skin was rough, raspy against hers, but she closed her hand around it and drew him unsteadily to his feet. "Come along, Pedro. I'll fix you a place to sleep and you can kill me tomorrow."

He wiped his face on his forearm. "I'll definitely be able to do that," he said. "I'm pretty drunk now."

"I can see."

She led him through the crowd. People parted at their approach, incredulous looks on their faces as they watched the victim-to-be escort her would-be assassin from the cantina. Someone asked her if she needed help, but she waved off the query.

Outside, the street was quiet. She saw a couple down the block, locked in an amorous embrace up against a wall. In the other direction, she saw the dark, silent bulk of the church. "It's this way," she said. "Across the plaza."

"I was over there earlier. Before I killed Pancho."

"I'm surprised no one told me."

"Maybe they were afraid I would kill them, too."

"That must be it."

Halfway to the end of the block, she stopped suddenly. Her abrupt halt almost made Vergara lose his balance, but she caught him and pressed him up against the nearest wall. Kneading dough and carrying trays full of bread built strong muscles, even in a slender woman. "One more thing, Pedro," she said. "Wait here."

"Wait for what?"

After arriving in Los Angeles, she had traded the Baby Dragoon that Joaquin had given her for a brand-new Philadelphia Deringer. The little pistol was more easily concealed. Before her parents had found success with the bakery, she had sold herself on city streets and in brothels, much like Elsa's Place. She knew how dangerous a man could be when he was alone with a girl or a woman. Paying for her company made many believe they could do whatever they wanted, and they didn't hesitate to use force to get their way. She'd learned early on that it helped to have a weapon close at hand, something the man wouldn't even see until it was too late. In those days, she had used knives, but when she'd first learned of the Deringer, she knew it was the ideal solution.

She tugged it from inside her sleeve and pressed it up against Vergara's forehead. The reality of his situation sank in slowly, and before he could react, she pulled the trigger. His head muffled the sound, and she didn't even see any blood until he fell away from the wall, leaving a ragged stain behind.

She hadn't killed many people—she was no Joaquin, no Pedro Vergara. Just a handful, when necessary for her own protection. But she had found that when a victim cooperated, it wasn't hard at all.

56

"Thirty men riding with Undersheriff Charlie Clarke," Tres Dedos was saying. "Wilmer Smith from Sacramento has a dozen, and Walter Dorton from El Dorado has twenty."

"I'm not worried about any of them."

"You don't worry enough, Joaquin. That's your problem. Well, one of them."

"I thought my problem was that my woman is missing."

"A missing woman is never as much of a problem as a woman looking over your shoulder. I could list your problems, but there's not enough time in the day."

Joaquin could tell that his cousin was joking. No matter how hard he tried to disguise it, Tres Dedos always had a twinkle in his eye when he taunted Joaquin.

That twinkle vanished as he turned serious. "But there's one more you should know about. You remember Harry Love?"

"Of course! I took him for a friend, once. But that was before he killed Hector."

"Friends are the worst," Tres Dedos said. He grinned. "I mean, when they turn against you. It's like they have to prove they were never really your friend after all, by being particularly spiteful to you."

"Like Pancho," Joaquin said. He hadn't heard anything from Los Angeles yet, and wondered every day when Vergara would return with news.

"That's right. The state legislature has just passed a bill. It hasn't been announced yet, but it will be, today or tomorrow. The state is hiring Love to form a team of California Rangers with just one mission. You. Apparently, they're still not sure how many Joaquins there are, or if they're all just you, but he's been tasked with finding and capturing or killing the bandit Joaquin, and any other bandits Joaquin he can come across. You can be sure that you're his main goal, though."

"I'd like to see him try. If I can get within gunshot range of that bastard, my smiling face will be the last thing he ever sees." Bold talk. Joaquin hadn't killed anyone since Bear Mountain, and he hadn't missed it at all. He had mostly stayed at the arroyo and sent others out on raids. Having seen Love murder Gonzales, he knew he'd be capable of killing the lawman. But he would be just as happy to never lay eyes on him again.

He knew there was more killing ahead, though. He had tried to steel himself for it. If need be, he would think of Rosita, and let the old rage fill him again.

"I just wanted you to be aware of what's going on," Tres Dedos continued. "And those are just the ones I've heard about this week. Even our spies can't keep track of them all. You're suddenly the most wanted man in California. In all of the United States, maybe."

"It's nice to be wanted," Joaquin said with a chuckle. "But perhaps not that way."

For the past twenty minutes, Tres Dedos had been filling him in on information gathered from his network of contacts in the state's Mexican communities. He had handed Joaquin a stack of cuttings from various newspapers, and told him the editorial leanings of those papers. Then he'd listed rewards offered by different towns and counties, and finished up by detailing the organized posses out looking for him.

Joaquin felt proud, in a way, to have achieved so much distinction after being born into poverty, in a hamlet the world had largely passed by. He tried to make light of the lawmen hunting for him, but he knew he should take them seriously. He'd had good luck evading the law thus far, but luck didn't hold out forever.

Tres Dedos sat across from him at the table in the canvas-roofed part of the house they shared, looking at him. The question on his mind was obvious: what now?

Joaquin took a few moments to compose his thoughts, then said, "It's time, then."

"Time for what, my brother?"

"Time to do what must be done. To drive the Americans from the state and return it to its proper owners. California should fly the Mexican flag, not that of the nation that stole it from us. I've been thinking about this for a long time, cousin. Now's the time. The Americans tremble at the thought of us. When they see us coming, they hand over their purses without us having to say a word. We need to use that fear against them, to send them back to wherever they came from. These shores, these forests and mountains and rivers and gold, are part of Mexico and no other."

"But they're so many, Joaquin, and more all the time. They're worse than rabbits, those whites. They're like weeds after a spring rain."

Joaquin laid his hand over his cousin's—its three fingers almost as familiar now as his own hands—and sighed. He'd been thinking about this for a long time. Maybe Pancho Dominguez had planted the seed; maybe he would have come to it on his own regardless. But the more he dwelled on it, the more obvious it became. He'd been holding it back until he fleshed out the idea more thoroughly, but now that he'd started talking about it, he couldn't stop. "We can't outrun an entire nation, if that's what they send after us. We might not get out of this alive. But I won't go down without a fight, and this is the fight I was put on this Earth for. I know that, as surely as I know anything in life. We need to call all our men back, from wherever they are. Then we need as many volunteers as we can get from among our supporters, and as many horses as we can steal. We need guns, and ammunition, too. With a force of five hundred or a thousand mounted soldiers, we can drive out every American. I'm certain of it."

Tres Dedos nodded. "I like it," he said. "As long as they don't all run. I want the chance to kill as many as I can."

Joaquin chuckled at that. "You'll have that chance. I'm sure of it. Now, let's get to work."

• • •

Three months wasn't very long to catch a bandit who'd been evading the law for almost as many years. Love didn't have time for selective recruiting—he rounded up the first twenty men he could find who knew how to handle a horse and a gun, looked halfway sober, and wouldn't eat too much. Although Joaquins had been spotted all over the state, the most recent reports had been from the north-central part, and most of the crimes attributed to Murrieta had been committed around the diggings. So that's where he decided to start looking.

He didn't have to look for long. A white rancher whose property fronted Murray Creek in Calaveras County reported that forty of his best horses had been stolen. The announcement of the California Rangers and their mission had been spread far and wide, and with it the urgency of reporting any suspected sightings to the state government for immediate dispatch to the rangers. The rancher had taken the announcement to heart and had telegraphed the capital. Love arrived at the scene the following morning. The tracks left by the rustlers and their ill-gotten gains were still clear and easy to follow, so follow it the rangers did.

Love's second-in-command was a lawman named Charles Ellas, from San Andreas, right here in the county. Ellas was a war veteran who'd come west from Georgia to kill Indians, and he had done so in Kansas and then Texas. When the war broke out, he was assigned to the Fourth Infantry. He had walked into the grinder at Resaca de la Palma, where a musket ball had shattered his upper left arm. Wounded, he had strayed away from the others, and a Mexican lancer had stabbed him in the abdomen and left him for dead. Somehow, he hadn't died, but had made it back to a medical tent. The doctor there had sawed off his arm at the shoulder, and given him the happy news that the lance had missed any vital organs. Still, the war had been over for him.

Ellas had drifted for a while before winding up in California. He found work for John Sutter in New Helvetia, guarding the Miwok and Nisenan workers so they wouldn't abandon the fort when their traditional herb- and acorn-gathering times came around. In that job, he had been able to do some more of the Indian killing that had brought him so far, and he'd stayed on until John Marshall discovered gold while supervising the construction of Sutter's sawmill on the American River. Then, like most of the white men in Sutter's employ, he left for the gold fields.

Instead of striking it rich, Ellas had struck out, but he'd been able to parlay his military experience into a position as undersheriff of Calaveras County. When Love, who'd heard of his exploits, had offered him the position—figuring that a lawman from the area Joaquin had most often frequented would be handy to have along—Ellas had jumped at the chance.

Now, Love summoned Ellas up to the front of the pack and pointed out the mass of hoofprints. They crossed Murray Creek about a half-mile from the spot where the fence had been knocked down—and quickly stood up again, as was Joaquin's usual pattern. On the far side of the creek, the trail led up the bank and out of sight. "You got any idea where they might be headed?" Love asked. "We're a day behind, so if there's a way to cut 'em off, that'd be helpful."

Ellas shook his head. His shirtsleeve was pinned at the left shoulder, and scars on his face indicated that he'd seen some rough times. "Can't rightly tell. Let's us cross over and foller 'em for a spell, see do they keep on in the same direction."

"That's the plan, then." Love gave a loud whistle and waved his arm to indicate their path. With Ellas just off his right shoulder, Love followed the trampled trail into the creek. It ran fast, but it wasn't too deep or too wide, and a minute later his mount heaved up the other side.

The afternoon stretched on. Summer wasn't far off, and the day was a hot one. The trail continued in a northerly direction, so easy to follow that a child could have led the way. What bothered Love was that there were so many prints, he couldn't tell which belonged to horses with riders and which the animals stolen from the ranch. He could only guess, but his guess could be wildly wrong. They might have been following a dozen men, or fifty.

He also couldn't determine how fast the bandits were traveling. Most of the horse droppings they passed had pretty well dried up, which indicated that they were still about a day behind. But the bandits would've spent some time herding the stolen animals, keeping them on the trail, which should have slowed them down a little. The landscape here was hilly, but not densely forested, although the trail was heading into more rugged country. A man could see a long way, and there was no visible cloud of dust in the distance that might have indicated a large party.

"Ellas!" Love called. The lawman rode up beside him. "Where are we headed here?"

"The Mokelumne River's an hour or so up ahead on this path," Ellas reported. "A little settlement called Chaparral Hill. Gold's mostly played out there, so it's pretty near abandoned. There's a few river crossings in the area."

"If these bandits are based to the south, as I believe they are, why would they be herding the horses to the north?"

Ellas shrugged. "Got a buyer for 'em, mebbe. Or they want to make a few more stops before they turn south, steal some more stock."

"Could be," Love agreed. He didn't like it, but with no good alternatives, he chose to keep following the well-trodden path.

The hour Ellas had mentioned passed, and they still hadn't reached the river. They were a ways from San Andreas, which was where Ellas hung his hat, so Love figured maybe he just didn't know the country that well. The trees grew taller and thicker, the land rocky, with steep slopes and rugged declivities. The trail narrowed, and natural barriers on either side jammed the horses even closer together.

Love's stomach complained loudly. They'd been on this path for the entire day, without stopping for lunch. He'd pulled some hardtack from a saddle bag and chewed on it from time to time, but he had tobacco in there, and a flask, and he wanted a nip of each as well as a solid meal. Some of the men were grumbling, too, though he tried not to hear them, or at least not to let on that he did. But they'd have to stop soon. Maybe when they reached the Moke River they could water and feed the horses and stretch out some of the saddle cramps.

The trail led into a canyon with rocky slopes on either side, dotted with pines and crested at the top with tall trees and plenty of scrub. Love was thinking about his bodily needs instead of about the situation; the ease of following the path had dulled his reflexes. So when he caught the flash of afternoon sunlight reflecting off of something metallic, up there on the hilltop, he didn't think twice about it until he heard the loud crack of a rifle.

That brought him back to reality in a hurry.

"Ambush!" he shouted. "Find cover!"

57

That first round slammed into the earth in front of Love's horse. The beast reared back, and Love gripped it with his thighs, fighting for balance. As the horse came down, he yanked hard on the reins and leaned to his left, trying to spin it around. But other riders still pressed forward, and the horse had nowhere to go.

The first shot was a signal to others, and a withering volley followed that felled men and mounts alike. Love's horse, on the verge of panic, took a ball in the snout and gave a piteous cry before dropping to its knees. Love leapt from the saddle, snatched his rifle from its scabbard, and ducked behind the animal's bulk. Lead buzzed around him like wasps after someone had poked their nest. More bullets thunked into his fallen horse, and the poor creature twitched and wheezed with each one. Love wanted to finish it, end its agony, but couldn't spare the time or the lead.

He spotted men on both of the surrounding hillsides. They were dug in, sheltered behind stout trees or boulders or the ridgeline itself. The only available targets were the barrels of their weapons, or the instant they showed themselves to aim and fire. Behind and around him, other rangers were pinned down. Those at the rear of the column had turned back, taking cover amidst the trees—or, for all he knew, riding hellbent for safety in some other state.

Staying put would be suicide. The greasers—he could see them well enough to know they were Mexicans—had every advantage. Eight or ten feet back, a chestnut mare with no rider shifted around, unsure of which way to go without a guiding hand. Four men were positioned between Love and that horse. Any of them might be able to reach the animal and escape on it.

But he was the captain of the California Rangers, the man charged with assembling the team and leading it to its rightful conclusion. Of them all, only he was indispensable.

He yanked his Colt from its holster and fired five quick rounds at the bandits, then whirled around and ran at a crouch past his other men, themselves sheltering behind fallen horses or dying comrades. A couple eyed him in surprise, and one of those raised his head too far and took a musket ball for his trouble.

Reaching the horse, Love grabbed the reins and shifted the animal so that its body was between him and the bandits. Lead flew past, but he was moving quickly, and none struck home. When he was safely out of range, he climbed into the saddle and rode away, calling for the other rangers who'd vanished from sight.

His team's first encounter with Joaquin—if that was indeed who led this band of horse thieves—hadn't turned out the way he'd hoped. All he could do was rebuild and try again.

But to do that, he had to survive.

• • •

It had been a long wait.

Scouts and spies had kept an eye on Joaquin's back trail and reported on the progress of the posse following it. It could have been the California Rangers or one of the many other posses Tres Dedos had warned Joaquin about, and it didn't matter one way or the other. Night would fall in a little while, and he wanted some rest. The Mokelumne River would be a good spot to let the horses drink, let the men bathe if they so desired, and give everybody time to gather their strength. The next day would be a long one, during which they'd cross over some rugged country as they looped around to the south.

But without knowing the plans of their pursuers, he couldn't take that chance. Instead, he guided the party into a narrow slot he knew of. Their trail would unmistakably lead right through it, but on the far side was a meadow where a few men could keep the stolen horses penned up while the rest took up positions on the flanking slopes.

This setup was almost a duplicate of the first operation with Tres Dedos's men, who had become his men—when they'd taken the payroll for the two sawmills. That one still gleamed in his memory as one of the most elaborate and successful jobs they had pulled. Of course, that one had also involved explosives. This one didn't, because they hadn't had time, but he wouldn't have minded if they'd been able to. Most of their escapades were simple affairs—catch a lone rider with a heavy purse, or charge into a small camp—French, Chinese, German, but ideally American—and demand treasure or blood. Most people willingly gave up treasure, and the ones who gave up blood wound up also giving up treasure, after the fact. In fact, Joaquin had learned, the more adamant a man was that he would rather die than hand over his wealth, the more wealth he probably had to hide.

Hours had passed and the sun started dipping behind western hills by the time the posse came into view. When they were in range, the ridges on either side cutting off easy escape, Joaquin fired the first shot.

Harry Love had been the most obvious first target, but

when he had tried to aim at the man, his hands had trembled and he'd missed the shot. A destructive barrage of lead from two-dozen rifles followed. Horses reared up, throwing riders, or fell atop them. Men fell, too—at least nine in the first volley. Biting white smoke clouded the clean, clear air. As the first group of bandits reloaded, the second opened fire, and more of their pursuers went down.

Some started returning fire, then, but the bandits had chosen their positions well and fired from cover. The men on the ground were shooting up, always harder, and most of their shots flew overhead or plowed into the earth in front of their targets.

After the first few minutes, the battle shifted. The remaining men from the posse found cover in the trees or lay behind fallen horses. They freed rifles and started to aim more carefully. A couple of Joaquin's men were hit, one by a shot that split the top of his head in half. Some of the posse members, who had been at the rear of the column, had turned tail and ridden away as fast as their mounts could carry them. Harry Love was one of those who'd escaped, because after his horse had fallen, he had snatched up the reins of another whose rider had been hit. He'd led the beast away from the field of fire, and the last Joaquin had seen of him had been his back. He had fired another shot at the deputy's retreating form, but the distance was too great, and his round fell short.

Now, men picked out their targets carefully. The crack of rifles was spaced out, not simultaneous thunder. Even so, more shots missed their targets than hit, on both sides. Some of the posse members tried to work their way up the slopes, covering one another for short dashes from rock to tree to a furrow deep enough to lie in.

Joaquin saw one who had made more progress than the

rest. He had already made it to a height that gave him an angle down on some of the bandits, and he'd shot two of them. He had almost reached the top of the ridge. Joaquin snugged the stock of his rifle into his shoulder and sighted down the barrel, but the man ducked behind an old pine with a trunk bigger around than he was. Glancing down the hillside, Joaquin saw almost a dozen of his men within the sniper's range, most still focused on enemies below, so unaware of the threat from above.

So much death, all around him. And more to come, if that man wasn't stopped.

He needed a better shot at him.

Just below the ridge on the far side, a ragged line of trees offered possible concealment. As long as the man didn't see him during the short sprint in the open, Joaquin could make his way nearer. And from the angle of the rifle barrel that Joaquin saw, the man was aiming downslope, about to kill another bandit from on high. Nothing Joaquin could do about that; he was a good shot with a rifle, but the gun barrel didn't give him enough of a target, and a missed shot would reveal his own location.

Instead of shooting, he took advantage of the moment to hurtle down the rock-strewn slope. His foot landed wrong on one step and slid out from beneath him. He landed hard and skidded, sharp edges tearing through his clothing and into the skin of his left leg and thigh. He held onto the rifle, though, and quickly righted himself. The pain didn't start to burn until he was upright again and behind the first of the trees.

They were more widely spaced than they'd looked. He still didn't think that was a problem, as long as his quarry kept his attention fixed on the bandits below him on the other side. From that tree, Joaquin darted to the next, and the third, pine boughs offering a screen, if only scant protection. As he worked his way across the slope, though, he heard shot after shot ring out from the sniper's position, and the anguished cries of his targets suggested he was picking his shots well.

Finally, Joaquin reached a position from which he had an angle on the sniper. Should the man look his way, he'd have an easy downhill shot at Joaquin, shielded only by a pine trunk a little less in diameter than twice Joaquin's thigh, but that Joaquin had to be on the near side of to take his own shot. He couldn't even lean on the tree for stability; the trunk was on his right side, where the rifle was. He took careful aim at the back of the man's head, then lowered his barrel slightly—the fellow's back was a bigger target, and a shot there would incapacitate him just as well.

He squeezed the trigger. The rifle boomed, and his ball thudded uselessly into the mighty tree's bark.

Not altogether useless, though; it alerted the sniper to his presence. The man swung around the big tree and pointed his gun at Joaquin. Joaquin dropped his own rifle and threw himself down, drawing his revolver at the same instant. When his left leg hit the earth, pain lanced through him, but he brought the pistol up and fired three quick shots at what he could see of the sniper.

At least one of them struck home. The man shouted and his rifle clattered to the ground. Pressing his momentary advantage, Joaquin charged.

But the slope was steep here, the footing treacherous, and his left leg throbbed. Coming down hard on that foot, the leg buckled, and Joaquin landed face-down in the rocks. On impact, he lost his grip on the pistol, which landed a few feet away and slightly downhill.

Scrambling for it, he caught a glimpse of the sniper

retrieving his rifle. Joaquin couldn't watch the other man and locate his revolver at the same time, so he hurled himself sideways, rolled across the jagged stones and snatched up the gun. He raised it and quickly aimed, only to see the sniper aiming down at him.

Both weapons sounded simultaneously. Joaquin was sliding down the slope, rocks lacerating his thighs and torso as he went. The sniper's shot fell short, throwing grit into Joaquin's eyes. But Joaquin's downhill travel hadn't affected his aim—the line remained true, and his bullet struck the sniper between nose and mouth. The rifle fell from limp hands and the man teetered briefly, then dropped to his knees. Joaquin planted his boots, arrested his slide, and aimed again. His next shot hit the sniper's forehead. The man collapsed in a heap.

Joaquin regained his footing and hurried to the top of the ridge. From the sniper's vantage point, he'd had easy shots at several of the bandits, some of whom he'd killed or wounded. If Joaquin hadn't stopped him, the man could have killed many more of his men. Still, as he looked at the dead man, he felt a pang of regret for the circumstances that had brought them together here, on opposite sides of the fight. But at least it was the last man he'd have to kill, for now.

The fighting had mostly ended; only Tres Dedos remained locked in combat. A white man gripped his rifle by the barrel and swung it like a club, trying to hold off Tres Dedos's machete. From here, Tres Dedos looked like nothing so much as a hulking grizzly slashing with huge claws at the smaller man.

The gun made an awkward club, though. The man's swings flew wild, and Tres Dedos waited until one upset the man's balance, then charged in with the machete. Sunlight caught the blade, then the spray of blood as Tres Dedos slashed it across his opponent's throat.

The battle over, Joaquin started down the hill. When he reached Tres Dedos, his cousin was still hunched over his enemy's body, no doubt desecrating it in some fashion. Hoping to calm him, Joaquin gripped his shoulder. "Let's go, cousin."

Tres Dedos spun around with a growl worthy of the bear he so resembled and drove the blood-caked dagger he held at Joaquin's heart. Beneath him, the dead man's head was sliced halfway off. The bandit leader stumbled backward, falling to the ground. "It's me!" he cried desperately, flailing with his feet. "Manuel!"

Tres Dedos was almost upon him before understanding finally flickered in his eyes. When it did, he halted his charge, lowered the blade. "Sorry, boss. Guess I got carried away. These son-of-a-bitches were trying to kill us, and I wanted to teach them a lesson!"

Joaquin looked at the corpse on the ground. "The thing is, it's hard for the dead to learn. They don't remember much."

"Well, if he sees me in Hell, he'll remember me, by God!"

"I have no doubt."

Tres Dedos eyed him from head to toe. Joaquin realized how he must look: clothing torn and ragged, flesh pretty much the same, all of it streaked with blood and filth.

"You look like shit," Tres Dedos said.

"That's much more like it, thank you." Having gotten out the words, Joaquin realized the lunacy of them and started to laugh. His laughter ignited Tres Dedos's, who threw his head back and let that infectious roar burst from his lips.

"God, I love to fight!" Tres Dedos bellowed when he was able. Then he let loose again. Within seconds, both men were sitting in the blood-soaked dirt, crying with laughter. Other bandits came over to see if their leader had gone completely mad. They stood in a wide circle, nobody daring to venture too near. The sight of them only made Joaquin laugh the harder, until the sounds he and Tres Dedos made filled the air and must have floated beyond the scattered white clouds and shaken the very heavens.

58

"You hear that?" Ellas asked.

Harry Love nodded. "I hear it. Don't rightly know what it is. I'm a practical man, but sometimes I wonder if them folks are human at all."

They'd stopped about a half-mile away from the ambush site, around a bend in the trail made by the stolen horses, the view blocked by a thick screen of pines. From the site of the battle, the furious roar of gunfire had dwindled until shots were scattered, then silence reigned. But now it sounded like a pack of hyenas had come upon the bodies of the dead and were overjoyed by the prospect.

Rand Lorenz, who despite his youth had experience as a ranch hand, a miner, and had briefly fought in the Mexican War, slipped almost soundlessly from the trees. He was tall and lean, still gangly, like a man who maybe would never fill out, and he shook his head slowly from side to side. Love had sent him to discern the result of the battle. "They're gone, every one of 'em," Lorenz said when he reached Love. "And two of them greasers are sittin' by a corpse, howlin' like banshees. I swear I never seen anythin' like it."

"Thanks, Rand." Love studied the survivors. Two had been wounded, but not seriously. Eleven in all.

Out of twenty-one.

Ellas seemed to read his mind. "Governor's not gonna be

happy about this."

"He'll never know about it!" Love snapped. "Not a word to anyone." He raised his voice a little, hoping it wouldn't carry all the way back to the killing field. It was a deep voice, rumbling like thunder, but at a register that didn't tend to be heard a long way off. "All of you are sworn to silence about this. Never speak of it. Not to loved ones, not to the press, and for damn sure not in Benicia. Those cowards in the legislature would rein us in if they knew our first encounter with Murrieta had ended in a rout. My mistake, I took on the first men who volunteered and looked halfway able, instead of recruiting one by one and finding the best men for the job. I'm sorry for that. I'll do it the right way this time, and we'll replace the men we lost and carry on like nothing's happened."

Ellas ticked his head back toward the ambush site. "What about those men?"

"They knew the risk. Buzzards and bugs'll take care of the corpses. And I'll take care of their families, if they got any, so don't worry about that." That was a lie; he had no intention of paying off the families of men who'd died in their very first battle. He had hit the outlaws' trail as soon as he'd formed up the force and hadn't even reported the names to the governor yet for payroll, so if these men kept their yaps shut, nobody ever need find out what had happened here.

Taking Ellas aside, he dropped his voice again. "What we need is to know where Murrieta's gonna be, not where he's been. We need to know what he's planning before he does it, and where he feels safe. Running around after him is pointless. We gotta get out ahead of him."

"How do we do that?"

Love waved a hand in a gesture that might have encompassed their immediate surroundings, or the entire world.

"Them Mexicans out there know more than they tell us. They hide Murrieta, help him when they can. He's like some kinda hero to them. They gotta know how to find him. We need to lean on them, harder than we ever done before."

Ellas nodded. "Makes sense, I reckon."

"Let's take a few days. You take the men home to San Andreas and press the greasers there. You know them folks, who's connected up and maybe how to persuade 'em. I'll start recruiting some men who know the butt end of a rifle from the barrel. In four or five days, we'll all meet up in San Andreas and go from there."

"It sounds like a plan. I don't have a better one."

"All right, then. Let's skedaddle, and I'll see you in a few days' time."

• • •

Ellas went slow and cautious, going to individual Mexicans he knew were making honest livings serving Americans, and who might not want those livings disrupted by cooperating with bandits. He figured the questioning would get more aggressive when he started visiting those he didn't know, and he was prepared to take whatever measures might be necessary to loosen tongues. But he also figured the honest ones would respond better to gifts than to threats, so he shot some turkeys and spent a couple of days taking them to the homes of sympathetic Mexicans. Every one was a dead end.

On the third day, he visited the home of a fellow named Juan Carlos Flores, who worked as a cook and general laborer at Mary Baskin's boarding house in town. There, his theory bore fruit.

"I don't know where Murrieta is," Flores said. "I keep away from those kinds of folks, you know? Those bandits give all Mexicans a bad name. I'm not even from Mexico, I'm from

Venezuela."

"That right?" Ellas asked. "I always thought you was a Mexican."

Flores gave an exaggerated shrug. A small man, short and extremely lean, he had the wiry strength that came from hard work. His skin was dark, his hair brown, and his bright eyes large for his narrow face. They sat in his modest home at a table he had probably built himself, with one leg somewhat longer than the rest. "To be honest, most of you Americans don't know the difference, but we do. Anyhow, all I know about Murrieta is what I hear. Most of it is complaining from Mrs. Baskin's guests; sometimes they been robbed on their way here and can't even pay for their rooms. And some of it is just what people—my people, not yours so much—talk about when it's just us."

"And what kinds of things do they talk about?"

"You know, laughing about Murrieta's crimes, how he keeps giving white folks fits because they can't catch him, and like that."

"That's going to change, Juan Carlos."

"I hope it does. It's hard for honest folks, when people think we're all thieves and murderers."

"If you can help me find him, it'll change that much quicker."

"Like I said, I don't know where he is. But I might know something."

Ellas shifted in his chair and put his elbow on the table. The chair squeaked against the pine floorboards, and the table rocked precariously. "Know what?"

"You know, people talk. Sometimes when they shouldn't, I guess. I don't know the man they were talking about—I think he has family here, but he's not from here. Anyhow, a couple days ago, he was told to deliver some food and whiskey to this abandoned shack, and also some bandages, I guess? Because there was this wounded fellow in that cabin. He went and bought some eggs and cheese from Mrs. Baskin, even."

Mary Baskin kept a small plot of land behind the boarding house with a few cows and hens, so she could always provide eggs, milk, and cheese to her guests. Such things were rare in the mining towns, and Ellas himself had breakfast at the boarding house once or twice a week just to enjoy them.

"Who is this man?" Ellas asked.

Another elaborate shrug moved Flores's bony shoulders. "I don't know. All I can tell you is what I heard. This man bought those things, and took them to that shack. I don't know who it was, so I don't even know if he ever came back this way."

Ellas found himself growing increasingly furious. Flores acted like he wanted to help, but he was so vague, whatever he knew—if he really knew anything at all—was useless. "Let me get this straight. You don't know who the man was. You don't know where he is. And you don't know who was in that shack, or how he might have been injured. I need something solid, Juan Carlos."

Another shrug only fueled Ellas's growing rage. "Well, I know where the shack is. Does that help?"

59

According to what Flores had told him, the shack sat alone near the banks of the Mokelumne River about a mile east of the crossing at Lancha Plana, a remnant of a strike that had seemed rich but played out early. Ellas set out the following morning, taking five of Love's rangers with him: Polkin, Lorenz, Katz, Hoover, and Emmons. Riding at a steady clip, it took most of the morning to get there from San Andreas, so when they arrived, the sun was high and warm, the air as still as the grave.

The little wood-framed shack sat on a clear patch of land, with trees about thirty feet away on three sides and tall grass all around. It was larger than Ellas had expected; he'd have called it a cabin, not a shack. But it was a crude affair; he was surprised the first stiff wind that came along hadn't leveled it. The men spread out to approach it from all sides except the south, where the river flowed. If he could believe Flores, an injured man had holed up inside, and like a wild animal, he could be dangerous in that condition. With all the men in place, weapons at the ready, Ellas called out. "You inside the cabin! I'm Charles Ellas of the California Rangers, with the legal authority to enter any building in the state. You're surrounded. We mean you no harm, but we wish to talk to you. We're comin' in and we don't want no trouble about it!"

He waited a few moments but heard no response. Had the

man already succumbed to his injuries? Again, he shouted. "Here we come!"

This time, he heard a noise. Then Lorenz started calling, "Window! Window!"

"What window?" Ellas asked. He couldn't see any windows from here, just a door that should have had a couple of steps leading up to it, and which someone would have to high-step to enter.

"The window back here!" Lorenz cried. "Someone came out!"

Now, Ellas saw a man running full tilt from behind the shack toward the river. He had a revolver in his left hand. "Shoot him, damn it!" Ellas screamed. At the same moment, he raised his own rifle and tried to lead the running man. He fired and missed.

The running man barely paused. He snapped off a shot toward Ellas, then spun and fired at two of the other visible rangers. Finally, Emmons and Katz fired back, and Polkin joined in. Ellas drew his pistol and fired three shots.

Somebody hit the running man, halting his progress. He dropped to one knee and fired again at Ellas, his shot missing by a wide margin. Ellas fired twice more, and Hoover and Lorenz both got off a shot. The man regained his feet, managed a few more stumbling steps toward the river, and collapsed on the bank.

"Get him away from that water!" Ellas shouted, afraid the man would slither in and drift away before he could be questioned. He looked none too capable of it, but appearances could be deceiving. "If there's anyone else in the cabin, we're comin' in and we don't want no trouble!"

Lorenz and Polkin dashed to the fallen man's side and dragged him away from the riverbank. "He's hurt bad,"

Polkin reported. "Dead, most like. Leastways, he will be soon."

"Stay with him, Barney. You others, with me."

"You don't think that was the fella we're looking for?" Hoover asked.

"He didn't look injured," Ellas said. "Not until we shot him."

He studied the cabin for a moment, then said, "Hoover, you and Emmons go around to that window in back, look in and make sure there ain't somebody inside aiming to shoot whoever comes through the door. The rest of us will go in the front."

Hoover nodded, touched Emmons on the shirtsleeve, and they hustled around to the rear of the structure. Ellas, flanked by Lorenz and Katz, waded through tall grass and approached the door.

"Coming in!" Ellas called when they stood outside it; just off to the left in case whoever was inside started shooting.

"You're clear!" Emmons shouted from the window.

"Come ahead," said a gravelly, accented voice from inside.

Ellas pushed the door open. A block of sunlight from the doorway washed out the light filtering in through the window. Both landed on a Mexican man sitting upright in a corner, a bed of dried grass beneath him and a threadbare blanket across his legs. Shirtless and sweating, probably feverish, he blinked as if having a hard time seeing what was right in front of him. A bloody bandage wrapped around his head was still wet at his right temple. Blood that had leaked from the wound covered his entire right side. On closer examination, he had suffered other wounds, though the blood from his head hid them—something that might have been a knife wound between his ribs, other cuts and bruises on his left arm.

On the floor near his right hand were the remnants of whatever food he'd been brought, along with a carbine and a knife and two empty whiskey bottles. He made no move toward either weapon. Ellas shoved them out of reach.

"How'd you get hurt?" Ellas asked.

"I was standing in the wrong place," the man said, his voice weak. He tried on a smile, but it didn't take.

"Looks like a bullet or a rifle ball grazed you. Another inch to the side and you'd have died on the spot."

"Would've been easier."

"Where were you standing?"

"In the middle of a gunfight."

"More precisely? We might could help you, but only if you help us first."

"A place called Chaparral Hill. Near there, anyhow. That's all I know about it."

"You're with Murrieta's band?"

The man looked about the empty cabin. The effort made him wince. "I'm not with anybody."

"You were, though. They leave you for dead?"

"I thought I *was* dead. I knew I didn't have long, anyway. One of the men stole a boat and put me in it, said he knew about this place. He rowed us here and told me he'd spread the word that I needed some supplies."

"Then Joaquin turned his back on you."

The man shook his head, despite the obvious pain it caused. "Joaquin told the other man to look after me, and he did. I know I'm dying. I can't ride. But he didn't abandon me."

Ellas couldn't suppress a grin. This was the first confirmation that they had, in fact, been on the trail of Joaquin Murrieta that day. He couldn't wait to tell Harry Love.

"So, this other jasper did what? 'Spread the word,' you

said. What's that mean, exactly?"

"Told somebody in one of the Mexican neighborhoods. That person told somebody else. Word gets around."

"I reckon it does. Especially where Murrieta's concerned. How does that work?"

The other man sat silently, mouth closed tight. Ellas couldn't tell if he was fighting off a wave of pain, or just determined not to give up any information that might hurt Murrieta. "We can help you, you know. Get you to a doctor, take care of that wound. You don't have to die just 'cause you been shot."

"You would do that? For me?"

"You help us, we help you. Simple deal."

The man sat there, eyes closed, for long moments. Considering, Ellas guessed, and he didn't push. Finally, the man opened his eyes. "Joaquin has supporters. Some call them spies, and maybe that, too. But people who look up to him. In every town from the Mexican border to Mount Shasta, there are them who'll keep their eyes open and pass on the word if anything happens that might be of interest to Joaquin. If Joaquin calls, they come. If he or his men need shelter, or food, or weapons, they provide it. If he needs them to fight for him, even to die for him, they do that."

"Is that what happened to you?"

The man nodded. The strain this encounter was putting on him was apparent in the weariness he showed. He was talking in hopes of saving his own life, but it was draining him fast.

"We keep track of rich finds, or big payrolls, or where there are horses that could be stolen. We supply horses if Joaquin or one of the others needs them. That's how come they can always outrun the law—they always have fresh mounts available. This time, they were taking some horseflesh in my area, so I joined in. Then we were chased, had to stand and fight."

"I know. We were there, too, at Chaparral Hill."

"You were?"

"We're California Rangers. Our job is to put a stop to Murrieta and his band, and by God, we will do it."

The wounded man offered a weary chuckle. "That's not so easy."

"You can help," Ellas said. "Where's his hideout? Where would he be now?"

"I think I've told you all I can."

"You want to die?"

"It's a little late to ask me that. I'm most of the way there."

"I told you, we can help you."

"I've said all I'm going to. Either get me to a doctor or let me die in peace."

Ellas shook his head. "I've known the sight of a hangman's rope to loosen a tongue or two." He caught Lorenz's eye. "Rand, tie a noose and pick one of those trees out there. Ought to be some good ones close by."

"Yessir," Lorenz said. He hurried out the door.

"I'm dying anyway," the Mexican reminded Ellas.

"Might be. Still, a decent sawbones oughtta be able to fix you up. That's a bad wound, but you might could still live."

"In jail?"

"Could happen. You'd rather be dead?"

"Dead and free is better than caged."

"Let's see do you still feel that way in a few minutes."

While they waited, the Mexican closed his eyes. His bare chest still rose and fell, albeit slowly, so Ellas knew he hadn't died. Probably best for the man that they had come along, though. The man outside—most likely dead, now—might have been able to nurse him back to health. That had probably been the idea, anyway. But Ellas doubted that he'd have lived without a doctor's help, and although that whiskey might have dulled the pain for a while, a real doctor could provide medicines that would work even better.

He heard the creak of the door and turned to see Lorenz standing outside, holding it open. "It's ready."

"On your feet," Ellas said.

The man opened his eyes. "I can't."

"Josiah, help me out," Ellas said. Katz stepped forward and looped his arm under the Mexican's left shoulder. Ellas took the right, and they hauled him to the door. Outside, Lorenz, Emmons, and Hoover waited, and they passed him through to those men. Sunlight beamed through branches and limned a noose dangling from a sturdy cottonwood branch near the river's edge.

"Ready to have your neck stretched?" Ellas asked. "Or would you rather tell us where to find Murrieta?"

"Joaquin never did me wrong. I won't do him that way."

"Your call. You change your mind in the next few minutes, sing out."

He didn't change his mind, even when they draped the noose around his neck and tightened it. When the men released him, his legs buckled beneath him. Pulling on the rope to lift him was almost unnecessary. The entire time, the Mexican stayed quiet, except when the rope started to choke him — and even then, he didn't speak, or try to.

Riding away with the late afternoon sun casting long shadows ahead of them, Ellas wondered what kind of man could inspire that sort of loyalty in others. He had never felt that in his life.

That Murrieta, he figured, had something special about him. The Mexican hadn't stayed mum out of fear.

He had done it out of something more like love.

60

Harry Love showed up in San Andreas two days later, bringing five new men with him, and found Ellas sitting in the sheriff's office where he had worked before Love lured him away. "It's just a start," he said. He pointed to two of the newcomers. "I figured I'd pick men who've reported running across Murrieta in the past. Joe Farmer and Lucas Rhodes, here, both got scores to settle with that greaser bastard. These other fellows served with me in the war, and I'd trust 'em with my life. Murrieta ain't likely to get the drop on us again, and if he does, we'll make him sorry."

"It's good to meet you men," Ellas said.

"It's a start," Love said again. "I got some more ideas, but I wanted to get back here and see what you've learned."

Ellas looked grim. "Nothing much. The Mexicans here either don't know how to find him, or they won't talk about it. I tried bribes, I tried threats, I even hanged a couple. I did find one man who was in the ruckus at Chaparral Hill, wounded and left for dead by Murrieta. He told me how Murrieta stays ahead of the law, through his contacts all up and down the state. But even with a rope around his neck, he wouldn't tell me where he hangs his hat."

"How many Mexicans you got here in town?" Love asked. An idea was forming in his mind, and he liked the way it unfolded.

"The whole west end of town is Mex," Ellas said. "Thirty or so houses. Men, mostly, but also families, women and some kids and old folks."

"I say we give 'em an ultimatum," Love said.

"What kind of ultimatum?"

"You'll see tonight. In the meantime, let's have our boys gather as much firewood as they can. Also pitch, or lamp oil."

"How do we get our hands on that?" Ellas asked. "Buy it?"

"We're California Rangers," Love reminded him. "We'll show our badges and take whatever we can carry."

"Folks aren't going to like that."

"Folks ain't gonna like anything about this, except the end result," Love assured him. "Best make sure we got a lot of buckets, too, and a clear path to water."

Ellas scratched his head. "What exactly do you have in mind, Cap'n?"

Love nodded toward the door. "Let's step outside and have us a look-see, and I'll lay it all out for you."

• • •

As darkness fell, the rangers and a few locals Ellas had roped into helping out built a bonfire in the middle of the road, right at the divide between the American and Mexican sides of town. Most of the townsfolk came out to see what was going on, and Love turned away all questions until he was ready. The fire snapped and flared, spinning sparks into the sky and scenting the air with smoke and char, and finally Love turned to the Mexican side. Pails had been set out, holding stout branches wrapped in rags and soaked in pitch or lamp oil.

"My name is Captain Harry Love, of the California Rangers," he declared. "We been commissioned by the governor of California to bring the bandit Joaquin Murrieta to justice, and any other brigands we might happen across on the way. We know certain there's some of you knows where to find Murrieta. Ellas here spent a few days talking to some of you, but none of you'd tell him what we need to know. So, we'll do it this way. You folks got some fine-looking homes here, and I'm sure some of you have jobs in town and the like. Your white neighbors might even put up with your noise and drunkenness and the way you all cat around."

Having said that, he paused, picked up a torch, and held it into the fire. "But here's the thing. I'm gonna count to ten, loud so's you can hear me. If somebody don't come up to me and tell me where to find Murrieta by the time I reach ten, then I'll throw this into one of your houses. While that house catches, you'll have another chance. But if nobody comes through then, why, me and these boys here will burn *all* of your houses."

He took another break. Some of the Mexicans stared in horror, others whispered among themselves. Love didn't care what they said, unless they were telling him what he wanted to know. He stood there, feeling the heat from the massive fire at his back and the lesser warmth from the burning brand in his grip, and looked at them. He was calm, relaxed. The idea had occurred to him in the past, in Santa Barbara, but the city fathers would never have allowed it. Now, though, he had the power of the governor at his back. He could gun down every last greaser in Calaveras County and nobody would say boo.

It might come to that yet. But first, terrifying them would probably do.

"Anybody?"

"You can't do that!" someone shouted from the crowd.

"Watch me."

"We've done nothing!" another Mexican said. "We work

hard! We get along with our neighbors!"

Love jerked a thumb over his shoulder. "Your neighbors are standing behind me. I don't hear any of them trying to stop me."

The presence of a dozen armed rangers between the townsfolk and them—and the fact that he had the blazing fire at his back—might have had something to do with that. But he didn't expect that the town's white citizens would object strenuously to an effort to capture the bandit who'd terrorized the county for so long.

He turned his back to the Mexicans and addressed the rangers, but spoke loud enough for everybody to hear. "Anybody tries to stop me, shoot to kill," he said. "You boys ready?"

The rangers, privy to the entire plan, hoisted their guns in the air. "We got your back," Ellas said. "Do what you must."

Love started toward the nearest of the Mexican homes. It was a wood-framed cabin, painted a light blue color, with yellow around the windows and on the door. A homey-looking place, he thought, that someone had put a lot of work into. Almost a pity to turn it to ashes.

He heard muttering from the gathered Mexicans, and more than a few curses. A couple of men started toward him, but the raised weapons of the rangers and the hands of their comrades held them back. He didn't delay, but stepped right up to one of those yellow-framed windows and threw the torch inside. It landed on a plank floor, a couple of feet from a wooden table and some chairs. He wanted to make a strong statement with this first home, so he drew a liquor bottle from his pocket, took a pull from it, then raised it high. He hurled it inside, with enough force to ensure its breaking. When the glass shattered, liquor splashed around the room and ignited with a low rush. Within minutes, flames licked up the walls and he laughed as personal belongings caught.

Turning back to the crowd, he held out his empty hands. "Anybody? It's not too late to save the rest of your homes, but it will be soon."

More men cursed him. Someone threw a rock, missing him. He drew a pistol. When he saw another rock sailing his way, he fired in the general direction from which it had come. A man cried out in pain, and more shouted. He could feel the tension in the air now, along with the smoke from the fire crackling in the house and from the contained bonfire in the street. Like the flames inside the house, it wouldn't take much to ignite the situation. But the rangers had guns and so did several of the white men arrayed behind them. No doubt some of the Mexicans did, too. They were outnumbered, though, outgunned, and used to capitulating to American lawmen. When they saw their homes and possessions burned to the ground, he was certain at least a few would fight.

When they tried, it would be a slaughter.

Once again, he showed the Mexicans his back, almost inviting an attack that didn't come. "Okay, boys," he said. "This is what you've been waiting for. Burn it down!"

Whoops and hollers came from the white side of the crowd—not just from his rangers, but from spectators. In the flickering light, he saw unrestrained grins on some faces. On others, he saw something akin to sexual desire; men licking their lips, rubbing their arms. He had anticipated the delight some would take watching the Mexican neighborhood burn, but he hadn't expected that. Some of the spectators would wear out their women later tonight.

White men crowded forward and grabbed torches, then fanned out toward the Mexican homes. Some of the Mexicans fought back then, charging the men to protect their homes. One or two drew guns, others wielded knives, rocks, or fists. But the rangers and their white supporters beat back any efforts, and when a few Mexican men lay dead in the streets, the fight went out of the rest.

In the uneven light, Love saw a large tent at the far end of the Mexican community. He stalked toward it, a torch in his hand and Ellas at his heels. "What is that place?" he asked.

Ellas clutched at his arm. "Leave it alone, Harry," he said.

"What is it?"

"It's their church. It's the only Catholic church in town. Lots of the white folks use it, too. The Irish, the French, and them. Let it be, please."

Love shook off Ellas's hand and kept going. When he got close, he could see a wooden cross tacked up over the opening. He swept aside the flap and raised his torch. Inside, mismatched chairs were lined up in uneven rows. A makeshift pulpit stood near the front, and behind it, an altar held candles stuck into empty wine bottles, and a few wood or brass candleholders. Behind that, straps of leather held up a larger crucifix.

The flap fluttered behind him, and he turned to see Ellas there. "Please, Harry, I'm begging you. The priest is a Mexican, but he's a decent man, and like I said, whites worship here, too."

"They'll find somewheres else to pray," Love said. He held his torch against one of the canvas side walls. It didn't catch quickly, so he pulled out his personal flask and splashed liquor over the tent wall, then threw some over the chairs and altar. When he touched the torch to it again, flames spread quickly.

"God damn you to Hell, Harry, *I'm* Catholic!" Ellas roared.

"This is sacrilege!"

"Sorry," Love said. He wasn't sorry in the least. Ellas shouldered past him and cut down the big cross. Wrapping his arms around it as one might a woman, he carried it out of the tent, glaring at Love all the while.

Ellas's tenure as a California Ranger, Love thought, might come to an end soon. It was too bad; the man knew this county well, and Murrieta had spent plenty of time here. But Ellas's loyalty had come into question, and Love couldn't risk having someone at his back who held a grudge.

He stood in the tent as long as he could, and watched it burn.

61

When Joaquin returned to Arroyo de Cantua with almost fifty stolen horses, he expected to see Pedro Vergara grinning and gloating about how he had killed Pancho Dominguez and Antonia. But although men gathered around the returning bandits and badgered them for stories from the road, many avoided Joaquin's gaze. Finally, Reyes Feliz, who Joaquin had left in charge, approached him with a glum look on his lean face.

"Where's Vergara?" Joaquin asked.

"He hasn't returned," Reyes said.

"Have you heard anything from Los Angeles? Did Dominguez kill him?"

"Yes, I have. But Joaquin—"

"We need to get in touch with some of our spies there, have them look into it."

"Joaquin!" Reyes was clearly exasperated. He had something else on his mind, but Joaquin didn't want to hear about it. The situation with Antonia had been weighing on him the entire time he was away from the camp, and he wanted it dealt with.

"Just tell me. What's the news?"

"Pedro killed Dominguez, but it was a close call. People are saying that Pancho laid a trap, expecting you to go to Los Angeles yourself."

"He meant to kill me?"

"That's what I've heard. He killed Pancho, but then Antonia killed Pedro. She's still there."

She knew about the trap, then. Had probably helped Pancho set it. She had to be punished. Nobody else could have hurt Joaquin in that way. Having done so, she'd earned the full weight of his wrath.

"Send Juan Borilda there to kill her."

"Borilda," Reyes repeated. "You're sure?"

Vergara was a skilled murderer who should have been able to do the job. But Borilda was a blunt weapon who made Tres Dedos look like a peacemaker. He had no interest in women or any of life's finer things. When he acquired treasure, he gave it away or used it to buy liquor. He ate only to live, and he lived only to drink and kill. She might try to kill him, but she'd get nowhere.

"I'm sure. Send him right away. He should kill her and report back to me directly."

Reyes nodded. He was obviously still agitated, wanting to talk to Joaquin about some other matter. "I will, Joaquin. But listen to me."

His tone was urgent. Joaquin realized he had been thinking only of himself, of his vengeance against those who'd betrayed him. He wrapped an arm across his brother-in-law's shoulders and drew him away from the crowd. "What is it, Reyes?"

"Have you heard what happened in San Andreas?"

"San Andreas? No, what?"

"The Mexicans there," Reyes began. "Their homes . . ."

• • •

Charles Ellas wasn't sure if he had quit the California Rangers, or been fired, or whether he was still on the payroll. After the night of the fires, Harry Love had barely spoken to him, and he'd left town early the next day to continue his recruiting. Love was angry that his efforts had been without result—every Mexican home in San Andreas burned to the ground, but still, not a soul had given up any information about Murrieta's whereabouts. Again, Ellas was impressed with their loyalty to the bandit—and somewhat dismayed that he didn't feel the same loyalty to Harry Love.

In Love's absence, and in case he was without a job, he had made arrangements with Sheriff Easton to get his deputy position back. He'd been tapped by Love to join the rangers in the first place because of his sterling reputation as a lawman, and he was by far the most effective deputy in the county, so that hadn't been a tough sell.

The days since Love's departure had been hard. The town's Mexicans had sifted through the ashes looking for any belongings that might have been spared. Then they'd left, no doubt looking for another town where their presence might be better tolerated. In their wake, San Andreas seemed almost lifeless. The jobs they'd performed went unfilled, leaving a hole in the heart of the town. At night, their music no longer resonated through the streets, and the fragrances of their spicy meals no longer wafted on the evening breeze. It wasn't a total loss; he believed there would be less petty crime in town, and fewer stabbings and shootings—greasers were forever getting into it over some imagined insult to themselves or their women. An all-white town might be a good idea, and he decided he'd talk to the sheriff about chasing out the few Chinese and blacks living there.

With the Mexicans gone, he was surprised to see an obviously Mexican woman walk into his office. She had on a long purple dress and scarves, and a black shawl covered her long hair and the lower half of her face. She was homely for a woman, but the dress hugged her curves and hinted at an impressive figure. The smell of her perfume accompanied her through the door with an almost physical presence, as if she'd bathed in it instead of just dabbing on a little here and there. "Morning, ma'am," Ellas said. "I don't believe I've seen you around town before."

"You wouldn't have," she said. Her voice sounded a little strained, making him wonder if someone had tried to throttle her. But where had she come from? "I'm not from here."

"What can I do for you?"

"It's what I can do for you that matters. Are we alone here?"

He ticked his head toward the cells, on the other side of a wall. "There's a drunk sleeping it off back there. You might hear his snoring, but he won't hear a thing you have to say. Otherwise, yes."

"Good. He has spies everywhere, and I'm putting myself in danger just being here."

That perked him up. "Who has spies?" Ellas asked, but he thought he already knew the answer.

"My brother," the woman said. "Joaquin Murrieta."

"You're Murrieta's sister?"

"That's right. I was really hoping to find you and Captain Love together, but . . ."

"The captain's out of town," Ellas said. This was getting more and more interesting. He had been sitting back in his desk chair, but now he sat up straight, hands folded on top of the desk.

"Well, I suppose I can tell you," she said. She looked away from Ellas, toward her feet, as if embarrassed by what she was about to say. "It's about my brother. He's brought shame to our family. His crimes—they're terrible. Just terrible."

"Indeed, they are," Ellas agreed.

"He must be stopped. I know you and Captain Love have tried, but . . . I can tell you where to find him."

"You can?"

She met his gaze again. "Yes," she said. "But . . . may I come closer? I don't want anyone to hear."

"There's nobody here but that drunk, and he's out cold."

"Still."

"All right. Come ahead."

He expected her to lean over the desk, but instead, she stepped around it and bent over him, as if to whisper it in his ear. She was, he realized, quite tall for a Mexican woman. In his experience, they were usually on the shorter side.

"Joaquin Murrieta is," she whispered, drawing the shawl away from her face and exposing a dark mustache fringing her upper lip, "right here!"

Ellas tried to react as the realization sank in, but he was too late. She—no, he, Murrieta himself—gripped the back of Ellas's head with one strong hand and with the other, sank a blade into his throat. He drew it across in a single swift motion, and Ellas watched his own blood spurt forth like a fountain, splashing his desk and spraying beyond it, almost to the door. Eyes still open, he felt his body twitch uncontrollably with each new spurt. He tried to rise to his feet, but couldn't, and succeeded only in kicking the bottom of his desk. Then his head drooped forward shoulders hunched, and the world started to darken from the edges and working in.

He didn't even hear Murrieta leave. The next-to-last thing he thought was, *I deserve this*. And the last thing was, *But Harry deserves it more*.

62

Dozens of the Mexicans driven out of San Andreas by Harry Love's brutal assault showed up at Arroyo de Cantua. So did dozens more, then hundreds more, from every corner of the state. They brought families, in some cases. Some brought horses or guns, or both; others arrived empty-handed but ready to fight. Most didn't know why they had come, only that Joaquin Murrieta had put out the word that he needed them. He had even called off Juan Borilda's mission of vengeance, because he needed every hand he could get.

These past years, he had been there when they were in need. He had provided gold, manpower, jobs. Whenever a Mexican had a dispute with a landlord, a banker, a miner trying to drive him off a claim, a lawman targeting the Mexicans in his town, Joaquin had been ready to help. Now it was their turn to help him, and they answered his call, in droves. Arroyo de Cantua filled up with humans and horses. Tents and makeshift structures went up in a hurry, until what was once a camp started looking more like a city. The livestock in the meadow were crowded together, though Joaquin promised that wouldn't last long.

As he had always done, he sized up the men as they arrived, to determine which would be best suited to joining his outlaw band. He wouldn't turn away any Mexican who came to the arroyo, but some would be more helpful to him than others. He had learned to judge quickly, from a man's stance, his demeanor, sometimes the number of visible scars or the way he carried his weapons, who would be valuable in a fight and who would be better off staying behind, tending the livestock and feeding the hungry.

Bringing so many people together resulted in disagreements, even fights. When the mood started to turn ugly, Joaquin spread the word that he would address them all, that night, under the full moon. That did the trick. With something to look forward to, some explanation for their presence forthcoming, bitter feelings faded. And he had the perfect explanation.

With the help of Reyes and Tres Dedos, Joaquin arranged a makeshift stage that elevated him several feet above everyone else, and positioned him so the full brilliance of the full moon shone upon him. It took a few minutes for the people to settle down and look his way, but soon a rare hush descended over the arroyo. Only crickets filled the quiet.

Joaquin cleared his throat and began.

"My friends, thank you one and all for coming to our aid at this hour of need. I'm no politician or speechmaker, but I want to share with you my reason for calling you to join us. For too long, our people have been mistreated on this land that is rightfully our own. We all know what happened recently in San Andreas, where an American lawman burned Mexicans' homes and place of worship, for no reason but cruelty.

"California was stolen from Mexico by means of a fraudulent war—a war that never had any justification but was itself merely a pretext to attack our nation and steal territory we had long held. Our government turned over California to stop the slaughter of our people.

"But Americans have developed a taste for slaughter, and

there's no indication that they'll ever lose it. When *they* came here from Europe, they slaughtered the natives. When *we* arrived in Mexico, we embraced the natives, and taught them the ways of Christianity. We saw them as brothers. Who among us doesn't have both Spanish and Indian blood mingled in our veins? But not the white Americans. When they reached Mexico, they slaughtered Mexicans. Having taken California, they continue the slaughter of Mexicans and Indians.

"We are gathered here—on this piece of ground that is part of Mexico, contained within the boundaries of California—for one purpose. To take back what is rightfully ours!"

This declaration brought a roar of approval from the crowd. Joaquin waited for it to die down, then raised both his arms high. "Together, we will rid California of the American scourge. What they took from us by force of arms, they will lose the same way. We will mount up and ride bearing torches and guns. We will kill every American we have to and set fire to every field, every house, every business. From north to south, we'll drive the interlopers out before us, until the survivors are forced to escape by sea or flee to the east. When we've reached the southern border, we'll declare that line nonexistent, and California will belong to Mexico once more!"

This was met by another roar, louder this time, and more sustained. Joaquin basked in it. He hated to admit it now, but Pancho had been right all along. This was what he was made for. He hadn't been put on this Earth to kill and steal, but to inspire his countrymen. To take back what had been lost. And he could do it. He was convinced. Mexicans would rise up from every town in the state, from north to south, ocean to mountains, and he would lead them to victory.

Maybe he was a politician, after all.

He stepped down from the stage and the people swarmed toward him. He accepted embraces and thanks. People reached across rows two and three deep just to touch his shoulders or to grasp his outstretched hand. For more than an hour, he accepted their adulation, until finally the crowd thinned. People returned to their own tents or cabins, though still, the arroyo was noisy with conversation about what they'd heard.

Joaquin watched the ranks of his supporters—his friends, his brothers and sisters—thin, then started toward his little house. His mind buzzed with vivid images: a thousand mounted warriors thundering across the rolling hills and meadows, hoofbeats echoing from the Sierra Nevada to the sea, putting the torch to everything in their path that had been built by the whites. They would cleanse the land with blood and fire. As depicted on his birthland's flag, the eagle of Mexico would devour the wicked serpent.

So engulfed in his own thoughts was he that he almost didn't see Florencio Cruz emerge from the shadows, just short of the house. But the big man spoke up, and then Joaquin recognized his friend. He wrapped his arms around the shorter man and drew him into a tight embrace. "Florencio, my brother. What did you think?"

Cruz seemed to tense up at that, and Joaquin released him. "Is something wrong?"

"They're right about you, Joaquin," he said. "You've changed."

"Who's right? Who says that?"

"Some of the men. The ones like me, who've been with you for the longest."

"Changed in what way? Of course, I've changed, we all change with time."

"Not like you," Cruz said. Disgust came through in his voice. "You've started believing the stories told about you. We're bandits, that's all. We ride, we rob, sometimes we kill. But we're not statesmen, and we aren't heroes. You think you're something special, placed here by God to restore Mexico's glory. You're a horse thief, Joaquin. That's all!"

"I never said I was special!"

Cruz's distaste seemed to have faded, replaced by a deep sorrow that slumped his shoulders, bowed his head. Then Joaquin realized his shoulders weren't just slumped, he was reaching for a gun. "Yes, you did," Cruz said as he brought up the pistol.

All thought vanished from Joaquin's mind. Instead, he reacted instinctively. He stepped quickly to his left, and at almost the same moment, moved closer to Cruz. Cruz tried to track him with the pistol, but by moving farther to Cruz's right, Joaquin forced him to hold the gun at an awkward angle. Then by stepping in close, he made the other man's shot even more difficult; had he squeezed the trigger now, his bullet would have flown far to the side.

Even as he moved, Joaquin was yanking his own revolver from its holster. He was close in, directly in front of Cruz. As Cruz tried to bring his weapon back around to where he could use it, Joaquin fired twice, point blank, into Cruz's belly and chest.

For almost half a minute, Cruz didn't move. Joaquin couldn't have missed, at that range, but he wondered if perhaps Cruz had tucked a frying pan or some other armor under his shirt. He was raising his gun barrel to point at Cruz's head when his old friend finally started to react. His fingers spread, and the pistol slipped from them, landing on grass already damp with nighttime dew. He took two awkward steps backward, his head tilting forward as if to examine his own chest. Then his knees gave out, and he buckled, pitching forward onto the grass.

By then, people were running toward them, and Tres Dedos had burst out of the house with a rifle in his hands.

"It's all right!" Joaquin shouted. "It's over. He's done!"

"Who is that?" Tres Dedos demanded.

"Florencio," Joaquin said. He couldn't disguise the disappointment he felt. "He thought I'd gone mad. He drew on me. I had no choice."

"He tried to kill you?" someone asked from behind.

"He tried to—" Joaquin stopped himself. He had started to say, "assassinate me." But to have finished that sentence would have proven Cruz right. Had he really lost his way? Did he think he was more than a man? More than the horse thief Cruz had described?

Was his entire plan delusional? The ravings of a madman who'd forgotten what he came from?

No, he couldn't allow himself to believe that.

California was Mexican. If the Mexican Army wouldn't fight for it, then he would. Perhaps once he set the example, the government would realize what he had started, and would send the army to help finish the job.

Mexicans in California needed a hero, and if it had to be him, then so be it.

He had never gotten anything without trying. This time, he had to try harder than ever. Lack of confidence expressed by his longtime associates would not dissuade him. He could spare no thoughts for defeat, but would imagine total victory, and he would make it real.

63

Lucas Rhodes didn't know what he was doing in Hang-town. Being there just reminded him of the massacre he'd survived at Garlin's Draw, and seeing its size reminded him that others had indeed struck it rich—though more often from selling things to the miners than from mining itself. In addition to its bevy of saloons, the town boasted several churches now, though the enormous stone Zeisz Brewery building suggested which establishment served more customers. Rhodes had only wanted to do the same as these people, to earn his fortune through hard work, one way or another. But Joaquin Murrieta had taken that opportunity from him. Love hadn't told him why they'd come, but he didn't care—if it was a step closer to finding Murrieta, then he was game.

Harry Love played his cards close to his chest, and all he'd told Rhodes was that he wanted to talk to a white man who might have an idea of Murrieta's location. He wanted Rhodes along because his passing familiarity with Murrieta might help Love know whether the man was telling the truth. Rhodes didn't know who the white man was, or why he would know anything about Murrieta, and Love refused to enlighten him.

They reached Hangtown in the afternoon. Love declared that his throat was parched, and he needed a drink. With no shortage of watering holes, that was easily accomplished. As the afternoon wore on and became night, Love kept drinking, and Rhodes grew increasingly concerned. Finally, he was able to convince Love to eat some dinner, and he did the same. The whole time, Love turned away every effort Rhodes made to get him to reveal who they'd come to see.

Finally, Love decided it was time to pay a visit. With some effort, he wrenched himself from his chair and made his way toward the door, bumping into other drinkers on the way.

"Are you sure we shouldn't put this off until morning, Harry?" Rhodes asked when they were outside. "Neither one of us is in any condition to interrogate somebody."

"I'm fine," Love growled. "You just have to sit there and listen. Tell me if you think the bastard's lying."

"I'll do what I can," Rhodes promised.

In a couple of minutes, he understood where Love was leading him. The offices of the *El Dorado Republican* lay dead ahead, and through a window, Rhodes could see lamps burning inside. Despite that, the place seemed still.

"Do you think there's anyone in there at this hour?"

"I'm sure of it," Love said.

The door was locked, so Love hammered on the glass with a burly fist. After a minute or so, when it became clear Love wasn't giving up, Rhodes saw movement inside, and a slender, bespectacled man emerged from an inner office. As he neared the door, a questioning expression on his face, Love pointed to the badge pinned to his shirt. The man nodded and unlocked the door.

"What can I do for you gentlemen on this fine solstice eve?" he asked as he tugged it open.

"Fine what?" Love asked.

"Tomorrow's the solstice," Rhodes said quickly. "First day of summer."

Love gave a brief nod, then asked, "Are you Springer?"

"I confess that I am," the other man said. "Thomas Springer, editor-in-chief and publisher, at your service."

Love started forward, even though Springer still stood in the doorway, holding the door. Acknowledging Love's obvious intent, Springer stepped away and Love strode into the newspaper offices. Rhodes followed, closing the door behind him. The place smelled of oil and what must have been printer's ink.

"Lock it," Love said.

Rhodes locked it.

"This is highly irregular," Springer protested. "We'll be open for business tomorrow at nine o'clock. If there's something I can do for you then, why—"

"Now's good," Love said. "Your office?"

Springer bowed to the inevitable. "Right this way."

He led them to the back office from which he'd originally come and seated himself behind a desk so buried in paper that none of its wooden surface could be seen. Rhodes wondered how he made any sense of what was in front of him.

The office contained two additional chairs, but they likewise served as resting places for piles of paper. Springer made no effort to clear them, so the two rangers stood.

"Now, how can I help you?" Springer asked.

"What I want to know," Love began, "is, have you had any more dreams lately?"

Springer couldn't keep the look of surprise off his face. "Why, I dream most every night. Nightmares, often, but not always. I don't understand—"

"I mean dreams about a specific murdering greaser," Love said.

"I'm afraid I don't—" Springer cut himself off midstream.

"Oh, I see. No, sir, I have not dreamed of Mr. Murrieta again."

Love stepped forward and put his big hands atop some of the papers crowding Springer's desk, leaning on them, his upper torso thrust almost all the way over it so he shadowed the journalist. "You can still help us, I reckon. Where's Murrieta's hidey-hole?"

"I have no idea," Springer said.

"You've been there. You didn't dream all that."

"You're correct, sir. I have been there. But I was blindfolded, lying trussed up in the back of a wagon like a Christmas goose, for the entire journey. I literally have no idea where I was taken."

"Tell me what you do know, then."

"May I ask on what authority you're making these demands?"

Love tapped his encircled star again. "We're California Rangers."

Enlightenment dawned in Springer's eyes, which his spectacles exaggerated. "Oh! You're Captain Love! I actually wrote to Governor Bigler's office requesting an interview when I heard about your recruitment. Do you have time to answer a few questions?"

"I'll ask the questions, and you'll answer 'em. What do you know about Murrieta's hideout?"

"I wish I could help you, but I just can't. As I said, I was taken there blindfolded. Murrieta spoke English with me, but most everybody else spoke Spanish, of which I know nothing beyond 'adios' and 'tequila.' It was dark when I arrived and dark when I left. I cannot help you, sir. I know nothing."

"I don't believe you."

"And yet, I'm telling the truth. We appear to be at loggerheads, don't we?"

"At what?"

Rhodes had been wondering when Springer's manner of speech would irritate Love past his breaking point. That moment appeared to be upon them. "Harry, he doesn't know anything," he said.

"He's lying!" Love roared. He reached across the table with his left hand and pinned Springer's right down on the papers. With his own right hand, he snatched a big knife from a sheath on his belt. "Now, I'm going to ask you questions, and every time you tell me you don't know something, you'll lose a finger. How's that sound?"

Springer tried to struggle, but he couldn't budge Love. His mouth opened and shut, but no words issued from it, only guttural sounds. Rhodes was both disgusted and fascinated by the way Love had turned conversation into combat, without hesitation, and seemingly without mercy. Almost oblivious to Springer's efforts to wrench his hand free, Love pressed the blade of his knife against Springer's little finger.

"Where is Murrieta's hideout?"

"You wouldn't!" Springer cried.

"Wrong answer," Love said. He put his weight down on the knife. Rhodes heard bones cracking, and blood spurted first against the blade as Love removed it, then across the scattered papers. Springer screamed.

"Jesus, Harry!" Rhodes said, stepping toward them. A glance from Love stopped him.

"You still got nine more," Love reminded Springer.

"My hand! I need my hands!" Springer cried.

"Then you better start talking."

"I told you, I don't know!"

Love moved the knife to the ring finger of Springer's right hand. "Where is it?"

"All right, all right!" Springer shouted. "I'll tell you what I know. Just stop this!"

Love released him and stepped back. "Have you any bandages?" Rhodes asked.

"There's a-a-a box in the press room!" Springer said. "It's painted red. Down on the floor under one of the tables."

Rhodes rushed out of the office, found the box, and brought the whole thing back with him. Springer was sitting back in his chair, his face almost as white as the papers on his desk had been before he'd sprayed them all with blood. Rhodes found some fabric bandages in the box and tried to hand them to Springer, but the journalist was holding his right hand with his left and wouldn't take them. Rhodes squeezed around Love and squatted beside Springer, holding the mass of bandages against the bleeding stump. The bulk of the digit still lay where Love had left it, on top of some blood-soaked pages.

Springer looked like he was about to faint. "Just tell him what he wants to know, so we can summon a doctor," Rhodes said. "You'll be fine." That last part might have been a lie. Springer didn't seem fine. He had lost a lot of blood, and if he passed out, he might never wake up again. He was slight of build, but apparently possessed an inner reservoir of strength that had, so far, kept him conscious.

"Out of the way, Lucas," Love said. It came out as mostly a growl, the words barely intelligible. Springer gave Rhodes a nod and took the bandages, pressed them against his own hand.

Rhodes, still at a crouch, moved between Springer and a stuffed bookcase behind him, staying close in case the man needed more help. Love brandished the knife again. "You've got nine more. Are we going to keep this up, or are you going to tell me what I want to know?"

"For God's sake, I *don't know* where it is." Springer's voice was weak, his tone less argumentative than it had been. "South of here, I think, perhaps in the central valley. All I could see were canyon walls, and inside a kind of vast meadow with a creek running through it. They had dozens of tents and little shacks, and there was one house built of stone. But it could have been anywhere."

"Nobody said the name of a nearby town, a river, anything like that?"

"I told you, they spoke mostly Spanish with each other. I only know a little, and they speak it so fast I couldn't have kept up even if I'd tried."

"You're not being very helpful," Love said. He got a grip on Springer's arm and waved the knife before his eyes. "Maybe you need to lose another finger."

"Arroyo!" Springer shouted. "I remember that word being used. Arroyo something."

"That's not much. There are probably a thousand arroyos in California."

Springer slumped back in his chair and closed his eyes. "It's all I have. I'm sorry. Take both my hands, take my feet if you will. I know nothing else."

Love released the arm, and Springer cradled it to his chest, still holding the bandages against his hand. They had turned almost completely red, and blood bubbled though them, dripping onto the newspaperman's pants.

"If I find out you've lied to me, you'll lose a whole hand," Love said.

"I'm not lying."

"And if you hear from him again, let me know. You can always reach me through the governor's office. Understood?"

"I understand." Springer's voice was weary, distant.

Rhodes wasn't sure he would last long enough to hear from Murrieta again. "Where's the nearest doctor?"

"His office is four doors down," Springer said. "He won't be there, but he lives upstairs."

"I'll bring him back in a few minutes. Stay with him, Harry." Rhodes hoped the implicit warning was good enough, its meaning clear. Deciding it wasn't, he added, "And keep him alive."

64

As the canyon filled with volunteers and horses, the camp took on the air of a military operation. Some of Joaquin's top lieutenants, men who'd fought in the American War, drilled the newcomers and made them practice shooting in multiple positions and while mounted—though usually dry-firing, saving real ammunition for the coming battles. The late-night drinking largely came to an end, as the men were expected to rise early for exercise.

Without knowing it, Harry Love helped. Having thus far failed to locate Joaquin's camp, he and his full force of rangers swept through Mexican communities throughout the state, demanding to know Murrieta's whereabouts. They killed random men to demonstrate the serious nature of their demands, torched homes and businesses. Still, no one gave up Joaquin to him—but in his wake, people streamed to Arroyo de Cantua from every town he attacked. Seeing Love's brutality for themselves convinced them of the righteousness of Joaquin's cause.

One warm day, Joaquin was watching Tres Dedos teach a class in knife-fighting when one of the volunteers approached him. The man could have been aged anywhere from thirty to fifty. His skin was dusky; fully Indian or nearly so, which contributed to the difficulty in discerning his age. He had a scattering of silver in his black hair, but he walked with his spine straight and his shoulders spread. A man who still had his pride, Joaquin thought, despite whatever hardships he'd faced.

"Señor Murrieta," the man said. His tone was hesitant, as if worried that Joaquin might be deep in thought, or else trying to learn the finer points of gutting one's opponent.

To put him at ease, Joaquin gave him a big smile and extended a hand. "At your service, sir," he said. "Please, call me Joaquin. And you are?"

"My name is Renato," the man said. "I'm sorry to disturb you."

"No disturbance at all, my friend Renato."

"Well, I wanted to thank you, for all you've done for me and my family."

Joaquin led him away from the lesson; the sound of Tres Dedos's instruction made it hard to hear him. "I'm sure it was nothing."

"It was everything! I have a farm, not too far from San José. I nearly lost it, two years ago, because of some debts that were called in during a bad year for the crops. But you heard about my troubles and stopped by with bags of gold. I was out working in the fields, but Iselda, my wife, said you were very kind. You gave her the gold and told her to pay off the debt. She made you some tea, and then you left. I never had a chance to thank you myself, so I wanted to do so."

"No thanks are necessary," Joaquin assured him. "I'm glad it helped. Who's minding the farm now?"

"My wife and daughters stayed behind. My sons and I came in answer to your call. We're ready to fight for California."

"Thank you, then, for coming to help."

"It is our duty. I am from Oaxaca, and my great grandfather

was nearly pure Mixteco. He told me that when faced with a decision, the only proper choice is to do what is right. He always spoke slowly, because he wanted to weigh his words, to say the right thing. This, I believe, is the right thing to do."

"I think so, too."

"I have only one question."

He paused, and his expression was almost sheepish. "Go ahead," Joaquin said.

"What happens if we die?"

Joaquin thought he'd been ready for any questions that might come up, but that one threw him. Instead of offering a glib response, he tried to consider the question. What happens, indeed? If they died, they died.

But that was no answer. Finally, he said, "You might. Any of us might die. If we do, we'll be martyrs to the best cause there is—the freedom of our people to inhabit land that is rightfully ours. I can think of no better reason to die."

The man seemed satisfied with that. He thanked Joaquin again, shook his hand, and went off to do whatever he'd been doing before spotting Joaquin.

And Joaquin was left to wonder how many of his volunteers would die. And would their deaths accomplish anything real? Was returning California to Mexican rule even possible?

He believed that it was both possible and necessary.

But yes, people would die in the trying. And those deaths would be on his head.

• • •

As it happened, the dying had already begun.

With the camp filling up, Joaquin was desperate for good horses, guns, and ammunition. To that end, he had sent trusted lieutenants across the state to steal what they could and buy what they couldn't steal, and to try to find out what

Love knew. But Love had eyes and ears everywhere, and other lawmen, inspired by the fact that the governor and legislature were taking seriously the threat of Mexican banditry, had become more aggressive in trying to root it out.

As usual, Tres Dedos sat him down and gave him the news as it came in. Claudio Feliz got into an altercation over a card game in Monterey. He drew a pistol in self-defense, but a lawman named John Cocks, happening onto the scene, shot and killed the only armed Mexican he saw.

Reyes Feliz was in Los Angeles with Cipriano Sandoval and Benito Lopez when General Joshua Bean, who had been the first American mayor of San Diego, was murdered by an unknown killer. The three Mexicans were in the vicinity, though, and a friend of the general's pointed the finger at them. They protested their innocence, but to no avail, and all three were hanged before Joaquin even heard about their predicament.

Joaquin had second thoughts about Antonia, and he recalled Borilda, and sent Atanacio Moreno and Juan Senate there with a message for her. Moreno was to tell her that Joaquin forgave her, and still loved her. But neither man ever returned, so Joaquin didn't know if the message had been delivered. While they were there, Senate killed a lawman and had a hefty reward posted for his capture or his corpse. Hoping to claim that reward and strike out on his own, Atanacio Moreno murdered Senate. He tied the corpse to a horse and led it to the nearest sheriff's office. Unfortunately for Moreno, he was recognized as having been drinking and carousing with Senate the night before, and under severe questioning, admitted to being part of Murrieta's band. Sentenced to death, a hangman's rope stretched his neck a week later.

Even at the arroyo, tensions were high. Fights broke out,

sometimes leading to death. As their leader, Joaquin couldn't turn away from the necessity of administering swift justice, even when it broke his heart to do so. None brought him more sorrow than when he had to kill Humberto Mota, who had himself killed two others in a fight over a woman's attentions. The woman, as it happened, had no interest in any of the three.

The deed done, he retired to his room in the little house, closed the door, and wept.

It had been easy to kill Ellas, the lawman who'd helped Harry Love burn an entire Mexican community. Florencio Cruz's death had been unavoidable, a matter of defending himself. But Mota had been a loyal friend. Having to put him down, like a dog that had turned rabid, had been one of the hardest things he had ever done.

A gentle tap sounded on the door, and Joaquin sniffled, wiped his eyes, and said, "Yes?"

"It's me." Tres Dedos's husky growl.

"Come in."

Tres Dedos did. He moved quietly for such a big bear of a man. He stopped beside Joaquin, who sat on his bed, and laid a hand on the bandit leader's shoulder. "It's a hard time," he said.

"It is, indeed," Joaquin agreed. "We're on the cusp of our greatest victory, but so many of those who brought us to this point won't be here to relish it."

"I know you grieve for them, Joaquin. They knew when they joined us what the stakes were. And the risks. It's a rare outlaw who dies peacefully in his sleep."

"I know that. But so many, and seemingly all at once. It's hard not to take it as an ill omen."

Tres Dedos sat beside him. His weight tilted the bed in his direction, and the slender Joaquin had to adjust his balance so as not to fall into the big man's lap. "I think we should take a trip, you and I," he said. "A change of scenery."

"To make me forget our fallen brothers?"

"Nothing of the sort, Joaquin. Just to refresh your spirits a little, and to show you what I saw on that recent journey I made."

"You went to San Francisco?" Tres Dedos rarely left Joaquin's side, but he had been summoned by an uncle and had to make a quick trip to that city.

"That's right."

"And that's where you want to take me?"

"Right again. Who knew you could read another's thoughts?"

Joaquin laughed. "Yours have never been hard to grasp," he said. "They usually involve killing or eating. Sometimes making love, but not so often."

"Not this time, though."

Joaquin pondered for a few moments. It wasn't a good time to leave the camp. Newcomers streamed in, two one day and ten the next. They needed training, which Joaquin left up to others, but they also needed welcoming and inspiration. They came because they knew Joaquin Murrieta had called for them. What would they think if he was gone when they arrived?

But perhaps Tres Dedos was right that some time away would do him good. And if Tres Dedos had something specific in San Francisco he wanted Joaquin to see, then Joaquin wanted to know what that was. His cousin had never steered him wrong.

"What about the volunteers?"

"I've been thinking about that, too. Let's split them up among the trusted lieutenants we have left. Send them out to acquire horses and whatever loot they can find. If they're going to join bandits, they need to see what it's really like. And we want them to have experience firing their guns at something besides targets. Some will desert, but we wouldn't want those anyway. The ones who prove themselves will be valuable, and we'll know who they are. Then we'll all meet up back here in a few days' time and prepare for what comes next. We'll leave enough here to mind the horses, and that's all."

"I like the sound of that," Joaquin said. "San Francisco it is. Leave tomorrow?"

"First thing."

"First thing. Thank you, my brother. Let's call our lieutenants together and lay out the plan. Then we'll sleep, and rise with the sun to begin our voyage. There's one stop I want to make first."

"I'll wake you," Tres Dedos promised. "You'll never get up that early on your own."

65

Thomas Springer had found Joaquin Murrieta once by putting the word out through the local Mexican community in Hangtown. That community was smaller than it had once been; the depredations of the California Rangers had driven many Mexicans into hiding, and even those who stayed tended to keep to themselves these days. But Springer still had contacts among them, so he wasn't as surprised as he might have been to see Joaquin walk through the door of the *El Dorado Republican* office one day in late June.

Jon Sheehan was working the press, but he stopped when the man came in. Springer couldn't hear the conversation, but he saw Joaquin point toward his office. After a brief couple of moments, Sheehan nodded and let Joaquin pass.

By the time he reached Springer's door, the publisher was already on his feet. "Señor Murrieta," he said, extending a hand. "Thank you for coming, sir."

Joaquin shook his hand, then released it but grabbed Springer by the wrist. He turned Springer's hand this way and that, studying it. "You've lost something," he said.

"Indeed, I have."

"If you were an outlaw, they'd call you Three-Fingered Tom."

"I suppose it's never too late to change professions," Springer said. "The newspaper business is a hard one, and not getting any easier."

"I recommend against banditry," Joaquin said. He released Springer's wrist, but he gestured toward it. "Appearances aside, journalism still seems safer. How did that happen, if I may ask?"

Springer went around behind his desk and indicated an available guest chair. "Please, sit. I'm glad you came. And I will tell you the story of my missing digit, because it has to do with why I asked to see you again."

"You're not planning another dream, are you?"

"Nothing of the sort." Springer lowered himself into his chair, putting most of his weight on his left hand, as he had learned to do. The right didn't hurt much anymore, unless he banged it against something, but he still treated it with special care.

Joaquin, likewise, sat, and looked questioningly at his host.

Springer began by raising his hand. "A man named Harry Love did this. You know who he is, I'm sure."

"Harry did that? Why?"

"He believed I could tell him where to find you. Of course, I couldn't. I told him that. He thought this would change my mind."

Joaquin shook his head. "I'm sorry, Tom. I know Harry, and I never imagined he would assault a white man that way. Did you tell the sheriff?"

"No local lawman will go up against Harry Love right now. I mentioned it to the town marshal, but he didn't seem inclined to take action. Love claims special dispensation from the governor to take any measures he deems necessary, and apparently, the local law agrees."

"And he did it to find me. That bastard."

"You seem to have gotten under his skin. He has a special hatred for you."

"We were friends once. Not anymore, though. The man is like the wind, blowing from this direction now, then changing without notice. Just another hateful gringo, Tres Dedos would say—cruel for the sake of cruelty. Seeing your hand stings, like an ice shard to my heart. If he was here now, I would kill him without an instant's hesitation."

"That's what I wanted to talk to you about," Springer said. He had been nervous about asking for this meeting—the fact that Joaquin had always behaved like a gentleman toward him didn't entirely outweigh the stories he'd heard about other, less fortunate individuals. But now that they were talking, he was glad he had made the request, and that Joaquin had complied. "I got a sense of the man, while he was here. Since then, I've talked to some others who know him well. I think he feels that you betrayed him, somehow. He takes everything you've done personally. He's a bulldog, Joaquin. He's been dispatched by Governor Bigler to capture or kill you, but I'm telling you, it's killing he has on his mind. And he has a deadline of three months, but I don't believe that he'll stop if he hasn't done it by then. I think he'll keep at it until you're dead, one way or another."

"Why do you say that?"

Springer hadn't known what to expect—a tantrum, threats, curses, perhaps. Instead, the bandit seemed genuinely curious.

"I don't think he's a happy man. He's a drunkard and a violent lout, and those things typically go along with deep dissatisfaction with one's life. I obviously don't know him—I've only ever had the one encounter. From what I've been told, though, he brims with hate for Mexicans. Not just them, but anyone who's not white and in a position to do him favors. And you in particular."

"I was an employee," Joaquin suggested. "A laborer for him. Perhaps he thinks that I should have stayed that, not tried to elevate my station in life."

"That's probably part of it. You represent something, Joaquin. Mexicans look up to you—and I daresay, a fair number of put-upon Americans do, too. You've become something of a folk hero in your own time. A Robin Hood figure, one might say. As that, you're like a beacon, a red cape to the bull that is Harry Love. Putting a finish to you is the only thing that keeps him going."

"Why are you telling me this?" Joaquin asked.

"I respect you. You've never done me a wrong turn. You've treated me like a fellow human being—which is more than I can say for Love. I wanted you to know that you've got to be on your guard. Don't let him get near you."

"I'll do my best." He let out a weary sigh. "I'm tired, Tom."

"Tired?"

"Tired of the outlaw life. The running, the killing, all of it. I have a goal in mind—one I'd rather not share with you, so please don't ask, and when you see it come about, please know that it's not directed at you. You've always treated me well, too."

"You can get out, can't you? Leave the state, perhaps, start a new life elsewhere?"

"Not yet. Soon, but not until I've finished what I've set in motion." He wrinkled his forehead and rubbed his eyes, like a man waking up from a long nap. Or perhaps a man in need of one. "I feel like I'm being torn in two, between the outlaw me—the folk hero you mentioned—and the man I want to be.

They're not the same person, and I don't know how to blend them inside one skin."

Springer nodded. "I think that describes the human condition," he said. "The person you are inside, and the one people see from without. Like you, I don't know how to bridge that gap. I wish I did."

"If you come upon an answer, let me know. I appreciate the warning about Love. Is that all you wanted? I'm afraid I can't stay in any one place for very long these days."

"Well, I should tell you that I'm planning to write a book about you. It was originally intended to be a history of California, but I've narrowed my focus considerably. I've been collecting interviews toward that end, and news clippings from all around the state, building my base of knowledge. There are some holes, though—I hope we'll be able to meet again one day and have a longer chat."

"As do I, Tom." Joaquin got to his feet. "Thank you for your concern. I hope Love doesn't hear that I've been back to see you again."

"That makes two of us."

He saw Joaquin to the front door, and watched the outlaw get on a horse and ride out of town. Only then did it occur to him that he should have mentioned the other man who'd came with Love. Rhodes, his name had been.

He shook his head. It probably would have meant nothing to Joaquin. At any rate, it was too late to worry about it now. He went back into his office to scribble some notes about the conversation while it was still fresh in his mind. Newspaper work paid the bills, but he had hopes that his book would attract attention nationwide, and maybe internationally.

A man could always dream, couldn't he?

• • •

The running battle had raged for more than twenty minutes.

Harry Love, along with the other rangers, had responded to a report of a rancher whose wagonload of beef had been stolen by armed Mexican bandits near Sonora. They'd raced to the scene and found the bandits' tracks. The wagon slowed their escape, and an hour's ferocious riding brought them into view. Once the bandits spotted their pursuers, they abandoned the wagon, but by then the shooting had begun.

Love was no fan of shooting from the saddle. He preferred a rifle to a pistol, and he liked to take his time about aiming and to make every shot count. But the bandits didn't seem inclined to provide that opportunity. He didn't know if Murrieta was among them, but he saw scattered sombreros and big Mexican star rowels on spurs, and he was determined to kill or capture every last one, just in case.

He'd grown weary of the chase, though. He was no young man, after all, and his arms ached almost as much as his ass did. His breathing was labored, as was that of the roan he rode. His nostrils hurt from the smoke he breathed in with every shot. Two rangers had been knocked from their saddles during the running fight, but he didn't know their condition—couldn't, without stopping and turning back. Until those bandits were dead or had surrendered, he wasn't going to do that.

More of the bandits had fallen, though, which he attributed to the fact that shooting targets ahead of oneself was marginally easier than behind. Only four remained, and the distance between them and the rangers had lessened considerably.

The bandits had left established trails far behind and raced cross-country, over oak-lined hills and grassy meadows, splashing through creeks and shallow ponds. For a few moments, he lost sight of them when they passed over a rocky ridgeline, but he kept up the pace, and soon they were back in view. Beyond them, though, was nothing—it was as if they'd reached the end of the earth. His vision skewed by the motion of his horse, it took Love a few seconds to realize they had come to the edge of a cliff. In the distance were more rolling hills, but there was plenty of empty space before one could reach those.

He allowed himself the briefest of smiles. The men hadn't jumped the cliff, so chances were it was too far a drop to risk. They were cornered, and outnumbered better than three to one.

Instead of waiting for the rangers to reach them, though, the four turned their mounts and charged directly at their pursuers, guns blazing. Now, everybody was shooting forward, and two more rangers fell, Bert Crider and Frank Noble. Love couldn't worry about them at the moment. He reined his horse to a stop and took careful aim at the nearest of the Mexicans. His first shot missed, and he only had one more before he'd have to reload. He corrected his aim and fired again.

The Mexican kept riding toward him, but something had changed. After three more strides of his horse, he slipped from the saddle and fell in a heap. Around Love, the other rangers kept firing, too, and within seconds, the fusillade killed all of the remaining Mexicans.

Now came the hard part.

Love and the others took a few minutes to rest, reload, and slake their thirst. But then the grisly task of checking each of the fallen bandits, and tending to the wounds of their own, lay before them. He kept Rhodes at his side, because the two of them were the only ones among them who could positively identify Murrieta.

Backtracking and eyeing each one who'd fallen took

another two hours. They found two rangers dead, and two more wounded but alive. They placed the wounded and the dead in the abandoned meat wagon to be taken to Sonora.

They checked every Mexican, killing those who hadn't already died. As they went, they searched pockets and scavenged anything of value, along with guns and ammunition. Murrieta was not among them. Nor did Love recognize any of the others.

They slept that night in a Sonoran hotel, and Love took advantage of the opportunity to visit a house he knew of, where the Mexican girls all spoke English and chased away the tensions of the day. Rhodes declined an invitation to join him, but that was fine.

Some things, Love didn't mind sharing, but others he preferred to keep to himself.

66

San Francisco was a revelation.

Joaquin and Tres Dedos reached it at nightfall and made their way through crowded streets laced with fog until they found the St. Francis Hotel at the corner of Clay and Dupont. They ate in the restaurant, then retired. Although they didn't expect to be recognized, in the morning, Joaquin streaked flour through his air to make him appear older, and Tres Dedos wore gloves to disguise his missing finger. Joaquin didn't get his first view of the city's breadth until they stepped outside after breakfast.

It was staggering.

A structure of some kind, from ragged tents to three-story wooden buildings to palatial mansions made of brick or native stone, occupied every bit of open space. Although Joaquin couldn't see where any room to build more could be found, he heard the sounds of construction everywhere—hammering, sawing, even a steady thumping sound that Tres Dedos said was a steam shovel leveling hills of sand near the coast. Leaving their horses stabled and dressed in finery, discreetly carrying only a few weapons, the two men set out to explore on foot.

The bay, they found, was jammed with ships, in places five or six deep, waiting their turns to reach the docks. Their masts formed a virtual forest; Joaquin thought a man might be able to leap from one to another, to reach the city without touching water. Smaller boats ferried passengers to shore from those farther out. "There must be hundreds of men on those ships," Joaquin marveled. "All of them coming to California."

"Hundreds on each ship, and more ships every day," Tres Dedos said. "Some are French, Italian, Chilean, even Spanish. But most are Americans. Thousands of arrivals every week."

"This is what you wanted to show me?"

"All of this." Tres Dedos swept his arms in circles, taking in the views from every direction. "Before Marshall found gold, this was a sleepy huddle of tents known as Yerba Buena. In the four years since, it's become a city to rival any other. You saw it last night, heard it when we were trying to sleep. This city never rests. All it does is grow."

He was right. People thronged the streets. Chinese and Africans and Mexicans, sure, but mostly white. Americans by the scores. Wide streets climbed hillsides and dropped down to the water, and not a one looked empty. Joaquin and his cousin strolled aimlessly, seeing every sort of business, from laundries to grocers to publishers to the American Theatre, where signs indicated that Lola Montez would soon perform.

They spent the morning just wandering, never by themselves on any street they crossed. Most people who acknowledged them at all greeted them cheerfully; here, it seemed, no one feared Mexicans. They stopped for lunch at a restaurant that had tables outside as well as in.

As they ate, Tres Dedos talked. "I'm glad you came with me, Joaquin. I saw this a few weeks ago, and it's been on my mind ever since."

"It's astonishing," Joaquin said. "I've never seen so many people in my life, or such a grand city."

"I understand how you feel about the Americans, my

friend. I agree with you. They're a scourge, and California should rightly fly the Mexican flag. But you'll never stop this. The California you and I know, the gold camps and the miners and the isolated communities—they aren't the threat anymore. This is the threat, and even with a thousand men on horses, we couldn't put a dent in it. We can't even slow it down. It will only grow and grow."

"So, you're telling me to give up?"

Tres Dedos laughed. "I've always been smarter than you, but since when have I been able to tell you what to do? I'm only suggesting that you look at this and consider your chances. You could kill five hundred Americans a day for the next year, and five thousand more would take their place. Their numbers are as limitless as their lust for gold. It's the same in Los Angeles, Monterey, even San José. It's happening everywhere. We've already lost California, cousin. Once change comes, it can't be turned back."

The suggestion formed a pit in Joaquin's stomach. He pushed aside his half-eaten lunch, afraid to take another bite. "What would you have me do, then?"

"If I were you? I'd go home. You have wealth beyond anything you ever dreamed of. You can spend the rest of your life as a hidalgo, a grandee. Didn't you say that was your ambition, when we came here? To return once you were richer than Rosita's father? You've achieved that, and more. Here, you'll always be a hated outlaw. There, you'll be an honored nobleman—a hero."

Joaquin remembered what Tom Springer had told him, and his sense of confusion returned. Who was he, really? Would he ever truly know himself? Did anyone?

"A hero?" he echoed. "You think so?"

Tres Dedos took a drink of wine, wiped his mouth with the

back of his furry hand. "You know how those people at our camp look at you. With admiration. I daresay some worship you. In Mexico, I'm sure people feel the same way. Go home, Joaquin. You might not have conquered California, but you've conquered the hearts of our countrymen. No man could've done more."

"Let me think on it," Joaquin said. "Thank you for being honest with me."

"I never promised you anything more, my brother."

"I wonder . . ." Joaquin began. "Do you think we can find anything here to amuse us for a day or two?"

Tres Dedos gave him a wide grin. "My friend," he said, "I do believe we can."

67

Love and his rangers stayed in Sonora for a few days, awaiting intelligence that would direct them somewhere else. Stories filtered through to them of raids throughout the state, from Shasta almost to the Mexican border, but without definitive proof of Joaquin's whereabouts. Anyway, after the mounted gun battle, the horses needed some rest, as did the men. But Love was anxious. Their three-month posting was up on August eleventh. They were more than halfway through July, and although they'd turned the state's Mexican communities upside-down and killed or arrested dozens of Mexican bandits, they still seemed no closer to Murrieta. It was almost like he had some kind of magical power that rendered him invisible when anyone with a badge came too close.

One early afternoon, Love was eating lunch with Rhodes in the hotel restaurant when a waiter stopped by the table and leaned over. "Captain," he said, "there's a woman asking to see you."

Love was at a loss as to who it might be. "Is she carrying a baby who looks like me?" he asked.

The waiter looked mortified, but at Rhodes's laughter, he relaxed. "No, sir," he said. "No baby at all."

"Show her in, then."

The waiter nodded and went outside, then returned with a young woman in tow. She was blond, slender, with a pronounced underbite. Love had never seen her before, he was certain. She looked like she had been traveling; her clothing was dusty and torn, and she wore boots caked with road grit. Mounted, then, not in a coach or wagon. But beneath the grime, her light brown eyes were lively and intelligent, her face well composed. He rose, as did Rhodes.

"Madam, good day," Love said. "I'm Captain Love, and this is Lieutenant Rhodes. The waiter says you're looking for me?"

"I am," she said. "I've come a long way. Governor Bigler's office told me where I might find you. May I sit?"

"Please." Love held out a chair for her. She sat heavily, weariness overtaking her, and he pushed her in nearer the table. "Something to drink? Water, coffee, something stronger?"

"Water would be lovely."

Love arched an eyebrow at the waiter, who hurried off, though he looked like he wanted to stay close and hear her story.

When he had brought her water and wandered away again, she took a long drink, set the glass down, and said, "My name is Amelia Bennett."

Love blinked a couple of times, searching his memory. "I'm sorry, should that name mean something to me?"

"I'm sure it wouldn't," she said. "Although I have served you, once. I'm a waitress at the Bella Union Hotel, in Los Angeles. You were there with two other lawmen, having lunch."

"Yes," Love said. "That does indeed ring a bell. That was a couple of years ago, though. Does your visit today have anything to do with that?"

"No, not at all. But it does have to do with my employment there."

"Go on, Miss Bennett."

"Well, sometimes when I'm serving customers, I pay a little more attention to the conversation than I should. Not with you—I made a point of not listening in while you were there. But a month or so back, I served two people of the, umm . . . the Mexican persuasion, you might say."

"And?" Love was losing patience, wanting her to get to the point.

"One of them was simply beautiful. She had a Mexican accent, but light hair, and brown eyes. I heard the man she was with call her 'Antonia.' Sometimes they spoke Spanish, but sometimes they spoke English."

"Who was the man?"

"Well, that's what made me remember the conversation. A few days after they were in the restaurant, he was hanged in Los Angeles, and I saw an engraving of him in the newspaper. His name was Moreno, and he was said to be part of the bandit Joaquin's gang."

"Atanacio Moreno?" Rhodes asked.

"Yes, I believe that was it."

"He killed another member of the band," Rhodes said. "And he tried to claim the reward, but he was recognized."

"I remember!" Love snapped. "Please, go on, Miss Bennett."

"Well, at the time, I didn't know who they were talking about. I heard the woman, this Antonia, say something about someone trying to have her killed, but failing. That made me interested, of course, so I listened more closely, and made a point of visiting the table often. To check up on them, of course, see if they needed anything."

"As an attentive waitress does," Rhodes said.

"Exactly. Then the man said that he—whoever 'he' was—had intended to send someone else to finish the job, but had called it off at the last minute. The man said that 'he' had forgiven her, that he was certain that 'he' still loved her. She said that perhaps she should visit, to try to mend things between them, and asked if 'he' were still in the same place."

"Did she name the place?" Love said. This had suddenly become most interesting.

"No. The man started speaking in Spanish again, but I caught the first part. He said, 'Sí.' Then, something something, and, 'Arroyo de Cantua.'"

"Arroyo de Cantua? You're certain of that?"

"I wasn't. They speak so fast, in Spanish. But when I saw the Moreno fellow in the newspaper, I started asking some friends. One told me that Arroyo de Cantua is a real place in California, so if that's what I heard, then that's probably what was said."

"We'll look into it. Anything else?"

"That's really all I heard. It eventually dawned on me that this might be helpful to you. It took me a couple of weeks to scrape together the funds to make the trip, but here I am. I hope it's helpful, and that I haven't put myself in danger by telling you this."

Love met Rhodes's gaze across the table. After everything they'd tried, every dead-end, every tip that turned out useless, could it be this easy?

"I'll station a couple of men with you to guard you until he's been dealt with, if that will put your mind at ease," Love assured her. "And they'll escort you back to Los Angeles. It won't cost you a penny."

"It will help," she said.

Again, Love met Rhodes's eye. "Arroyo," he said. "Springer wasn't lying." Turning back to the lady, he added, "Can you tell us how to find it?"

"That I cannot do," Amelia Bennett said. "I've told you all I know. What you do with that, sir, is up to you."

• • •

Love ordered two men to take Amelia Bennett back to Los Angeles and to stay with her until Murrieta was in custody, and left the wounded rangers behind. He found Arroyo de Cantua on a map, and the ride there took only a few hours. The night was almost cloudless, with only high, thin wisps occasionally drifting over a bright, three-quarter moon. At the head of the column of rangers, Harry Love looked at the narrow opening of the canyon. Those rocky outcrops could be hiding dozens of men, and likely were.

At this time of night, he hoped, Murrieta's men would likely be carousing, drinking themselves silly. But awake. Come morning though, they'd be groggy, hung over. That was the time to strike. They'd been decimating Murrieta's forces, and had never known him to have more than forty or fifty men at the most. And Murrieta wouldn't be expecting an attack in what he still believed to be a secret hideout.

"This is near enough," Love said. "Any closer and their guards might spot us." He pointed to the west, the far side of the valley. "We'll camp in those trees over there, and wake before dawn. No fires!"

The men turned their horses and headed across the broad valley, riding at an easy pace as quietly as fifteen men could travel. Tall cottonwoods lined a narrow river near the foothills marking the valley's edge, and they made camp, drank from canteens and ate hardtack and jerky, and caught a few hours' sleep.

By the time the sun cleared the peaks of the Sierra Nevada, they were riding through the canyon's mouth at full charge, bristling with weapons. No guards raised an alarm, no shots met their approach.

Inside the canyon, the morning light showed a bizarre tableau. Hundreds of dwellings were scattered across the grassy plain, in no discernible pattern. Tents, shacks, lean-tos of every description had been thrown up willy-nilly. As the journalist had claimed, one stone house stood amidst the others, sporting half a roof, with the rest open to the sky. A Mexican flag fluttered in a light breeze that carried the fecund scent of manure.

This was the place, then, and the camp, where they'd expected to find at a couple dozen outlaws, could have held several hundred.

But—luckily for them, Love realized belatedly—it didn't.

One end of the little valley was fenced, and full of more horses than he had ever seen in one place. But at first glance, he saw no humans at all.

Then one emerged from a tent, a rifle in his hand. A couple more looked over from near the horses. A shirtless man stepped out of an area that could only be the camp's latrine, buttoning his trousers.

Love brought the column to a stop near the greaser with the rifle, who was scratching his head and blinking as if he'd just woken up. Probably he had, his slumber disturbed by the thunder of the charge. "I'm Captain Love, and we're the California Rangers. Is this the camp of Joaquin Murrieta?" Love demanded.

The man looked this way and that. "Do you see him anywhere?"

"I only see a few scraggly-looking hombres I wouldn't turn my back on. Answer my question."

"There's nobody here but us," the man said. "I don't know who this Joaquin fellow is."

"Then you don't mind if we look for him in those tents and houses?"

"Only one house here, and it's empty," the man said. "Look all you want."

Love ordered some rangers to watch the man and the few others around, then went to the stone house. Springer had told him that Joaquin slept under the roofed part. He and Rhodes and three other rangers went inside, but the man with the rifle had told the truth. It was empty, the stove cool. Someone lived inside there, all right, but nobody was there now.

Love emerged, furious. Could this have been a trap arranged by Joaquin, and Amelia Bennett part of the plot? But if it was a trap, when would it be sprung? He studied the canyon walls, seeing nobody. The handful of men they had found posed no threat.

He returned to the man, whose rifle the rangers had confiscated. "Those horses," he said. "I have no doubt they're stolen."

The man simply shrugged. "Could be."

"We're taking them. At San Juan Bautista, we'll examine their brands, try to determine their rightful owners. Do you have any intention of trying to stop us?"

"Not me," the man said. "I couldn't even if I wanted to. There's too many of you. You'd kill me."

"You're right about that," Love said. "I ought to do it anyway, just because I don't like the looks of you. But I'm in a generous mood this morning, so I'll let you live. Unless you try anything, of course."

The man sank to the ground and sat there, legs crossed in the damp grass. "I'll be right here," he said. "Help yourself."

Love eyed the man, considering whether to shoot him as an example to the rest. But the man hardly seemed worth the bullet. Rangers had checked a few of the tents and other structures, but there didn't appear to be more than six or seven men here in total, and none of them looked inclined to make trouble.

"Round up those horses!" he called. "I hope some of you have worked ranches before, because we've got us a good-sized herd to drive to San Juan!"

It wasn't how he had expected the attack to go, but it was something. If these were indeed Murrieta's men, and the stolen horses that'd been reported from every corner of the state, then at least he could deprive the outlaw of the treasure he would make from selling them. And he would make sure to visit again soon, when his quarry might actually be present.

"One more thing," Love said. He climbed down from his horse and handed the reins to Hardy Bowman, youngest of his recruits, who he'd taken on in order to honor the young man's uncle, Sergeant John Bowman. John had died of dysentery at Corpus Christi Bay before the war even broke out, leaving his wife Sarah, who'd signed on as a laundress with the Seventh Infantry. In the years since, Sarah had earned her own kind of infamy, so Love heard of her exploits from time to time. But it had been John he'd served with, and John he remembered most fondly.

Ignoring the stares of the handful of Mexicans, he crossed to the flagpole standing outside the stone house. Instead of lowering the Mexican flag with the line and pulley, he simply cut the rope and watched it drop to the ground, then worked it into the earth with his boots.

When he took his reins back from Bowman, he said only, "This ain't Mexico."

68

The first thing Joaquin noticed as he and Tres Dedos rode into the canyon was the noise. The ride back from San Francisco had been quiet, contemplative, only occasionally broken by conversation. He had thought about what he'd seen, there, and about his conversation with Tom Springer. As they passed through the opening, though, he heard voices, a din so loud that he was surprised people ever passed within ten miles of the place without wondering what was going on. But there was something strange about the sound. Something hollow.

Inside, the camp looked normal at first glance. People milled about, moving from tent to tent or chatting in the open areas. Horses stood in the meadow. But a second glance showed him that those horses numbered perhaps three hundred or a little less.

When they'd left, there had been almost eight hundred. Most of the men had gone out raiding, taking the new volunteers along to show them what the outlaw's life was like, and even with them gone, the horses stolen to outfit Joaquin's proposed cavalry stayed behind. He'd hoped to have a thousand horses, in case he could raise the thousand men he expected. Now, though, he could see about four hundred men, and not even enough horses for everyone to ride.

Gregorio Lopez spotted their approach and came running

to meet them.

"What happened here?" Joaquin asked.

"California Rangers came while most of us were away," Lopez said. "They took all the horses. Said they were driving them to San Juan Bautista to return them to their owners."

"The rangers were here? How long ago?"

"Three days, they say. We just got back yesterday. Most returned the day before, and there are still a few groups who haven't made it back yet."

"All those horses we gathered, over weeks and weeks . . ."

"Gone, boss. All gone."

Sudden fury engulfed Joaquin. "Was it Love? Did he say his name?"

"Yes, they said the leader called himself Captain Love. He's also the one who . . ." Lopez didn't finish his sentence, but he glanced at the flagpole in front of the house. The flag was gone. Joaquin dismounted and stormed over there to find it draped over a chair, torn and filthy.

"I hate that man. I've never hated anyone more." Even as he spoke the words, he knew it wasn't true. The men who had defiled Rosita had earned his undying hatred, and that still burned within him. Everything he had done since, every man he'd killed, and every favor he'd done for his own kind, had grown out of that. Hatred had ruled his life for years now. Antonia had probably recognized that in him, and more than anything else, that had probably driven her away. He hoped his message had reached her.

"You know this man, Love?" Lopez asked.

"I knew him, in Sawmill Flat, when I first came to California. We were friends. But now this."

"There's no enemy like a former friend," Lopez said. "You chose the other side of the law. You remind him of his own failure."

"I hope he continues to be a failure," Joaquin said.

"Now that they know this place, they'll be back," Tres Dedos pointed out. "Won't take long, either. Getting all those horses to San Juan and sorting them out will take a little time, but he knows you'll be back here. I wouldn't be surprised if he'd left spies behind, and even now they're racing to let him know you've returned."

As usual, Tres Dedos was right. This place, so long a haven, was safe no longer.

Joaquin looked at the people scattered around the camp. Several of his most trusted lieutenants were dead or in jail. These volunteers were farmers, miners, laborers, but not hardened warriors. They had the spirit, perhaps, but lacked the necessary skills. And instead of nearly a thousand horses, they had only a couple hundred, at best. His vision of Mexicans tearing up and down California's hills and valleys, putting American property to the torch, was only that—a vision, never to be realized.

All the way back from San Francisco, he'd been pondering his next move. He had been loath to give up his dream of returning California to Mexican rule, but seeing how many Americans were already here—and seeing the sheer numbers arriving every day, not only in San Francisco, but as Tres Dedos said, in other port cities as well, and doubtless overland—he had begun to recognize the impossibility of it.

"Gregorio, call everybody together. I have something to say. Call me when they're ready."

As Lopez turned to obey, Joaquin walked into the house, head down, to gather his thoughts. He felt overtaken by a deep and profound sadness, but within it lurked a surprising twinge of something like hope.

• • •

Tres Dedos tapped on his door. "They're ready."

"I'm not," Joaquin said.

"The sooner you get it over with, the sooner it's over."

"Why do you have to be so smart, Manuel?"

"I can't help it. It comes naturally to me."

Joaquin wiped sweat from his forehead. "I wonder what that's like. I think my brains are leaking out of me. Why is it so hot?"

"Because it's July in California. Do you know you always ask questions when you don't want to do something difficult?"

"It wasn't this hot in San Francisco."

"That's on the coast. It has some elevation, and it's cooled by fog and sea winds. You're free to go back."

"That's a good idea. I'll leave immediately."

"*After* you've addressed the people who are waiting for you," Tres Dedos said with finality.

"Fine, all right." Joaquin opened the door. He had changed from his traveling clothes, put on a black silk shirt and black pants, with a red sash about his waist. He wanted, at this moment, to look at least moderately impressive. Tres Dedos was still wearing a serape caked with road dust. The heat never seemed to bother him. Neither did the cold. Joaquin wondered what it was like to be so comfortable in one's own skin.

He let his cousin lead him outside. The people waited, spread out across the meadow but all looking his way. The hush was remarkable. The sadness hadn't left him, but something about all those people gathered to hear him speak sent a thrill through him. He meant something to them. They had come here, left their lives behind, because he'd asked them to. He'd given them something to believe in.

In turn, they helped him believe in himself.

He stopped when he was in a spot where he believed everyone could see him. They stretched out across the meadow, so he'd have to shout to be heard. No intimate conversation, this. He would only have this one last chance to address them all together.

"My friends," he began. "I called you here to attack the Americans, to burn them out of their homes and businesses, to drive them from California and return it to Mexican rule. And you came, by the hundreds. You came, and you made me so proud. But I'm standing here today to tell you that I was wrong.

"I was wrong to want to burn them out—just as wrong as they were at San Andreas and Yaqui Camp and all the other places where they burned your homes. Just as wrong as they were at Matamoros and Monterrey when they invaded Mexico, in a war they fought only because they wanted to steal California from us. And that was before they even knew about the gold. Now that they do, they'll never let it go. They would kill every one of us to keep it, and they have the numbers to do it.

"The way to take revenge on the Americans is not to fight fire with more fire. It's to live among them, to upset their expectations, and to never let them forget you're here. My mistake was in becoming what they expected me to be, an outlaw.

"They called me a horse thief, and I became one. They called me a killer, and I kept on killing. But no more. As of today, I will be only who *I* want to be, not who *they* want me to be. I bid you do the same.

"The more Mexican outlaws they see, the more convinced they are that it's the only thing we're good at. And that's not true. Mexicans can do anything. Anything at all.

"My friends, you should sing, dance, drink, make love, be happy. That will confound them more than anything else could. That will drive them mad.

"I brought you here for a revolution. I've learned that the revolution I had in mind is impossible. Instead, we need thousands of revolutions. Personal ones. You can each be a revolution by yourself, by showing the Americans that you're honest, hard-working, peaceful, loving, and kind. As I know you are, because that's the Mexican way."

He wasn't sure how to end. Once his feelings had started spilling out in words, he'd gone on longer than expected, and felt like he could keep talking until the end of time. He had held so much inside for so long, certain that the bandit's life required a man of actions instead of words. He had read great books, studied the poets, but never really thought he had the gift of language. He still didn't, but the people before him seemed rapt, wanting him to deliver deep wisdom.

No, he decided. Keep it short. If he went on, they would only get bored. He took a deep breath, raised his hands high, and shouted, "Thank you! Thank you all for coming! Thank you all for showing me the strength of our people. Viva Mexico!"

That raised a cheer from the crowd that seemed to shake the stones from the heights. Joaquin turned away from them and saw Tres Dedos standing to one side, clapping softly, a huge grin on his face. Joaquin strode to his friend and embraced him. "And thank you, brother. You were right, as ever. I'm lucky to know you."

"Yes, you are," Tres Dedos said with a chuckle. "And I, you. I could never speak to a crowd like that, much less spur them to action."

"We need some action ourselves," Joaquin said. "We need

to clear this place out before the rangers return. If they know how many are here, they might bring an army with them. It would be a massacre."

"I've already spread the word among our men. They've been passing it throughout the newcomers. By nightfall, this camp will be empty. I have just one question for you."

"Yes?"

"Where are *we* going?"

"I'm not going anywhere. Home, soon, but first I have one more thing to do."

"What's that?"

"I have to kill Harry Love."

"He's riding with a dozen men or more, hoping to kill you," Tres Dedos pointed out.

"Many have tried that. I'm still here. Perhaps I can't be killed. But Love can be, and I mean to do it. Hatred has driven him mad—killing, burning, even attacking his fellow white men. He needs to be stopped, and I'm the one to do it."

"You mean *we* are," Tres Dedos corrected. "Where you go, I go."

"You should go home," Joaquin answered. "Back to Trincheras, where it's safe. I'll join you as soon as Love is dead."

"But nothing ever happens there. There's no one there to kill."

"You don't need to do any more killing. You've done enough. So have I, as soon as I'm finished with Harry."

"Hmm. Sounds strange," Tres Dedos said, shrugging. "No more killing? I guess I could give that a try."

69

Getting the horses off his hands at San Juan Bautista tied Harry Love up for a few days before he could return to Arroyo de Cantua. The men rode through the central valley on one of those summer days when the air is so still and hot, it feels like the world is a stove and the Lord himself is stoking the fire with one sun after another. Grasshoppers tormented the horses and the men, sweat coated everything, and Love's neck and chin itched something fierce. When he earned that reward Bigler had promised, he thought he might spend some of it on enough blocks of ice to build a chair and sit on it until it melted.

The Mexicans they'd questioned claimed that Joaquin had a few hundred men at the camp. Having seen the sheer number of tents and other dwellings there, Love didn't doubt that it had been true at one time. On the other hand, when he and the rangers had dropped by, there had only been a handful, and none of those terribly intimidating. Recognizing the possibility that they might encounter a massive force, he decided to risk it. If they got close and saw an army, they'd turn tail and come back with a bigger American army. But he didn't want to take a chance on humiliating himself by requesting military accompaniment, only to get there and find the same half-dozen or so.

When they reached the point at which they'd camped, the

night before their early-morning raid, they stopped in the welcome shade and Love scanned the entrance to the canyon with field glasses. He looked for the smoke of fires, for lookouts hidden around the entrance, and for any traffic in and out. Seeing none, he handed the glasses to Lucas Rhodes. "Can you see anything?"

Rhodes held the field glasses to his eyes and slowly tracked across the distant hills. "Looks clear."

"What I thought, too. Reckon we should go make sure."

He reluctantly gave the signal to cross the open plain, exposing his men once more to the heat, the insects, and potentially the buzz of lethal rounds from the guns of hidden snipers. Short of scaling the treacherously steep heights defining the canyon, the only way in was through the front door, which was easily defended. Murrieta had chosen his hideout well.

As they neared it, he saw the alluvial fan of tracks: horse, wagon, and human, that he'd noticed on their earlier visit. This time, there were many more—his own mount's among them; no rain had fallen since then to smooth out the land. But the freshest tracks indicated people leaving the camp, not entering it. That could account for the lack of visible guards or any sign of human activity within those walls.

But it would also make this trip another wasted effort. He spat once and scratched under his beard. Had that Mexican bastard dodged him again?

At the entrance, he raised his hand and paused the column. "Hear anything, Lucas?" he asked. All he heard from within was the incessant buzz of insect life.

"Nope. Bugs is all."

"Same. Let's go see." He glanced over his shoulder. "Weapons at the ready!"

He listened to the racket of men drawing rifles from

scabbards, pistols from holsters, shifting in their saddles. When that stilled again, he started into the narrow defile.

Two minutes later, he stopped again and viewed essentially the same scene as before. Fewer tents were in evidence, though. No horses remained in the fenced-in meadow, and the gate stood open. No humans were present, either. In front of the house, the dirty, torn Mexican flag had been run up the pole again, the rope tied in a knot where he'd cut it. Murrieta's parting gift, he figured.

They were too late. The bandit was gone.

"Damn him," Love said. "Damn him to Hell." Speaking those words reminded him of the time Ellas had said that to him. He was starting to think Ellas had the power to make it come true. Time was running out on their three-month commission, and he had not laid eyes on Murrieta once during that time. For that matter, he couldn't be certain that he ever had. He still believed Murrieta was the young man who'd worked for him, but he had no proof. He had found himself, more than once, hoping he was mistaken about that. Given the stories he'd heard about Murrieta's treatment at the hands of Americans, he could understand why his one-time friend would have chosen the outlaw's path. But if and when the time came to pull the trigger, he hoped this Joaquin was someone else entirely, and that his Joaquin had returned to Mexico and lived there still.

The sun had passed its zenith and started its slow summer descent. He gave brief thought to looking inside the house, but it wasn't as if Murrieta would have left behind a written description of his plans, or a map with a handy circled spot and a note saying "Hide out here."

"Let's light a shuck out of here," he said to no one in particular. He turned his horse around and started for the entrance. The other rangers followed.

Just past the opening, he stopped again and studied the view. The valley was long, stretching north to south for what seemed like hundreds of miles. East to west it was considerably shorter. Mountains hemmed it in on both sides and, as here, occasionally rose from the valley floor.

He studied the tracks left by what could've been hundreds of people. Once they cleared the canyon's mouth, they trailed off into every direction. Sometimes just a few, but in other places seemingly dozens.

"What do you think, Lucas?" Love asked.

Rhodes hopped down from his mount and studied the tracks. He walked back and forth, eyes down, for a good twenty minutes, while Love fanned himself with his hat and wished the man would get on with it.

Finally, Rhodes settled on a line of hoofprints heading almost due west. "These look familiar," he said. "The way this shoe's worn, I've seen this before. Ten animals, two carrying burdens, eight people. Could be Murrieta."

"Or not," Love said.

"You got a better idea, Harry, spit it out."

"Good enough for me, Lucas. We'll follow these a spell."

Within an hour, the tracks split up, some continuing west and others turning south. The sun was lower still. Love watched it, thinking it symbolized his three-month assignment. July was almost over. The commission's sunset was August eleventh. If he hadn't found Murrieta by then, all he'd have to show for his efforts was his regular monthly pay—and the national humiliation that would accompany his defeat.

As they followed the faint trail, hopelessness set in. He longed for a cool, quiet saloon where he could drink himself into oblivion. What good was a lawman who couldn't find his own behind with a map and a compass?

Another hour passed, and now they rode straight into the setting sun. It was blinding, making it hard to follow even the scant hoofprints that hadn't peeled off one way or another. They'd also passed stretches of bare earth where the sun had baked the ground so hard, hardly any tracks existed. Love wondered if Rhodes was only guessing, and they were still heading west without any solid reason.

"This man's a damn ghost," Love complained.

"He's real, Harry," Rhodes countered.

"Then why can't we find him? Why can't any lawman in this whole damn state lay a hand on him?"

Rhodes pointed out a rise up ahead. "Let's go up there, get some elevation. Maybe we can see something."

"Best hurry, then. Be dark soon."

"If there's space enough, we can make camp up there and continue come morning."

Love thought of the flask in his saddlebag. "Makes sense, Lucas. Come on." He put his heels to the horse and hurried up the slope, racing the dying of the light.

And he was too late. As he topped the rise, the sun blinked out behind the coast range, painting the evening sky in shades of indigo, salmon, and gold. Love kept going, to the edge of the little, grassy plateau, dodging a few live oaks. At that edge, he dismounted and wrestled his field glasses from their case, trying to survey the valley floor in every direction before all light had fled.

He saw scattered farms and plenty of empty space, but no groups of riders. Discouraged, he started to put the glasses away. Then, Rhodes said, "Harry."

"What?" Love snapped.

"Over there, in those hills. Is that smoke?"

Love followed Rhodes's pointing arm, keyed in with the field glasses. It was indeed a thin ribbon of gray against the darkening sky. He tracked down it and found a spot of light that could have been a small fire.

A fire such as men on the move might build to cook an evening meal.

"What is that place?" Love called out. "Those hills!"

"That's the Gabilan Range," Rand Lorenz said.

"You from hereabouts, Rand?"

"I lived in Monterey for a spell."

"Near enough. Anybody live up there?"

"Not around *there*."

"Can you get us up there in the dark?"

"Sure," Lorenz said quickly. Then he added, "I think, any-how. There's a trail around there."

Love tucked away the glasses and got back on his horse. "What are we doing sitting here? Time's wasting!"

70

Joaquin had wanted to leave Arroyo de Cantua at first light. But the night before, after his speech, many of the men had gotten drunk. And in the morning, people who weren't too sickly wanted to speak to him, to touch him, to thank him for all he had done for them. He tried to press coins into the palms of the poorest ones, knowing they might have left their farms or their jobs to come when he'd called. Some refused it, others accepted with even more profuse thanks. All in all, getting out of there took hours.

He rode with seven of his most trusted friends. Tres Dedos, of course, and Joaquin Valenzuela, Luis Vulvia, and Antonio Valenci, who'd been with Tres Dedos since before Joaquin even knew them. Antonio Severino, Gregorio Lopez, and Gustavo Zaragoza rounded out the group. Severino had a cousin in Monterey that he wanted to see, so they were heading there first, to drop him off. From there, they would travel south. Valenci and Zaragoza wanted to stop in Los Angeles. The rest were bound for the border and Mexico. Tres Dedos had refused to go back to Trincheras alone; he was determined to stay with Joaquin until Harry Love was dead.

They started out too late to make it in a day, so stopped for the night in the Gabilan Mountains, where Lopez was able to shoot a white-tailed deer for dinner, with the remainder intended as a gift for Severino's cousin. They cleaned it where it died and left the remains, carrying the meat a fair distance away so as not to attract the predators and scavengers after the offal. They made camp in a clearing near the edge of a ravine with a creek flowing through it, so fresh water was close by. After they cooked and ate as much as they wanted, they sat around the fire, sharing a bottle of mescal and talking intermittently about past exploits and future plans.

"I know a pretty French girl who deals cards in Los Angeles," Zaragoza said. "I want to see if she'll make an honest man of me."

Tres Dedos burst out laughing. "A French card dealer? Not likely! But you'll enjoy her corrupting influence, just the same."

"If she th-throws you out, Gustavo," Valenci said, "you can always c-come and work at my uncle's ranch. The pay isn't m-m-much, but it's every month, and the only ones trying to kill you are the cows."

"I think I'd rather take my chances with people," Zaragoza countered. "At least I know what they're up to. I think cows are probably sneakier than anybody knows."

"I guess you've never met a c-cow," Valenci said.

"Not a live one. I've eaten plenty, though, and I don't want them to smell it on me."

They all laughed at that, and Tres Dedos passed around a flask. Conversation continued, but Joaquin was thinking about the lawman. Moving alone, or just with Tres Dedos, he should be able to get close enough for a clean shot. Perhaps even near enough to use a knife, so Love would know in the end who had killed him.

And why.

Another hour or two passed, and everyone started getting sleepy. The talk dwindled and the laughter died out. Zaragoza was the first to curl up on the ground, with a blanket under him and some of it wrapped around on top, his head on his saddle.

Vulvia volunteered to take first watch, so Joaquin tried to quiet his racing mind and finally drifted off, surrounded by the rustling, throat clearing, and gentle snores of his closest friends.

• • •

They'd tethered the horses a half-mile back, at the foot of the rocky rise, and left young Hardy Bowman to mind them. Fifteen strong, they wended their way through the pines with pistols drawn or rifles at the ready. When Love buttoned the top two buttons of his army jacket—the day had been a hot one, but a chill had set in—his hand grazed the California Rangers badge on his chest. Having ridden most of the day, then most of the night, he was tired, on edge, and saddle-sore, but the closer they drew to the campfire he'd spotted, the more anxious he became. Soon, he reckoned, they would put an end to this grim task, one way or another.

"Hey, Harry!" That was Rand Lorenz, not much older than Bowman, who never tired of hearing Love's war stories. "Is it true Augie Winrow tried to bushwhack you, but you killed him with his own gun?"

"I ain't one to talk about folks I might or might not have killed," Love said. "Especially when he might could still have friends or family about."

"Way I heard it, you snatched his gun from his hand and beat him to death with it."

"Might've done. Or not."

"Winrow killed eleven men, right?"

"Thirteen. Hush, now."

Hushing Lorenz was no easy task. "I never heard if he got

buried. Where is he now?"

Love waved vaguely north and east, a gesture that could have encompassed the bulk of the Coast Ranges and the entirety of the Sierra Nevada, at minimum. "Out there somewhere, I guess."

"Alive?"

"Seems unlikely. I only ever heard of one man could pull that trick, and he weren't the killing type."

"What do you mean, Harry?"

"We get back home after this, spend some time with your Bible," Love said. "Luke twenty-four." He shot Lorenz a fiery glance. "Enough blather, now, we're close."

Some of those at his back were, he knew, unlikely lawmen. Lorenz was a cowhand who'd left his last job to try mining, and failed at that. Wilson Hurwitz was an occasional horse thief who'd shot three men at a poker table. Josiah Katz owned a dry-goods store. Barney Polkin hadn't been sober five days straight in years, and he was showing the effects. Mexican War veteran Lucas Rhodes and Joe Farmer both owed Murrieta for past crimes. Love had drawn the team together in a hurry, once he had the go-ahead from Governor Bigler, and he'd had to settle for less than perfect. The man he trusted most—Rhodes, who had an admirable record from the Mexican War, and whom Harry had made his lieutenant in the rangers—was bringing up the rear, in case Murrieta knew they were coming and was circling around behind.

It wouldn't do to underestimate their quarry. Others had done so, and usually only learned of their mistake moments before death snatched away the surprise.

A new scent wafting through the trees brought Love up short, and he raised a hand to halt the others. Fire, the fragrant aroma of burning pine. He stood still, and under the whisper of the breeze through the pine boughs, he could hear its faint crackle and the occasional snap of the burning sap. He took stock. They'd neared the top of the slope. To his right—to the east—a steep embankment dropped toward a stream that they'd been level with before starting the climb. In the gray gloom of morning, he could see that the trees were thicker up there. They were pines, so their fallen needles made a soft carpet, and kept the undergrowth to a minimum. They could approach without being heard.

Lorenz was still at his shoulder. "Fan out," Love said softly. "Into a half-circle." He backed the words with gestures, and the men obeyed without question. They'd performed this maneuver before, circling around packs of outlaws, but never closing in on the real object of the hunt.

This time, Love swore, something was different. He could feel it. Murrieta was in there. He took a few more steps and stopped again, sniffing the air. Coffee.

So close.

He moved with new caution, always looking forward, checking his footing, watching for movement. The other men did the same, those at the ends of the wings spreading out ahead of the others. Taking his Colt Navy in his left hand, he wiped his right on his pants, then gripped it again, forefinger against the trigger guard.

Birds flushed from a pine with a flutter of wings, and Love froze again. Ahead, a horse gave a nervous snort. Love sniffed the air again. The fire and coffee scents were gone. The breeze had shifted.

"Harry?" Lorenz, at his left shoulder. He glanced back. "What are we waitin' for?"

"You rather kill or get killed?"

"Rather do the killin', myself."

"Then wait. And shut the hell up."

They waited. After a few moments, Love felt the breeze in his face again, bringing the scent of woodsmoke with it. Stronger than ever.

Again, Love started forward, taking slow, cautious steps. The other men did the same. The first tendrils of golden sunlight started to thread through the pines. Love heard the creak of leather, the *ting* of a coffee pot against rock, men snoring, the gurgling of the nearby stream.

Then, there they were. Love counted seven men. One squatted by the fire, watching the pot. Another—a hulking brute, ugly as sin—sat on a fallen tree, smoking. The hand holding the cigar was missing its little finger. Five others still huddled in their bedrolls, two of them snoring loud enough to mask the Rangers' approach. They all looked swarthy. Mexican.

Love stepped into the clearing. Around him, forming a semicircle around the camp, his men did the same.

The guy at the fire looked up in surprise. "Who are you? What do you want?"

"I'll ask the questions," Love said. "Who's in charge here?"

The man on the log flipped his cigarette into the fire, started to reach under his serape. "I am," he said.

"I wouldn't try that," Love cautioned. "There are twenty guns on you." A lie, but the man wasn't going to count.

"I've seen worse."

"I imagine you have, Jack. That's your name, right? Three-Fingered Jack?"

"My name's Manuel Duarte. What's yours?"

"I'm Harry Love. These men are California Rangers, and we've been charged with arresting you and your compadres."

"Good luck." Three-Fingered Jack—Love was certain of it

now—snaked a hand under his serape and it came out blasting.

Love fired back, catching Jack in the upper chest. The other rangers opened up at the same time. The man by the fire pitched forward into it, knocking over the coffeepot. Some of those in the bedrolls struggled to get free, or simply started shooting guns they'd burrowed in there with. Others died where they lay.

Rangers fell, too. Lorenz cried out and dropped to his knees, clutching his chest. Out of the corner of his eye, Love saw Polkin keel over, and he heard other men go down. Then he felt the whisper of a bullet scraping his sleeve, and he saw another Mexican with a rifle at the far side of the clearing, amidst the trees. This man was clad all in black, with a black hat pulled low over his brow. Love thought it was Murrieta, but the man was just a black form in the shadows. The man dropped his rifle and pulled a revolver. It barked twice, and Farmer and Katz fell.

Love took aim and fired, catching the newcomer in the shoulder. At the same chaotic instant, Three-Fingered Jack— who'd already taken three bullets that Love had counted; two, he'd fired himself—lurched off the log and lunged toward the rangers, a Bowie knife in one hand and a pistol in the other.

The man on the other side of the clearing staggered back into the pines, where his black clothes blended into the shadowed boughs. Love couldn't watch for long, because too much was happening around him. Jack fired his gun into a ranger's skull, at close range, spraying pink mist out the other side. Love shot Jack again, his bullet powering through Jack's left arm and into his ribs. Even so, Jack drove the big knife deep into Bob Cooper's chest.

Love fired twice more, hitting Jack both times, and finally

the man went down. But the newcomer was shooting again, and with each crack of his gun, another ranger was hit. Flat on his belly, aiming his rifle over the bulk of one of the dead Mexicans, Wilson Hurwitz took aim and fired, catching the man in the hip. He spun away, lost his balance, but made it back into the relative safety of the trees. Even then, he kept shooting.

Then, as abruptly as it had begun, all was quiet. A thick layer of smoke hung over the clearing, from all the gunfire and from the smoldering clothing of the man lying next to the fire, having managed to roll away from it before he died. Love eyed the pines on the other side, looking for any sign of the eighth man.

71

Joaquin wasn't sure what had awakened him, but he glanced over and in the light from the dying fire, saw Vulvia sitting up with his chin on his chest, sound asleep. Then he heard it again, a loud snort and a quieter kind of gulping sound. Both came from where the horses were picketed nearby. Joaquin had long known the sounds that horses make when they were anxious or scared, and those were two of the most common.

Joaquin rose quietly, lifting the gun belt at his side. The smell of the excess deer meat might have drawn any number of predators, despite leaving the considerably more substantial bulk of the animal where it fell. A big cat, a wolf pack, or bears could injure or kill the horses, and the men if they got that far. He buckled the belt around his waist and grabbed a rifle, too. Out of habit, he donned his hat, pulling it low over his brow.

"What is it, Joaquin?"

That was Tres Dedos, sitting up.

"Something spooked the horses. I'll go look."

"I'll be here," Tres Dedos said. He shook Vulvia. "You're supposed to be watching."

"Sorry," Vulvia said. "I better make some coffee."

"You do that." Tres Dedos sat on a log and started to light

a cigar.

With those two awake, Joaquin stepped into the trees, listening for any unexpected rustling in the brush. He heard another snort before he reached the horses. They were definitely aroused; one standing stock still, staring at something off in the darkness, another scraping at the ground over and over with the same hoof. At the sight of Joaquin, who they knew well, a few of them relaxed.

"Easy, everyone," Joaquin said. "I'll see what's out there." He kept going, past the horses, every sense on high alert. Seeing nothing, he stopped and tested the breeze. At the moment, it blew from beyond the horses, toward them and the camp on the other side, so he kept going in that direction. Better to intercept whatever they smelled before it reached them.

So intent was he on what might be waiting ahead that although he vaguely felt the shifting of the breeze, uneven here atop the low mountain, he paid no attention to it.

He was still walking away from the camp when he heard muffled voices.

Then the shooting began.

Heedless of the fact that he might be turning his back on dangerous predators, he spun around and ran headlong toward the camp. In the shadows of the tree canopy, he ran smack into a tree. It was a pine, not a hardwood trunk, but he took a needle in the eye, or sap. The pain was ferocious. Half-blinded, he pushed off and continued.

Guns were still going off. Far too many shots fired to just be his men, shooting at wolves or bears.

No, this was an exchange of fire between people.

When he was close enough to the camp, he saw more than a dozen men in a U formation, surrounding most of his friends.

Blood everywhere.

Tres Dedos was facedown beside the fire. Vulvia on his back, one arm smoldering in the coals, with his beloved coffeepot tipped over beside him, its nectar mixing with his blood. Lopez sprawled out with a gun near each hand; he'd gone out shooting. Zaragoza, Valencia, and Severino taken in their sleep. If any yet lived, he couldn't tell.

Almost directly across from Joaquin stood Harry Love.

Joaquin pressed the rifle to his shoulder and aimed. Pulled the trigger. But the man was in motion, and Joaquin's round only nipped his sleeve. He threw down the rifle and yanked the Colt, firing at closer targets.

A round crashed into his left shoulder, staggering him. White heat followed, and he knew that was going to hurt. He let his left arm hang and fired at men he knew he could hit. Head shots; with each one, another attacker went down.

Then he tried for another shot at Love. Before he could pull the trigger, another bullet or ball hit him in the right hip. The pain was instantaneous. He made for the relative safety of the trees as best he could, limping, hoping his black clothing would let him melt into the shadows.

The gunfire stopped.

Were all of his men dead, then? A profound sorrow came over him, but he pushed it away and let his growing fury take its place. The men who did this had to pay—especially Harry Love. He leaned against a tree and reloaded the Colt.

Then, barely able to walk, Joaquin tried for a new angle on the men, now advancing into his camp. He only made it a few steps before several of them got a bead on him and fired. One round knocked off his hat, grazing his scalp. He wasn't even sure how many times he'd been hit; he felt them all at once, as if a stampeding bull had charged into him.

Half-blind, blood in his eyes, off balance, his hip screaming, he tried to hurtle toward cover.

Then the ravine yawned in front of him. Unable to stop his forward motion, he went over the edge, tumbled and rolled, finally came to a stop at the bottom, lying on his back, with his right side half-submerged in the cool water of the stream.

He tried to rise but couldn't. He sank back down. Pain defined his entire world.

A rustle of brush from the top of the ravine caught his attention. He blinked away blood, tried to see. Pale moonlight showed a figure standing there, a blur in the night. A big man, one arm raised, something in his hand. This was it, then. The kill shot. He almost appreciated the coup de grace that would end his pain, vanquish his sorrow.

But instead of shooting from his elevated perch, the man started down the steep declivity, clutching at brush for balance.

Joaquin's vision blurred, then sharpened. At last, he recognized the man: Harry Love.

He pawed at his hip, but the Colt was gone. Somewhere up above, or lost in the fall. As Love reached level ground, Joaquin tried to rise, intending to rush the man and choke the life from him.

He couldn't. His arms gave way beneath him. He had no strength in his legs, could barely scrape his heels back and forth in the dirt. Looking up at Love, blackness closed in until all he could see was the big man's face, and then not even that.

"Joaquin," Love said. At the sound of his voice, Joaquin's vision cleared again. He lifted his head an inch or two off the ground. It took every bit of strength he possessed.

"Harry," he managed.

"I had to, Joaquin. You understand that, don't you?"

"We were . . . friends, once."

"We were," Love agreed. He might have been smiling, but Joaquin couldn't be sure. "I always liked you."

Joaquin felt empty. Cold. For a few moments he forgot where he was, forgot that Harry Love stood before him with a pistol in his hand. Then he became aware again. The ground was damp, the air still. Love wavered, as if Joaquin was looking at his reflection in a pond into which someone had thrown a stone.

"I'm . . . I'm finished, Harry."

Love leaned closer, holding one hand to his ear.

"I said, I'm done. Dying."

"I can see that, Joaquin."

"Can you do . . . one thing, for me?"

"What's that?" Love asked.

"In my p-pocket." Joaquin was shivering now, the cold causing him to stammer. "A scarf. I c-can't . . . r-reach it."

"What about it?"

"I want to h-hold it."

"Hang on, then, I'll get it for you."

Love holstered the revolver. He approached Joaquin slowly, as if anticipating a trap. But he seemed to understand that Joaquin had no strength left, couldn't have attacked him. Still, Love kept the hip with the gun on it turned away as he fished in Joaquin's pocket.

"This old scrap?" Love lifted it, looked it over.

It was true, there wasn't much left of the thing. Joaquin had worried it almost to nothingness.

But it was enough.

"Yes, that. P-put it in my h-h-hand. Please."

Love leaned in, near enough that Joaquin could smell the rank breath of a man who'd been riding and fighting with little water and no rest. He pressed the bit of silk into Joaquin's hand, and Joaquin closed his fist around it.

"There you go, Joaquin."

"Th-thank you, Har-Harry."

"I'll let you be, now. Let you die in peace."

Harry turned away, took a couple of steps, then stopped. He faced Joaquin again, looking down at him. "I can't tell if I'm sorry it turned out this way, or glad. I mean, I knew I'd have to kill you. But I figured . . . I don't know. That it'd be easier, I guess."

Joaquin couldn't answer. He felt the bit of silk in his hand, and the cold and the darkness swallowing him.

Then consciousness slipped away like a sweet dream, forgotten upon waking.

• • •

A sudden rustle in the trees had alerted the rangers. The man was on the move, heading west. A fusillade of lead changed his course; and he abruptly darted the other direction. For a moment, he became visible through a gap in the trees, and four rangers drew beads on him at once. All four fired. The man's hat blew off and blood spurted from his head. He staggered a few more steps, then fell over the edge of the embankment. The racket that followed suggested that he was rolling down the steep slope, coming to a stop somewhere below.

"I'll check on him," Love said.

"Good," Rhodes agreed. As Love headed for the rim,

Rhodes took stock. All seven of the Mexicans in the clearing were dead. So were five of his fellow rangers, with four more wounded. Lorenz had both hands clapped over a gaping hole in his chest; a river of blood bubbled out between his fingers.

"L-Lucas," he wheezed. Tears streaked the grime on his cheeks. "I'm...I'm hurt bad."

They were hours of hard riding from any serious medical help. The kid would never last that long. "You're not going to make it, Rand."

"But...but I gotta..."

"You're in pain?"

"Yeah. It h-hurts somethin' aw-awful."

"Quick is better." Rhodes held the barrel of his pistol inches away from the side of Lorenz's head. The young man's eyes went huge and he started to quake. Rhodes squeezed the trigger. The shot pierced the quiet, and everyone who could swung around toward him. Lorenz slumped over, out of pain. At almost the same moment, he heard two more shots, away from the circle. Love, he guessed.

"Kid couldn't travel, and he wasn't gonna last more than an hour at the most," Rhodes said by way of explanation. "Anybody else so hurt they can't ride?"

He got no takers. A couple of the men were in bad shape, but none as badly injured as Lorenz had been.

"Mayfield, find their horses and bring 'em here," Rhodes ordered. "We can load our dead on them, and any wounded as can't walk out. Meanwhile, go through their gear and see what they got that's worth keepin'." He walked over to Three-Fingered Jack's corpse, kicked it.

Then Love returned, made his way through the carnage and stopped in front of Rhodes. "What about the one went over the edge?" Rhodes asked.

"I climbed down to take a look," Love said. "He's dead."

"Well, you wanted Joaquin Murrieta. I guess you got him."

"I was hoping to take him alive, but he dealt the cards."

Love's words were clipped. He seemed sullen, even angry. Men reacted in different ways to gun battles, Rhodes knew. They left him feeling excited, energized, glad to have survived. Love probably took it otherwise.

"We need to be able to prove to the governor that we got him. I don't want to haul his corpse all the way to Benicia. How about we just take his head?"

"Could do, I reckon," Rhodes said. He rubbed his chin. "Might take Jack's hand, too. To sort of confirm Joaquin's identity."

"Makes sense. I'll get Joaquin."

"Guess I'll do Jack."

Love turned away without another word, tugging a knife from the sheath on his belt.

While he worked, Rhodes eyed the growing pile of belongings the other men had gathered. Along with the eight horses and fine Mexican saddles and bridles—nobody made tack like the Mexicans—there was a good brace of weapons and ammunition, a few small pouches of gold and currency, some tobacco, coffee, and other foodstuffs, and some usable boots and fancy spurs with those big Mexican rowels. Not a bad haul.

But the main prize was Joaquin Murrieta. Joaquin the Terrible, scourge of the gold camps, the most-wanted outlaw in the brief history of the state of California. Governor Bigler had ordered Love to form the California Rangers, for the specific purpose of bringing in Joaquin. Dead or alive, as the saying went.

Dead would have to do.

Rhodes looked up from his mental tabulation of the loot and saw Love walking toward him, holding a human head by its long, black hair. A trail of blood formed a glistening wake in the early-morning sun. The head was slender, light-skinned, with a thin black mustache and a scar on the right cheek. That was Murrieta, all right. He rose, unable to hold back a grin. "That's just great, Harry," he said. "That head's worth a thousand bucks to us. Split—" he made a quick mental calculation. "—fifteen ways, if everybody back in Sonora pulls through. Plus another four hundred-fifty for our pay."

Love's face screwed up in disgust and he dropped the head at Rhodes's feet. "Blood money. This whole business makes me sick."

"You been chasin' him for months, Harry."

"That's right. And the whole time, I wasn't sure he was who I thought he was. Now I know, and it don't set right with me."

"You and him was partners for a spell, right?"

"He worked for me," Love corrected. "We became friends."

"Friends with a murderous son of a bitch like that?"

Love's gaze swept across the campsite, encompassing dead Mexicans and dead and wounded rangers. "That's right, Lucas. Friends with a murderous son of a bitch like that. You want to make something of it?" He turned his back and walked toward his horse.

He could feel that way if he wanted. Nothing Rhodes could do about it. This wasn't murder, this was law enforcement, and if Harry Love chose not to see the difference now that he'd caught his quarry, that was his own worry.

He put Jack's hand on the ground beside Murrieta's head. Getting the hand was a good idea, but not absolutely necessary. The reward was for Murrieta, and they clearly had him. Edgar Leach, the post surgeon at Fort Miller, across the San Joaquin Valley, could come up with a way to preserve the head for the trip to Benicia.

Rhodes looked at the head again. Money in the bank.

And of course, as lieutenant, he deserved the second largest cut.

"Joaquin Murrieta," he said, addressing his grisly prize. "You only thought you was famous before. Just imagine what's in store for you now."

72

When Joaquin opened his eyes again, the sun blazed down. He closed them again. Too bright.

"Am I alive?" he asked of no one in particular. The sound of his own voice startled him. It sounded wrong, foreign. He lay there, trying to figure out his physical condition without moving around too much. After a few moments of consideration, he realized one reason his voice sounded so strange; his right ear was full of something. Gingerly, he raised his right hand to it and poked around. Mud.

He remembered Harry coming down to him. They'd spoken, briefly. He opened his left fist, and saw the scrap of scarf Harry had fetched for him.

Then he remembered Tres Dedos and the others, back in the camp.

That memory spurred him to his knees. And that motion made him vomit, again and again, until there was nothing left in him but clear, viscous fluid. The motion of vomiting made every part of his body burn with pain, especially the wounds at his shoulder, hip, and scalp.

And all of it brought back the first great loss of his life. His Rosita. His friends, his band, even Antonia, for a while, had filled some of the emptiness inside him, but nobody could fill all of it. She had left behind a hole that was walled off against everything but hurt.

Joaquin slumped back onto the mud and gravel of the streamside. Why had he lived, he wondered, when everyone else in his world had died? What had he done wrong? Had he so angered God that eternal life on Earth was his punishment?

If he'd had a gun at that moment, he'd have held it to his own forehead and pulled the trigger. But he didn't. He remembered that he'd been carrying his Colt when he fell, and the empty holster was still buckled around his middle. The gun might have gone into the stream, or almost anywhere when he went over the side, arms flailing.

There were guns aplenty back in camp, though.

That thought, more than any other, forced him to his feet.

The wall of the ravine looked like the tallest of mountains. Could he possibly climb it?

"You are Joaquin," he reminded himself, out loud. Still strange. He dug more mud from his ear. "There's nothing you can't do."

Even as he spoke the words, he knew them for a lie. Not only that, but his wounds were relatively superficial. The worst, he thought, was that left shoulder, but the round seemed to have hit only muscle and passed through. The head wound, a graze, had bled a lot. The right hip was also a graze, tearing his pants and flesh. All of it hurt, and the fall had compounded the pain, leaving him cut and bruised all over.

He didn't think any permanent damage had been done to his body.

His heart? His soul?

Another story altogether.

The thought of the guns up there lent him strength. Anyway, they'd done the climb the night before, all of them, after coming down to the stream to fill their canteens. He tried to remember the route they had taken and climbed the slope—

not really as steep or as high as it had seemed at first—grabbing onto bushes with his right hand, pulling himself up a little at a time. Twice, he thought about giving up, just letting go and dropping back down where he'd been. But lying there until he died—or worse, recovered—seemed like too much trouble.

He pressed on.

Finally, he reached the top and scrambled over.

Not far now to the camp. Through the trees. He was able to walk almost upright, limping but in a more-or-less straight line.

Then he smelled it.

The closer he got, the worse it became.

Charred flesh.

Spilled blood.

All the other smells that went along with men dying.

Closer still, he saw that animals had been there. Ragged bits of flesh were scattered here and there. Somebody's bare foot, under the lowest boughs of a pine, with no leg attached. Bloody tracks on the earth.

Then the camp itself came into view, through the branches. The vibrant colors of blankets and serapes and blood, painfully bright in the sunshine. He stopped, closed his eyes. Why was he doing this? Why torture himself?

The question answered itself. Because he deserved it.

No, because *they* deserved it.

His friends.

He pushed on, limping, hurting, into the midst of it.

Not even aware yet that his eyes had overflowed, that tears ran down his cheeks, snot bubbling from his nose. Not until a great, gulping sob escaped him and the pain in his shoulder felt like someone had stabbed him with a sword.

Zaragoza, still in his blankets.

A headless body near the fire. Blood turning the dirt brown and black in a wide circle. From the clothes, he knew it was Gregorio Lopez. But why take his head?

And Tres Dedos, still where he'd been, face down. But his hand was gone, and a smaller stain marked the ground near his wrist.

Then he knew. For identification.

Three-Fingered Jack's hand. The head of a man who somewhat resembled Joaquin Murrieta.

The reward promised the California Rangers if they captured or killed the bandit Joaquin.

He fell to his knees beside Tres Dedos, laid his head on the man's broad, still back, weeping.

"I was never as good a friend to you as you were to me, Manuel," he managed, between sobs. "Do you forgive me? Can you?"

No answer. He sat back on his haunches and howled at the sky.

After a while, his throat ragged and aching, he prayed, for the first time in what seemed like forever. Years, anyway.

He prayed for the souls of his friends, of these men who had died because they had been close to him.

He prayed for doom to befall those who'd mutilated their corpses.

He prayed to die, here, with the only people he still loved.

That prayer, at least, was not granted. Exhaustion overcame him, and he fell asleep for a while, his head on his beloved cousin's back.

• • •

When he woke again—still alive, then—the sun had moved in the sky. An hour gone, maybe two. He remembered the guns.

But those were gone. The rangers had carried away the bodies of their own dead, and from the bandits had taken guns, ammunition, knives, even boots. The horses were gone, along with whatever gold the men had packed into their saddlebags.

Thieves, then, as well as murderers.

All of it under the color of the state. All of it not only legal but sanctioned by the legislature and the governor.

An earlier Joaquin—younger by a few hours—would have sworn revenge.

He looked for that Joaquin, but couldn't find him. He was gone. Dead. The Joaquin who lived now was weary to the bone.

Vengeance was for younger men.

He made another quick pass through the camp, and on impulse, turned over Tres Dedos's body. His friend's face, almost peaceful, as if in repose. Maybe a slight smile on his lips, like he'd killed one of the gringo bastards right before he died.

Joaquin laughed. Tres Dedos could always make him laugh. Even in death.

He pulled back the man's sleeve and found it, the sharp dagger Tres Dedos always kept strapped to his forearm. When the rangers had found four or five knives, they probably figured they had them all.

Not even close. Joaquin knew there was another one, shorter-bladed, down his pants, but he decided to leave that one. Manuel might want it in the afterlife.

He removed the straps from Tres Dedos's arm and unsheathed the knife. As always, Tres Dedos had kept it razor-sharp. Joaquin briefly considered plunging it into his own heart, but that moment had passed. Instead, he slid it back into its leather sheath and put it on his belt, across from the empty holster.

He had lost everyone that mattered to him, in this country. But that didn't mean he didn't have people elsewhere. Lopez and Tres Dedos had left him the greatest gift they could offer: Freedom. He felt like an almost unbearable weight had been lifted from him. He owed nobody, and nobody owed him.

For once, no one was chasing after him. The authorities thought they had killed the bandit Joaquin.

"Joaquin Murrieta is dead," he said aloud. His voice sounded better now, so he tried it again, shouting it to the skies. "Joaquin Murrieta is dead! Long live Joaquin!"

For a moment, everything went quiet. Birds stopped singing, crickets silenced their trilling. Then he heard the soft, liquid rush of the creek and a light breeze sloughing through the pine boughs. As the sounds of other creatures resumed, he was struck by the beauty of this place, which they had missed when they'd arrived here at dusk. Sunlight filtered through the trees. White, yellow, blue, red, and purple wildflowers pushed up through the grass, and two black-and-orange butterflies played tag just above them. Through the pines, he caught glimpses of other mountains in almost every direction, blue and purple in the distance. The sky overhead was a crisp blue broken by wispy white clouds.

Beyond what he could see from here, he knew, lay other landscapes, part of California's seemingly infinite variety. Coastlines hemmed in by sheer cliffs and others with wide, sandy beaches. Towering mountains eternally cloaked in snow. Vast, sunbaked deserts that seemed empty until one stood inside them and saw the resilience of life. Meadows lush with tall grasses, hills that turned golden in the autumn, rivers that brought gold to those who worked for it.

Once, he had thought it all belonged to him.

Now, he knew better.

He could never be more than a visitor here. This wasn't his place, after all.

He had no horse, no money, no weapons but a knife. But he knew places where he'd buried gold, for just such an occasion. And he had friends out there, people who would help him if he knocked on their doors. He poked around the wreckage of the camp until he found a canteen, tucked beneath the saddle Zaragoza had been sleeping on. Still full, from the night before.

One more thing. He went back into the trees where he'd been shot and scanned the ground. There it was! He picked up his hat, dusted it off, fitted it onto his head. His scalp was still gummy with blood, but that would just help hold the hat in place.

He stopped by the camp once more, to say goodbye.

And then, stepping as lightly as he could manage, Joaquin climbed down from the hillside.

Once he reached the valley floor, he turned so the sun beat down upon his right side. He had hours yet before nightfall, time enough to make some good progress.

Joaquin wasn't done with California. Not yet. But he was on his way.

Limping, aching, one step at a time, he headed south.

South toward Mexico.

South, toward home.

73

December 1853, San Francisco

Despite the chill, Sansome Street was busy. People moved in and out of shops, some laden with packages. Christmas was coming, after all. Harry Love had no one to buy presents for this year.

Blood money. He'd accepted his reward and his salary. Some of it went to gambling debts, but he still had plenty left over. That had trickled out, though; a room, a bath, a meal, a woman, and so on. Bit by bit.

None of it helped him forget what he'd been a party to.

They had presented their trophies to Governor Bigler and received their pay, along with considerable acclaim from the press. For a while, they'd been feted in Benicia and San Francisco. Then the rangers had split up, gone their separate ways. Love was glad of it. He couldn't stand to see the faces of the others. He couldn't stand for them to see him, knowing what he'd done.

Ahead, at the corner of Sansome and Halleck, a long line of people snaked out of an open doorway. He knew the place—King's, the saloon owned by John King. Curious, he bypassed the line and peered inside. Then he saw the banner above the door: "Today only—See the Head of the Bandit Joaquin!" In smaller type below that: "And the Hand of Three-Fingered

Jack!"

Despite everything, Love hadn't been able to bring himself to throw away his ranger badge. He reached into his coat pocket and withdrew it, holding it up to the man at the door. At the same time, he put a finger to his lips.

The doorman winked, smiled, and said, "Come on in, Cap'n." When a couple of the people waiting in line started to object, he silenced them with a stern glance. Love pushed past him and inside.

Here, the smells of sweaty bodies crowded together wrestled with the aroma of liquor, making him crave a drink. The tables and chairs had been stacked against one wall, except for a single table on which stood two large glass bottles. King and a couple of his bartenders held court at the bar, pouring drinks for men who consumed them on the spot. But most of the crowd inside paid no attention to them; the attraction was on that table.

The line curled around it, so the viewers—many of them Mexicans—could ogle not only the fronts of the items on display, but the sides and backs as well. From Love's position, he could only catch a glimpse, between the people in line, of long black hair floating in a solution of some kind. In the other jar, half-hidden from here, floated four fingers of a bloated hand, likewise encased.

All in all, not much different from the last time he'd seen them.

During his brief spell of fame, Love had become accustomed to being looked at. People either recognized him, or thought they did, no matter where in the state he went. That was part of why he'd decided to stay in San Francisco for a while; here, people were busy with their own lives, the city filled with more newcomers every day, and he believed that his novelty was wearing off. People mostly left him alone, which was what he wanted more than anything.

But now, he felt eyes on him. Trying to be casual, he lifted his gaze from the jars. A man across the way was looking directly at him. Their eyes met briefly, then Love looked away. He heard whispers that sounded like "*el patrio*."

He shifted his angle, pressing in closer to the table holding the grisly prizes, and took another discreet glance.

The man had already started toward the door.

He had shoulder-length, dark hair, streaked with gray. A thin mustache on his upper lip and a bristly beard likewise. His face was lined with age. He was slender, a little shorter than Love, but not much. He walked with a slight limp. His clothes were black, even the greatcoat he wore over his suit. He went through the door without looking back.

Despite the man's age—from the quick glance Love had, the man looked fifteen or twenty years older than himself—he seemed strikingly familiar. And he was spry, in spite of that limp.

Realization set in suddenly. The man was already outside, and the crowd blocked the doorway. Love shoved through, almost pulling out the badge again. He didn't need it; the doorman parted the mob for him, and he burst out.

Heedless of the horse and carriage traffic in the road, Love stepped into it so he could see beyond the pedestrians crowding the street. He looked up and down Halleck, then Sansome, before finally spotting the man up the block, almost to the next corner. Love hurried after him. A buggy almost ran him down; its driver shouted curses at him in his wake. He paid no mind.

When he reached the corner, the man—moving too fast for one of his seemingly advanced age—was almost to the next one. Love raced after him, and shouted, "Hey! You there!"

At that, the man stopped, turned around. A smile crossed his face.

Love knew that smile.

Closer up, he could see that the lines on his face had been drawn there, and the white in his hair and beard probably applied with powder or flour.

"Yes?" the man said as he approached. "Did you want something?"

"Damn it, just to see you!" Love said. "What are you doing here? Are you crazy?"

"I don't think so, no," the man said. "Who is it exactly that you take me for?"

"I'd know you anywhere, Joaquin. Don't play games with me. We've both been through too much for that."

"I'm sorry," the man said. "You've confused me for somebody else. Someone from your past, perhaps? You look like a man with a rich past. Memories of your friend, eh?"

"Memories, yes."

"Good ones, I hope?"

"Some. Not all of them, but mostly."

"Well, what could be better, then? Sometimes good memories are all we're left with. Best to enjoy them, isn't it, than to try to create others that might replace them?"

"I don't . . ." Love stammered. "What are you . . .why?"

"I'm not sure how to answer that."

"Joaquin, it's me, Harry. Surely you know me."

"Please don't call me that name," the man said. That smile flashed again, then vanished. "I'm afraid I must be going. So much to do. The season, you know? I'm sure you're busy, too."

"I'm not," Love said. "Can't we go somewhere quiet, get a

drink or a meal? It's been so long, and I . . ." Love let the sentence drop. The man was looking at him curiously, almost as if trying to remember where he might know him from. Or else to memorize his features. Either way, he wondered if he was wrong about it all. He hadn't thought the lines aging the man's face looked natural, and neither did his hair color. Could he be mistaken about those things, and everything else?

"I'm sorry," the man said. "I can't stay."

"But . . ."

The foot traffic had been flowing around them, but now the man stepped into its midst and started away again. Before he went, he spun around and said, "I owe you my thanks, Harry. This will be the last time we meet, but I'll always think fondly of you."

"Joa—" Love started, then remembered the other man's request not to use that name.

Then the man was gone, lost in the crowd. Love thought about chasing him down again, but he decided not to.

He'd made clear that he had someplace else to be. He had been here, and now he was gone.

And wasn't that just like him?

Here one minute, then vanished. A drop of water in a flowing river, a mote of dust in the wind. Never still.

Grinning, Harry Love turned and walked the other way, back toward Sansome. His original errand forgotten, he decided it was a good day to spend some of what money he had left.

He could use a drink, after all. It was almost Christmas, after all, and he didn't think he wanted to meet it sober.

EPILOGUE

October 1860, Trincheras, Sonora, Mexico

"But why, Papa? Why did you go back there, after you were safe?"

Joaquin chuckled. Now that Manuel was almost five, he loved to hear the story, but he always asked the same question. Little Tomás, only three, rarely spoke, but it was obvious that he was always listening, soaking in every word and filling his mind with it. Sometimes, Joaquin suspected that Manuel asked the same thing over and over because he truly didn't remember the answer, not that he wanted to hear the *whole* story, every time. But Tomás didn't ever ask, because having heard it once, he would recall it for the rest of his life. He was, Joaquin supposed, a bit like his namesake that way. And Manuel, who always loved a good tale, was like his.

He leaned forward in his chair and held out his hands. Manuel came into them, and Joaquin lifted the boy onto his knee. "Having heard that my head was on display, I had to go and look!" he said. "Wouldn't you, if it was your head? Wouldn't you want to see it in a bottle, and people lined up for blocks just to look?"

Manuel made a face. "*Eeew*," he said. "A head in a bottle? I wouldn't want to see that."

So, he wasn't like his namesake in every respect. Probably for the best.

"Well, I had to see it for myself. And I'll tell you, for a moment, I was almost convinced it *was* my head. I had to touch my own face, to make sure it was still there. I was pretty sure it was floating in that bottle!"

"No, you weren't!" Manuel shouted. "You knew it wasn't yours! You couldn't see it if it was, because your eyes would be in the bottle!"

That, too, was typical of Manuel, and the cousin for whom he was named. Always the realist.

"You're right, Manuel. It was the head of my friend Gregorio, who happened to look like me. I knew it was his."

"But why would you want to see that?"

"To thank him," Joaquin said. "For the gift he gave me."

"He gave you a gift? After he was dead?"

"He gave me you!" Joaquin said, bouncing his son on his knee. "And Tomás, and your mother. All of this. Without him, I could never have had any of it."

"And if the captain was your friend, why did he hunt you?" Manuel asked. Another of his usual questions.

"Friendship is funny," Joaquin said. "Sometimes your friends can hurt you the most. But you can forgive your friends, if you try. Your mother forgives me for something or other just about every day."

Manuel clapped a hand over his mouth. "Mama! I forgot! She said to tell you that lunch is ready! Come on!"

"Yet another way you're like my cousin," Joaquin said. "Always hungry. How about you, Tomás? Are you hungry, too?"

Tomás blinked and rose from his spot on the floor, headed

for the kitchen.

Joaquin started to follow, but then stopped, as a dream from the night before flooded back into his thoughts. It was ugly. Harry Love was passed out, his legs hidden in the bushes at the edge of someone's yard, his body splayed out in the road. His snores were so loud, that they could've been used to warn ships on foggy days off San Francisco's coast. He'd vomited in his sleep; it flecked his lips and chin and one cheek was pressed into a pool of it.

Joaquin knew it was just a dream, but it felt like a premonition.

Instead of going in to lunch, he went to the door and looked out at the village where he had been born, and to which he'd returned, sleepy in the noontime sun. A few chickens roamed past on a mission of some kind. A neighbor carried a pail of water around behind his house, where Joaquin knew two burros waited. A passing breeze lifted some dust and dropped it again. His gaze shifted, looking northward for a moment. Then he turned his back on the north and headed into the house, toward the aroma of fresh tortillas and beans.

He didn't need anything from that direction.

Everything he needed—everything he had ever needed—was right here.

And it always would be.

AUTHOR'S NOTE

Some of what you've just read—unless you're one of those who turn to the back of a book before the first page—is true. Some of it isn't. The rest might be. Or it might not. That's the thing about legends, and about fiction. What's true isn't as important as what could, in the right circumstances, be perceived as true.

Historians and fictioneers have been digging into the story of Joaquin Murrieta since his name first surfaced in California in the early 1850s. Having done massive amounts of research about the man and his times, the best conclusion I can reach is that, while much is known, much, much more isn't. What I've tried to do is to paint a picture of what might have been, while staying as true to the known history of early California as possible. Historians will doubtless argue over pieces of this, and they're welcome to.

I've been fascinated with the story of Joaquin since I lived in San Jose in the early 1970s. That interest was deepened during the course of numerous visits to the Gold Country, where his known exploits began. I'm deeply indebted to Russell Binder for finding a way to convince me to finally sit down and write this book, and to Peter Murrieta for sharing stories that have been passed down through generations of his family, and for his massive and meaningful contributions throughout. Great thanks also to the scores of historians whose work I referenced, to my friend Bob Boze Bell and the True West archives, to Stephen Andes, to the Calaveras County Historical Society, and to various online sources. Finally, I couldn't have written this without the love and support of my wife, Marsheila Rockwell, and our family.

And I'm grateful to you, reader, for making it this far. In the end, that's what this is all about.

ABOUT THE AUTHORS

Jeffrey J. Mariotte has written more than seventy books, including original supernatural thrillers *River Runs Red*, *Missing White Girl*, and *Cold Black Hearts*, horror epic *The Slab*, and the Stoker Award-nominated teen horror quartet *Year of the Wicked*. Other works include the acclaimed thrillers *Empty Rooms* and *The Devil's Bait*. With his wife and writing partner Marsheila (Marcy) Rockwell, he wrote the science fiction thriller *7 SYKOS* and *Mafia III: Plain of Jars*, the authorized prequel to the hit video game, as well as numerous shorter works. Three of his novels have won Scribe Awards for Best Original Novel, presented by the International Association of Media Tie-In Writers. He's also won the Inkpot Award from the San Diego Comic-Con and is a co-winner of the Raven Award from the Mystery Writers of America. He's been a finalist for the Spur Award from the Western Writers of America, the Peacemaker Award from the Western Fictioneers, the International Horror Guild Award, and the Bram Stoker Award from the Horror Writers Association.

He is also the author of many comic books and graphic novels, including the original Western series *Desperadoes*, some of which have been nominated for Harvey, Glyph, Stoker, and International Horror Guild Awards. Other comics work includes the horror series *Fade to Black*, the action-adventure series *Garrison*, and the original graphic novel *Zombie Cop*.

He is a member of the Western Writers of America, Western Fictioneers, International Thriller Writers, Sisters in Crime, the Horror Writers Association, and the International Association of Media Tie-In Writers. He has worked in virtually every aspect of the book and publishing business, as a bookstore manager and owner, VP of Marketing for Image Comics/WildStorm, Senior Editor for DC Comics/WildStorm, and Editor-in-Chief for IDW Publishing. When he's not writing, reading, or editing something, he's probably out enjoying the desert landscape around the Arizona home he shares with his family and pets. Find him online at www.jeffmariotte.com, www.facebook.com/JeffreyJMariotte, and on Twitter at @JeffMariotte.

Peter Murrieta is two-time Emmy Award winning producer, writer and showrunner with a career mission—to expand and further legitimize the entertainment value of telling stories about diverse cultures that are about more than their trauma. His credits include *Wizards of Waverly Place, Superior Donuts, One Day at a Time, Greetings from Tucson,* which he created, *Mr. Iglesias* on Netflix, and has recently completed working with Mike Schur and Shea Serrano on *Primo*.

After teaching and touring with Second City Chicago, Peter moved to Los Angeles and was accepted into the esteemed ABC writing fellowship. His success in this program led to professional writing positions on multiple shows before selling *Greetings from Tucson*–a story about an upwardly mobile family of mixed ethnicity. The Latino cast and lighthearted examination of his culture within the predominantly white television landscape was a large step towards making his career's mission a reality. This success made it easier for him as a producer to ensure underrepresented persons had more opportunities on both sides of the camera, as evidenced by his work on Disney's award-winning *Wizards of Waverly Place*.

Peter was honored in 2018 with the Imagen Foundation's Norman Lear Writer's Award for his dedication to broadening the diversity of the entertainment industry. Along with the projects he is currently working on, he has been a fellow of screenwriting at AFI and is currently the Director in Residence of the Sidney Poitier New American Film School at Arizona State University. Peter finds himself continually surprised and inspired by the horizonless rewards found through giving back to the diverse next generation of storytellers.